Follow the Heart is filled with delightful characters that set out on a mission to marry well . . . if only their hearts would stay out of it! Dacus has created a rich Victorian setting filled with fresh characters whose backgrounds include everything from the poorhouse to aristocracy, adding charm and depth to this romantic tale. A thoughtful takeaway is watching Kate discern the difference between her obligations to duties—duties both fair and unfair—and listening to God's direction. This is one story I'll never forget!

—Maureen Lang, author of *Bees in the Butterfly Garden*

Kaye Dacus has created a wealth of memorable characters in this charming story of love, duty, and sacrifice. Sent to England to marry a rich man and save her family from financial ruin, the heroine can't allow her growing feelings for the handsome gardener to keep her from her obligations. The fast-paced plot and tender love story are bound to delight and leave you eagerly awaiting the next book.

—Margaret Brownley, *New York Times* best-selling writer and author of the Rocky Creek and Brides of Last Chance Ranch series

Follow [Your] Heart to pure magic! Kaye Dacus has penned a dual love story—twice as tender, twice as romantic, twice as sigh-worthy as a proper Victorian tale should be . . . and I devoured every heart-fluttering page!

—Julie Lessman, award-winning author of The Daughters of Boston and Winds of Change series

Follow the Heart is a delight! Kaye Dacus has written a richly layered romance and given us characters who readers want to find both love and happiness. I couldn't wait to see whether or not they would follow their hearts!

—Robin Lee Hatcher, best-selling author of *Belonging* and *Betrayal*

In *Follow the Heart*, Kaye Dacus takes readers on a romantic journey through some beautiful homes and lush gardens in her English setting, while letting her readers get to know and love her engaging characters.

The story had me cheering for Kate and Christopher to do just what the title says and follow their hearts.

—Ann H. Gabhart, author of *The Outsider,*
The Believer, and *Angel Sister*

Kaye Dacus has once again crafted a tension-filled love story that will keep you turning the pages. *Follow the Heart* will have you cheering for characters who hold fast and exhibit sacrificial love for their family while temptations rise at every turn.

—Judith Miller, author of *A Hidden Truth*

Charming, delightful, and captivating are three words that come to mind when describing Kaye Dacus's newest novel, *Follow the Heart.* Her characters spring to life in old England, and her romance is more than satisfying—with the added pleasure of an equally enjoyable secondary romance. I heartily recommend this book to any lover of historical romantic fiction. It's my first book by Kaye but certainly won't be my last.

—Miralee Ferrell, author of *Love Finds You in Sundance, WY*

In *Follow the Heart*, Kaye Dacus gives us a love story set in the age of Queen Victoria when the English aristocracy ruled. Not only has she created characters who will grow on the reader, but she has placed them in extraordinary circumstances that will test everything they ever believed. With beautiful settings, characters true to the times, and actual events, Dacus paints a beautiful story with words that will capture the reader's imagination.

—Martha Rogers, author of the series
Winds Across the Prairie and Seasons of the Heart

Follow the Heart

A NOVEL

Follow the Heart

Kaye Dacus

PUBLISHING GROUP

Nashville, Tennessee

978-1-4336-7720-5

Published by B&H Publishing Group
Nashville, Tennessee

Dewey Decimal Classification: F
Subject Heading: LOVE STORIES—19TH CENTURY
\ ROMANTIC SUSPENSE NOVELS \ INDUSTRIAL
REVOLUTION—FICTION

Scripture reference is taken from The Webster Bible: Title:
The Holy Bible, Containing the Old and New Testaments, in
the Common Version. With Amendments of the Language, by
Noah Webster, LL. D. | New Haven: Published by N. Webster. |
M.DCC.XLI. Date: 1841. Publisher: N. Webster: New Haven.

1 2 3 4 5 6 7 8 • 16 15 14 13

For Ruth and Liz—two of the dearest friends anyone can have. Thanks for all of your love and encouragement.

ACKNOWLEDGMENTS

*H*ow would this even be in readers' hands if it weren't for my fabulous agent, Chip MacGregor, and my wonderful editor, Julie Gwinn? I owe both of them so much. And I must also take this time to publicly laud adulation upon my copy editor, Kathy Ide. There were a lot of times in the revision process in which I was infuriated by her questions, suggestions, and changes—but then I realized that she was only challenging me to become a better writer. And that's a gift she probably doesn't even realize she gave me. Thanks, Kathy. I also can't close this without giving a huge shout-out to Middle Tennessee Christian Writers for all of their encouragement. It's wonderful to have such a close-knit and supportive community of writers with whom I get to spend so much time.

PROLOGUE

Philadelphia, Pennsylvania
New Year's Eve, 1850

*W*ould the rustle of her skirts against the floorboards give her away?

Kate Dearing lifted the burdensome bulk—pink silk-taffeta flounces over layers and layers of starched petticoats—and padded down the hall in her soft kid dancing slippers. Christopher, her younger brother, said he'd seen Father and Devlin Montgomery head toward Father's study.

Devlin wanted to ask for Father's blessing before he proposed to her. At least Kate assumed so. Devlin had been courting her for almost a year now. And even though she could hardly tolerate being in the same room with him for the hour his calls lasted, at twenty-seven years old, she had no alternatives—for no other man had paid court to her in more than five years, despite the family's wealth and her large dowry. Devlin was wealthy and somewhat handsome. His family owned hundreds of thousands of acres of land in western Pennsylvania and eastern Ohio.

The railroad company in which Father had invested his fortune wanted to lay new rail lines through it.

She squeezed through the narrow door of the storage room behind Father's study. She and Christopher had discovered the hiding place years ago.

Trying to mash her bell-shaped skirt flat to keep it from catching on any of the old, framed paintings stacked against one wall, Kate sidled down the cramped space toward the thin beam of light that trickled through a chink in the wood-paneled wall. Too high to see through, it carried sound from the adjacent room quite well.

"You lied to me." Devlin's voice held a venom she'd never imagined the staid young man possessed.

"Lied?" Her father sound shocked—offended. "Is Kate not beautiful and accomplished? Intelligent and well capable of running a large household?"

Devlin snorted at her father's words. "When she keeps her mouth closed and her radical beliefs about abolition and voting rights for women behind her teeth, yes, she is passing pretty."

Kate stifled a gasp. Only passing pretty? Then she shrugged. She'd always known she'd never be a great beauty like her mother, God rest her soul.

"It is not of Miss Dearing that I speak," Devlin continued. "It is of you and the deception you used your daughter to try to draw me into."

Kate frowned. Father had nothing to do with Devlin and her meeting each other. Aunt Kitty arranged the introduction.

"I am certain I do not take your meaning," Father said, though Kate recognized the tremor of fear in his voice. It was the same as when he'd tried to convince seven-year-old Kate and four-year-old Christopher that their mother and newborn sister would be just fine—and the same as when he'd told them the next day of Mother and Emma's passing. Now, as then, her heart caught in her throat.

"You may have everyone else in Philadelphia fooled, but we Montgomerys know better."

Father laughed nervously. "I do not know to what rumors you have been listening—"

"They are no rumors. The front page of the paper announced the land commission's decision to vote against allowing a railroad to be built through that part of the state. That means everyone who invested in the speculation, in buying up all of that land, lost everything. And since you boasted to my father of how you invested all your wealth in the speculation, trying to get him to go in it with you, it is obvious you are also now penniless. And you intended for me to marry your spinster daughter—whom no man with use of his senses would have before she possessed no dowry—to save the railroad and your fortune." A loud thump followed Devlin's pronouncement as if he'd hit his fist against the table or desk. "I will not be your dupe."

The thud of footsteps followed by the opening and slamming of the study door masked the whoosh of Kate's skirts as her knees gave out and she sank to the floor.

Bankrupt? Penniless?

Surely not. Yet . . . the invitation list for tonight's ball had been kept suspiciously small. Father had spent more time than usual away from the house in recent weeks. And when he returned home, his haggard appearance made her wonder if he was coming down with a chill.

Bankrupt. Penniless.

Kate pushed and pulled herself back up to her feet and squeezed through the small space and back out into the wide hallway. The *dark* hallway. Never before during a social event had so few candles been lit. And when had the exquisite Persian rug that had dressed the hall floor since before her birth been removed?

Though not a proper ballroom, the salon in the back of the house served the purpose well, looking much larger tonight with the pared-down number of guests who had come to celebrate the advent of the new year.

Maud gave her a questioning look when she stepped into the room. Kate smiled at her stepmother, hoping to keep her believing everything was fine.

How soon would all of these people know that the Dearings were ruined? How soon would they turn their backs on Father and Maud, on Christopher and her? On her young half-sisters, Ada, Clara, and Ella? Once Philadelphia society discovered their new financial status, doors would be closed, connections severed. No one would want to be associated with a man who invested unwisely and lost everything.

Devlin had been correct—no man would want to marry her now, with no dowry.

Ignoring the cold of the winter evening, Kate escaped through the back doors to the solitude and peace of her garden, its wildness beautiful even in the light of the half-moon and covered in snow.

Dear Lord, what am I supposed to do now?

CHAPTER ONE

SS Baltic
Off the Coast of England
February 9, 1851

*Y*ou should come back down to the saloon, where it's warm."

Kate did not turn from the vista of gray, choppy water in front of her at her brother's voice. The last fourteen days seemed as nothing to Christopher—a lark, an adventure, not the exile Kate knew it to be.

An exile that came with an edict: Find someone wealthy to marry.

"I do not see the point in sitting in the grand saloon, pretending as though everything is fine when I know it is not. I have no talent at pretense." Kate wrapped her thick woolen shawl closer about her head and shoulders at a gust of icy wind. "If any of those other passengers knew we were being sent to England as poor relations, they would shun us."

Just as everyone in Philadelphia had. Word of Graham Dearing's financial misfortune spread like last summer's great fire that consumed the Vine Street Wharf—quickly and with almost as much destructive force. Kate and Christopher's step-mother had been too embarrassed to come down to the train station to see them off to New York two weeks ago—too afraid she would see someone she recognized on the street and not be acknowledged. Only Father had come with them to New York to say good-bye. And to remind Kate why she was being sent to her mother's brother: to find and marry a fortune that would save their family. The memory of their argument on the platform before she joined Christopher to board the ship burned through her like the coal that powered them closer to her destiny.

"What's wrong with enjoying the trappings of money while we can?" Christopher sidled up beside her and leaned his fore-arms against the top railing. "Besides, from Uncle Anthony's let-ter, it doesn't sound like he plans to treat us any differently than his own children, just because we're 'poor relations,' as you put it."

"But they'll know. *Sir* Anthony and his daughters and what-ever house staff they have—they'll know that we're completely dependent upon their charity. It will be written in their eyes every time they look at us. Every time we sit down at a meal with them. Every time they take us to a ball or party. We will be creating additional expense for them." Kate trembled, not just from the cold.

"You had no problem with our creating additional expense for Father when we lived at home. Why start worrying about it now?"

Kate finally turned to look—to gape—at her brother. Certainly he was younger than she, but only by three years. However, he was a qualified lawyer, a man full-grown at twenty-four years old. How could he speak so juvenile? Did he not realize what Father and Maud had done to afford to send them abroad? Had he not noticed the missing paintings, carpets, and silver—sold so Father could afford their passage? Kate had a suspicion that much of their stepmother's heirloom jewelry had met the same fate. Not to mention Father's sacrifice of pride in begging his first wife's brother, the baronet Sir Anthony Buchanan, to take them in.

Christopher's light-brown eyes twinkled and danced. "Come on, Kate. I've heard that wealthy men can be plucked up on every corner in England, so you've nothing to worry about. They will take one look at you and be lining up at Uncle Anthony's door to court you."

Heat flared in her cheeks. "You can stop that nonsensical flattery right now, Christopher Dearing. It will get you nowhere." But she couldn't stop the smile that forced its way through her worry.

"It got me exactly what I wanted." He put his arm around her shoulders and gave her a squeeze, then turned and forced her to walk back toward the stairs leading down to the grand saloon on the deck below. "We will be docking in a few hours, and you've been sulking the entire voyage. I insist you come below and enjoy yourself, just for a little while. Or pretend, on my account."

Tiny snowflakes floated down and landed on Kate's shawl and the mittened hand holding it to her chin. "Oh, all right. I will come. But only to get warm before we dock."

It took her eyes several moments to adjust to the darkness of the stairwell. Reaching the grand saloon, Kate slowed and waited for Christopher to regain her side. Though not yet noon, the candles in the hanging lamps and wall sconces had been lit against the gloomy gray skies outside. The large, etched-glass columns in the middle of the room, which connected to the skylights above, brought in little light to reflect from the mirrors lining the walls between the doors to the sleeping cabins.

Several younger men, playing cards in the corner near the foot of the stairs, called out to Christopher, entreating him to come join the game.

He waved them off with a laugh and then offered Kate his arm. "Come, there are a few people who would like to speak to you."

At the opposite end of the long room, partially hidden by one of the glass pillars from the card players near the stairs, sat a group of middle-aged women and a few men. The rest of the men, she assumed, were in the smoking room.

"Ah, here is your beloved sister, Mr. Dearing." An older lady patted the seat of the settee beside her. "Do, come sit, Miss Dearing." Mrs. Headington's clipped British accent made Kate more nervous than she usually felt before strangers. That, and learning the woman had been governess to their cousins many years ago. Mrs. Headington was so particular and exacting, Kate worried she and Christopher would disappoint their extended family at every turn.

Kate removed her mittens and shawl and perched on the edge of the sofa. "Thank you, Mrs. Headington."

"We were just speaking of the Great Exhibition." The plump former governess waved a fan in front of her flushed, moist face, her more-than-ample bosom heaving against her straining bodice with each breath.

"The Great Exhibition?" Kate folded the shawl and set it on her lap, where she rested her still-cold hands on it.

"Oh, Kate, I've told you all about it. Prince Albert's Great Exhibition. It's to be the largest display of industry and arts from all over the world." Christopher's eyes took on the same gleam as when he talked about laws governing the railroads. "Imagine— delegations are coming from as far as India, Algiers, and Australia and bringing displays of their industry and manufacturing, their artwork. Some are even bringing wild animals."

He lost the dreamy expression for a moment. "And I have heard there will be agricultural exhibits, Kate. You may find some exotic plants for the garden."

She smiled at the memory of her garden, her favorite place in the world—but melancholy and reality struck down the moment of joy. She might never see her garden again. For either she would marry some wealthy Englishman and stay in England for the rest of her life, or Father would be forced to sell the house.

Talk continued around her, rumors of fantastical exhibits and inventions supposedly coming to this great world's fair, which would open in just under three months.

What would she be doing by then? What about Father and Maud and the girls? She shook her head, trying to stave off the unwanted visions of her father, stepmother, and little sisters begging on the streets of Philadelphia.

The steward entered the saloon and called everyone to follow him in to luncheon. Christopher offered Kate his hand. When she gained her feet, he bent over, placing his mouth close to her ear, as if to place a kiss on her cheek.

"I know what you're thinking about. Don't let it get you down. Everything will be all right. You'll see." He tucked her hand into the crook of his elbow and led her through the steward's pantry, where the beautiful silver trays and chargers displayed there winked in the candlelight, mocking her with their opulence.

Mrs. Headington invited them to sit at her table for the meal, and Kate sank gratefully into the chair Christopher held for her. Though her brother knew almost all of the hundred or so first-class passengers traveling with them, Kate had kept to herself most of the voyage, unable to laugh and flirt and pretend the way Christopher could.

"You appear sad, Miss Dearing." Mrs. Headington gave Kate a knowing look. "Is it a young man you have left back home who occupies your thoughts?"

Kate latched on to the question. "I had—have a suitor, ma'am. He courted me for over a year. I believed he would propose before . . . before Christopher and I left for England. But alas, he did not."

Christopher's jaw slackened, and Kate felt a kindling of amusement at his astonishment over her ability to spin the story in such a manner. Perhaps she did share some of his abilities, buried deep within.

"I do not know what the fellow could have been thinking, allowing a woman like you to slip away with no firm commitment.

Does he realize how easily he could lose you to one of our fine English gentlemen?"

If only Mrs. Headington knew what Devlin Montgomery knew.

"If the blighter is not man enough to propose before you left, you should consider yourself free to accept other suitors, Miss Dearing. Though you must allow me to caution you against those wicked men who want nothing more than to ruin virtuous young women like you." Mrs. Headington raised her teacup in emphatic punctuation to her warning, though speculation filled her gaze. "There are plenty of lords who will look beyond the lack of a title when it comes to a pretty face, so long as she has a substantial dowry."

Kate hoped one of them would also look beyond the lack of a dowry. Rather than let Mrs. Headington's unintentional disparagement send her back into the doldrums she'd been in since that awful discovery on New Year's Eve, Kate continued smiling and trying to engage in conversation with Mrs. Headington and the other travelers who joined them at the marble-topped table.

It would do her no good to show up on England's shores dour-faced and hung all around with melancholy. She had little enough to work with as it was—being too tall, with average looks, and angular features. Oddly enough, for Kate, the Old World meant a new life. Here, where no one knew her, where no one could recount the names of the men who had courted her and then decided not to marry her, she could forget the past, forget her failure to find a husband. In England, she could become *Katharine* Dearing, the woman who could not only carry on a conversation about botany or politics with any man, but who could dance and flirt as well.

For ten years, since her debut at seventeen, she'd turned her nose up at the young women who simpered and giggled and flattered all the young men. Well, most of those young women were now married with families of their own.

She glanced around the table and studied the interactions between married couples and among the few unmarried young women and men. Could she remake herself in the image of the debutante across from her with the blonde ringlets, whose coy, soft eyes and sweet smiles drew the men's attention like bees to nectar?

To her right, Mrs. Headington argued with Christopher about the politics surrounding the Great Exhibition and the worry of many that Prince Albert would bankrupt the country with the lavish display of agriculture and industry.

Kate Dearing would have joined in the conversation of politics. *Katharine* Dearing, however, turned to the balding, middle-aged man on her left. "What part of England are you from, Mr. Fitch?"

She lowered her chin and blinked a few times, trying to imitate the blonde's batting eyelashes. The man beside her almost choked on his wine before setting down the goblet to answer, obviously no more accustomed to being flirted with than Kate was to flirting.

Dowry or no dowry, she must and would find a wealthy husband. And as her stepmother was so fond of saying, practice makes perfect.

Andrew Lawton drew his coat collar higher around the lower part of his face and pulled his hat down, wishing it would cover his ears, exposed as they were to the frigid winter air. Beyond the inn's small front porch, snow blew and swirled on the indecisive wind—first toward, then away; left, then right. White dust skittered this way and that on the cobblestone street.

He closed his eyes and took a deep breath, longing for spring and the orderliness and discipline he would bring to the gardens at Wakesdown Manor. He had the plans all laid out on paper and was prepared to begin construction of the new gardens so they would be ready to burst into bloom when warm weather arrived. But instead, he was in Liverpool. And on a Sunday, no less.

Who would choose to travel by steamship in the middle of winter?

He'd only just managed to get away from Mr. Paxton and the Crystal Palace in time to catch the train from London to Liverpool yesterday. Eleven hours on an unforgiving wooden seat in the unheated third-class car—not wanting to part with his hard-earned wages in order to ride in the warmth and comfort of second class or the luxury of first—followed by a night on a lumpy bed in a freezing inn had done his back and his temper no favors.

Rather than go to the expense of a hiring a cab for the mile walk back to the train station, Andrew adjusted his collar again, hooked the handle of his valise over his left wrist, stuffed his gloved hands into his coat pockets, and leaned into the swirling wind with a brisk pace. The inn's distance from the station had made it economically attractive for the overnight stay—half the cost of those within a block or two of both the train station and the Mersey River ports, where everything and everyone came in and out of Liverpool.

By the time he reached his destination, the swirling white dust had turned to hard, pelting ice. According to the timetable written on the board in the ticket office, the *Baltic* had docked ten minutes ago, shortly after one o'clock.

If he caught the two o'clock train, he would arrive in Oxford near eleven tonight. He desperately wanted to sleep in his own bed after so many nights away. He purchased three first-class tickets, as per his employer's instructions, tucked them into his waistcoat pocket, then went to the telegraph office and wired Sir Anthony so he would know to be expecting his guests to arrive tonight.

Back out on the platform, he noticed the ferry from the steamship had landed at the far end. Passengers disembarked while crew unloaded baggage through a lower-deck portal.

He scanned the passengers coming toward him, looking for a young man and young woman traveling together. Americans. That was all Andrew knew. Dismissing several older people and a couple of women traveling alone, Andrew released his breath in frustration.

"You look lost, young man." A woman in a dress too tight and juvenile for her ample form and age stopped in front of him.

Andrew doffed his round-crowned bowler hat—and the woman frowned at it a moment. If Andrew had known he would be making this side trip when he left Wakesdown, he would have packed his top hat, since the more serviceable bowler served to emphasize his working-class roots.

"Good afternoon, ma'am." Andrew tucked the hat under his elbow. "I am supposed to be meeting a Mr. and Miss Dearing. You do not, perhaps—"

"Christopher and Kate. Of course I met them. It is hard not to get to know all the other passengers on a two-week voyage."

Andrew inclined his head in relief. "Would you mind pointing them out to me?"

"No, not at all." She squinted at the ferry. "Yes, there they are. Good-looking fellow in the indigo coat. The young woman is, alas, much plainer than her brother." The woman leaned closer and dropped her voice. "And if what I heard in Philadelphia is true, their father, wicked man, just lost all his considerable fortune in a railway speculation that failed. Poor dear. Only way she would have caught a husband at her age and with her lack of beauty would have been with a substantial dowry."

Andrew scanned the passengers coming off the boat. There—a young man in a dark blue overcoat. But that could not be Christopher Dearing. For the woman beside the man in the blue coat was anything but plain. Not beautiful like Sir Anthony's daughters—but far from plain. A straw-brimmed bonnet hid her hair, but her brown cloak and shawl emphasized her bright blue eyes, even from this distance.

"Now, if you will excuse me, I must arrange my travel to London."

Andrew gave the older woman a slight bow, then stepped forward to meet the Dearings.

Andrew stepped into the man's path. "Are you Mr. Dearing?"

A smile replaced the look of consternation. He stuck out his gloved hand, which Andrew shook in greeting.

"Christopher Dearing." He pulled the arm of the young woman in the brown cloak, who'd stopped a full pace behind him. "And this is my sister, Kate—I mean, Katharine."

Katharine gave a slight curtsy, red tingeing her cheeks.

"Andrew Lawton." He inclined his head, then dragged his gaze from the woman—whose face was, perhaps, a bit too square for her to be considered truly handsome—back to her brother. "Sir Anthony sends his apologies for not coming to meet you personally. But his youngest daughter fell ill two days ago, and he did not want to leave her." He glanced back at Katharine Dearing, to keep her from feeling excluded from the apology.

Concern flooded her striking blue eyes. "I hope it isn't a grave illness."

Andrew reminded himself that Miss Dearing was Sir Anthony's niece and, therefore, no one who should garner his interest in any capacity other than as one of the masters—fortune or no. "When last Sir Anthony wired, he did not believe it to be more than a fever due to the wet winter we are having and Miss Florence's insistence on riding every day no matter what the weather."

"I am sorry she's ill, but it is good to know it isn't dire." Katharine looked as if she wanted to say more, but at the last moment lost her nerve.

"So . . . did I hear you correctly?" Christopher asked. "The name is pronounced An*tony* and not An*thony*?"

"Yes, Mr. Dearing, you heard correctly."

Miss Dearing transferred a tapestry bag from one hand to the other.

"May I take that for you, miss?" Andrew pushed his hat back down on his head and reached for her bag.

"Oh, you don't—" But she let the protest die and handed him the bag with a sudden doe-eyed smile. "Why, thank you, Mr. Lawton. We arranged with the steward to have our trunks transferred directly to the Oxford train. The schedule they had aboard ship indicated there is one that leaves at two o'clock."

"Yes, that is our train."

Katharine looked up at her brother. "We should get our tickets now so that we are ready when it's time to board."

"No need." Andrew shifted her bag to his left hand, along with his own, and patted the waistcoat pocket through his frock and overcoat. "I have already taken care of the tickets. The train arrived just moments ago, so we can go find a compartment." He motioned with his free hand for Christopher and Katharine to join him, and he led them down the platform.

"My, but you have already thought of everything, haven't you?" Katharine's flirtatious expression seemed odd, like a daisy growing from a rosebush.

And the look of confusion on her brother's face only added to Andrew's. Surely she realized from his humble attire he wasn't anyone who could offer her the wealth she apparently needed in a husband. So why would she overtly flirt with him?

"How long a trip is it from here to Oxford?" Christopher asked.

"Almost nine hours, so long as the tracks are clear." Andrew looked past the roof of the station. Snow mixed with the icy precipitation from half an hour before, and it looked to start piling up quickly. Hopefully, traveling south and inland from here would mean away from the snow.

He found a compartment in the first-class car, set his and Katharine's valises on the seat, and turned to assist her in. She thanked him profusely. Once she was settled, he and Christopher lifted the small valises onto the shelf over the seat opposite Katharine, and then sat, facing her.

Katharine wrapped her shawl tighter around her shoulders and arms. Christopher leaned over and opened the grate of the small heater and stoked the glowing red coal. "I'd hoped maybe to see one of those new heaters I've been reading about—where steam heat is pumped from the fire in the locomotive throughout the cars in the train."

"Have you an interest in the railway, Mr. Dearing?" Though he had no desire to make the sister feel left out of the conversation, Andrew was in great danger of allowing himself to stare at her now that she was in such close proximity. Upon second thought, the squareness of her jaw did not detract from but added to the symmetry of her face. And above all else, Andrew appreciated symmetry.

"Yes—my apprenticeship was with a firm that specializes in railway law. It's fascinating to see how, in a matter of just ten or twenty years, the railroad has changed our way of life." Christopher stretched his lanky frame into a position of repose, obviously accustomed to the comforts of first-class accommodations.

"I was twenty years old when the railroad came to Derby—my home—in the year '40. It has quite changed the way of life for everyone there." Andrew removed his hat and gloves and set them on the seat beside him.

Christopher's eyes—brown, rather than blue like his sister's—flashed with curiosity. "Really? I hardly remember when the first railroad opened in Philadelphia in 1832."

"That's because you were not quite six years old when it came." Katharine's soft voice reminded them of her presence—as if Andrew needed reminding. "I remember it well. Father took us to the parade and to see the locomotive take off. It was the first time we were all happy since Mother and Emma died." Katharine's focus drifted far away along with her voice.

Andrew stared at her. In the space of mere minutes, she had changed entirely. No longer did she seem a vapid flirt, but a woman one might like to converse with.

Katharine's eyes came back into focus. "I do apologize. I didn't mean to cast a melancholy pall over the conversation." The strangely foreign flirtatious smile reappeared. "What is it that you do for Sir Anthony, Mr. Lawton? You must hold quite the position of importance for him to have sent you to meet us and escort us to Wakesdown." Her long eyelashes fluttered as she blinked rapidly a few times.

"I am a landscape architect. I am redesigning all of the gardens and parks on Sir Anthony's estate."

At the mention of gardens, something miraculous happened. A warmth, a genuine curiosity, overtook Katharine Dearing's blue eyes. Ah, there was the rose pushing the daisy out of its way.

"You've done it now." Christopher sighed dramatically. "One mention of gardening, and Kate will talk your ears off about plants and flowers and weeds and soil and sun and shade."

Katharine gave a gasp of indignation, but quickly covered it with the flirtatious smile again. "I am certain I do not know what you mean, Christopher. I would never think to importune Mr. Lawton in such a manner." She crossed her arms and turned to gaze out the window.

The train lurched and chugged and slowly made its way from the station.

Andrew couldn't tell if Katharine was truly angry at her brother or not, but he determined a change of subject might be in order. "Will you continue to read the law, Mr. Dearing?"

Christopher nodded. "I brought some books with me to study, yes. And I expect I'll pick up many more on the British legal system while I'm here."

Andrew opened his mouth to ask if Christopher were joking with him—but then pressed his lips together. Perhaps they had a different term in America for the pursuit of education in the legal system other than *read*. "Will you seek out a lawyer to apprentice with?"

"If Uncle Anthony doesn't mind, I might do that just to keep myself busy."

Katharine made a sharp sound in the back of her throat.

"Oh, right, I'm supposed to call him *Sir* Anthony until he gives us permission to call him *uncle*." Christopher grinned at Andrew. "Though really, in this modern era, why anyone would stand on such formality is beyond me."

Under the wide brim of her bonnet, Katharine rubbed her forehead with her fingertips, now freed from the mittens she'd worn earlier. Upon first seeing the Dearings, he'd assumed Christopher the older and Katharine the younger—from the way Katharine hovered behind her brother when they first met. Now, however, from Katharine's memory of something that happened almost nineteen years ago, she was obviously the older sibling. And if Christopher had been six years old in 1832, that meant he was now around five-and-twenty. Meaning Katharine must be in her late twenties, if not already Andrew's age of thirty.

That was what the woman he'd met at the station meant by "at her age." Andrew was not certain how things were done in America, but here in England, Miss Dearing would be considered well past the prime marriageable age. And if the rumors that woman heard in Philadelphia were true, without a substantial dowry, Katharine had no chance of marrying well.

For the first time in his life, Andrew felt true pity for another person. The last thing he'd promised his mother before she died of lung rot was that he would not end up like her—condemned to live out her days in the poorhouse. He'd worked hard to get where he was today, and he would do whatever it took to continue bettering himself and his condition.

He thanked God he had not been born a woman.

CHAPTER TWO

Wakesdown Manor
Outside Oxford, England
February 9, 1851

*W*hy had God made her be born a woman?

Honora Woodriff crumpled her brother's letter. Off in California, making a fortune selling supplies and dry goods to gold seekers. If only she'd been born a brother instead of a sister, he'd told her when she saw him off in London a year ago, he would have been happy to take her with him as his business partner.

Instead, she would have a life of solitude, caring for and teaching others' children.

She glanced at the clock on the mantel. Almost nine o'clock. Time for Florie's medicine. Tucking a stray wisp of hair back into the braids pinned low at her nape, Nora picked up the bottle the physician had left behind earlier this afternoon. At the door she stopped, returned to her desk and picked up the book from the top of the pile there, and then started across the house to her charge's bedroom.

Though Florie had been moved from the nursery to the family wing of the manor house a few years ago, she would still be Nora's charge until her fifteenth birthday in August, when she would leave for school, relieving Nora of her responsibility—and her employment.

She paused, reaching out to steady herself against the wall. It was a miracle she had been hired as governess to Sir Anthony Buchanan's two youngest children five years ago. Only twenty-one at the time and having taught for a scant eighteen months at Mrs. Timperleigh's Seminary for Deserving Young Women in Oxford, she had applied for the position at Mrs. Timperleigh's urging, who knew how overwhelmed Nora could get being surrounded day in and day out by the gaggle of girls at the school.

Despite Nora's certainty her letter would not garner a full reading, Sir Anthony had interviewed and then hired her. Now, here she was, five years later, preparing to send her last charge off to be finished at one of the finest schools in London.

And still, after five years, the rumor that she intended to become the next Lady Buchanan followed her whenever she went into town on her day off each week. After all, the gossip-mongers whispered, why would Sir Anthony have hired so young a woman with no experience as a governess, unless an ulterior motive were at the root of the decision?

She straightened, squared her shoulders, and continued toward Florie's room. In a few months, the rumor would no longer matter.

Miss Florence Buchanan sat up in her bed, supported and surrounded by pillows. Her black hair hung in two limp braids, and bright red patches on her cheeks emphasized her pallor.

"I see the maids have got you set up and comfortable as a queen." Nora forced cheerfulness into her voice. "I brought your medicine. And I thought I'd check to see if you finished the book I brought earlier and wanted something else to read."

Florie waved a limp hand toward the book under the lamp on her bedside table. "I finished it before supper. Where have you been, Nora? I've been frightfully bored."

"I was told your father planned to spend the evening with you."

Florie sighed. "He did. We played chess and then backgammon. But he left *hours* ago, and I have been here by myself since."

Nora set the medicine bottle and spoon on the table, hiding her smile over Florie's penchant for hyperbole, then perched on the edge of the high bed, the book she'd brought on her lap. "I am sorry. You should have had one of the maids fetch me, and I could have brought you something earlier."

Florie wrinkled her turned-up, freckled nose. "Please don't make me read anything for lessons while I am ill. I'd like to read novels—like *Udolpho* . . . or maybe, do you think, perhaps, I might read *The Tenant of Wildfell Hall*? I heard Edith and Dorcas discussing it last week, and they said it was scandalous."

Nora hid her smile behind an arch expression. "And you want to be scandalized?"

Florie nodded, eyes wide. "So may I read it?"

"That is a request I must clear with your father. Here is one you may read—and it might scandalize you, just a little bit." Nora handed over the book.

Florie angled the cover so that the light from the lamp glowed off the embossed title. "*Jane Eyre*. Oh, I've been longing to read this one. Even more than the other. Thank you, Miss Woodriff." She snuggled down into the pillows and opened the book.

"Before you get lost in that . . ." Nora picked up the medicine bottle and measured out a spoonful.

Florie pinched her nose but took the medicine without protest, though she did give a delicate shudder after swallowing it. Nora handed her the glass of water the chambermaid had left on the bedside table. As soon as Nora took it back from her, Florie once again wiggled down into the pillows and started reading.

"I shall return in one hour to put out the lights and see to it that you go to sleep instead of staying up all night reading." Nora picked up the medicine bottle to take it back to her own room. The doctor had warned Nora of the medicine's strength—and the possibility of coma or death if Florie accidentally took too much. Best not to leave it lying around.

"Miss Woodriff."

She stopped and turned at the voice of Wakesdown's housekeeper. "Yes, Mrs. Trevellick?"

The severe-looking woman gave her a kindly smile. "Young Mr. Lawton will be arriving with the master's niece and nephew in less than two hours. The staff will be lined up to greet them. I wanted to invite you to join us if you so desire."

"To see the Americans up close to find out if they're as wild as Indians, as all the penny dreadfuls make them out to be?"

Mrs. Trevellick chuckled. "Aye, more than few of the footmen and chambermaids read those stories and have spent the day leaping from one wild fancy to another of what the Americans will be like."

Nora opened her mouth to decline the invitation but stopped. She railed against the forced solitude of her position—not part of the family, but not part of the household staff, either. Yet if she turned down Mrs. Trevellick's invitation, the solitude would be self-imposed. "I believe I will join you. I'll get a good look at these Americans so I can describe them in full to Miss Florence in the morning, since she will not be allowed to see them until her fever is gone, I would imagine."

She and the housekeeper parted ways, and Nora returned to her chambers. The schoolroom seemed unusually dark and quiet tonight—as if Florie's absence the last two days had drained its essence.

Yes, she would see these American relations of Sir Anthony's. And, if she could work up the courage and find the appropriate means to do so, she would ask them about the need for governesses in America. For America, her brother wrote, was indeed the

land where dreams came true—if only one had enough gump-
tion to follow her heart.

⸙

For Christopher, the hours he spent on the train listening to
Andrew Lawton talk about his work as an apprentice to Joseph
Paxton, designer of the Crystal Palace, was the first time since
leaving Philadelphia two weeks ago that he had not been almost
utterly consumed by a sense of dread. He simply had a different
way of dealing with it than Kate.

Though almost three years his senior, Kate had always looked
to him to take the lead socially, as he was far more gregarious and
outgoing than she. Those who did not know the family well usually assumed Christopher to be the older and Kate the younger
sibling. He hoped that would continue to be the case here in
England so her age would not be an issue in trying to find a
wealthy husband.

Christopher almost groaned at the thought. His poor sister—
with as much as she wanted to help and protect the family, her
only recourse now lay in finding a wealthy man to marry her and
overlook the fact she had no dowry and the family had no money.
When she'd explained to him after luncheon that she wished
him to call her Katharine in public, deeming it to be more proper
and acceptable to English society, he'd shrugged and agreed. But
after seeing how his sister behaved toward Mr. Lawton, simpering and batting her lashes—*flirting* with him—he wasn't certain
he liked *Katharine* Dearing.

"So you came straight to Liverpool from London?" Christopher
kept his voice low to keep from waking her. Only minutes after
the train pulled out from the station, she fell asleep, rousing
briefly the few times the train stopped along the way.

"Yes. Mr. Paxton recalled me to London a week ago to help
transplant some of the trees and shrubs from inside the Crystal
Palace to a hothouse nearby, where they will be tended until the

palace is dismantled when the Exhibition ends in October." Over the past several hours, as Christopher and Andrew had talked and gotten to know each other, the Englishman had transformed from stiff and formal to relaxed and friendly. Christopher quite liked him, especially as he had firsthand knowledge of the goings-on surrounding the Great Exhibition.

The train jolted and began slowing.

"This will be our stop, then." Andrew stood, carefully, and shrugged back into his greatcoat.

Christopher was about to reach over and shake Kate awake, but withdrew his hand when her eyes opened and she blinked a few times to clear the sleep from them. "We're pulling into Oxford station, Kate. Let me help you with your coat."

Unlike most of the women he'd seen on the boat, who seemed to believe their wide-skirted dresses, with as many petticoats under them as possible, were just perfect for traveling in close quarters, Kate's brown traveling suit featured plenty of skirt, but not one that stood out from her two or three feet in all directions. She stood and turned so he could help her into her coat. She topped it with the matching cloak and shawl, looking, when she finished, like a brown triangle.

Not that he minded seeing her in something that hid her physical attributes. She'd inherited her extraordinary height from the Dearing side of the family, but from the life-size portrait of their mother that hung in the back parlor at home, it was obvious she'd inherited her figure from the Buchanan side. He hoped she had not brought with her the pink dress she'd worn to the New Year's Eve ball. It had taken all his willpower to keep from dragging her upstairs and finding something to drape around her exposed shoulders and chest. That the cut of her gown had been more modest than any other woman's in attendance that night had not mattered. She was his sister, and he did not want men ogling her.

Christopher shrugged into his own coat, though with all three of them standing and wavering about as the train jerked and hissed its deceleration, elbowroom was limited. Finally, the train came to a stop, and someone on the platform called, "Oxford! Oxford station, end of the line."

"Mr. Dearing, if you would take your sister to wait in the station house, I will find Sir Anthony's driver and we will see to the luggage." Andrew pressed the round bowler hat onto his head, nodded at Christopher, and touched the brim of his hat to Kate before opening the compartment door and disappearing into the night.

Kate stared through the window at the dark platform beyond. "I'm sorry I left you to the entertainment of a stranger." She stifled a yawn behind her mittened hand. "I don't know why I should be so exhausted."

Christopher reached across the narrow compartment and settled his hands on her shoulders. "Most likely due to the fact you have not been sleeping but a few hours each night for the past month."

Kate looked startled and then ashamed at Christopher's words. He gave her a quick hug. "Never you mind. If anyone has a right to lose sleep over this situation, it's you."

She pushed him away. "Don't coddle me, Christopher. I'm not a child. And please, do remember to call me Katharine. Wealthy men do not marry Kates. They marry Katharines."

Taken somewhat aback by his sister's sharp tone, as well as her reasoning, Christopher let his hands drop to his sides. Assuming she was grumpy because she was so tired, he said no more, but instead turned to pull down their two valises, Andrew having taken his with him.

Christopher opened the compartment door and, taking the handles of both bags with one hand, assisted Kate out onto the platform. Bitterly cold wind whipped around them, and Kate huddled close to him, pulling her shawl up to cover her mouth and nose. He wrapped his arm around her and hurried her over toward the light beaming through the window of the station house.

Though they could not get close to the coal heater inside, the congregation of travelers kept the room warm. Just when Christopher was thinking about getting impatient enough to go look for Andrew and the driver, the door opened and Andrew entered, coat collar held up to protect the bottom half of his face and ears.

"Mr. Dearing, Miss Dearing, the luggage is loaded and the coachman is eager to take us home to Wakesdown." Andrew held the door for them and then led them to the carriage. Christopher was glad for his sake—and for Kate's—that it was a closed coach, and hot bricks had been wrapped in the lap blankets to give them added warmth on the ride to their uncle's country house.

With Kate leaning on his shoulder, and a long day of travel behind them, Christopher found himself fighting a stupor on the half-hour drive from Oxford to Wakesdown.

When the carriage finally pulled to a stop and Christopher climbed out, an obscuring darkness surrounded them, blinding him to anything but the light coming through the open front door of the house. He turned to assist Kate down from the coach and then gave her the support of his arm to the front door.

"Katharine, Christopher, welcome to Wakesdown." The man who greeted them had close-cropped, curly hair of a silvery gray hue.

"Sir Anthony, thank you so much for your kind invitation to let us visit with you." Kate dipped into a courtesy without releasing Christopher's arm.

Christopher had to admit that what Kate lacked in expertise at flirting and small talk, she more than made up for with her ability at formal greetings. He removed his hat and bowed. "Yes, thank you, Sir Anthony."

The man guffawed and raised his hand in protest. "Come, come. We're not so formal when it is just family. Do call me uncle." He stepped back and motioned for them to enter the house.

Kate released Christopher's arm, lifted her skirts, and stepped over the threshold, Christopher following directly behind. He blinked against the bright, glittering lights of the dozens of candles in the chandelier overhead and the sconces that lined the walls of the wide entry hallway. He turned to accuse Andrew of vast understatement in describing the house, but the landscape architect was nowhere to be found.

Also lining the walls of the wide hallway were dozens of men and women—the men in formal suits, the women with frilly white aprons over black dresses. Christopher tried not to gape at the sheer number of staff. He had imagined Wakesdown to be similar in size and scope to their house in Philadelphia, at which they employed—had once employed—only around a dozen.

Sir Anthony stopped in front of two beautiful, raven-haired women dressed in full-skirted, fancy gowns that marked them as part of the family, not staff.

"Miss Edith, Miss Dorcas, I'm pleased to present your cousins, Mr. Christopher and Miss Katharine Dearing."

Though Christopher could admire Sir Anthony's daughters' beauty, the cold haughtiness in Edith's eyes kept him from finding her the least bit attractive. He remembered to bow a split second after Kate began her curtsy. The younger sister, Miss Dorcas, seemed friendly enough—though cowed by Miss Buchanan's intimidating manner.

"Of course, we will not expect you to stand on the ceremony of titles when among the family." Sir Anthony took a position beside his daughters. "I do apologize for the absence of my youngest daughter, Florence. But we expect the fever will be completely gone tomorrow, so you will get to meet her then. You will meet my older son and his new wife when we travel to London for Dorcas's presentation at court in April. Indeed, the only family member you will most likely not get to meet is my second son, an army captain who is off making his fortune in India."

For someone who went by the title *sir* and lived in a house that required such a large staff to run it, Anthony Buchanan sure did smile a lot. Of course with everything he had, why shouldn't he smile?

The rest of the introductions passed in a blur. The butler, the housekeeper, the footman who would be serving as Christopher's valet, the maid who would be assisting Kate. What was not a blur was the young woman in the simple gray dress standing near the housekeeper, hands folded demurely in front of her, her brown hair in a plain, almost severe style.

"And this is Miss Woodriff, Miss Florence's governess."

Curiosity filled Miss Woodriff's golden-brown eyes before she dropped them as she curtsied to Christopher and Kate. Though nowhere near as beautiful as Cousins Edith and Dorcas, nor even as pretty as Kate, something about Miss Woodriff drew Christopher's attention like iron shavings to a magnet.

Kate was not the only one who had been sent to England to try to marry money. But if Christopher could parlay his education and work experience from his apprenticeship into finding a job here, he could make his own money instead of trying to marry it.

CHAPTER THREE

*K*ate lay still, her eyes closed. Surely it had all been a dream. A vivid, horrible dream. Devlin casting her aside upon discovering she had no dowry. The tense weeks in which precious items disappeared from the house. The train ride to New York. Twelve days on a steamship surrounded by strangers. Another train ride. And more strangers.

A soft whoosh preceded a clatter. Kate's eyes popped open and she sat up in bed, heart pounding.

"I'm so sorry, miss." A slender blonde woman in a gray dress and white apron, kneeling in front of the fireplace, full skirt still billowing, adjusted the screen. "I didn't mean to wake you."

No. It had most definitely not been a dream. Kate swallowed past the thickness in her throat. "I was already awake." She knew she'd met this young woman last night, but everything blurred in her mind. "I'm sorry, I've forgotten your name."

The maid dipped a quick curtsy. "Athena, miss."

At the expression of surprise Kate couldn't conceal, the fair-haired maid smiled. "My mother was fascinated with Greek mythology when I was born. I'm to be your lady's maid while you're here. Since I hadn't heard from you by the time the rest of the family had breakfasted, I thought I'd better come up and make sure you knew where the cord is for the bell."

Athena approached the bed and pointed to a long, narrow strip of tapestry cloth with a gold silk tassel hanging from the end. "From now on, you just give this a yank and I'll know when you're up and ready for your breakfast."

"Ready for my . . . ?" Kate's gaze followed the maid back to the table in front of an enormous paned window.

Athena turned. "Do you want to have it in bed or sitting here?"

Except for when she was too ill to move, Kate had never been indulged with taking breakfast in bed. In fact, she had rarely taken breakfast alone in her room in her night clothes rather than downstairs with the rest of the family. "I'll sit at the table, thank you." She reached for the dressing gown draped across the foot of the bed and pulled it on before sliding off the high bed. Shivering, she slipped her feet into the bed shoes Ada, the middle of her three younger half sisters, had embroidered for her Christmas present.

"I've stoked the fire, miss, so it should be toasty here soon enough." Athena indicated the chair closest to the hearth that surrounded a fireplace so large, Kate's entire bedstead at home would have fit into it.

Everything about Wakesdown Manor seemed oversized. And Kate had never felt more insignificant in her life.

She choked down the food without tasting it as Athena bustled about the room, making the bed, adding more wood to the sluggish fire, and straightening the toiletries Kate had left scattered on the vanity last night as she'd pulled them out of her valise in the search for her sleeping gown.

"Shall I unpack your trunk for you, Miss Dearing?" Athena stood at the end of the bed, hands folded at her waist—though the position of inactivity seemed unfamiliar to her.

"No, I—" Kate closed her eyes and took a deep breath. *When in Rome* . . . "Yes, Athena, I would appreciate that."

Athena seemed pleased by Kate's change of heart—and to have something to busy her hands with.

"How long have you worked here, Athena?" Kate leaned against the oval cushion on the back of the chair and sipped the dark tea. She preferred coffee in the morning, but this tea was almost as strong.

"Me, miss? I started here as a between maid when I was thirteen." Athena pulled one of Kate's gowns out of the tissue paper layered between them and shook it out.

"A between maid?"

"Working either in the kitchens or house as needed. Then a parlor maid, and now a chambermaid. Though, with you here, now I'm acting as a lady's maid. That's rising pretty smartly through the ranks in ten years, my ma would say." Athena spread the dress on the freshly made bed and reached for another.

"Do your parents live nearby?"

Athena had a soft, tinkling laugh that made Kate feel close to laughing for the first time in days—no, weeks. "Oh, no, miss. Ma's a lady's maid for a countess over in Ipswich. My pa's the butler for a viscount in Norwich."

Kate poured another cup of tea, frowning. "Is everyone in your family a—" She couldn't bring herself to say *servant*, feeling the word would somehow devalue Athena and her family.

"In service? Oh, aye, miss. Me, and my two brothers as well. Ma and Pa used to work in the same house—that's how they managed to marry and have the three of us. But then the old baron died, and the heir sent all of his uncle's servants away so he could bring in his own people. We all had to take work wherever we could."

Kate had so many more questions, but asking how much the maid earned and how hard it was to get a position in a large household like this would probably be better kept for another day—once she'd gotten to know Athena better and knew if she could trust her to keep her confidences. For, if worse came to worst, Kate could always try to find work.

"This one should do quite nicely." Athena held up a dark purple afternoon gown. "Yes, I believe you will look quite fine in it when receiving callers, miss."

Kate dragged her mind out of the mire of worry about her family's financial problems. "Callers?"

"Yes. There's many hereabouts who will want to come by and see the newly arrived Americans. And though Miss Buchanan will turn most of them away, there may be one or two she will want to see, so you'd best be prepared."

After a quick sojourn behind the dressing screen with a washcloth and the basin of water Athena had heated beside the fire, Kate allowed herself to be corseted and dressed by a young woman who was, in Kate's estimation, better off than Kate herself. At least Athena knew what her future held—and that she had a way of earning her own living. Marrying money was a much riskier prospect.

After being layered into her undergarments, Kate sat at the vanity and tried to feign interest as Athena chattered about her family and their places of service while she brushed, twirled, and pinned Kate's hair.

"Beautiful hair you have, miss. The color of copper." Athena smoothed the wings that swept down to cover the tops of Kate's ears before pulling up again into the cluster of ringlets she'd arranged at the back of Kate's head.

"Thank you, Athena." The hairstyle was much fancier than the braids Kate usually wore pinned in a thick coil between her crown and nape. But, again, she reminded herself that things were done differently here.

Athena helped her into the gown, remarking on the exquisite lace collar, the fine stitching of the gathers of the full skirt, and the beautiful slope of Kate's shoulders, emphasized by the dropped seams of the bell sleeves. Kate adjusted the chiffon undersleeves so the cuffs hit the base of her hand.

"You look right pretty, miss." Athena turned her toward the freestanding mirror near the dressing screen.

Kate tried to judge herself objectively, but turned away from the mirror with the lingering impression of a very plain girl trying too hard to look beautiful.

"It looks to be a pretty day today—sun's out and last week's snow is gone. Perhaps after calls, you might want to take a walk in the gardens." Athena picked up the dresses from the bed, draping one after the other over her long, slim arm.

"The gardens?" Kate's heart lifted. Yes, outside, in nature. That was where she would find solace, comfort, and peace. "I think that would be lovely."

"Then I'll have your coat and winter boots ready for you, miss." Athena headed toward the door with Kate's wardrobe wrapped in her arms. "I'll take these downstairs now to be pressed."

"Thank you again, Athena." She followed the maid toward the door.

"No need to thank me, miss." Athena opened the door and started down the hallway, then paused and turned back toward Kate. "If you'll take the main stairs down that way"—she pointed the opposite direction from where she'd been headed—"you'll find yourself in the entry hall. The drawing room is directly opposite the foot of the stairs. That's where you'll find Miss Buchanan."

"Thank you, Athena."

Athena grinned and shook her head but didn't tell Kate not to thank her this time.

Not wanting to draw attention to herself, Kate stayed on the soft toes of her shoes, to keep the clack of the heels from echoing down the wide stone staircase. At the bottom of the stairs, the entry hall ceiling soared above her and the room spread out, looking twice as large as it had in the shadowy candlelight last night.

Kate stopped in the center of the hall and drew a deep breath—as deep as she could with how tight Athena had pulled her corset. She closed her eyes and pictured herself in her garden in the middle of the spring bloom. Calm crept in like ivy and wrapped around the worries and fears that had taken root the last six weeks. She wasn't certain what her future held, only that she would never find a husband if she continued on in the withdrawn and sulking manner she'd exhibited since learning of the family's financial ruin.

Raising her chin and forcing herself to smile, she crossed to the double doorway directly opposite the foot of the stairs.

The drawing room reminded Kate of the enormous lobby of the hotel in New York where she, Christopher, and Father had stayed the night before boarding the ship. She clung to the thin vines of calmness and continued into the room, with only a small hesitation in her gait.

The two black-haired young ladies she'd met last night sat in the seating cluster near one of the two fireplaces in the room, along with two women in bonnets and shawls.

"And here is our cousin, Miss Dearing." Miss Buchanan's voice rose above the soft din of conversation.

Kate stopped when the two visitors turned to gape at her. She curtsied and folded her hands at her waist, proud of herself for not wringing them.

Miss Buchanan made the introduction of the two women— one the wife of an important local squire and the other the wife of a dean at the university in Oxford. Kate repeated their names to herself as she took the empty chair beside her cousin. Panic overtook her. She'd committed her cousins' names to memory in preparation, but now faced with two of them, she couldn't remember what name went with which cousin. She could call the older of the two "Miss Buchanan," but what was the middle sister's name? Perhaps one of the guests would say it before Kate would have to betray her biggest social weakness.

During the voyage over, Kate had prepared herself for the rapid-fire questions that now came her way. Who was her family? What was life like in Philadelphia? Did they still have trouble with the Indians? Had she known what a train was before arriving in England? Had she ever seen a modern city like Liverpool or Oxford before? Did she think she'd ever be able to return to so primitive a place as Philadelphia once she had experienced life in Oxford?

"I did not get to see much of the city last night, as it was very late when the train arrived." Kate ran a finger down a deep fold in her soft wool skirt. "I understand that it is much smaller than Philadelphia, so it might take me some time to get used to living in more of a rural setting."

From the way the squire's wife's lips disappeared, she did not like to think of Oxford as rural. Kate hid her amusement. She would be cautious and not shame her cousins by insulting Oxford . . . or England. But she would not sit here and let anyone belittle her beloved Philadelphia by assuming it was primitive.

The two visitors turned their attention back to the Buchanan sisters—effectively ignoring Kate, which she much preferred.

She stood when the two visitors took their leave. As soon as they disappeared through the wide doorway, the middle Buchanan sister took hold of Kate's arm.

Kate's heart pounded, but she steeled herself for the coming reprimand and vowed she would not betray any emotion other than remorse.

"Rural?" A furtive smile brought a sparkle to the young woman's pale blue eyes. "Well met, Cousin Katharine. I would not have sat there so long as you did and listened to those women insult my homeland that way. They know Philadelphia is not out in the middle of the wilderness—as we all do."

The middle sister—oh, what was her name?—flinched when the elder cleared her throat. Kate turned in time to see the withering glare Miss Buchanan gave her sister.

The sister dipped her head and slunk back to the sofa, where she picked up her embroidery without a further word.

"While I understand no one wants to hear ill spoken of their home, unfortunately, those two women hold sway with a great many others in their social circle—low though it may be—and

we do not want them spreading the word that you are impertinent." Miss Buchanan glanced at her sister. "Do we, Dorcas?"

"No, Edith, we don't."

The tension in Kate's shoulders eased. "I do apologize, Miss
Buchanan—Miss Dorcas. I meant no harm. I would never want
to do anything that would—oh, this is terrible."

Edith adjusted the fire screen and then picked up a book from
the small table beside her chair. "Do not worry about today's
interview, Katharine. You will have many more opportunities to
establish that you are not an impertinent, uncivilized American."

Even though several years older than Edith, Kate suddenly
felt like an eighteen-year-old debutante once again, and vowed
to keep her opinions to herself. Desperate to rectify her error—
and to chip away at the ice hanging in the air between them—
she searched her mind for a neutral topic of conversation. "I do
not believe I have yet told you that we met your former governess on the voyage from New York."

Edith looked up from the pages she flipped through too fast
to have been reading them. "Which governess? I had five before
my fifteenth year."

As soon as her cousin asked, the woman's name slipped from
Kate's mind. Something that started with an H. Maybe a J? "She
. . . she said she had care of you until you were three years old."

"Ah. Miss Chatman. She left us to marry a merchant. Name
of Headington, or some such. I believe my father has maintained
contact with her over the years." And with that, Edith returned
her attention to the book she wasn't reading.

Kate tried to engage Dorcas in conversation, but the young
woman, just home from finishing school, seemed leery of opening
her mouth in her sister's presence. So Kate sighed and explored
the room while they waited for another visitor.

During the next two calls, Kate kept her opinions and wit to
herself, offering no more than general information and pleasant
nothings to add to the conversation.

After the final callers left, Dorcas and Edith excused them-selves. Kate returned to her room for her cloak, bonnet, and stout boots and escaped to the beckoning sunlight outside. The only door she knew of was the front. The footman who opened it for her bowed, but not before she glimpsed the curiosity in his eyes.

The gardens would most likely be behind the house. And just walking around the house proved a great task. Finally, she found a gap in the tall shrub row she'd been following and entered the garden. The gravel path split to go around a fallow fountain, and Kate took the right fork.

The footpath led her into a setting that reminded her of Fairmount Park in Philadelphia, though this park had the misfor-tune of too much attention from shears and clippers.

Farther down the path, Kate saw something that made her forget the last few hours. A gloriously overgrown boxwood bush, bright green against the winter browns surrounding it, lay on its side, ignominiously uprooted.

She knelt and, not caring that it would ruin her mittens, pulled the cold soil apart and worked to set the three-foot shrub upright, back in its rightful place again.

"I do beg your pardon, but may I ask what you think you are doing?"

The male voice so startled her, she lost her balance and ended up sitting in the pile of muddy dirt she'd been trying to push over the shrub's roots. Above her stood one of the most hand-some men she'd ever seen, the light from the waning sun shining behind him, creating a golden halo effect to his crown of brown curls.

Though vaguely familiar, his work clothes and heavy boots—and the long-handled spade on which he leaned—confused her as to how she would have met this man. He reached out his free hand toward her.

And Kate suddenly remembered him. "Mr. Lawton?"

"Miss Dearing. Do let me help you up." He wiggled his fingers.

As he was wearing work gloves, Kate didn't bother removing her soiled mitten before taking his hand. "Thank you."

Once back on her feet, she turned to examine the damage to her clothing. The long cloak had protected the gown, thankfully, and the mud barely showed against the dark brown wool.

"Is there a reason you decided to replant the shrub I just dug up?" Andrew Lawton leaned against the spade handle again. His eyes encompassed the colors of their surroundings—green and brown and golden, all at the same time.

Kate wanted to sigh in appreciation of his appearance but stopped herself with a reminder of why she was here. "I saw that the bush had fallen over, so I was putting it back into the earth— you dug it up? Why?"

Mr. Lawton's expression turned pitying. "Because it is an eye-sore, and it has no place in the plan I have for this area of the new garden."

"But . . ." Kate glanced around the otherwise pristine area. "It is rough and wild-looking, and it adds character and charm this garden desperately needs."

She turned back to Mr. Lawton when he made a choking sound. Those green-brown-gold eyes danced with amusement, and Kate felt none of it. He was laughing at her.

"Miss Dearing, you are not a gardener, so you do not under-stand. It is not roughness or wildness that makes a beautiful garden. It is through the control, the discipline, of nature that true beauty is achieved." Pity laced his deep voice.

Kate crossed her arms—no longer feeling the need to control her tongue or hide her true opinions. "Mr. Lawton, I will thank you to not make assumptions about me and what I do and do not understand. From what you said, I *understand* you are of the Italianate school when it comes to garden design. Artifice and architecture, formality and precision, but no passion. Nature was not meant to be controlled or disciplined. True beauty comes from allowing nature to take its own course, to be what God intended it to be."

Andrew kept smiling at her in that infuriatingly superior way. He straightened and hefted the spade over his shoulder. "And that, Miss Dearing, is the very attitude that leads to overgrowth and destruction in nature—and chaos and ill discipline in people." He inclined his head and walked away, whistling.

Kate stared after him, speechless. Had he just called her chaotic and ill disciplined? She took a few steps after him, desperate to ask him to clarify—but two other men approached him and she stopped.

She looked down at the shrub, which had started falling over again. With determination, she crouched and shoved the dirt Andrew Lawton had dug up back over the shrub's roots, then pounded it back into the hole with all of her frustration.

Next time she saw Andrew Lawton, she would be the one to walk away whistling. Just see if she didn't.

CHAPTER FOUR

*C*hristopher stared at the portrait of the dour, bewigged man, hoping against hope it wasn't one of his ancestors. He would hate to think he came from such stock. He moved on to the next life-size image hanging from the towering wall—and it took him a moment to realize it was a woman not a man, the tall, ruffled collar dating the image to the time of Queen Bess.

"Excuse me—are you . . . ?"

Christopher turned at the female voice. A girl—possibly a teenager—stood halfway down the enormous gallery hall, wringing her hands . . . though she looked curious, not worried. He flourished a bow toward her. "I'm Christopher Dearing. And you are?"

The pale face broke out into a huge smile. "I am Miss Florence Buchanan." She made a slight curtsy. "You're my American cousin."

"I am? Well, if that don't beat all." He grinned and winked at her.

Miss Florence Buchanan giggled and flushed to the roots of her black hair. Even the bell shape of the skirt of her green dress couldn't mask the languid lankiness of her frame—especially with two skinny stocking- and boot-clad ankles sticking out under the skirt and petticoats. She looked like she was better suited for playing baseball—or what did they call it here . . . cricket?—on the lawn than wandering about the portrait hall with her hands folded demurely at her willowy waist.

"I am sorry I was unable to greet you last night with the rest of the family." She edged closer to him.

He tucked his hands in his pockets and rocked from heel to toe. "I understand you weren't feeling well. I hope you are better now."

"Much better, thank you." She took another cautious step forward.

"Now you've had a chance to look me over, do I meet with your approval?" Christopher turned side to side, as if offering her the chance to inspect him fully.

She nodded. "Yes—I mean, I did not expect you wouldn't. I mean, I rather expected—hoped—you might be dressed in buckskins and wearing a raccoon hat."

He laughed. "A coonskin hat, you mean? I see you've been reading up on my fair land."

"Did you know him? David Crockett?" She closed the gap between them, warming to her topic.

"No, to my utter disappointment. Davy Crockett died when I was very little. But I too enjoyed reading about him."

"How far is Tennessee from Philadelphia? Miss Woodriff has a map, but it is not a very good one."

"Tennessee is quite a distance from Philadelphia. And as it is a large state, parts of it are very far from Philadelphia."

"As far as from here to London? It takes *hours* to get to London on the train."

Christopher bit the inside of his cheek to keep from laughing. "It's a bit farther than that."

Her blue eyes grew wide. "As far as to Paris?"

"Even farther than that—though we don't have the burden of crossing the English Channel, only the mountains."

"But the train could take you there, so you could see where he came from?"

He affected a deep sigh. "Alas, the railway system in America is not nearly as advanced as it has become in England. We have many more miles to cover, and most of it is through hazardous, rough terrain."

"Filled with Red Indians?"

He gaped at her. "Miss Florence, what does your governess allow you to read?"

"You may call me Florie. And Miss Woodriff gives me the most wonderful books. But Matthew sneaks his penny dreadfuls to me after he is finished with them."

"Matthew . . . the footman?"

"Yes."

No wonder this conversation had been very much like the one he'd had this morning with the young footman assigned to be his valet.

"Matthew is ever so desirous of going to America. A year ago when Miss Woodriff's brother left to go to California to get rich, Matthew almost went with him."

Christopher's interest piqued at that detail. So the governess's brother was off in California seeking gold. Though Christopher considered the endeavor foolhardy, he admired the man for the foresight of leaving Miss Woodriff behind where she would be comfortable and safe, rather than dragging her across the continent on a difficult journey only to put her at risk—from the environment and those populating it—once they arrived in California.

A clock chimed, echoing through the gallery. Florie gasped. "I had no idea how late it was. Miss Woodriff despises tardiness."

Christopher offered his cousin his arm. "Then let me escort you, and I will explain how I detained you. That way, she can be angry with me instead of you."

Florie took his arm with another giggle. "She tries to be stern, but deep down, I don't think Miss Woodriff could truly be angry with anyone. Not for long, anyway."

After several minutes, Christopher was glad of Florie's chattering company—he never would have found his way. They left the main part of the house and went into an older wing—colder, damper—and up two more flights of stairs.

When they reached the top of the second flight, the echoing clip of footfalls met them. They turned a corner, and Miss Woodriff came to an abrupt halt before she ran headlong into them.

She stared at Christopher for a moment, astonishment clear in her golden-brown eyes. With a little shake of her head, she turned her attention to Florie. "Miss Florence, your Latin lesson was to have started five minutes ago. You know how I feel about tardiness."

Florie gave Christopher a what-did-I-tell-you glance, then let go of his arm. "Thank you for the escort, Cousin Christopher. I will see you at dinner."

"My pleasure, Cousin Florie." He waited until the young woman disappeared into the classroom before turning his focus on the governess. Shorter than he'd remembered, she barely came up to his shoulder. "My apologies for making Miss Florence late. She found me in the gallery, and I kept her talking when she should have been returning here for her lesson."

Miss Woodriff—severe from her tightly drawn-back hair to her high-necked, long-sleeved indigo gown—closed her eyes. Before she bowed her head, the hint of a smile eased the straight line of her lips.

She looked up at him again. "I have been Miss Florence's governess for five years. I know it is she who kept talking to you, rather than the other way around. I do apologize if she kept you from anything important, Mr. Dearing."

"Nonsense. It was a highly educational conversation. We discussed geography, an American politician, and the aboriginal peoples of my country. I learned quite a bit." He ducked his head and grinned at her, trying to coax the corners of her mouth up farther.

It worked. Though she kept her lips pressed firmly together, Miss Woodriff gave him what most would consider to be a smile. "In other words, she asked you about Davy Crockett, Tennessee, California, and Indians." She shook her head. "Though the penny dreadfuls Matthew brings her contain a vast variety of shocking stories, those are her favorite subjects. Once again, I apologize, Mr. Dearing."

"Don't. I enjoyed it. I like that she's taken an interest in America. But perhaps I might be allowed to disabuse her of some of the more fantastical stories she may have read about my country." He looked over Miss Woodriff's head toward the classroom. "I quite enjoyed history and geography when I was a university student."

A glimmer of keen interest sparkled in the governess's eyes. "I believe that would be a wonderful idea. Would you consider coming to one of Florie's lessons and answering her questions? I am sometimes hard put to find the answers in my limited library on the subjects. Or would that be too much of a bother?"

He gave her a slight bow. "I would be delighted. Just let me know when, and I will be here."

Miss Woodriff's lips parted slightly when she smiled this time. She backed down the short hallway. "Thank you, Mr. Dearing. I look forward to learning more about America under your tute-lage—for Miss Florence's sake, of course."

"For Miss Florence's sake." Christopher waited until Miss Woodriff closed the classroom door behind her before he turned and skipped down the stairs, humming a jaunty tune he'd heard the sailors singing on the voyage over.

In the light of day, Miss Woodriff was more attractive than he'd thought last night. And if she let her hair down and wore a more becoming color, she could even be considered pretty.

But no, he couldn't allow his mind to travel in that direction. Though he'd never considered himself a great catch—too tall, too angular, not wealthy enough—for some reason, women did seem drawn to him. But now, with no promise of money and only his wits to guide him, he couldn't set aside his father's edict that he find a wealthy woman to wed.

The burden of marrying money and saving the Dearing family could not fall solely on Kate—who, though pretty, didn't have the most outgoing or flirtatious personality. Christopher wanted nothing more than to find a woman who matched him for wit, intelligence, and demeanor. Someone like Miss Woodriff might fit the bill quite well. But he could not allow himself the luxury of finding out. Like his sister, his fate was sealed. Marry money.

Of course, unlike his sister, he did have one small chance of escape. If Andrew Lawton would agree to introduce Christopher to his mentor—Joseph Paxton, designer of the Crystal Palace in London—he could possibly find well-paying employment.

⋘⋙

Kate tried to pull the shawl collar of her dinner dress higher up onto her shoulders, but the gray-blue silk taffeta would not budge. Athena fussed over Kate's hair, arranging a few long ringlets to rest over her bare right shoulder.

Though only Christopher and the Buchanans would be at table, Kate dreaded this dinner as much as those her father and Maud held for which the dining table had to be extended to seat more than twenty. She had a healthy appetite, but her stepmother's admonitions to "eat like a lady" in front of others kept Kate's stomach growling at meals taken in public. And though the Buchanans were blood relations, they were also strangers whose good opinion of her could be the making or death of her future here.

The butler called everyone into the dining room shortly after Kate arrived downstairs. She knew enough to hang back and allow her cousins to precede her into the dining room. Even as a young girl, she'd been taught by her mother how much emphasis the English put on arranging everything by social rank, even for something as simple as processing into the dining room. Sir Anthony took Edith's arm, and, with a shy giggle, Dorcas took Christopher's.

The youngest Buchanan sister hooked her arm through Kate's. "I think you should probably walk in ahead of me, as you are an adult, but let us go in together, and then we do not have to dither about whether you or I have precedence."

"I believe that is a wonderful idea, Cousin"—her heart caught in her throat a moment before the name popped into her memory—"Florence." Kate towered over her youngest cousin, though Florence stood a few inches taller than her elder sisters.

"It's Florie, please, Cousin Kate."

Kate raised an eyebrow. No one in this household called her Kate, except . . . "I take it you have been talking to my brother about me."

"Not about you, no, but we were the first two to arrive in the sitting room and he called you Kate. Is it all right if I call you that as well? Katharine seems too formal."

Florie reminded Kate forcefully of her little sisters; and, as she did with them, she let the young woman have her way. "Of course, you may call me Kate."

Kate nodded her thanks to the footman who held her chair. The superfluous length of the dining table made the party of six seem even smaller, all seated at one end with Sir Anthony at the head, Christopher and Dorcas to his right, Edith, Kate, and Florie to his left.

To be polite, Kate sampled a little of each dish, and found most of it to her liking. When she noted that Dorcas and Florie ate heartily, she too ate until satisfied.

Christopher and Sir Anthony spoke of railways and factories and, as Kate anticipated, ended up talking about the

Great Exhibition—Christopher's favorite topic since arriving in England.

"What you must understand, dear boy, is that the Exhibition threatens the peace and prosperity of London—of all England, in fact. Why, just think of the thousands upon thousands of people thronging into London, blocking up traffic, filling the city center in unwashed masses. I have already prepared my house staff to guard the doors and windows around the clock to protect against the thievery certain to be happening." Sir Anthony motioned for the butler to refill his wineglass.

Obviously crestfallen, Christopher sputtered a moment. "But . . . think of all there will be to see and learn . . ."

"And then there is the construction of the building itself. Crystal Palace, indeed. Why, one strong storm and it shall shatter and fall to the ground. No, we shall not be attending, not I nor my daughters, for fear of our lives. And if you and your sister are wise, you will follow our example."

Dorcas heaved a dramatic sigh. "This is my debut season—and it will be ruined by this spectacle conceived and put on by a foreigner."

Kate frowned. "I thought Prince Albert was the driving force behind the Exhibition."

Edith pressed her napkin to her lips, then pinned Kate with a pitying gaze. "He is the foreigner of whom Dorcas speaks."

"Prince Albert is German, Katharine, and he never allows any-one to forget it." Sir Anthony's voice held a trace of disdain. "He believes himself—indeed all Germans—to be superior to the English. It is even rumored he is a spy for the emperor of Russia and his uncle, King Leopold of Belgium."

"I have heard that he and the queen both champion the rights of the working class and campaign for the abolishment of slavery." Several speakers whose lectures Kate attended in Philadelphia supported their abolitionist and social-reform platforms with the example of how the leaders of Britain also fought for the same things.

Sir Anthony made a sound halfway between a grunt and a snort. "And they forget that it is with the aristocracy and land holders of this country that the power lies." He sighed and held up his hand when Kate took a breath to respond. "My dear, we in England have seen too much revolution, too many heads lost amongst our European cousins over the ideas you so freely espouse in America—the rights and conditions of the working class, political access for the common man, voting rights, and the like. You would do well to remember sentiments flow in different directions here."

Her uncle softened his rebuke with a kind smile. "Now, on to a more pleasant subject. Over the next few days, our guests will be arriving."

"Guests?" Christopher asked.

"Yes, for the house party. Young men and women of appropriate social standing and wealth will be coming to stay for four weeks of dinners, balls, and entertainment. It is customary in winter, when it is too early to go to London to immerse ourselves in society, to bring society to the country. And this year there will be a ball to honor your arrival in England." He glanced at Kate to include her.

Kate silently thanked the Lord that the house party had not begun before their arrival, giving her a day or so to acclimate herself to the customs and culture here. She had a lot to learn.

In the sitting room after dinner, Kate entertained Florie and Dorcas by answering their many questions about Philadelphia as best she could. They had a good time teasing her about her accent and trying to mimic it. Edith sat apart from them, a book in her hands and a scowl puckering her brows and lips.

"There is entirely too much laughter coming from this room." They all startled, but Sir Anthony entered wearing a wide smile that belied his reprimand, Christopher directly behind him.

"Cousin Christopher, come, sit." Dorcas tapped the arm of the chair beside her. "Katharine has been telling us about Philadelphia, but she said you attended college near New York

City." She and Florie dived into questioning him about Yale and his years at college and law school.

Sir Anthony sat beside Kate. "Katharine, I hope you are not upset by what I said at dinner. I did not mean to scold you, only to guide you in how our ways are different here than what you might be accustomed to in America."

Though Kate still struggled to push back the feeling of being an awkward adolescent—always saying the wrong thing and tripping over nothing but shadows—she smiled at Sir Anthony. "Think nothing more of it, Uncle. I am grateful for your guidance, as I do not want my behavior to reflect poorly on you or the Misses Buchanan during my time here."

His eyes crinkled when he smiled, just as her father's did. She couldn't help but smile back. "If you choose your husband wisely, you will most likely find him to being amenable to discussing some matters of politics behind closed doors."

Her smile twisted into a grimace. "I shall take that as a great compliment, sir."

He cocked his head, confusion filling his eyes.

She leaned toward him. "The idea that I will have a choice of husband—that there will be more than one man who will ask for my hand in marriage."

Sir Anthony chuckled. "Tosh. The guests who will be here for the next month have been carefully selected as those who will make suitable husbands." He now leaned toward Kate, their foreheads almost touching. "Though I will admit that I hope you are not the only young woman of my relation who will be finding a husband amongst them." His gaze slanted toward Edith, still aloof from the rest of the family, glowering at her book.

Kate bit the inside of her lower lip to keep from speaking. Could it be possible that Miss Edith Buchanan, heiress to a large dowry no doubt, was having trouble securing a husband too? Perhaps the affliction ran in the family.

CHAPTER FIVE

*A*ndrew smiled every time he passed the replanted boxwood. Seeing Katharine Dearing leaning over it, defending the eyesore, had given him a glimpse at a much different woman from the strangely flirtatious one he'd spent hours with on the train from Liverpool.

And every time he set his spade to the earth to dig the bush up again, the memory of the indignation in her clear blue eyes stopped him.

He hefted the tool over his shoulder, gave the trunk of the shrub a nudge with the toe of his boot, then headed back toward the gardener's lodge, breaking into a jog when the drizzle turned into a steady rain. He propped the shovel against the wall before entering.

The head gardener greeted him with a smile. "The boxwood still stands?"

Andrew nodded and stepped over to the large fireplace to warm himself. "The boxwood still stands."

"I can send one of the lads to do it for you, if you like."

Perhaps that would be a better solution. Andrew sighed. "No, 'tis something I need to do myself." He pulled off his heavy leather gloves and scrubbed his hands over his cold cheeks. "The new hothouse is completed. I've just come from inspecting it, and it is holding steady heat, even in this rain. I will spend the afternoon tagging the plants to be moved, then tomorrow we can work on moving the ornamental plants from the kitchen greenhouses and many from the conservatory into it. Sir Anthony is much desirous of having the plants throughout the house changed for new ones before his guests arrive. And daily fresh floral arrangements as well."

"The additional space in the new hothouse will be quite the boon with the extra work a house party generates. And now we can increase production from the kitchen hothouses—a blessing, that, with all the guests to feed." At the tall worktable in the middle of the room, Tom unrolled Andrew's initial sketch of his plan for the organization of the plantings in each of the hothouses, including the one yet to be built, which would utilize Joseph Paxton's sectional glass-and-iron construction innovation.

The three foremen came in from their duties of supervising the undergardeners in the existing greenhouses and joined Andrew and Tom at the table.

All had taken the time Andrew had been in London to familiarize themselves with the new design. Roland shyly presented a piece of paper on which he'd sketched a few suggested improvements. Of the four men he worked with most closely here, Andrew had always believed Roland—youngest of the foremen—to be possessed of the most creative and progressive mind. And while Tom had been reluctant to include the three in the planning stages of the project, none of the young men gave Andrew a moment's regret for giving them the same opportunity Mr. Paxton had given him.

"Well done, Roland. This will increase the stability in the iron structure and reduce the time spent in construction. If we place an additional door here . . ." Andrew paused when he realized he no longer had the attention of the four gardeners. He looked over his shoulder toward the door, straightened, and turned.

Christopher Dearing stepped forward. "I'm sorry. I didn't mean to interrupt. I was exploring the grounds and ducked in out of the rain. I can leave if I'm keeping you from your work."

"No, Mr. Dearing. Please, do join us." Andrew motioned him toward the table. "We are reviewing the final plans for a new hothouse. You might find it interesting as an admirer of Mr. Paxton's work, as it's inspired by his designs of the conservatories at Chatsworth and his design of the Crystal Palace."

The younger man's eyes sparkled with interest, and his long legs made fast work of the space between them. He bent his tall frame over the high table to examine the plans and maps.

"Why so many greenhouses? Does Wakesdown raise produce to sell?" Christopher frowned over the plans.

"No. These"—Andrew indicated the four structures closest to the house—"produce food for the family, their guests, and the house staff during the cold months when it cannot be raised in the outdoor kitchen gardens. These two, and the orangery attached to the manor house, contain exotic flora that would not survive in our cold climate—citrus trees, pineapples, peaches, and ornamental plants and flowers for the young ladies to decorate with. All need much warmer temperatures than what we have in England naturally. So we grow them indoors."

"But what about these acres here?"

"Sir Anthony does have orchards and grain fields—wheat and rye. There is a mill here." Andrew pointed at the rendering of the building at the far corner of the property. "The rest is pastureland. Wakesdown uses what they need of the flours and livestock; the remainder is sold at market in Oxford."

Christopher nodded and studied the chart in silence for a moment. Andrew's mind bubbled with questions—about America and the opportunities there for someone like him; about how the use of railways could drastically improve the ability of small farms to sell their produce and livestock outside of their local market towns. Conversations started but not explored with any depth on the train several days ago. And the one subject not broached, which Andrew would never allow himself to indulge in—finding out more about Dearing's sister. Pretty despite her exhaustion when he first met her; stunning when passionately defending a scraggly bush, her gloves and coat caked with mud.

"What you need is a spur line here"—Dearing traced a line on the map of the entire estate—"to connect Wakesdown to the main rail line in Oxford, and you could become one of the leaders in exporting your produce to the rest of England."

"Could you just imagine?" Foreman Harry leaned closer and traced the line between pastures and fields. "Not loading up the wagons time and time again and taking our goods to market, but just sending it all off in a train car . . . like Granny going to London to see the queen."

Andrew had to laugh with the others. "It would not be quite so simple, would it, Mr. Dearing?"

Dearing launched into an explanation of spurs and gauges and hand-powered carts, while the three foremen hung on his words—Tom listening with crossed arms and a speculative expression.

Andrew examined the overview map of the estate's several thousand acres, more than half of which were given to cultivation and livestock. Sir Anthony had complained to Andrew more than once about how much more the estate could be producing in foodstuffs and animals if only they had an easier, more economical way of getting it all to market.

Mindful of the passing minutes, Andrew pulled out his watch. He gathered the plans and maps, effectively ending Christopher's lecture on railway technology.

"Mr. Dearing, I have an appointment at eleven o'clock with Sir Anthony. If you are not occupied, I would invite you to attend him with me and explain your idea of a spur line to the estate."

The American straightened from the edge of Tom's desk where he'd perched. "Tell Sir Anthony? But I have no firm figures or estimates. Without knowing the laws—or even who owns the land between Wakesdown and the rail line, or the railway's laws concerning spurs—I don't know if it can be done."

Andrew tucked the papers and maps in his canvas bag and slung the strap over his shoulder. "I know. But I believe Sir Anthony would be pleased to entertain the idea, even if it turns out to be impossible." He raised his brows. "So will you come?"

Dearing grinned and rubbed his hands together. "Let's go."

Andrew buttoned his coat and tugged his gloves on, then led the way back through the field, which would become a hedge maze in a few months, toward the manor.

Approaching the house, Andrew hesitated.

"What's the matter?" Dearing stopped.

How honest could he be with a relation—and guest—of the people in the big house? Andrew decided to take a risk on the friendship Dearing seemed eager to offer. "I have entered Wakesdown through the front door only once—six months ago, when I first came to be interviewed by Sir Anthony. And then I was allowed to enter that way only because Mr. Paxton was with me."

"They make you use the servants' entrance?" A hint of scorn laced Christopher's voice. Andrew wasn't certain if it was meant for him or for the Buchanans.

He shrugged. "It is appropriate. I am neither family nor guest. I am a hireling, of no higher stature than any other person in Sir Anthony Buchanan's employ. Lower than many, in point of fact."

"I find that hard to believe."

Andrew tried to find an example Dearing would understand. "The housekeeper must run the entire household staff—dozens of maids and men—as well as manage the household finances. Surely she is of much higher importance than a man who, a scant two years ago, was nothing more than an undergardener at Chatsworth when Mr. Paxton made me his apprentice."

He shifted the strap of his bag to a more secure position on his shoulder. Someone who grew up with wealth and privileges could never understand.

Dearing swept the vista of the enormous Georgian facade of the east wing of the manor with a frank, appraising gaze. He looked back at Andrew. "Well, as I am nothing more than a poor relation without employment, I should not be eligible to enter the door trod by you and the housekeeper. But I shall take it as a reminder to pursue my quest for employment with all due passion so I may be worthy to count myself as one of your peers." He swept into a deep, groveling bow.

At first Andrew was affronted, believing himself mocked. But when Dearing rose, grinning, Andrew's ire eased and he found the humor in Dearing's words.

Andrew led him down the path leading to the lowest level of the house—one not visible from the front—and in through the gate leading to the kitchen courtyard.

Yes, even if the spur rail line turned out to be impossible, the discussion of it would allow him to spend time with another man of passion for building and innovation. Dare he think of Christopher Dearing as an equal—as a friend?

Christopher hadn't been this nervous since his final examinations at Yale. He followed Andrew from the kitchens and into the main part of the house, wishing he'd never stepped into the building at the end of the rows of greenhouses. As much as he longed to make friends here, the thought of telling his uncle about his crazy, ill-conceived idea made him wish he'd avoided the landscape architect.

Sir Anthony answered Andrew's knock with a booming, "Enter."

Andrew turned and gave Christopher a tight smile before opening the heavy door into the study. Unlike the bright library at the front of the manor, where Christopher had spent most of the past few days, the study was dark—walls lined with mahogany paneling and shelves holding hundreds of books, with only two windows on either side of the massive, heavy desk at which Sir Anthony sat.

He looked up, his creased forehead easing as he smiled at them. "Andrew, Christopher. Do come in." He motioned them to two of the four club chairs flanking the crackling fireplace.

While Sir Anthony had seemed affable in all of their interactions so far, now that Christopher faced him in his capacity of landlord and potential patron—and Andrew's employer—his uncle looked severe and imposing.

Andrew launched into his explanation of the changes marked on the plans for the new hothouse, then for the gardens and plantings.

"Which is why I asked Mr. Dearing to come with me." Andrew straightened from leaning over the maps spread on Sir Anthony's desk.

The baronet looked at Christopher with undisguised curiosity.

Christopher cleared his throat. "It was merely an idea—a fancy, really—and may not be feasible."

"Do not apologize for wild dreams, Christopher. How many advances would have been lost if the inventors had been afraid of expressing their fancies?"

While Christopher didn't believe he was an innovator, he appreciated his uncle's attitude. He took a deep breath and pictured himself back in the head gardener's lodge. He explained spur lines and showed Sir Anthony three likely places—relatively flat and close to the main line into Oxford—where a Wakesdown spur could possibly be built.

Sir Anthony was silent for a long moment after Christopher finished, tracing the routes Christopher had detailed with his finger.

Finally, the baronet straightened. "I understand your concerns as to why this might not be possible. But I want you to work on this. I will inform my steward you are to have whatever resources required to get the land surveyed or to acquire information or permits or anything else you need."

He turned and perched on the edge of his desk. "Andrew, do you return to London soon?"

"Within the next few weeks, to order and gather materials for the gardens."

"I would like Christopher to travel with you—to meet Mr. Paxton and his colleagues. We must do all we can to assist this young man in establishing himself here, since he was pulled away from what I am certain would have been a stellar career in America."

Heat crawled up Christopher's throat to his face. "Thank you, Uncle."

Sir Anthony smiled and rounded his desk to sit in the well-worn leather chair behind it. "And should this venture not come to fruition, I am certain that the contacts you make through Joseph Paxton, as well as others you will come into contact with in the course of your research, will be beneficial in securing you employment that suits your social standing."

Christopher started to frown, but quickly hid it. Something that suited his social standing? What exactly did that mean? Something suited for a poor relation here only to sponge off wealthy relatives until they were able to get rid of him by forcing him into a somewhat respectable job, of which they would not have to speak or think?

Sir Anthony continued. "We must be discerning and ensure you take a position only if it is suitable for a member of the Buchanan family. For though you bear a different surname, I will never forget that your mother was my dear sister, even if our father did sever all ties with her when she married. Did you know, Christopher, that Louisa and I shared a nursery and then a governess until my twelfth year? She was only a year younger than I, and she was my dearest and closest friend. But when she met Graham Dearing, there was no reasoning with her. Our father tried every argument he could think of. But Louisa was in love."

Christopher perched on the high arm of one of the chairs flanking the fireplace. "Had you no other siblings?"

Sir Anthony tapped his steepled fingers against his chin, his eyes glazed over with memories. "None. Our mother died when we were quite young, and our father's second and third wives gave him no children." His gaze snapped up to Christopher as if in sudden realization. "You have younger siblings from your father's second marriage, do you not?"

Christopher nodded. "Three sisters."

Sir Anthony grimaced. "All the more burden for you and Katharine, then. Boys do not create as much expense to raise as girls, I believe. My wife died when Florence was but a babe in arms. My two eldest, my sons, seemed to cost very little—a new suit of clothes here or there. Schooling, naturally. But my daughters . . ." He shook his head with a grimace. "Always wanting new gowns, shoes, hats, the latest fripperies and fobs. If a seamstress tells them something is fashionable, they must have it. I am certain your father, with four daughters, must feel the same pinch, especially now."

Christopher wondered how much his uncle was able to sympathize with the Dearings' situation. With a baronetcy and a family legacy of wealth, land, influence, and power going back generations, the Buchanans had never wanted for anything. The Dearings' money hadn't come into the family until late in Christopher's grandfather's life. Before the coming of the railroad, the Dearings had been nothing more than farmers and lumber and fur merchants, trying to carve out a life in the wilds of Pennsylvania.

Christopher glanced at Andrew, who stood as far away as the small room would allow, hands clasped behind his back, looking as if he'd blend into the bookcases behind him if he could.

Christopher rose and started rolling up the maps, and he and Andrew made their farewells.

"Ah, Christopher, one more thing," Sir Anthony said as Christopher was about to exit.

He turned to face his uncle.

"Do not forget that the ball in your and your sister's honor is in a week. Please make use of my tailor in town. Morency can arrange for a carriage to take you this afternoon." Sir Anthony nodded in a way that brooked no opposition.

Christopher exchanged a glance with Andrew. As if the other man understood what Christopher must say, he took the maps and excused himself, disappearing down the dim hallway.

Christopher stepped back into the study. "Sir Anthony, while I appreciate your kindness in allowing my use of the carriage, I must decline the offer. I cannot . . . I have not the money for a new suit of clothes for the ball."

Sir Anthony's expression changed from curious to sympathetic. "I should have made myself clearer. It is my understanding from my valet, who has spoken with the man serving you, that you have no suit of clothes appropriately formal for such an event. Therefore, you *will* go to my tailor to be fit for the new suit I have already ordered and purchased for you. It has only to be altered for your specific measurements before it will be ready to wear."

Christopher opened his mouth to protest, but Sir Anthony held up his hand with a sigh. "I understand your American pragmatism and unwillingness to accept charity from others, especially we English. However, by agreeing to have you in my home and to take you publicly by the hand before society, I have also agreed to do what is necessary to make certain you—and your sister—look like members of my family. It will not do for Katharine, in her quest to find a wealthy husband, if either of you look anything less than aristocratic, would it?"

"But the clothing we brought with us is almost new, and it served us just fine at the last balls we attended."

One side of Sir Anthony's mouth quirked up. "Yes, well . . . in America, I am certain you were the height of fashion. But you are no longer in America. You are in England. Styles and sensibilities are different here."

Christopher's shoulders sagged with the burden of charity.

"Once you have established yourself in a career, you may repay me if you like. Until then, however, please allow me to care for you as for my own children. I would not have agreed to your father's request if I had not been willing to do so."

Though it rankled every American nerve in his body to accept such charity, Christopher nodded. "Thank you, sir."

"Your mother would have had it no other way."

Christopher must take his word for that, since he had few clear memories of her. Inclining his head, he once again made his farewell, this time making it to the other side of the door without being recalled. The click of the latch shot through him like a spike through a rail.

He was certain Andrew had returned outside, most likely to the gardeners' lodge, from whence he likely conducted most of his work. But Christopher couldn't face him right now—knowing that Andrew had correctly interpreted the meaning behind Sir Anthony's words.

Instead, he headed upstairs, taking the marble steps two at a time. He counted the doors on the right-hand side of the hallway until he came to the fifth, at which he stopped and knocked.

"Come in," Kate's voice came faintly through the door.

He entered, glancing around at the suite. Slightly larger than his own room, it had definitely been decorated with a woman guest in mind: lace and frills and flowers on any surface that would countenance fabric covering or hanging from it. Kate must hate it.

"Christopher!" Kate set aside her book and hopped up from the shepherdess chair beside the wide fireplace. She took his hands in hers and squeezed them. "I feel I haven't seen you in ages—even though we share the same table for dinner every night." She motioned him to pull over one of the chairs from the table.

She looked different. He'd noticed the past few evenings that her hairstyles were fancier. But despite the intricate twists and curls her hair had been coaxed into, which should have given her an air of confidence and poise, she seemed withdrawn, nervous—almost sad.

Sir Anthony's words echoed through Christopher's head. It would not help Kate in her mandate to find a wealthy husband if Christopher refused their uncle's offer of new clothing from his own selfish sense of pride and independence.

Looking at his sister, he resolved to do anything to ensure her success in the marriage mart, no matter the blow to his pride or what steps he must take.

CHAPTER SIX

$\mathcal{K}$ate frowned, watching a myriad of emotions and thoughts cross through her brother's warm brown eyes. He'd come here with a purpose, of that she was certain. But now he seemed to be waging an internal war with himself over his mission.

"How—how are you faring here, Kate? Are you and our cousins getting on well?"

"Well enough, I suppose, for people of such different backgrounds and ages. And you? What do you find to fill your time with?"

Christopher's thick brows raised and lowered. "I have been over most of the house in the past five days. I have also started exploring the grounds. I came across Andrew Lawton in the gardener's lodge this morning."

Kate's attention wandered as Christopher told her about his morning's activities. Andrew Lawton. She could not get the handsome, square-jawed gardener out of her head. Her mind slipped back to that first morning when she found herself on the ground looking up at him, that superior smile on his face.

That superior smile that showed the dimples in his cheeks and the cleft in his chin. And when he helped her to her feet and she was close enough to gaze into his eyes . . .

She shook her head to clear the thoughts of the man she'd already spent too much time thinking about. Thankfully, Christopher didn't notice.

"So I suppose I will be going into Oxford this afternoon to have my new suit fitted."

New suit? What had she missed? Not wanting to let him know she hadn't heard a word he'd said after Andrew Lawton's name, she frowned but nodded.

"You can understand my frustration, can't you? I want to do what's best, for you and for our uncle and cousins, but it's hard for me to accept such charity when I haven't been accustomed to it."

Ah. So that was the problem. And it was *his* problem. But he seemed to want to make it hers. Anger bubbled in Kate's throat until she couldn't contain it. "Christopher, keep in mind that the brunt of this situation falls on me. I am tired of your acting as if this is hampering your plans or keeping you from doing something more important. Do you think I *wanted* to come here? That I enjoy putting myself on the marriage mart like a slave on the block? I have never asked you for anything in my life, but now I am. I need your help. I need your support in this venture. And if that means you must sacrifice your pride and accept Sir Anthony's charity, then that's what I'm asking you to do."

Christopher stared at her as if he no longer recognized her.

Guilt flowed in, but Kate resisted the urge to apologize and retract her request—her demand. She needed to know he was on her side, that he would help her in how best to present herself, the persona she was required to put on.

He took her hand in his, giving it a squeeze. "I'm sorry, Kate. You're right, I'm being selfish."

Talk returned to his activities of the morning—and of his time spent with Andrew Lawton. Kate's mind wandered again down the garden path where she was certain to run into the handsome young architect.

"... to London."

Kate's attention snapped back to her brother. "London?"

"Yes. Uncle Anthony believes Andrew's mentor, Mr. Paxton, might have connections that would be beneficial to me in securing employment. If I can find a position that pays well, then you and I need not be dependent on our relations."

But she still needed to marry. And raised as she had been with wealth and privilege, she knew she would make no good wife to a poor man. No matter that she had availed herself of all the schooling available to women in Philadelphia, her training was as a hostess, as someone fit only to become a matron of society, a woman who managed the household but didn't keep it herself.

Christopher stood, stretched, then leaned down to kiss the top of Kate's head. "I shall leave you now, Sister. And I will do whatever I can to support you. You have my word."

For several minutes after the door clicked shut behind her brother, Kate tried to return her focus to the novel she'd been reading. But to no avail. Rain still tapped against the tall windows, which had kept her from taking her usual morning walk.

Christopher said he had been all over the house. Why could she not do the same? So far, the only rooms she'd seen were her bedroom suite, the sitting room, and the dining room. But she knew from her walks outside Wakesdown just how far the manor sprawled, and she imagined it would be grander inside than the gray-stone exterior hinted.

Outside of her room, she paused a moment, tempted to take the back staircase down to what she was certain would be the more interesting part of the house—the areas off limits to family and guests, such as the kitchens, laundry, and servants' halls. But as she was uncertain Edith had forgiven her for her impertinence to the guests the other day, she couldn't afford another faux pas.

At the bottom of the main stairs, instead of going directly across the wide entry hall—itself as large as the salon that served as the ballroom at home—Kate turned right and headed toward the back of the house. The hallway led her past the billiard room, an informal gentlemen's sitting room, and a large library before it ended at the entrance of a grand room even larger than the front hall. With the ceiling soaring at least twenty feet above her, Kate's feeling of insignificance increased. Crystal sparkled from the enormous chandeliers lining the center of the room, even though the windows, as wide as double doors and twice as tall, revealed gray skies and continued rain.

The wall opposite the windows displayed larger-than-life portraits of people she assumed were her ancestors. She chuckled at their morose expressions. If she had to wear starched ruffs and corsets like that, she probably wouldn't have smiled much either.

Her heart leapt when she reached the doors at the other end of the gallery and discovered they led into a good-sized conservatory. The room, with windows making up most of the walls and ceiling, had probably once been the main indoor greenhouse for Wakesdown many years ago. It still held plenty of plants, but it had been made into a pleasant sitting room, with groupings of chairs in each corner, separated by a fountain in the center.

A door opposite caught her eye, and she stepped through it—only to stop in rapture. An orangery. Wakesdown had an orangery!

More than twice the size of the conservatory, the orangery featured a mostly glass construction, but this room had been kept to its true intention—growing delicate fruits, vegetables, and flowers all year through.

Closing her eyes, she let out a sigh of appreciation, then drew her breath in slowly through her nose, separating and cataloging all of the different aromas as best she could.

"Smells wonderful, does it not?"

She jumped, pressing her hands to her chest and taking a quick step back to keep from falling over.

"Sorry. I did not mean to startle you. I thought you saw me." Andrew tied a piece of twine around the delicate branch of a small tree. When he released it, a white tag fluttered at the end of the string.

"I . . . I was exploring and . . ." Kate hated the way her voice squeaked when she was nervous or upset. She wasn't sure which affected her more—the memory of their last encounter, with her falling in the mud in front of him, or the way his shirt clung to his chest, shoulders, and arms. She closed her eyes again and took a deep breath. "Yes, it smells wonderful in here."

"Tell me what you smell." His voice sounded closer, but she dared not open her eyes.

Slowing her breathing, Kate tried to separate the riot of scents surrounding her. "Jasmine. Orange blossoms. Fuchsia. Peonies." She turned her head to the side to see if she could distinguish more. "Sweet peas. And . . . lilies. I know there are more I recognize, but the fragrances are all mixing together." She opened her eyes and almost took a step back.

Andrew stood not five feet from her, tying the twine of another white tag to a small wooden stake, which he stuck down into the soil of a potted aspidistra. He turned toward her. The sardonic expression he'd worn at their last meeting had been replaced with one of respect. "I am impressed you could distinguish so many. I recognize most of the scents because I know what flowers and plants are in here."

"My stepmother was quite fond of strongly fragranced flowers, so our hothouse smelled like an expensive Parisian perfume." She smiled at the memory. "Well . . . like five or six different perfumes all mixed together."

Melancholy clouded Andrew's expression. "When I was a boy, I would pick flowers for my mother, to give them to her when she returned home from work. Now I know they were weeds, but she acted as if they were the most beautiful blooms from the royal hothouse."

"Is that where your love of gardens came from?" Kate trailed her fingertip along the long, flat leaf of the aspidistra nearest her to keep from staring at Andrew's long, nimble fingers as he tied another tag to a stake.

"Partially." He stuck the wooden peg into the pot closest to Kate. "Part of it comes from learning how to bring something that can be so wild and destructive as nature under control, and how the discipline of pruning and repotting and replanting can make something even more beautiful."

"Destructive?" Kate swung her arms wide and turned in a slow circle. "How can you call any of this destructive?"

Andrew cocked half a smile at her and moved on to the next table of potted plants. "I have seen ivy grow so dense and thick that it pulled down a brick wall. The job of the gardener—and of the garden designer—is to create a balance between the beauty of nature and the power of it."

Kate picked up a tag he'd dropped and curled it between her fingers.

He glanced over his shoulder at her. "You must admit, you would not enjoy a garden so overgrown and wild that it has overtaken all the paths and hinders you from walking in it."

She pressed her lips together and wouldn't look up from the small piece of paper. She couldn't admit that he was right, but she couldn't think of a counter-argument, either. "What are you doing with these tags, anyway?"

He had the good grace not to look too triumphant. "Construction is completed on a new hothouse. The plants I am tagging will be moved into it tomorrow. Feel free to look around. I can tell you what something is if you do not recognize it."

As if she would ask. She turned and strolled down the next aisle, stopping to inhale the strong, spicy fragrance of the jasmine blooms. Halfway down the aisle, she stopped. She'd forgotten her plan. This tête-á-tête with Andrew provided a perfect opportunity to practice her flirting techniques. Sir Anthony had mentioned guests coming—male guests so Kate could try to find a husband. And if she couldn't flirt convincingly, how would she ever catch one? However, seeing Andrew, talking about plants and flowers, had put all thoughts of *Katharine* and the need to find a wealthy husband out of her head.

Pushing aside fern fronds, she peeked at Andrew. Her heart skipped, and she let the greenery obscure him from view again. It wasn't just that he was handsome—Devlin Montgomery had been even more distinguished. It wasn't that she could talk to him about plants. She'd spoken with the gardener at home all the time without feeling the least palpitation in her pulse.

He came around the end of the row and started toward her, tagging plants.

Every time she opened her mouth to say something flirtatious, it died in the back of her throat. She couldn't do it. She couldn't flirt with Andrew Lawton.

Finally, she looked down at her pin-watch. "Oh, dear. The hour has gotten away from me." She hurried toward the door to the conservatory. "Good-bye, Mr. Lawton."

He tipped an imaginary hat to her. "Good-bye, Miss Dearing."

The portraits in the gallery glared at her as she hurried past, not slowing her pace until she reached the main stairs.

She'd always hoped she'd marry for love but was pragmatic enough to realize that her marriage would more likely be a business arrangement. She'd debuted into Philadelphia society at age seventeen, marking her official entrance to the marriage market. Because of her father's wealth, her mother's aristocratic pedigree, and the dowry Kate was destined to bring, she'd been introduced to most of the wealthy young men in New England. Tall, short, thin, stout, homely, and handsome, she'd seen them all.

Not one of them made her heart skip or beat faster. Not one of them made her tongue-tied by his mere presence. And not one of them had a gaze that could penetrate the layers of refinement and poise and see who she really was inside.

No one but Andrew Lawton. And no matter how he affected her pulse and her speech, she must push those reactions aside and forget about him. Because he was most definitely not the wealthy, titled man her father had sent her here to marry.

Kate returned to her room to find Edith and Dorcas riffling through her gowns. She stepped forward and grasped the post at the foot of the bed to keep from yanking her gray-and-purple plaid dress out of Edith's hands. The only wealth Kate now possessed was her wardrobe and her mother's jewels. Perhaps it was vanity, but she felt the need to jealously guard the only material possessions she had left. "What is going on?"

"Dorcas and I needed to see if you had any gowns suitable to be seen in society." Edith tossed the afternoon gown onto the bed. "It is a good thing we checked. You have a few that are acceptable, and I do believe Miss Bainbridge will be able to alter others into something presentable before next week. Papa said we are to have Miss Bainbridge fill out your wardrobe with whatever else is necessary." Edith tossed another gown onto the bed. "What have you in the way of jewelry?"

Kate clenched her teeth tightly to keep her jaw from hanging open at her cousin's audacity. Taking a deep breath, she turned to the dressing table and took the large lacquer jewelry box out of the bottom drawer. She set it atop the vanity, opened it, and stepped away.

Dorcas smiled and exclaimed over several pieces, but her older sister seemed harder to impress. After fingering every piece in the box, Edith turned with a sniff.

"From what I can tell, there are many fine stones, but the pieces are small and terribly out of date. Have your maid take the box to the steward and tell him I said to have Father's jeweler reset all the stones into more fashionable pieces."

Kate rushed forward, slammed the lid of the box closed, and grabbed it to her chest. "I will do no such thing. These were my mother's, and they will remain as they are or I will wear no jewelry at all."

A flash of fury flickered in Edith's icy eyes before her face settled into an expression of haughty indignation.

"Edith, I think the jewelry is lovely just the way it is," Dorcas rushed to say before Edith could speak. "Once her gowns are altered, any jewelry she wears will look lovely."

Kate had suspected since the day they met that Edith was not accustomed to being crossed. And rather than conciliatory, Dorcas's tone just now had been nervous, as if she were unaccustomed to gainsaying her sister.

Fortunately, Edith backed down and didn't fight with her over the jewelry, so Kate decided to give in on having her gowns altered. She would be the first to admit that the majority of her wardrobe was plain and out of date, most of her everyday gowns being more than five years old. She saw no reason to spend money on new clothes when what she had was serviceable. Also, Dorcas and Edith wore brighter colors and bolder patterns than her muted grays, lavenders, blues, and browns.

Right now, in fact, Edith wore a gown in a glaring blue-and-orange plaid—though with Edith's black hair and flashing blue eyes, she could handle the strong colors and large pattern. Kate had fought with her dressmaker in Philadelphia over the garish pink taffeta of the ball gown her father had forced her to have made for the New Year's Eve ball. Kate had seen a burgundy she'd much preferred, but the dressmaker had been ordered to put her in a bright color.

She shuddered, remembering the night of the party. No matter what the Buchanans' seamstress did to Kate's gowns, she'd still be the old maid no man in his right mind wanted to marry. Especially not when standing beside her younger, much prettier, wealthy cousins.

"Girl!" Edith snapped.

Athena stepped from the shadows behind Kate, with a timidity and fear that riled Kate's anger toward her cousin. The maid bobbed her knees in a quick curtsy without raising her eyes from the floor.

"Fetch Miss Dearing's trunk."

Athena scurried from the room after another curtsy. Kate would apologize to her later, when Edith wasn't around. Dorcas seemed to notice nothing amiss with her sister's high-handed manner. Would something happen every day to remind Kate of how differently things were done here—and how much she missed her old life?

The next two hours were spent with Kate watching Edith and Dorcas—mostly Edith—go through every thread of clothing Kate owned and deciding which gowns were "serviceable," "salvageable," and "not fit for the rag heap."

Much to Kate's dismay the only garment Edith took no issue with was the pink ball gown, with its flounces and ruffles and fripperies that made Kate feel like mutton masquerading as lamb. She had a feeling her experience with the dressmaker would be even less agreeable.

"The first of our guests arrives within the hour." Edith looked down her long nose at Kate's afternoon dress, a light blue with a darker blue floral print. "I suppose that will have to do. But have that maid do something else with your hair. Ringlets do not become you. Your face is too long and narrow—the ringlets on the side make it look longer. See what she can do, but do not be late coming down to the great hall to greet our guests." Edith swept from the room.

Dorcas followed her sister, throwing Kate an apologetic glance. "I think when your hair is swept up from the sides and the curls cascade down the back, you look lovely." She raised her hand in a wave and closed the door behind her.

Kate dropped into one of the chairs at the small table. Every gown she owned lay draped across the bed, the second tall-backed chair, and the shepherdess chair beside the fireplace.

Crossing her arms on the table, she laid her head down. But instead of weeping, she laughed. Laughed at the absurdity of her life. Laughed at the cruel joke God seemed to be playing on her, allowing her to develop feelings for Andrew when she could never marry him. Laughed—because if she didn't, she might not ever leave this room again.

CHAPTER SEVEN

*K*ate climbed out of the carriage in front of a row of buildings on a side street in Oxford. She turned to wait for her cousins to join her—but neither seemed at all in a rush to alight to the street.

Edith leaned forward, her ice-blue eyes matching the frigid air. "Dorcas and I have many calls to make, so it will be a few hours before we return for you. If you finish with Bainbridge before we return, there is an acceptable tea shop next door at which you can wait and watch for us."

The footman snapped the carriage door closed at Edith's nod.

Well, that was that. With a shake of her head, Kate lifted her skirts and turned. Overhead hung a shingle with faded blue lettering indicating this was indeed the establishment of *Miss Bainbridge, Seamstress*.

Kate turned in a slow circle, taking in the picturesque scene. On either side of the narrow, cobbled street stood two blocks of three-story row houses, each one differentiated by color or style, and each with a shingle hanging over the door to indicate the business that took place inside: Miss Bainbridge's seamstress shop—with its tall windows, each displaying a ready-made dress to show her skill and knowledge of the latest fashions—the tea shop next door, a music shop across the street, a flower shop beside that with a display of hothouse flowers in its wide windows.

This street was Oxford's High Street in miniature, and Kate quite liked the quaint quietness of it. She wondered if the greenhouses at Wakesdown provided flowers for the shop across the way, and whether Andrew's plans for expanding the hothouses took into account providing flora and produce for the benefit of those who did not have the luxury of year-round growing. She would ask him next time she saw him—it would give her the perfect excuse to strike up a conversation.

Kate entered the seamstress's shop. She paused just inside, allowing her eyes to adjust from the watery gray glare outside.

"I will be with you in a moment. Please feel free to browse the fabrics and notions while you wait." A dark-haired woman looked up from where she measured ribbon for a customer.

Miss Bainbridge was apparently not only a seamstress, but a shopkeeper as well, with dozens, nay, hundreds of bolts of cloth piled from floor to ceiling on shelves lining all four walls of the room. Down the middle of the room were tables displaying spindles of ribbons, lace trims, buttons, ready-made collars and cuffs, undersleeves, and every other accessory a woman's gown might need.

The bell on the door sounded, and Kate looked up in time to see another customer exiting. The dark-haired woman came out from behind her cutting table, sliding her shears into a deep pocket in her apron. Kate guessed the woman to be about her own age.

"I am so sorry to keep you waiting. Miss Dearing, I presume? I am Cadence Bainbridge"

Kate nodded. "It was no bother to wait. You have a lovely shop, Miss Bainbridge."

"Oh, please, call me Caddy—everyone does." She looked around the room with a critical eye, as if seeing only tasks needing doing rather than the wonder of fabrics in every color nature provided. "My shop girl is away visiting family." She sighed, then turned a smile on Kate again. "But no matter. Shall we retire to the back room to get started, Miss Dearing?"

At Kate's nod, Caddy Bainbridge turned over a wooden plaque hanging in the window of the front door so the word *Shut* showed to the street. She withdrew a key from another pocket and locked the door. "Now we shan't be disturbed. Follow me, please." She led the way to her workroom in the back where three young apprentices worked diligently on various projects.

After Kate declined tea or other refreshments, Caddy had her strip to her chemise and drawers—insisting on the removal of even Kate's corset so she could get her true measurements.

Caddy moved around with an economy and speed Kate wished all dressmakers possessed. Even though a coal brazier glowed red in the corner of the room, Kate's skin crawled with the chill creeping into the room by the time Caddy finished measuring her.

"You are very nearly perfectly proportioned," Caddy declared, making a final notation in her book. "I was not certain when you came in—but now I realize your corset was doing you no favors." She crossed to one of the many chests of drawers lining one wall of the room. She set her book and pencil atop it and opened the middle drawer.

The corset she withdrew was similar to the ones Kate owned, looking to be of white cotton; however, it appeared a different shape—and it had no straps to go over her shoulders.

Holding the front of it in place so Miss Bainbridge could lace it in the back, Kate could feel the differences. Rather than ending just below her waist, the front came to a point that almost reached the juncture of her legs. At the sides, the waist nipped in severely before flaring out over her hips.

"Blow out all your breath." Caddy caught Kate's eye in the full-length mirror, a determined glint in her eyes.

Kate took in a deep breath, then released it in a rush and held it while the seamstress pulled the laces as tight as she could.

Kate's ribs protested the pressure of the new shape, and she wasn't certain she liked the additional tightness around her hips and lower abdomen. She closed her eyes and prayed for Caddy to be finished tugging and pulling on the strings soon.

"Now . . . breathe."

Breathe? Kate's chest and stomach felt so constricted she wasn't certain air would be allowed in. But by taking in slow, shallow breaths, she managed to right herself before dizziness could overwhelm her.

Opening her eyes, she saw herself in the mirror—and gasped. She set her hands to her newly defined waist, shocked at how much smaller it looked. Surely that was worth the pain she now experienced, wasn't it? Her stepmother had always told her how much men prized women with small waists; thus the need for corsets. Would this help her gain a husband?

"Now, let us see what we can do about your gowns." Caddy crossed to Kate's trunk and opened it so the lid rested against the wall.

"What is wrong with them, really?"

She watched Caddy debate between giving an honest answer or a flattering one. Thankfully, she opted for honesty. "Most of your gowns seem to be several years out of date. You may have noticed that rounded waistlines are no longer popular. The style is now for the dropped point—though with the advent of ever fuller and wider skirts necessitating more and more petticoats and crinolines underneath, the deeply dropped waist of just a year or two ago is rising again. And the skirts on most of your morning and afternoon dresses are too narrow."

"And what is to be done about narrow skirts? It isn't as if they can be let out, can they?"

Caddy shook her head and helped Kate step into a plain linen petticoat. "The note Miss Buchanan sent over with the trunk said that if I was unable to match the fabrics or alter the gowns, new ones were to be made."

Kate's skin burned with embarrassment—and no little frustration—over the way her younger cousin was directing her life at the moment. "I see."

Several starched and quilted petticoats later, Kate finally donned the first of many gowns under examination. With the new corset, the bodices of most of her gowns needed to be taken in. Yet most did not work with the addition of layers beneath.

She learned that her sleeves were all wrong—no one wore straight sleeves anymore. The rage was all for bell or pagoda sleeves, necessitating the undersleeves that covered her arms from wrist to just above the elbow. The shoulders rode too high, too close to her real shoulders. And the dinner dresses and ball gowns—why, the necklines were completely outdated. They should be rounded in front and covering just the tips of her shoulders, not coming to a point in the center and cut high enough on the shoulder to cover the straps of her old corset.

With each gown Kate donned and Caddy marked and pinned, the seamstress's expression grew more grave. And Kate could understand why. With the new undergarments, none of her gowns fit her the way they should.

Finally, Caddy, who had been ripping out the hem of Kate's brown traveling dress to try to make it long enough to cover the bottoms of the petticoats, sat back with a sigh. She pushed up to her feet, gave Kate's figure a long look in the mirror, then met her gaze.

"I have an idea. Take this off, and I'll be back in a moment."

The dress buttoned down the front, so it proved easy enough to remove—though she did so with caution, since she had no desire to be stuck with any of the pins now glittering throughout the fabric.

Caddy returned with an armload of fabric in a blue-and-gray pattern. "I was making this for someone else, but when she saw the fabric, she decided she did not like it and chose something more colorful." She held up the dress.

Kate's breath caught in her throat. The blue print on a light gray organdy fabric was just the type of palette she liked—and the types of colors she'd been afraid her cousins would not allow her to continue wearing.

Caddy helped her into the dress. The pleats of the bodice fanned from her waist up and over her shoulders—making her waist appear even smaller, and giving a demure slope to her shoulders. The double-tiered bell sleeves dropped away dramatically from her elbows, with blue-and-gray silk fringe emphasizing the width of them. The demure check pattern of the bodice gave way to an intricate block-printed floral motif in the double-tiered skirt. White undersleeves and a lace collar finished the look.

The dress fit as if made for Kate. "Oh, Caddy . . . it's exquisite."

"It's a wool organdy, so it will serve you for much of the year." Caddy fluffed the skirt over the petticoats, then stepped aside to admire her handiwork. "Thankfully, I had not yet gotten around to hemming the bottom, so with a narrow hem, it will be perfect for your height. If you like it, it is yours. I cannot imagine anyone doing it better justice than you."

Kate eyed herself critically in the mirror. With her hair swooped back at the sides into a cascade of curls in the back, a more feminine shape to her figure, and a beautifully made gown, a new sense of confidence filled her—something she hadn't felt in a long time.

The woman looking back at her in the mirror, with her blue eyes and oval face, would be able to capture the attention of any man she set her sights on. This was Katharine Dearing.

If only Andrew Lawton could see her like this.

No. She could not allow herself any more indulgent thoughts about him. Beginning tomorrow, she would be introduced to English society, and she must begin her quest for a husband. A *wealthy* husband. And if he were not as good looking as Andrew, or if he did not share her love of the outdoors and green, growing things, well, then, that was a regret she would have to learn to live with. For the regret of knowing her family suffered through her selfishness was one she could not live with.

While one of Caddy's assistants hemmed the gray-and-blue dress and the other worked on taking in the waists of three of Kate's existing gowns, Kate and Caddy picked out fabrics and notions for new dresses, including a ball gown that Caddy promised would be ready for a fitting by the beginning of next week.

Caddy had just finished fastening the hooks at the back of Kate's newly altered day dress when the Wakesdown driver knocked on the door. Thanking the seamstress profusely, Kate draped herself in her navy wool cloak and hurried out to the carriage. As usual, Dorcas gave a friendly greeting while Edith acted as if she resented the necessity of stopping to pick Kate up on the way home.

By the time they got back to Wakesdown, the clouds eased and strips of sunlight filtered through. Eager to get out of doors, Kate did not bother changing clothes, but only replaced her shoes with her old, comfortable walking boots and headed out into the grounds.

Before she realized what she was doing, she found herself stopping beside the scrubby little boxwood. She smiled over the fact that it still stood—though the leaves remaining on it were mostly brown.

"You realize now, certainly, why the shrub cannot remain."

Kate drew in a breath of cold air until her lungs felt fit to burst. With as pleasant an expression as she could muster, and ignoring the pounding flutter in her chest and heat in her cheeks at his deep voice, she turned. "Good afternoon to you as well, Mr. Lawton."

He doffed his round felt hat. "I do apologize. Good afternoon, Miss Dearing."

"Tell me, Mr. Lawton, do you wait here every day just to see if I will come by?"

Andrew Lawton's thick brows raised a fraction. Once again, Kate found herself mesmerized by his eyes, unable to draw her gaze away. How had she never noticed before the chip of brown in the green iris of his left eye? She leaned forward as if to step closer to examine his eyes more carefully, to ensure her own did not play tricks on her, but managed to stop herself before doing so.

"Waiting for you? No. Truthfully, I had come to finish the job you interrupted."

"That was days ago. Why have you not completed the job before now?"

Andrew looked away, but the rising color in his planed cheeks wasn't just from the chill mid-February wind.

He tapped the point of the long-handled spade against the gravel path.

Kate couldn't hide her amusement, guessing the reason for his embarrassment. "Did you leave the shrub at my request?"

He turned his gaze heavenward before heaving a sigh and giving her a pointed look. "Yes, Miss Dearing. I found myself unable to dig the shrub up again—though it has no place in the design for this section of the park. But now—"

"But now it is dying and a blight to anyone's gaze. Here—give me the shovel." She reached for it.

He stared at her mittened hand, brow furrowed. "Give you the spade? Whatever for?"

Kate allowed a derisive sound to escape her throat. "What for? Why, to dig up this dead shrub, of course. I replanted it; therefore, I should be the one to dig it up again."

When Andrew did not seem inclined to give her the tool, Kate stepped forward and took it from him, waiting until she turned her back to him before smiling. Though physically on his feet, the way he reeled from her surprising action had figuratively knocked him to the ground, more than making up for the embarrassing position in which she'd found herself the first time the boxwood shrub had come between them.

Andrew stood back and watched as Kate set her mittened hands just so on the wooden handle and set the tip of the spade at an angle to the root of the shrub. A booted foot—by no means small and dainty—appeared from under the voluminous skirt and petticoats, like a bee emerging from a June rose.

His amusement turned to surprise when she pushed the blade into the hard ground with more force than he'd expected her to possess. With at least as much skill as the gardener's young apprentices, Kate made short work of loosening the soil around the bush. Andrew moved forward to offer assistance only when she'd dug sufficiently for the boxwood to start listing to the side. He held it straight so she could finish what she'd started.

He didn't realize how firm a grasp he had on the branches until the roots gave way and he reeled backward, taking several steps to regain his balance without ending up on the ground.

Finally he gave up on balance—and dignity—and let gravity have its way with him. The cold, hard ground rose up to meet him as he fell back, the bush landing in his lap.

From the way Kate tried—and failed—to hide her amusement at his situation, he knew his downfall had the desired effect. Her indignity had been recompensed in kind.

He pushed himself to his feet, leaving the shrub on the ground, and brushed the dirt from his trousers.

Katharine stacked her hands atop the spade's long handle and rested her chin on them. "I do hope you aren't injured, Mr. Lawton." A lilt of laughter laced her voice.

"Do not worry about me, Miss Dearing, I come from a hearty stock."

"As your chosen career is a physically demanding one, I have no doubt that it would take much more than a stubborn bush to knock you off your feet."

He examined her expression closely, finding not simply humor but understanding and camaraderie in her blue eyes.

"My brother tells me you have quite a plan for the gardens and park."

Andrew looked down and shook the loose dirt from the boxwood's roots. From their previous conversations, he knew Miss Dearing had a different idea than he on what comprised beauty in nature. Was she baiting him, or would she be able to see how order and structure created the perfect showcase for nature's true beauty?

He tossed the skeleton of the shrub onto the sledge he'd brought with him for that purpose, then turned back to Miss Dearing. "I would be more than happy to show you my plans for the park and gardens, either on paper or by touring you around and explaining the designs for each area." He gave a slight bow. "I am at your service anytime."

Katharine gave a slight curtsy. "Thank you, Mr. Lawton. I shall remember your invitation, and when I have time I would enjoy a tour of the grounds." She glanced over his shoulder and grimaced, then looked back at him, stretching the spade toward him.

He took the tool and looked over his shoulder also. A housemaid scurried toward them down the path.

"And now, if you'll excuse me, I do believe I'm being summoned." Katharine inclined her head, stepped back onto the gravel path, and hurried away to intercept the maid who had no doubt been dispatched to find her.

Andrew watched her depart until he realized just how much he liked watching the sway of her full skirt, even with her long cloak obscuring her figure. He lay the shovel onto the sledge, capturing a few branches of the bush under it to keep it from falling off. Once again he had found himself captivated by the American woman. And once again he had to remind himself that he was in no position to act on his feelings.

No matter how much he liked Katharine Dearing, he must—and would—conquer this attraction.

CHAPTER EIGHT

*Y*ou're supposed to be educating me—making sure I'm ready to go off to finishing school. And all the girls there will laugh at me if I don't at least know a few basic dances."

Sighing, Nora closed the book of French verse she'd been trying for the past half hour to get Florie to recite. "What dances do you think you need to know before you go off to finishing school, where you will have dancing lessons?"

"The waltz, certainly, as that is said to be the queen's favorite. And then . . . a minuet and a quadrille?"

At almost fifteen years old, Florie probably should know the steps of those dances most popular at the balls she would be attending in just a few years' time when she made her debut. Nora had learned those and many more as a student at Mrs. Timperleigh's Seminary for Deserving Young Women when she was Florie's age.

Not that an opportunity to use that knowledge had ever presented itself to Nora, who had progressed from the classroom to teaching at Mrs. Timperleigh's to becoming governess to Dorcas and Florie the year before Dorcas went off to finishing school in London.

Nora set the book on the table and stood, holding her hands out to Florie. "Very well. The waltz is a three-step figure—"

"Not in here!" Florie looked disdainfully around the school-room. "Besides, what will we do for music?"

Nora dropped her hands to her sides. "I cannot very well show you the steps and provide music."

"That's true. You have not the voice for singing."

From anyone else, the comment would have been insulting. But the grin that Florie gave her made Nora laugh. Florie had long ago given up trying to learn to sing.

"I have an idea." Florie dashed from the room with a whirl and a flare of skirts and ankles.

"Miss Florie—" Nora followed her young charge as fast as she could walk. Obviously, they needed to repeat the lesson on deco-rum and the speed at which a lady moved.

Every time Nora rounded a corner, it was just in time to see the pink ruffle at the bottom of Florie's skirt disappear around the next. She slowed when she reached a corridor and did not seeing the young woman ahead of her.

Voices came from a room ahead on the left moments before Florie exited, pulling Christopher Dearing by the wrist behind her. Florie did not pause—in her stride or her speech—as she passed Nora in the hallway.

Face burning, Nora lowered her eyes, unable to hold Mr. Dearing's confused gaze. She followed them downstairs, through the gallery and morning room to the music room.

"Miss Woodriff will play for us and you can show me the steps to the waltz." Florie pulled her cousin into the middle of the room.

Embarrassment trickled down into Nora's stomach, where it solidified as a knot of horror. Her talent at the piano hardly sur-passed her talent for singing. And Florie wanted Nora to play in front of Christopher Dearing? The self-assured American who now stood in the middle of the room in his waistcoat and shirt-sleeves, looking devastatingly handsome?

"Miss Florence, I do not think it prudent to impose upon Mr. Dearing's time—"

"Oh, he doesn't mind, do you Cousin Christopher?" Florie beamed up at him. It wasn't an expression of infatuation, but one that bespoke high esteem.

"I—no, I don't mind at all, Cousin Florie." He grinned down at the fourteen-year-old, and Nora's skin tingled. He turned to look at Nora. "Although if Miss Woodriff does not believe this to be a good idea, I will respect her decision."

"Thank you, Mr. Dearing, I—"

"She thinks it's a wonderful idea." Florie pulled on her cousin's sleeve to regain his attention.

Heart pounding so hard she could feel it pulsing in the tip of her nose, Nora made her way to the piano. Unlike Florie and the older Buchanan sisters, Nora could not play from memory, so she stepped to the bookcase beside the instrument to choose a piece of music. She found "Bouquets" by Johann Strauss and carried it to the piano, at least familiar with the main melody of the waltz.

With her pulse providing the tempo, Nora set her fingers to the fine ivory keys as Christopher, with Florie in his arms, showed the young girl how the dance began.

He glanced over his shoulder at Nora. "Let's start slowly, shall we?"

She nodded, unable to speak under the force of his grin. She read through the first line of the music twice before she started playing, visually digging out the melody so she could concentrate on it.

Wincing at each misplayed note, Nora kept her attention pinioned to the page in front of her, not wanting to look over the top of the small cabinet piano and see the look of disappointment—or worse, disgust—on Christopher Dearing's handsome face at her lack of accomplishment.

Not that it should matter. A man like Christopher would never deign to think of someone in Nora's position. His background, his relations, made him too far above her station in life.

Slowly, she got a feel for the song and, though it sounded wooden and hollow to her own ears, she managed to play the main theme of the song through until she no longer had to concentrate so hard on reading the notes.

Now she could hear Christopher's voice. "One, two, three. One, two, three. Ow. No. Step back with your left foot. One, two, three. Step back first, not forward."

Though Nora did not dare take her eyes from the music, the friendly, encouraging tone of Christopher's voice conveyed his patience and kindness. Nora's fingers tripped over the next three notes, and embarrassment flamed in her cheeks.

"I just can't get it," Florie wailed. "But maybe—"

Nora jumped at a tap on her shoulder. She stopped playing and looked up, surprised to see Florie standing beside her. "If I watch you and Cousin Christopher dance, maybe I'll be able to get the steps better."

About to protest, Nora's voice stuck in her throat when Christopher extended his hand toward her. "It can't hurt."

Trembling, Nora placed her hand in Christopher's large, warm one and stood, joining him on the opposite side of the piano. Florie sat on the vacated bench and pulled the music off the stand so she could see over the top of the instrument to watch them.

Unlike Nora, Florie had mastered every musical instrument in the house by the age of twelve. And it had only taken her that long because her father had brought home a new instrument every time he went to London for several years, trying to see if he could stump her with one. She had finally turned her nose up at the large brass horn called a euphonium, and he had stopped.

Trepidation settled with a nauseating lump in the pit of Nora's stomach as Christopher's hand settled just below her shoulder blade. She ignored the temptation to wipe her hand down her skirt before placing it in his.

He was so very tall. Though not short, she still found herself at eye level with his cravat, admiring the silver filigree pin holding the folds of blue silk in place.

And his shoulder. She stifled a shudder. Through the smooth cotton shirt, she could feel the contours of his muscles in a way she'd never thought to experience.

Beautiful music drifted toward them from the piano, and Christopher's hand tightened around hers. Nora tilted her head to look up into his eyes.

He moved, and she followed his lead, trusting him to lead her through the steps she hadn't used in more than eight years.

As if she'd been born to do it, Nora danced—though she wasn't certain her feet touched the floor. Strength, stability, and sensuality flowed through Christopher's arms and hands into hers, creating a sense of comfort and belonging Nora never knew existed.

Forever. Eternity. A lifetime.

The music faded and the forever ended. Christopher stepped back and bowed. On unsteady legs, Nora curtsied.

At the piano, Florie applauded. "That was beautiful. I think I may have it now."

Unable to meet Christopher's eyes again, Nora replaced her charge at the piano, opened the music, and plunked out the melody.

"I don't think we need the music, Miss Woodriff." Florie took her place in Christopher's arms—the place Nora selfishly wanted back. "If Cousin Christopher can keep the time . . ."

He nodded. "Ready? And . . . one, two, three. One, two, three."

Florie sashayed around the room, waltzing as if she'd been doing it for years, never taking a single misstep, even when Christopher stopped counting out loud.

Nora found herself fascinated with Christopher's feet. His well-shined black shoes slid across the wood floor like a leaf skimming the surface of a creek, with a lightness that belied his size and strength. Never before had she considered a man graceful, but that was the only apt description.

Eventually, Christopher ended the dance, bowing to Florie as he had done to Nora.

Florie flounced a curtsy with a giggle. "Thank you, Cousin Christopher."

"My pleasure, Cousin Florie." When he turned toward Nora, still seated at the piano, his amused grin slid into a more serious smile. "Miss Woodriff. Thank you for allowing me to assist you in Miss Florence's tutelage."

"Thank you, Mr. Dearing. I am sorry for interrupting your day with something so trivial."

"Dancing is never trivial, especially for an accomplished young lady. Isn't that so, Cousin?" He winked at Florie, who giggled and simpered at him.

Never before had Nora felt jealousy toward one of her charges—envy at the ease of their lives, certainly, but never outright jealousy. She must not allow these feelings to develop further. Not toward Florie, and most definitely not toward Mr. Dearing.

Christopher stretched his fingers, then balled them into fists. The raccoons still romped in his stomach, his head whirling with the rhythm of the waltz. How could someone he hardly knew affect him so?

Female voices faded as his cousin and her governess disappeared in the opposite direction. Christopher returned to the small room Sir Anthony had set up as a study for him. But after staring at the tome of English railway law without comprehending a word on the pages, he turned the wooden swivel chair until he faced the window.

Outside, rain fell thickly, obscuring everything beyond the low shrub that marked the border of the small garden outside this mainly unused wing of the house. The navy dress Miss Woodriff had been wearing made her eyes gleam golden in the pale gray light that had filtered into the music room through the tall mullioned windows. The center parting and smooth wings of her hair, pulled back into a plain knot at the back of her head, served only to emphasize her fine cheekbones and delicate features.

Turning back to the desk, he leaned his chin on his fist over the law book and allowed his mind to drift back, allowed Strauss's lilting tune to fill his mind as the memory of taking Nora Woodriff into his arms and waltzing her around the music room made him sway slightly in his seat.

She was nothing like the debutantes and socialites his father and stepmother had pushed on him every time he'd been home from Yale. Thus her attraction. Unlike her young charge, she didn't simper or smirk, flirt or flatter. Though shy, when she looked at him, she did so with wide-eyed innocence, not with eyes that tried to calculate his pecuniary worth.

But if the footmen were to be believed, perhaps the reason Miss Woodriff showed no artifice when she looked at Christopher was that she had her sights set higher—toward the master of the house. Though if that were the case, she'd had many years in which to try to secure him, with no outward results so far.

One thing he had learned in his short time here was that the life chosen by Miss Woodriff was one of isolation and loneliness. Not in the family's social circle yet not one of the servants, she lived in a suite attached to the schoolroom, where she spent all of her time when not discharging her duties with Florie.

And when Florie went off to London for finishing school in a few months, Miss Woodriff would be without employment, without a place to call home.

The image of himself rescuing her from such a fate made him smile. He could be like the heroes of the bedtime stories his little sisters loved—swooping in to save Nora from a life of tedium and loneliness. He could marry her and take her back to America, where he would find work with one of the many railroad companies springing up all over the western part of Pennsylvania and into Ohio, make his fortune, and then return home, where she would become queen of Philadelphia society—for everyone would love her for her kindness and gentleness. Just like in the fairy stories.

Love. Was it possible to love someone he'd met not even a week ago? Clara, Ada, and Ella would say yes; however, Christopher knew his heart was not yet lost to the governess. He'd been around enough women in his life to realize the pull of attraction he felt toward Nora Woodriff was different from that caused by a beautiful face and lithe figure. Something more surged through the air between them whenever they were in the same room. He knew—or hoped, anyway—that she felt it too. It could be the beginnings of love, though he had never experienced the emotion outside of his family, so he couldn't be certain.

It might help if he got to know her better. And he would begin by taking her up on her offer to come to Florie's lessons to teach his cousin about America.

CHAPTER NINE

$\mathcal{T}$he loamy incense of soil and growing things, along with the sweet and spicy aromas of flowers, fruits, and herbs, greeted Kate with a warm, moist embrace at the conservatory entrance. She breathed deeply and leaned back against the doorframe, letting her eyes drift shut.

Silently, she thanked God for the bustle and demands of preparing for a house party that would keep Edith and Dorcas busy all day, which meant freedom for Kate to do whatever she wanted. And what she wanted was to see the gardens. However, the rain still had not eased, so she'd come to the conservatory, hoping against reason that *he* might be here.

She pushed away from the jamb and strolled down the center of the conservatory, lifting her hand to run her fingers along the cool, smooth fronds of the overarching palms. She paused in the doorway between the conservatory and orangery and breathed deeply of the citrus-scented air. The precious orange and lemon trees, with their dark-green foliage and colorful fruits, almost made her forget the gray chill beyond the windows and glass ceiling of the large room. In a corner, several of the pineapples looked ready to be harvested. And a riot of jasmine and other flowers added their color and fragrance to the scene.

Kate's spine tickled at a rustling noise. She turned, heart racing, breath caught in her chest, hoping to see Andrew coming toward her. Instead, she saw the gray-clad governess rising from the bench under a vine-covered arbor, a book closed over her index finger.

"Miss Woodriff, I do apologize. I did not mean to disturb you."

"It is no disturbance, Miss Dearing." She raised the hand holding the book. "I am simply reviewing this book to see if it is appropriate for Miss Florence. *The Biographical Memoir of Daniel Boone.* Mr. Dearing recommended it to me, and Sir Anthony was kind enough to send to London for it."

Christopher was recommending books to the governess? Kate tried not to let her surprise show. "That was one of Christopher's favorite books as a boy. There has been much debate in the twenty years since its release over the accuracy of some of the anecdotes related in it. But as a piece of folklore, it is unrivaled."

Miss Woodriff looked relieved. "That is good to know. I found myself questioning the veracity—even the plausibility—of some of the stories. Miss Florie and I will discuss the difference between history and folklore once she reads this. We have many figures in England's history around whom myth and reality have become so interwoven, it is difficult to discern truth from fantasy." She motioned toward the bench. "Will you join me, Miss Dearing?"

Though Kate had come out here seeking someone else, the governess's hopeful expression drew Kate toward her. "I would enjoy that." She settled herself on the bench beside the governess, then cast about for something to say. "How long have you been at Wakesdown?"

"About five years. I came about six months before Miss Dorcas left for finishing school." She sighed. "And in another few months, Florie will be off to school herself."

"What will you do then?"

Nora gave a delicate shrug. "I am uncertain. I know Sir Anthony will give me a good reference. I think I may see if Mrs. Timperleigh can take me back at the seminary."

"Mrs. Timperleigh?"

"She is the proprietress and headmistress of a seminary for young girls in Oxford. She takes only girls whose families cannot afford to send them to school elsewhere. *Deserving young women,* she calls them. It has grown into quite the concern in the fifteen years since she started it." Nora smiled. "I was one of her first students, and then I taught there for almost two years before becoming governess here."

"So you are from Oxford?" Kate found herself more at ease with this stranger than with her own cousins.

"No. Manchester. My father worked in the wool and cotton mills, but when he was injured and couldn't pay rents, my parents sent us children out to find work. Since they did not want their daughters working in the factories, like my brothers, they sent us south. I came to Oxford seeking a position as a chambermaid or kitchen maid, though I was older than most girls looking to enter service. I finally gave up on trying to find work in one of the fine homes and started knocking on the doors of businesses. I eventually made my way to Mrs. Timperleigh's school. She told me that she would give me room and board and a small wage and allow me to train as a maid, but only if I also agreed to become a student at the seminary. Six years later, I was teaching."

Just as Athena's story had, Nora's story put Kate's circumstances into perspective. She'd had such a privileged upbringing—maids to dress her and arrange her hair and clean up after her, cooks to prepare her meals, a seemingly bottomless purse from which to purchase anything she wanted or needed. Athena and Nora had both grown up working since they were old enough to carry and tote—Athena learning to become a maid, Nora in her parents' home. Until recently, Kate would have looked on the two of them with pity and a measure of disdain. Now, however, she found herself envying their ability to earn wages, to support themselves.

"I would love to meet this Mrs. Timperleigh. She sounds like quite the philanthropist." And if all else failed, perhaps Kate could find some subject on which she was well versed and convince this saint of a woman to hire her as a teacher.

Tired of the dark turn of her thoughts, Kate tried to shake herself out of the melancholy. "Do you spend time in the orangery often?"

"During bad weather, I come here often to read on the afternoons when Miss Florence's French tutor is here. When it is pleasant outside, I walk in the gardens and the park. Nothing refreshes me quite so much as fresh air and God's creation."

Kate found her first genuine smile of the day. "I find being surrounded by nature soothing. But it is nothing compared to getting my hands in the soil, planting and weeding, pruning and trimming."

Nora's pale brows raised in surprise. "You worked in the gardens at your home?"

Kate grimaced a little. "Not so much as I make it sound. I had my own potted plants in the greenhouses and flowers outside in the garden that I cared for. But we had a gardener. He graciously allowed me to putter about, getting underfoot. I think he sympathized with my need to work out my problems and concerns by getting dirt between my fingers and grass stains on my apron."

"Do you know a lot about flowers and plants—how to identify them as well as how to care for them?" Nora set the Daniel Boone book aside and turned so she angled toward Kate on the bench. "Would you be willing to meet me here and teach Miss Florence what you know of botany? We have studied the language of flowers, but only from books, so she knows what they mean, and what drawings of the blooms look like, but she would not be able to identify the shrub or tree from which they come.

I have asked the gardener and Mr. Lawton, but they are too busy. Would you . . . could you make time to do it?"

A sense of purpose quickened Kate's heart. "I would enjoy that. When?"

"Monday?" Nora caught her bottom lip between her teeth, her golden-brown eyes hesitant.

"What time shall I meet you here?"

"Oh, thank you." Nora's hand shot out and clasped Kate's, taking both of them by surprise. After a shared moment of laughter, Nora withdrew back into her calm, dignified manner. "Would two o'clock fit with your plans?"

The guests for the house party would not begin arriving until after four Monday afternoon. "Two o'clock would be perfect."

Kate spent another pleasant half hour in the orangery with Nora. Beyond her understated, elegant exterior, she had a gentle humor and calmness of spirit that made Kate feel as refreshed as if she'd spent hours walking in an enchanted forest.

After Nora returned to the schoolroom, Kate closed her eyes and breathed deeply, trying to separate and identify the aromas surrounding her. But instead of inhaling the fragrances of flowers and plants, a phantom of the woodsy, spicy scent of Andrew Lawton filled her mind. She shivered at the memory of his smile, his slightly crooked front teeth making it all the more charming. Not for the first time in her life did she wish she'd mastered the skill of drawing portraits, for she would love to be able to capture his square jaw and the way the light and shadows emphasized his planed cheeks. And his eyes . . . oh, his eyes. Dark hazel or mossy green, depending on his surroundings, with that mesmerizing chip of brown in the left iris making it so hard for her to look away.

Why couldn't he be heir to a vast estate, earl of something or other?

Rubbing the tightness in her neck, Kate stood and left the orangery. On her way back to the main part of the house, she stopped, bent, and picked up two fallen jasmine blossoms. Rising, she tucked them into the swoop of hair over her left ear. She had not worn flowers in her hair since last summer, and it made her homesick.

Instead of allowing herself to wallow in melancholia, she spent the rest of the afternoon in her room, writing down ideas of how she would share her knowledge of plants and flowers with Florie and Nora. She lost herself in the task so much that Athena's appearance to help her dress for dinner took her by surprise.

The gown Athena put her in was a new one Miss Bainbridge had sent over this morning, burgundy wool gauze fabric decorated with a pink floral-and-ribbon motif. Athena wove ribbons through Kate's hair, and an ivory silk shawl with a paisley border finished the look.

Unusually for him, Christopher did not arrive until a moment before the butler stepped into the room to announce dinner. Kate fell in beside Florie, bringing up the rear of the small procession into the dining room, accustomed now to her place in the line of precedence behind all of the other Buchanans.

Over dinner, Christopher and Sir Anthony discussed what they'd read in the day's newspapers—mostly concerning London and the preparations for the Great Exhibition. Kate kept her attention on Florie, who was as animated as Edith was petulant. Apparently the duties of preparing for so many guests did not sit well with the eldest Buchanan sister. Kate tried not to smirk. As a wealthy woman who would probably marry a wealthier, if not titled, man, Edith would be responsible for planning such events for the rest of her life. Kate pitied Edith's future husband and hoped he was not someone who would want to entertain many guests often.

Kate did her best to answer Florie's seemingly endless questions about America and personages both historical and mythical. Christopher usually answered Florie's questions, but with his attention fully occupied by Sir Anthony, Kate found herself grateful for Florie's inquiries, as it kept her from having to try to engage Edith in conversation.

Until Edith interrupted. "Katharine, after dinner, we will retire to your room to ensure you have something appropriate to wear to greet Lord Thynne when he arrives tomorrow."

Kate set her wine glass down carefully. "He is coming two days early?"

Apparently the aristocrat's name was important enough to draw Sir Anthony's attention. "Stephen Brightwell, Viscount Thynne, is coming at my invitation. His father was a dear friend, before his passing. Though not as ancient as I"—Sir Anthony's eyes twinkled—"Thynne is a bit older than all of you. There shall be plenty of young people in attendance to keep you all company. I thought I would invite someone to keep me company. Thynne is coming to us from London, as Greymere, his Oxfordshire home, is under renovation."

"Lord Thynne inherited the title after his older brother's passing, and he has recently returned to England from . . . somewhere foreign." Edith waved her hand as if in dismissal of the thought of any place other than England.

"Argentina." Florie turned to Christopher. "How far is that from Philadelphia?"

Christopher grinned at her. "Probably farther than England."

"Oh."

Kate, Christopher, and Sir Anthony all chuckled over Florie's disappointment.

"Lord Thynne is one of the highest ranking members of Oxford society, so it is very important he have a pleasant visit." Edith's voice acquired a pitch of annoyance.

"Not to worry." Sir Anthony reached across the corner of the table and patted his eldest daughter's arm. "I will see that he is kept entertained. After all, he is here as my personal guest. So I shall take his entertainment upon myself."

"Good." Edith shrugged her father's hand away. "He may be a viscount, and one of the wealthiest men in this part of England, but from what I recall, he is a right old bore, and not in the least handsome. It is no wonder he is still a bachelor at his age."

Kate hated herself for the way her stomach leapt at Edith's words. A wealthy bachelor viscount coming here? Boring, she could compensate for. Old, she could live with. Not handsome, she could overlook. But could she make someone like him fall in love with her? It would be the only way to get a marriage proposal that came with an agreement to help her family financially.

"There shall be ever so many more wealthy, titled men— handsome and young—in town this season." Edith gave Dorcas a clearly patronizing look. "You are fortunate to be debuting this year. London will be a whirl of activity because of the Great Exhibition. We shall have to review our invitations quite carefully to ensure you and I are seen at only the best events."

Kate ignored the obvious insult her cousin meant by excluding her from these hypothetical social activities.

Sir Anthony smiled as he dabbed at the corners of his mouth with his napkin. "Perhaps your good fortune will continue, Dorcas, and you will find a husband in your first season, unlike your sister, who will be entering her fourth season with not one offer of marriage yet."

Kate held her breath to suppress her urge to laugh at her uncle's comically tragic expression.

Edith's eyes narrowed to slits and her mouth pursed into a small bud. The lines in her forehead and around her eyes and mouth created white streaks through her flush.

After several shallow breaths to control her reaction, Kate swallowed and pressed her napkin to her lips, eyes downcast. She would not, could not, look across the table. If she caught Christopher's eye and he betrayed any reaction to Sir Anthony's comment, she would not be able to restrain herself further.

"Now, Papa, you know that is not true." Dorcas rose to her sister's defense. "Edith has received an offer of marriage from Mr. Brockmorrell."

Edith gave a shrill gasp. "Dorcas!"

But for once, Dorcas would not be intimidated by her sister's remonstrative glare. "'Tis true. When we saw him in Oxford this week, I heard him tell you that he still awaited your answer."

"As if I would consent to marry someone like Linus Brockmorrell—social climber that he is. No rank, no family of any account."

"A fine gentry family," Sir Anthony said pragmatically. "And his grandfather took that farm and turned it into quite an estate."

Kate thought herself sufficiently disciplined to set her napkin in her lap and look up again. While Edith's color had evened out, anger—or was it petulance?—still contorted her face into unattractiveness.

"And who was his grandfather? A man who came up from nothing by selling mutton and wool to the Royal Navy during the war."

Kate made the mistake of glancing at Christopher. Grandfather Dearing had made his fortune by raising pigs and cattle to sell to the American army for meat during the War of 1812. Christopher cocked his head and raised his eyebrows, apparently thinking the same thing. Kate choked on a laugh and pressed her fingertips to her lips.

Edith pushed out of her chair, sending it teetering backward. A footman jumped forward to keep it from crashing to the floor and pulled it back. She threw her napkin onto the table. "If you find that so amusing, Miss Katharine Dearing, why don't *you* marry him? After all, it's your family who are poor relations and need the money, not mine." She straightened, raising her chin and looking down her nose at Kate. "Besides. I have my sights set much higher than the grandson of a sheep farmer." She stalked from the room.

"Do not take her words to heart, Cousin Kate. Edith is tired and bad-tempered from seeing to the arrangements today." Dorcas folded her napkin and placed it on the table. "Once she gets a good night's sleep, she will calm down and remember herself. I should never have mentioned Mr. Brockmorrell. Edith cannot abide him, and I knew it would make her angry. I am sorry she took her anger out on you." She smiled across the table at Kate, then motioned for a footman to pull out her chair so she could rise. "Now, how about you and Florie and I go up to your room and pick out what you will wear to meet Lord Thynne tomorrow?"

CHAPTER TEN

$\mathscr{R}$unning late for his meeting with Sir Anthony, Andrew ducked into the entrance to the orangery from the garden path rather than wasting additional time going around and entering through the service wing. He prayed everyone in the house would be occupied with the pending arrival of the important guest and not notice his presumption.

He drew up short, however, at the sight of a silhouetted figure near the door that led into the grand gallery that connected the conservatory with the rest of the house.

At the sound of his footsteps, the figure turned, the wide bell-shaped skirt catching on the low palms growing in large pots on the floor beside her.

He stared at Kate. He couldn't decide if it was that he hadn't seen her for a few days or if there truly was something differ-ent about her. Or perhaps it was that he usually saw her outside with a diaphanous brown cloak covering her from shoulder to hem. The deep-purple gown with black lace, like fine tendrils of ivy growing over it, clung to her torso in such a way that she appeared narrower in the waist than he remembered; it made her look taller too. Rather than clinging to her willowy arms, the long sleeves fell away at the elbows, revealing pristine white undersleeves with lace cuffs that brushed the backs of her hands.

Remembering himself, he inclined his head in greeting. "Miss Dearing."

"Mr. Lawton." Her voice had a breathless quality to it he hadn't noticed before. She pressed her left hand to her side as if her ribs pained her.

"Are you all right?" He stepped forward, concerned at the grimace that crossed her face. "Shall I call for someone?"

A heated blush replaced the brief expression of pain. "No, thank you, Mr. Lawton. I am . . . I will be just fine." She clasped her hands before her. "Have you come to inspect the conservatory? Anything to dig up in here?" Her blue eyes glinted with humor now.

He looked around the room as if he took her question seriously. "I do see a few ferns that should be cut back, and a fichus in need of pruning." He returned his gaze to her, trying to hold his pulse—and his heart—steady. "I do not suppose I could talk you into assisting me with such a task."

She cocked her head and her full, rosy lips pulled into a smile. "You know my views on allowing plants to grow freely, Mr. Lawton."

"You sound like someone in the anti-slavery movement— freedom for plants!" He raised his hand in exclamation.

Her laugh was contagious, but then her expression grew serious. "Though I am not an abolitionist, I do support their cause. All living things—plants, animals, people—deserve to live and grow freely, to be what God intended them to be without interference from others."

While he agreed with her to a point—especially on the matter of slavery—he could see the fallacy in her argument. And it worked to his advantage. "So you are saying, then, that we should have no government, no laws? That the church should not endeavor to teach us right from wrong? That children should be allowed to run amuck and never be disciplined?"

Kate made a derisive sound in the back of her throat and crossed her arms. "You know that is not what I meant. What I mean is . . ." She narrowed her eyes. "You are trying to get me to support your position of pruning and trimming and shaping every branch and leaf of every last plant on earth. I shall never agree with you on that point, sir."

He stepped close and bent his head down to whisper in her ear. "I am no *sir*, ma'am." He could see the gooseflesh raise on the side of her neck and he quickly stepped back, his own skin tingling in response to the heady scent of her.

He cleared his throat. "In truth, I am late to a meeting with Sir Anthony."

"Do not let me keep you longer, then." She stepped out of the middle of the path, allowing him room to pass her.

As he did, he saw a bloom from the purple China aster behind her had fallen to the low table on which the planting tray sat. He bent, picked it up, then straightened and turned to face her.

The edge of her skirt covered the toes of his boots. His heart beat an irregular pattern. Unable to resist the temptation, he tucked the flower into the soft wing of hair just over her left ear. The velvety petals brushed her temple and cheek—much like he wished he could do with his fingers.

Their gazes locked, and Andrew lost himself in the summer-blue of her eyes. He slowly lowered his hand to his side and stepped back. Not trusting his voice, he bowed his head toward her, then spun on his heels and forced himself to walk away.

He did not ease his pace until he reached the door to Sir Anthony's study. Nor did his heart slow its pace. He toyed with fire in indulging his attraction to Katharine Dearing. She was not for him. He had nothing to offer her, even if there were no difference in their stations. And as he was just beginning his life as an independent man, one who had power over his future, he could not begin to think of sharing that life with another. Not yet. Not for a long time to come. Too long for someone like Miss Dearing to wait.

Kate held on to the back of a wrought-iron chair for several minutes after Andrew departed, trying to catch her breath. The new corset coupled with her pounding heart made that task nearly impossible. Never before had she reacted thusly to a man's mere presence. Yet just the sight of Andrew Lawton made her as giddy as a child with a new toy. And when he drew nearer to her and she caught his scent—a mixture of soap and soil and outdoors—her knees had grown so weak she feared she might collapse from the pleasure.

The aster brushed her temple and she shivered, pulling the flower from her hair. The simple blossom reminded her of the daisies that grew wildly in her garden at home.

And that reminder choked her with regret. The only reason she had met Andrew, the reason she was in England, precluded her from allowing anything to come of the attraction she felt toward him—an attraction she now knew was mutual. She'd seen it in his eyes.

Tears stung the corners of her eyes, and she blinked against them. How unfair could God make her life? For the first time she'd had a taste of what falling in love might be like—and because of her family's need for money, she must put all thoughts of him away, must turn mercenary and find a man with money, and flirt and pretend attraction to snare a husband.

As her father had said to her on the dock before she boarded the ship to England: She was just like the pigs her grandfather had sold to the army during the war of 1812—a commodity to be sold to the highest bidder to bring an infusion of money into the family coffers.

Tossing the flower back onto the table, she escaped outside, wishing she'd brought a shawl to ward off the late-winter chill, but needing the bracing air and exertion before she could face anyone else. However, she didn't walk far. Just to a rise that overlooked the main garden behind the house. Neat. Orderly. Tidy.

Disciplined. She grimaced. Everything a garden, and a person, should be.

If her father had been more disciplined, Kate would not be here now. If he had tended his finances the way Andrew and Wakesdown's gardeners tended this land, the Dearing fortune would still be intact.

Uncertain how long she stood there, gazing over the winter-browns and evergreens of the landscape, Kate finally returned inside. After fully embracing the chill, the conservatory felt hot, like Philadelphia in July.

Footfalls drew her attention. Taking as deep a breath as she could, Kate steeled herself against another encounter with Andrew. But instead of the man who could never be more than an acquaintance, a maid bobbed a curtsy to her. "Miss Buchanan requests your presence in the hall, miss. The carriage with Lord Thynne was spotted entering the park."

"Thank you." Kate couldn't remember the young housemaid's name. Servants seemed to pop up like dandelions wherever she turned—too many to keep up with, and so similar in their plain dresses and white caps and aprons that she had a hard time telling them apart. The maid bobbled again and vanished back into the house.

Kate took a few steps toward the door, paused, then returned to pick up the aster before fleeing from the conservatory. At the other end of the portrait gallery, she took a hidden set of stairs and rushed through the upper wing to her suite. In the bedroom, she pulled a thick book from the shelf beside the fireplace. It fell open to her favorite poem by Lord Byron. With the flower folded into a handkerchief, she tucked it into the book, which she pressed closed and returned to the shelf.

Turning, she caught a glimpse of herself in the long mirror beside the dressing table. The image reflected there was one she barely recognized. The only thing about her that had not been changed by her cousins was her face—and it showed the changes that regret and responsibility had wrought over the last few months. She looked every year of the twenty-seven to her credit.

She should have long been wife and mother by now. And yet . . .

And yet no man had ever wanted to take her to wife. She pressed her palms to her hot cheeks. What was wrong with her that no man had ever even acted as if he wanted her?

No man saved Andrew Lawton.

She glanced at the book of poetry.

Andrew Lawton could not have her, unless he suddenly found himself in possession of a great fortune. And that was as likely to happen as the sun falling from the sky.

She smoothed her hands over her newly tiny waist to the fullness of the skirt over her hips—and the multiple petticoats and crinolines pushing it out to an extreme width she still was not accustomed to.

She grimaced at her own reflection, then turned and hurried back downstairs. While she could not compete with Edith's and Dorcas's black hair and ivory skin for beauty, she took pride in knowing her figure was at least as good as theirs in her new apparel.

Reaching the bottom of the stairs, she drew a look of admonishment from Edith and a welcoming smile from Dorcas. And, surprisingly, Florie stood with them. Her small feet, encased in soft brown boots, tapped on the carpet.

Dorcas reached up to touch Kate's hair where the flower had been. She smoothed the tendrils that rested against Kate's cheek.

Heat flared in Kate's face, but not because her coiffure needed attention and she hadn't noticed. The feeling of Dorcas's hand there was so different from Andrew's that she almost pulled away from her cousin to keep from losing that memory.

"There. Now you are perfect." Dorcas nodded at her in satisfaction.

As they had when Kate and Christopher arrived, the entire house staff lined the two sides of the hall, leaving the family to stand at the base of the stairs. Dorcas took her place between

Edith and Florie, and Edith motioned for Kate to stand on Florie's other side. The girl looked up at Kate with a grin that revealed her excitement at being included in the welcoming party for someone of Lord Thynne's importance.

Within moments, Sir Anthony and Christopher joined them from the direction of his study in the back of the house. Christopher settled his arm around Kate's waist and gave her a quick squeeze. The new suit he wore fit him to perfection, showcasing the width of his shoulders and his height while deemphasizing the lankiness of his long limbs.

"I like your new dress," he whispered, then kissed the top of her head before dropping his arm from the hug.

"And I like your new suit," she whispered back. But his attention was no longer on her. His eyes shifted toward the head of the line of servants. Kate followed his gaze and noticed the young woman standing beside the housekeeper. Nora.

Kate glanced back up at her brother's face and concern squeezed her heart. She should speak to him, remind him that he, too, was under edict from their father to find a wealthy spouse.

Christopher looked down at Kate and grinned. She smiled back. Perhaps she'd misread the glance. Maybe she'd projected her own ill-advised attraction onto her brother. She hoped so.

A flurry of activity at the door wiped all such thoughts from her mind, and she smoothed her hands over her waist again before clasping her hands in front of her and trying to adopt the pose of nonchalance her cousins bore.

The footman opened the front door, and a man entered with a whirl of his great cloak. Sir Anthony moved forward, the butler behind him, to greet his guest.

"My Lord Thynne, welcome to Wakesdown."

"Thank you, Sir Anthony. So good of you to invite me." The newcomer shrugged out of his caped cloak and let the butler take it along with his hat and gloves.

The viscount turned to face the family after Sir Anthony finished his greeting.

"Thynne, I believe you remember my eldest daughter, Edith."

Edith seemed a different creature in the lord's presence from the one who had spoken so disparagingly of him at dinner the other night. She dropped into a curtsy with what could only be termed a simpering expression. "My lord, we are honored by your presence in our house. If there is *anything* that you require, please do not hesitate to let me know." Her long, dark lashes fluttered, and she ducked her chin when she rose from the deep obeisance.

If Kate had been dependent on Edith's description of the viscount to try to pick him out in a crowd, she never would have managed the task. She found him handsome, but in a rugged way that seemed strange for a member of the aristocracy. He was not overly tall—no taller than Kate, though she stood at least half a head taller than most women—but his muscular frame gave the appearance of a larger man. His blond hair and pale eyes were offset by a lined, ruddy complexion that bespoke someone who spent quite a lot of time outdoors. He looked . . . well, he looked like a Westerner. A cowboy or a frontiersman. Not an English lord.

He seemed a bit taken aback by the overheated warmth in Edith's greeting. "Th-thank you, Miss Buchanan. I am certain I will find all of your preparations more than adequate for my needs."

"My younger daughters, Dorcas and Florence."

Dorcas and Florie both executed perfect curtsies—but not as deep or reverential as Edith's had been. "My lord," they chirped in unison.

The viscount bowed to the two young women, his expression reserved but pleasant.

"And this is my niece and nephew, come from America, Miss Katharine and Mr. Christopher Dearing."

Christopher bowed and murmured his greeting.

Kate dipped into a curtsy. "My lord." That was how her cousins had addressed him. And since she'd be hard pressed to get his real name to form on her tongue at this moment, she decided she might actually appreciate the requirement of titles rather than names among her uncle's set. When she straightened, the viscount's intense gaze drew heat into her face again. But a warning sounded in her mind—a warning in the overly sweet, somewhat sensual voice Edith Buchanan had used to greet him. *Stay away; he's spoken for.*

"Miss Dearing." He dragged his eyes away to Christopher. "Mr. Dearing."

Sir Anthony bustled the viscount off to his study. A chattering Florie joined the governess and they vanished into the back of the house—and this time, when Kate saw Christopher's gaze linger on them as they walked away, she knew it was not her imagination.

The house staff dispersed, and Edith and Dorcas returned to the sitting room.

Kate grabbed Christopher by the sleeve before he could disappear into the recesses of the massive house.

He turned, his expression full of innocent questions.

"Christopher, I see how you look at her."

"Her?"

"The governess."

"Miss Woodriff?" He glanced over his shoulder toward where Nora and Florie had disappeared.

"Yes, Miss Woodriff. I hope you aren't thinking . . ." She couldn't bring herself to finish the statement. More than anything, Kate wanted to see her brother happy. But the thought of their little sisters being forced from their home, not having enough to eat, made her stand firm in the need to discourage him from this path.

Christopher's expression closed, darkening. "I am thinking nothing that should be of any concern to you, Kate." He stalked away, leaving Kate standing alone in the cold, echoing hall.

Fighting both anger at Christopher and anxiety for her own lot, Kate returned to the orangery. But even the loamy, moist smell of soil and mulch, mingled with the sweet spices of the flowers and herbs growing there, could not raise her spirits.

She found herself standing by the table holding the trays of purple China asters. She fingered the velvety petals.

I will think of you. That's what the cheerful little flower meant when given from a man to a woman. *I will think of you.*

Turning her back on the blooms, she closed her eyes and hugged her arms around her abdomen. The expression on Andrew's face when he'd so gently tucked the flower in her hair would be etched in Kate's memory forever.

"I will think of you too," she whispered.

CHAPTER ELEVEN

$\mathscr{K}$ate pressed her left hand to her side and maneuvered her shoulders to see if she could find any relief from the corset boning that insisted on digging into her lower ribs. Athena was even stronger than Miss Bainbridge; the gowns that had arrived yesterday, altered to Kate's measurements with the new stays, did not fit as tightly to her torso as they had when pinned for taking in. And she found breathing harder after Athena laced her up than she had in the seamstress's shop.

But if it helped her catch a husband . . .

Kate paused at the top of the stairs. *Lord Thynne. Stephen Brightwell, Viscount Thynne. My lord.* . . . At each step on her way down to the entry hall, she mentally rehearsed the guest's name and title. Though, after Edith's greeting of him this afternoon, Kate had no reason to believe anything she said to the man would matter. The viscount had obviously been invited by Sir Anthony for Edith's benefit. And Kate did not want any more animosity from her cousin than what was already there due to Edith's obvious annoyance with having poor relations living at Wakesdown.

"Good evening, Miss Dearing."

Kate's heel slipped and she lost her balance. A strong arm whipped around her waist to keep her from tumbling down the remaining half-dozen steps.

Gasping for air, Kate looked around at her rescuer. "Oh! My—my lord . . . Bainbridge. No." Mortification blazed across her face. "Lord Brighton. I mean . . ." Heart in her throat, she closed her mouth before she could embarrass herself further with additional incorrect names.

"Lord Thynne," he corrected, voice gentle. Amusement creased the soft skin around his eyes, though he didn't actually smile. "Although the title is so new to me, it is hard to remember to answer to anything other than Stephen Brightwell."

Kate nodded. "I am terribly sorry, sir—my lord. Please forgive me. Calling people by the wrong name is a malady I have been cursed with since childhood." She looked down at his arm, still encircling her waist.

He pulled his appendage back. "No forgiveness is necessary, Miss Dearing." He leaned closer, his expression conspiratorial. "I, too, often forget names after being introduced the first time." He stepped down beside her and motioned toward the main floor below. "Shall we join the others in the sitting room?"

If he'd offered her his arm, Kate would have been tempted to take it. But he did not. And the withering glance Edith gave her when she and Lord Stephen—no, Lord Thynne—walked in together confirmed for Kate that she should have as little to do with him as possible.

Kate joined Christopher and Florie near the fireplace and left the viscount to the attentions of Edith.

"You have been away from England for so long, my lord. It must be a relief to have returned to the civilized world from the wilds of the East Indies and years of living among savages." Edith's voice took on a shrill pitch that carried through the room. Kate looked over in time to witness Edith resting one hand on his crossed arms.

Kate would have sworn that he flinched at Edith's touch. Edith, however, seemed not to notice the man's discomfort. And with a face like his, set in an almost perpetual scowl, who could be sure what he was thinking?

Distance muffled Lord Stephen's response—no, not Lord Stephen. Kate wanted to rap her knuckles against her temple to try to get his names and titles to settle into her memory. Why were some people's names so easy to remember and others' so easy to forget?

For now, until she became accustomed to hearing him addressed by name, at least she could get away with saying *my lord* and leave it at that, with no insult given or taken. She hoped.

Edith latched onto the viscount's arm as soon as the butler appeared in the doorway to announce dinner.

Christopher offered his arms to Kate and Florie, and they followed Sir Anthony and Dorcas into the dining room.

But when they sat, Kate ended up exactly where she did not want to be—beside the viscount. She hadn't remembered that with another guest, the seating arrangement at table would necessarily change. As not only a guest but the highest-ranking one, the viscount took the place of honor at Sir Anthony's right hand. The seat Edith had occupied until now. Edith now sat at her father's left hand, with Christopher and Florie beside her. Dorcas sat to Kate's right.

"I understand you are from Philadelphia, Miss Dearing."

Swallowing a dainty bite of peas, Kate turned her head toward the viscount. "Yes, sir—my lord. Have you ever visited America?"

"Twice. Once to St. Louis by way of a paddle steamer from New Orleans, and once to New York. The city reminded me much of London."

A high-pitched laugh made them both look across the table.

"Surely you jest, my lord." Edith pushed her plate of untouched food away. "There is no city in the world like London."

And no women in the world like Englishwomen, Kate mentally added for her cousin.

"Then you have traveled extensively, Miss Buchanan?"

Kate dropped her gaze to her plate and bit the tip of her tongue to keep from smiling over the barb in Stephen Brightwell's voice.

"To London, yes. Not only did I attend finishing school there, we have a town house near Mayfair at which I have spent every season since I was presented at court." The last word choked off as if Edith remembered that it might not be wise to remind Lord Thynne she had seen more than one or two seasons. Though at his age, which Kate guessed to be around forty, would he care if a woman were not fresh from her debut ball?

"I see. Then you have seen much on which to compare London to other cities, such as Paris or Rome or"—he glanced at Kate with a nod—"Philadelphia or New York?"

Edith's lips drew into a pursed bow that did her sharp features no favors. "I have no need to see other cities to know that London far surpasses them."

"Lord Thynne." Sir Anthony cleared his throat. "Tell us of the renovations to Greymere. Wakesdown is also in the midst of renovations, though ours are out-of-doors—to the hothouses and gardens and park."

Kate's attention strayed from the description of construction of a building she had never seen, using architectural terms unfamiliar to her. She was, however, amused by Edith's feeble attempts to interject herself into the conversation with questions and comments that, even to Kate, sounded inane.

When dinner came to a close, Kate followed her cousins into the sitting room so Sir Anthony, Lord Thynne, and Christopher could talk about manly things.

Kate chuckled.

"What is funny, Cousin Kate?" Florie sidled up next to her and drew Kate to a settee near the fireplace. Dorcas joined them. Edith took the armchair at the far end of the seating arrangement—with them, but as far away from them as she could get.

"I was just remembering something. When I was eighteen, at one of the dinners my father and stepmother gave that season, I sneaked out of the sitting room and into the hallway outside the dining room and eavesdropped on the men's conversation after dinner."

Dorcas and Florie gave astonished gasps. Edith's scowl grew.

Kate would not let her cousin's displeasure deter her story. "The talk of politics intrigued me so much, I started to read my father's newspapers and periodicals. I became interested—nay, passionate—about many issues, including slavery and women's suffrage."

Edith released an inelegant snort. "A woman with a husband has no need of voting."

"And what of a woman with no husband?" Kate raised her brows and cocked her head.

"Her father will do so for her."

"And if her beliefs and views are different from her father's? Then what? Are we to have no say in the future of the place in which we live? My country fought a war over that very idea— that no one should be governed without representation to voice his, or her, concerns."

A pained expression overcame Edith's face, and she closed her eyes and turned her head away. Kate thought to remind her that the United States had won that war. But she let the subject drop. After all, America was a country that still allowed human beings to be held as slaves because of the color of their skin. Best not to scratch too far into the shiny surface of American idealism, or it would surely tarnish.

Florie turned the conversation to one of her favorite topics—the American West and the "Red Indians"—and Kate shared some of her sisters' favorite stories with her cousins.

Her third story was interrupted by Edith's piercing voice. "My Lord Thynne, please, do come in and sit by the fire." Edith glowered at Kate, Florie, and Dorcas until they stood and allowed Edith to force the viscount into the chair closest to the fire while she arranged herself on the settee.

Florie instantly found Christopher's side, and her seemingly endless questions about America flowed freely once again.

Dorcas sat on the settee beside Edith, hands folded, head bowed. Kate pitied the middle sister—and recognized many of her own traits in the young woman. A preference for solitude. A self-consciousness that came across in nervousness and unease around strangers.

If Kate had an older sister like Edith, she, too, would most likely have turned into an apprehensive mouse of a creature like Dorcas. But Kate had been blessed with Christopher, who wouldn't allow Kate to pull in her petals like an evening primrose when the sunlight of attention shone on her.

However, playing the shrinking moonflower to Edith's showy camellia in Stephen Brightwell's presence might serve her best for now.

Were there any moonflowers in the conservatory or orangery? Next time she saw Andrew Lawton, she would ask.

She took the chair beside Sir Anthony and engaged him in an unremarkable conversation about his sons, and the cousins she had yet to meet, and tried to clear thoughts of the landscape architect from her head.

꧁꧂

The next morning, the weather took a turn for the better, with rain clouds fleeing and the sun making an appearance after several days' absence. Kate blinked against the glare and accepted the footman's hand for assistance into the coach.

She took the space in the far corner of the backward seat, not wanting to usurp Edith's or Dorcas's place. She'd just settled her skirts and cloak so she didn't take up more than half of the bench when the coach jostled and Florie climbed in. The young woman's pink cheeks were almost the same shade as her fur-trimmed cape.

"Good morning, Cousin Katharine." Florie dropped onto the seat in a billow of pink wool, white fur, and petticoats. She stood and started over, carefully arranging her clothing before sitting again. "We might have a wait. Dorcas told me she saw Edith scolding one of the housemaids before she—Dorcas—came down."

The carriage jostled again, saving Kate the necessity of a response.

"Yes, that poor creature." Dorcas sighed. "Edith had her by the wrist and had leaned down in her face to berate her for something. She probably found fault with the way her fire was laid this morning or something else trivial. She's so cross these days." Dorcas settled herself across from Kate. "Father, Lord Thynne, and Christopher just climbed into the other coach, so we should be under way as soon as Edith joins us."

"Edith said Lord Thynne wasn't handsome, but I thought she was mistaken." Florie's eyes sparkled. "I thought he was quite handsome, especially with the way he looked at Cousin Kate."

Kate guffawed. "He looked at me no differently than any of the rest of you."

"No, I believe Florie is correct." Dorcas looked up from arranging her cape so it would not crease too badly in the confines of the coach. "His entire demeanor changed when Papa introduced you. And you saw how Edith tried flirting with him last night. I am certain she also noticed how he looked at you."

"I suppose age and looks do not matter to Edith after all, so long as a man possesses sufficient wealth." Florie frowned. "And while she would prefer a man with a title, I would imagine that if he has enough wealth, the title is not a requirement. For, as she is fond of reminding me, even a king can be deposed if he has no money. It is wealth, not title, she says, that truly gives a man power and status."

"Hmm." Kate tilted her head with a half-smile. "She would do well in Philadelphia society." She straightened. "However, I do not wish to interfere with Lord Thynne's courtship of Edith."

Dorcas let out a snort Kate was certain Edith would have reprimanded her for. "You'll be doing Lord Thynne a favor if you do."

The carriage jostled, and Kate's heart quickened, hoping Edith had not heard their discussion.

"Dorcas, do move over. Florence, sit up straight and pull your feet back under your skirts as much as possible." Edith's crimson cloak was understated compared to the green and red stripes of the skirt showing under it. Once settled, she looked across and gave a little start of surprise, as if not expecting Kate to be present. "Oh, good morning, Cousin Katharine."

The air inside the coach seemed to crackle with the chill in Edith's eyes. "Good morning, Cousin Ed—"

"Why are we not yet moving?" Edith leaned forward and opened the window in the door. "Footman, tell the driver we are ready."

The coach lurched forward, nearly dislodging Kate's feet from the hot brick—the only means of keeping the wait for Edith comfortable inside the chilly carriage. However, walking to the church would probably have been warmer than facing Edith's cold silence.

"There should be good attendance this morning." A nervous undertone laced Dorcas's voice, and she gave her older sister a sidelong glance before continuing. "All of the mothers with daughters in need of a husband will be there to see Lord Thynne."

Edith kept her face turned resolutely toward the window, her neck stiff, mouth pursed. Kate wondered if anyone had ever hinted to Edith that she lost most of her beauty with her face screwed up in petulance like that. She doubted it. And she wasn't about to be the bearer of bad news.

To fill the time, Kate allowed Florie to draw out from her descriptions of the church she and Christopher had attended in Philadelphia.

First to enter meant last to leave, and Kate held her impatience until Florie finished adjusting her skirt and cape and climbed out. Kate took a fortifying breath and stepped down from the coach. As soon as her feet steadied on the ground, she leaned her head back to take in the full aspect of the church. A square, gray-stone tower rose into the blue sky on the left end of the building, looking like a medieval castle turret—and making the rest of the building seem to hug the ground.

"It's Norman in design. Twelfth century."

Kate turned. "Good morning, Uncle."

Sir Anthony, only an inch or so taller than she, smiled and offered her his arm. The church bells echoed over the sunny countryside, and he led Kate into the church. The inside matched the outside—save that the stone walls were whitewashed and the nave at the end of the long, narrow sanctuary featured finely carved woodwork that could not possibly be as old as the rest of the building.

When Kate neared the Buchanans' bench, her heart quickened. But it was not the sight of Lord Thynne standing with Christopher and Edith that made her pulse race. Two rows behind, she recognized the curly hair and square jaw of Andrew Lawton.

If only she could catch his eye, maybe she could somehow convey the message that she would enjoy meeting him out in the grounds this afternoon. Of course, how she could convey that without revealing just *how much* she would enjoy that meeting, she wasn't certain.

He looked up. A slow smile spread from his lips—oh, those full, perfectly proportioned lips!—to his eyes. Kate's pulse chimed with the church bells. Cheeks burning with pleasure, she turned and sat, but she would have sworn she could feel Andrew's eyes on her throughout the entirety of the church service.

Taking his sketchbook with him, Andrew tried to convince himself that he only wished to work on the design of the elliptical garden he had planned for the lower part of the grounds to the west side of the house this afternoon. However, it was not the sight of that perfect plot of land that quickened his step several minutes later.

Though draped in a dark blue cape today instead of the brown he'd grown so accustomed to seeing her in, Kate's profile quickened his heart.

At the crunch of his footsteps on the dry, brown grass, Kate turned. A smile expressing what could only be termed pure joy flashed across her face before she could school her emotions.

"Is this where the elliptical garden will go?" She turned and surveyed the plot of ground with her eyes, made more intensely bright blue by the cloak.

Her chin might be a little too pointed, her nose a bit too sharp—but to Andrew, the flaws made her all the more beautiful. Hers was a natural beauty, an effortless grace, like a flower garden where weeds could not grow and which needed no tending to produce the sweetest-smelling blooms.

Those blue eyes turned toward him again. "Mr. Lawton? Is everything all right?"

He shook himself from his thoughts, embarrassed to be caught staring at her. "Y-yes, yes, this is where the elliptical is going." After opening his sketchbook and pulling his pencil from his coat pocket, he sketched his plan for the elaborate concentric circles of plants and shrubs and pathways he had planned. Kate asked him about two varieties of flowers he was unfamiliar with and suggested a few others he had not thought of that would fit well into the planned color scheme.

"May I?" Kate reached for the pencil. Andrew handed it over without hesitation. "What if instead of breaking up this section by putting a path through it, you divert the path here." She sketched in the new direction that took the path around the bed in question instead of through it, connecting it to the main walkway in a much more flowing, less grid-like design.

"Brilliant. Now, why didn't I think of that?" He glanced over and grinned at Kate. Only then did he realize they stood with shoulders touching, arms pressed together as they bent over the sketchbook. As much as it pained him to do so, he stepped away, breaking the contact.

"Here you are."

The sketchbook fell to the ground as Andrew and Kate both jumped and turned at the man's voice.

"Lord St—Bri—my lord." Kate made a slight curtsy to the newcomer. Andrew bowed. So this was the viscount who had come to visit Wakesdown. The lord whose grounds were reputed to be at least four times the size of these.

"Good afternoon, Miss Dearing. I learned from your brother that you like to walk in the gardens, and I had hoped to find you before you returned to the house. So I have been walking around looking for you. And finally I came upon your path." Lord Thynne's gaze turned on Andrew.

"My lord, this is Mr. Andrew Lawton. He is the architect my uncle hired to redesign the gardens here at Wakesdown."

Had that been a note of pride in Katharine Dearing's voice as she introduced him to the viscount? Andrew inclined his head to the aristocrat. "My lord."

"You are the young architect who apprenticed with Joseph Paxton, are you not?"

Pleasure rose in a wave of warmth from Andrew's throat up into his face. "Yes, my lord, I am."

"Sir Anthony seems quite pleased with the additional greenhouses and the plans you've drawn for the gardens. I look forward to seeing those sometime during my visit." The viscount returned his attention to Kate before Andrew could answer. "Miss Dearing, might I entreat you to show me some of the best walking paths? You must have your favorites by now."

While Andrew had not been certain if Kate's tone had conveyed pride when she introduced him to the viscount, he had no doubt that he saw interest in the aristocrat's face when he looked at her. Andrew's stomach twisted; he had no one to blame but himself. He knew Kate Dearing's situation, knew why she had come to England, knew himself an idiot to indulge this infatuation he felt toward her.

He used the excuse of retrieving the sketchbook from the ground to separate himself from Kate and Lord Thynne. "If you'll excuse me, my lord, Miss Dearing, I must be getting back to my work."

Kate turned as if to say something, her expression clearly apologetic, but Andrew walked away before she could. He had no other choice. He must walk away. He could not afford a wife, and Kate could not afford a husband like him.

≈≈≈

"I hope I did not interrupt anything important."

Kate dragged her attention away from Andrew's retreating back and smiled at the viscount. "No, my lord. Mr. Lawton was simply showing me the plans he has for this plot of ground."

With a sweeping gesture, Lord Thynne wordlessly invited her to start walking. She set her pace slower, more ladylike, than the brisk walk she usually took through the grounds.

"Are you interested in garden planning, Miss Dearing?" Lord Thynne turned up the fur-lined collar of his caped greatcoat against the wind they now walked into.

Kate pulled her arms inside her cloak. "Oh, I love gardens. But I leave the planning and tending of them up to others. I had my own few little plants at home in Philadelphia. And I enjoyed spending time in our garden. Of course, it was nowhere near as grand as this, being a city home. And you, Lord Thynne, are you interested in gardening?" She felt like an idiot, blithering on in such a manner.

He chuckled, a deep gravelly sound. "I enjoy gardens insofar that I prefer spending time outdoors. Although I find the gardens here in England to be too tame, too structured for my tastes."

"I, too, thought that when I first arrived. However, now that I have spent time in Wakesdown's gardens, I've come to discover a certain restfulness and beauty in the order and structure—" Kate swallowed the laugh that attempted to burst forth. If only Andrew could hear her now.

She turned onto the path that would take them back to the house. "Have you traveled abroad much, then?"

"In the sense of what many here would consider 'traveling abroad'—which means in Europe—no. I spent the last ten years in Argentina overseeing my father's properties there."

Kate glanced up at him and tried to simper. "Argentina? Truly? How different that must be from England. If it is not rude of me to ask, what manner of properties does your father have there?"

"A cattle ranch and a cotton plantation."

The words *cotton plantation* nearly made Kate stumble. It conjured too many images of slavery from the pamphlets and newspapers she'd read over the past few years.

"More than thirty-five years ago, when the war with Bonaparte came to an end, my father decided to put his wealth to considerable use as well as provide employment opportunities for a few hundred out-of-work sailors and soldiers returning from the front. He wanted to do it here in England, so as not to force men to leave their homeland. However, cotton is not suited to grow here, and cattle need much more land to graze than what he would have been able to attain here. It took almost two years to settle on Argentina and secure land there, and when he was ready for workers, he put advertisements in the papers in London, Plymouth, Portsmouth, Liverpool, and a few other cities. More men willing to leave England for the chance of a new life put forth their names than he could put to work at that time." He grimaced and squinted up against the glare of the sky above. "I have a list of men waiting for a chance to go to Argentina to work, many of whom are the grown sons of men who were on my father's list waiting for their chance."

Kate was not only relieved to know Lord Thynne was not a slaveholder, she was amazed at the philanthropic purpose of the ventures. "After ten years there, was it hard for you to return to England?"

"Yes. But with the passing of my older brother a scant six months after my father's death, I had no choice. My responsibility now lies here." He glanced around, then smiled at Kate. "Well, not here, but at Greymere Hall." He launched into a further description of his home and the changes and innovations he was bringing to it.

Once again, Kate's attention wandered. Every so often, she thought she heard footsteps on the path behind them, and in turning to look at Lord Thynne, she would glance over her shoulder to see if Andrew had decided to follow them after all. But if he had, he stayed out of sight.

By the time they reached the orangery at the back of the house, Kate knew more about Greymere's improvements than she wanted to—more than Lord Thynne had shared with Sir Anthony at dinner last night. The heat and steam of the greenhouse seemed to collect on Kate's cool skin.

"Thank you for walking with me, Miss Dearing." Lord Thynne made a slight bow. "I hope . . . I hope the weather stays pleasant so you can show me more of the gardens."

Kate wasn't certain if the stinging in her cheeks was due to the heat in the room or the heat of her self-consciousness. Why would a viscount want to spend time with someone like her? Lord Thynne was meant for Edith Buchanan. And Kate had already learned enough of her cousin's temperament to know she didn't want to cross the black-haired beauty.

"I hope the weather stays nice as well, my lord. However, if you truly want to see the gardens, you should ask Miss Buchanan to show them to you. After all, this is her home. She must know them much better than I do." She pressed the backs of her hands, still cool from outside, to her hot cheeks.

An inscrutable expression entered Lord Thynne's pale eyes, but he quickly masked it with a tight smile. "I do not believe Miss Buchanan is much of a walker. So you may be my only hope, if I am to see the grounds, Miss Dearing."

She didn't want to cross Edith . . . but she would not turn Lord Thynne away in case he did not want Edith. "In good weather, I walk every morning after breakfast, and you are welcome to join me whenever you wish."

The lines around his eyes deepened along with his smile. "I shall hold you to that, Miss Dearing." He inclined his head and left the orangery.

Kate stood for a moment among the palms and citrus trees. Could her task be accomplished so easily? Her stepmother had insisted that the removal to England was God's will and that if they all prayed hard enough and often enough, God would quickly bring about the solution to their dilemma. Could Lord Thynne be the answer to her stepmother's prayers?

CHAPTER TWELVE

$\mathcal{N}$ora straightened the stack of books one more time. Then she moved them off the main table onto the window seat. She moved them back to the table. Took the Daniel Boone book off the top of the stack and slid it into the middle so it might be seen but would not be too obvious.

The ticking of the clock competed with her pounding heart for volume.

A moment after the first chime sounded to mark eleven o'clock, the door opened. Nora folded her hands at her waist, prepared to congratulate Florie on her punctuality.

Instead, Christopher Dearing came through the door. "I hope I am not late." He looked around the room. "Ah, I see Cousin Florie isn't here yet."

Nora swallowed hard, wishing she did not have such a reaction every time she saw him. But ever since dancing with him last week, she had been unable to get him out of her mind—or to stop her heart from racing whenever she caught a glimpse of him. Or thought she might catch a glimpse of him.

"Thank you for coming, Mr. Dearing. I am certain—"

"Sorry. So sorry!" Florie dashed into the room, skirts flying.

Nora fixed her pupil with a stern expression. "You know tardiness will never be acceptable once you are at school."

"I know. You tell me every day." Florie grinned and took a seat at the table.

Christopher crossed his arms. "Cousin Florie, I must say, I am disappointed."

The young woman's face fell, eyes wide. "Why? What have I done?"

"I thought you were a caring, considerate person."

"I am. I promise, I am." Florie looked as if she might burst into tears at her cousin's disapprobation. Nora was torn between wanting to find out what Christopher meant and defending her charge. After all, she was a young woman, not a child to be berated so—though her position as youngest in the family, as well as being her father's special pet after her mother's death, meant Miss Florence acted younger than she was, holding on to the vestiges of the role as the baby of the family longer than she should have.

Christopher shook his head, then braced his hands on the edge of the table opposite Florie and leaned toward her. "If you want to prove to me that you are the young woman I thought you were, you need to be not just on time but early to your lessons every day. By giving Miss Woodriff that courtesy—by showing her you respect her time and the effort she has put into preparing your lessons—you will prove to me that you are the kind, thoughtful person I hope you to be."

Nora's heart pounded in a paroxysm of palpitations she thought would make her faint. She grabbed the back of the nearest chair and took several deep breaths. Not since she'd left her position at Mrs. Timperleigh's school had anyone afforded her the honor of such respect for her position. And she hadn't realized just how much she missed it.

Unshed tears sparkled in Florie's blue eyes when she looked at Nora. "I am so sorry, Miss Woodriff. I meant no disrespect. I promise I will be on time every day."

"Early," Christopher prompted, straightening.

"Yes. Early." Florie nodded as if making a solemn oath.

Christopher's gaze lingered on his cousin a moment longer before he turned and smiled at Nora again. She squeezed the chair back's rung until the carved wood bit into her skin. "Now, Miss Woodriff, how would you like me to begin?"

"We . . . we have an atlas there"—she pointed to the large book on a stand—"which has maps of America. Perhaps you would like to start with geography?"

Christopher picked up the stack of books Nora had left on the table and moved them to a shelf, then brought the large atlas over and spread it open on the table, pulling a chair over to sit beside Florie. He carefully turned the pages until he came to a map of the eastern portion of America.

"Cousin Florie, pay very close attention, because I am about to show you the most important city in the United States of America. Are you ready?" His brown eyes sparkled, but his facial expression was serious.

"I'm ready. But I think I already know what it is."

Nora had taught Florie all about Washington, DC, the capital city of the United States.

"Good." He pointed to something on the map. "This is Philadelphia, Pennsylvania. Not only is it the most beautiful city in America, it's also the most important because it's where I am from." He grinned. "Did you know that it was the first capital of the United States?"

Nora hid her smile, took one of the books from the pile, and sat on the window seat, pretending to read but hanging on every word Christopher Dearing said about his homeland. The longer he talked about it, the more she wanted to see it.

"How would someone get from Philadelphia to . . . where is it your brother has his shop, Miss Woodriff?" Florie's question pulled Nora back to the table.

"Sacramento, California."

"Your brother has a shop there?" Christopher looked up from the pages showing the entire continent of North America. "When I heard he was in California, I assumed he'd gone as a gold seeker."

"That was why he went, originally. But when he arrived in New York and discovered how many others had gone with the same plan, he decided he would make more money by opening a mercantile to sell supplies and dry goods to the prospectors. It seems to have been a good plan. He has done well for himself." So well, in fact, she was certain she would never see him again, as his letters were full of his love for his new home.

Christopher propped his chin on his palm. "It seems a long time, but mark my words—in another twenty or so years, there will be trains that can take someone from Philadelphia to California in a matter of days, rather than months."

"Twenty years a lifetime from now." Florie's voice contained a petulant whine.

Pulling his gaze away from Nora, Christopher squeezed his cousin's shoulder. "I know. But it's a big country."

"Show me how he would have gotten to California from New York." Florie leaned over the atlas again.

Nora and Florie had traced the route in pencil as Jack's letters arrived during his journey, but Florie had gone over it so many times since then, running her finger across the pages, the markings had been rubbed away.

Christopher looked at Nora again. "Do you know what route he took?"

As if she could forget. Worrying about him as the weeks passed between each correspondence had etched the names of the places he'd been indelibly in her mind.

She started naming cities and watched in fascination as Christopher's long, elegant fingers traced the route. With a delicious shudder at the memory of those hands, those strong arms, holding her as they'd danced, Nora swayed, catching the edge of the table before she lost her balance and embarrassed herself by swooning.

She tried to tell herself her extreme reaction to a man she barely knew was because she had never spent so much time in the company of a young, handsome man in her life. But even if that were the case, she still wanted to stop, to cease reacting to him. Because she knew, before long, he would move on to someone else, someone more befitting his social standing, his situation in life. And when he did, Nora would be left disappointed.

At least she would have the memory of him to keep her company during her long future as a spinster schoolteacher.

Five young women and six young men. Kate would never be able to keep all the names straight. She perched on the edge of the settee and allowed the newcomers to speak around and over her but did nothing more than observe and try to remember if the blonde in the garish orange-and-blue plaid gown was the knight's daughter or the earl's granddaughter. And while none of the women outranked Edith—the eldest daughter of a baronet— all were younger, prettier, and wealthier than Kate. And they all knew how to flirt.

The young men Sir Anthony invited ranged from sons of wealthy landholders—though not Mr. Brockmorrell of the unwelcome proposal to Edith—to the second son of a marquess, who just happened to have a sickly older brother.

And Edith Buchanan was the sun around which all the men orbited, the other women merely moons reflecting Edith's glow.

If they were sun and moons, what did that make Kate? The dark expanse of empty space between the heavenly bodies.

Smiling at her own fancifulness, she accidentally caught the eye of one of the young men. He inclined his head, then rose and came over to sit in the armchair beside the sofa. "Miss Dearing, I feel I hardly had a chance to greet you, as we all arrived in such

a gaggle. May I introduce myself again? I am Oliver Carmichael."
His brown hair curled over his ears and about his collar—but the
rest of his hair wasn't curly.

Kate could imagine the man's valet pinning Mr. Carmichael's
hair in curl papers every night before bed. She almost laughed.
"It is very nice to make your acquaintance, Mr. Carmichael. And
from where in England do you come?"

"I have the very great privilege of being a neighbor of the
Buchanans. Not a near neighbor, but at Chawley Abbey, about
five miles away. Perhaps you have heard of it?" He appeared
assured of her assent.

"No, I am sorry to say I have not." Though not so very sorry,
given the amusing way his expression fell. *No. I mustn't be Kate. I
need to be Katharine.* "Is it really an abbey?"

Pride swelled his chest. "A former one. It has been in my family since Henry VIII awarded it to the first Oliver Carmichael,
who served as a gentleman in the king's privy chamber."

If Kate remembered correctly, the current Oliver Carmichael
was an Honorable Mister, indicating he was the son of an aristocrat, and his family must be one of prestige in the neighborhood.
"My, but that is impressive, Mr. Carmichael. Do tell me about it."

As she knew would be the case, that was all the invitation
Carmichael needed to launch into a description of just how
favored his great-great-great-something grandfather was by the
Tudor king whom Kate knew only as a man who divorced or
killed all of his wives save the sixth one, who escaped with her life
only because Henry VIII died before he could have her arrested
and tried for something trivial. Oh, and the one who died from
childbirth complications. At least, that's the way Mother had
told the story so many years ago.

It had been one of Kate's favorite stories, one she asked for
almost every night when Mother came in to kiss her good night.

Since most of the stories her mother told her at bedtime were
meant to be instructive—encouraging Kate to be kind, loving,
humble, and generous—Kate had always been curious why her

mother had first told her the story of the Tudor king and his wives. Years after her mother's death, when Kate had been able to read the history of Henry VIII for herself, she thought she finally understood the lesson her mother wanted her to learn from the tragedy—to be cautious and wise and not let a man's flattering tongue lead her down a path of destruction.

Kate blanched. If that was truly the lesson her mother wanted her to learn, then her mother had been a hypocrite, telling Kate not to be guided by her heart but by reason alone. After all, Mother had married for love, against her family's wishes. And Kate knew her mother had loved Father dearly until the day she died. So why would she repeatedly tell her daughter a story that taught that following her heart could be dangerous and have a tragic end?

She nodded and murmured appropriate responses at Mr. Carmichael, but her insides roiled. As soon as he paused to take a breath, she stood. "Please, do excuse me, Mr. Carmichael."

She escaped the sitting room and didn't slow her pace until she exited the house through the orangery. The setting sun cast a rosy haze over the landscape, and her breath fogged around her head in the cold air. She shivered but kept walking.

Had Mother known? Had she learned that Father was the kind of man who could—and would—eventually lose everything? Had she come to view following her heart a mistake? Did she regret marrying Father? Envy her brother who'd inherited not just the family title of baronet but also the family fortune?

Was the cautionary tale of the six unhappy wives of Henry VIII the reason Kate had never been able to find a husband?

The image of a man with curly brown hair flashed into her mind . . . but it was not Oliver Carmichael. Kate could not count the number of young men she'd met in her life, prospective suitors her father paraded in front of her, hoping one of them would catch her interest—or that she would catch theirs. But it wasn't until she came here, until she met Andrew Lawton, that she'd ever felt a stirring in her heart, that she'd ever had the temptation to throw caution to the wind and follow her emotions rather than her reason.

Her mother had been able to choose love over caution, with no concern over wealth or what the future would hold for her family. Would Kate be able break her own heart by giving up the man she was falling in love with to find one who could offer financial security?

"Miss Dearing?"

She gasped and turned. Lord Thynne pulled his coat off and wrapped it around her shoulders. "It's far too cold to be out here without a coat."

"Th-thank you." Her teeth chattered together. "I guess I was too lost in my thoughts to realize how cold I was."

He led her back into the house, making her stop and stand in front of one of the coal braziers in the conservatory until she was warm enough to give the coat back to him.

"What was it that drove you outside on an evening like this?" He folded the greatcoat over his arm.

"I . . . something came up that reminded me of my mother. I haven't thought about it—haven't thought about her in that way—in a very long time."

At a distance a bell gonged. "That's the dressing signal. I should go." She skirted around Lord Thynne, but he fell in step with her.

"I shall walk with you, if you do not mind."

How could she refuse? "Of course."

"I do not wish to pry, but it sounds like you lost your mother at a young age."

"I was eight years old when she died. Complications from childbirth." Somehow, explaining it to the viscount allowed Kate to distance herself from the memories and shove the grief—and the worries over just what her mother had meant by telling her those stories—back into the corner of her mind.

"I understand your parents' marriage was a love match. How fortunate that you were old enough to experience their relationship."

Lord Thynne seemed intent on not allowing her the comfort of putting those thoughts away. "And your parents, my lord? Was theirs a love match also?"

The viscount let out a sound akin to a snort. "My mother and father could barely tolerate being in the same room with each other for longer than five minutes. Many say it is a miracle they managed to have three children, and an even greater miracle we were all sons. Of course, now that my elder brother is no longer with us, my mother is determined to cajole my younger brother into resigning from his position with the embassy in India and returning to England."

Louisa Buchanan had been visiting New York with her parents when she met Graham Dearing at a ball. They knew each other for less than a month before they decided to elope—because they knew her father would refuse them permission to marry. After all, who was Graham Dearing's father but an upstart cattle and pig farmer?

Kate had been born a scant nine months later.

If her mother had been more cautious, if she'd followed reason rather than romance, Kate would never have been born. Because Kate was certain her mother, with time for her family to influence her against the match, would have followed their wishes instead of her heart.

She gave Stephen Brightwell, Viscount Thynne, a sidelong glance as they parted at the top of the marble staircase. Though she wasn't certain she believed Florie and Dorcas that he had shown greater attention to her at his arrival than to the others, she could not escape the fact that he'd shown interest in her by twice coming out to the gardens to find her.

One path led to Stephen Brightwell, life as a viscountess, and financial security for her family.

The other path led to Andrew Lawton, a life as a hardworking wife to a hardworking man, and the constant worry of when and where his next job might be.

Head or heart? Given a choice, which would she follow?

CHAPTER THIRTEEN

*A*ndrew paced the edge of the area again, this time determined he would not lose count of his steps. A rustling. Was that a footstep on the gravel path?

Never before had anxiety crawled over his skin like ants. But the sight of Katharine Dearing coming toward him made every hair tingle. She increased her pace, coming downhill, and he met her halfway, offering his hand to help her over the sinkhole in the path caused by rain or melting snow, or both.

"I hoped I might find you out and about this morning." Kate's blue eyes sparkled, and she did not pull her hand out of his for a long moment after she steadied herself on solid ground again. "I've brought you something, and I hope you will not be upset at my presumption."

Right now, there was nothing she could do that would upset him. "I make no promises."

She narrowed her eyes, but the corners of her finely wrought lips raised in a smile. She pulled a scroll of parchment from under her cape. "I . . . I took the liberty of sketching out some ideas for that piece of land between the grape arbor and the sunken garden."

He took the scroll from her. "Would that be the piece of land where one lone boxwood shrub once stood?"

Kate laughed. Not a simper, not a giggle, but an honest laugh that warmed Andrew to his toes. "Yes. That would be the one."

The blue ribbon securing the scroll of paper very nearly matched the color of her eyes. Andrew slid it up the cylinder, but Kate stopped him, her mittened hand over his. "Don't look at it now. I . . . I'm afraid you won't like it, so I don't want to be here when you see it." She backed away, lifting her skirts to leap over the hole again. "I cannot stay anyway. I am expected back at the house to help entertain the guests."

Andrew moved as if to follow her but stopped when she held up her hands. "When will I see you again?"

She ducked her chin and smiled. "Have you not realized I walk in the garden every morning after breakfast? Or pass the time in the orangery if it is raining?" A few steps backward, then she turned and hurried away.

Andrew almost ran back to his cottage. After stoking the fire in the main room, he pulled up his favorite armchair beside it and unfurled the scroll.

Kate's sketch of her idea for the garden looked as if it had been drawn by an artist based on real life, not sketched from imagination. Not only could he visualize the layout from it, he could tell from the fine detail the types of plants she envisioned in many of the planters.

Of course, he would never allow them to become so over-grown, but he could definitely make this work.

He ran the ribbon through his fingers and turned the paper over. Katharine's handwriting wasn't nearly as refined as her drawing, but it was clear and concise. She explained not just her vision for the garden but suggestions as to the plants he could use, which would allow for varying color schemes in the spring, summer, and autumn. Her heart sparkled through her plain but passionate prose, and her knowledge of flora impressed him yet again. And below the note, she'd signed her name.

Kate. Not Katharine. But Kate. His Kate.

A knock at the front door drew his attention from the drawing. He set it in the chair before entering the cold hall to answer.

"Mr. Lawton, good, I hoped to find you at home on such a day as this." Lord Thynne stood on the other side of the threshold. "I asked the gardener where your cottage was when I could not find you out in the grounds. I hope you do not mind."

"No, my lord, I do not." Andrew stepped back. "Please, come in."

"Thank you." Lord Thynne ducked under the low lintel.

Andrew closed the door. "May I take your hat and cloak, my lord?"

"No, I can manage, thank you."

Because he usually ate in the servants' hall, Andrew did not have much in the way of refreshment to offer a guest. "I was about to make tea. Would you care for some?"

"I . . ." Lord Thynne tapped his hat against his leg before hanging it on the peg in the hall atop his coat. "Well, if it would not put you out of your way, a warm-up would be appreciated."

"If you would like to have a seat, my lord, I will be with you shortly." Andrew motioned toward the small sitting room, which served also as his office.

"There is no need to stand on ceremony with me, Mr. Lawton." Lord Thynne followed Andrew into the kitchen. He pulled out one of the two mismatched wooden chairs at the small, scarred-oak table and looked as at ease as if visiting in hovels like this were something he made a habit of.

Andrew turned his back on the viscount, for every time he looked at him, all Andrew could see was Kate walking away with the man, seemingly enthralled by him.

"Miss Dearing told me of your plans for the gardens and parks here—some of them, anyway. She said she found the gardens here beautiful and restful, and that is what I want at Greymere. So I wanted to come talk to you in person, for the grounds at my home are in much need of refurbishing."

Andrew pulled an old, white porcelain teapot down from a shelf beside the hearth, and the lid clanked in his trembling hand. He'd assumed that the recommendation to Lord Thynne would come from Sir Anthony, not from Kate. He sent silent thanks her way, not only for putting his name forward to Lord Thynne, but also for talking about him to the aristocrat. The fact that she had talked about him enough for Lord Thynne to be interested in possibly hiring Andrew to create a new design for his grounds filled him with pride and pleasure.

"What is it that you have in mind, my lord?" Andrew set about making the tea while Thynne described his estate, on the opposite side of Oxford from Wakesdown.

By the time the viscount was ready to depart, Andrew had made two additional pots of tea and the table was littered with sketches on the paper Andrew had retrieved from the other room.

"Thank you for allowing me to take up your morning, Mr. Lawton. As much as I would enjoy continuing this conversation, I must be going." Lord Thynne smiled at Andrew over his shoulder as he shrugged back into his caped greatcoat. "After all, I promised Miss Dearing at breakfast that I would see her at luncheon, and I would not want to disappoint her."

Every charitable thought Andrew had for the viscount over the past few hours popped like soap bubbles, to be replaced with an acidic burning in his stomach. "Yes. It would not be good to keep someone like Miss Dearing waiting."

Lord Thynne turned and leveled his gaze at Andrew, his expression inscrutable. "She is a most fascinating woman, is she not? I do not know if it is because she is American or if it is just her nature, but she is so . . ."

Beautiful. Charming. Intelligent. Well-spoken. Strong-willed. Self-assured. Andrew's mind filled in words as Thynne seemed to search his brain for an apt description.

"Refreshing." Thynne quirked a brow. "I know that is not something most women would want to be called, but . . . there it is."

Refreshing. Yes. She did bring a refreshing difference that most English women did not possess. But Andrew would go to his grave before agreeing aloud with Lord Thynne. He returned the lord's expression with a tight smile of his own.

"Again, thank you, Mr. Lawton. I shall have my head gardener send over the plans for the grounds and bring them to you so that you can create a plan for me to look at. I have a few other landscape architects who have done so already, but none have met with my approval. From our talk I am certain you understand the vision I have for the place, but, of course, before I hire you, I would like to make certain."

"I understand, my lord. I will be happy to do so, though you do understand that the time line would be dependent on my finishing my work here first."

"Oh, yes, naturally. I would expect no less dedication to your commitment to Sir Anthony as I would hope you would show to me." Lord Thynne inclined his head, then settled his hat atop it. "Mr. Lawton."

Andrew made a slight bow. "My lord."

A puff of cold air rushed in when Andrew opened the door to let Lord Thynne out. He waited to close it again until Thynne turned into the main lane leading back to the house.

Returning to the kitchen to clean up, Andrew considered the past hours. Had Lord Thynne truly come to discuss his gardens, or had he, as it seemed at the end, come to inform Andrew of his interest in Kate?

It seemed as if Kate must have talked about him to Lord Thynne enough to make the viscount believe that an attachment existed between them. Which, given Kate's situation, was impossible.

Though, Andrew admitted to himself, if he had Lord Thynne's position and wealth, Andrew would be considering asking

Katharine Dearing to become his wife, even though he had met her not quite two weeks ago. For he knew in his heart he would never meet another woman who would make him feel the way he did when he was with her.

Complete.

After a tedious morning of needlework and gossip, followed by an uncomfortable luncheon at which Edith managed to separate Kate from Lord Thynne and then monopolized everyone's attention, Kate gratefully escaped to her room for a bit of a rest before changing into her afternoon gown.

No sooner had Athena helped her out of the overskirt of her walking gown than Dorcas entered the bedroom.

"Edith wanted me to remind you that the seamstress is coming today to fit your ball gown for Friday night." Dorcas perched on the edge of the chest at the foot of Kate's bed, her voluminous skirt ballooning behind her.

Kate blinked and glanced away from the garish green-and-yellow plaid of the dress, so happy she'd stood her ground on choosing her own colors and patterns for the new gowns in the making. They might not be as fashionable or eye-catching as those worn by Edith and Dorcas and the other young women now in residence, but Kate would not feel ridiculous wearing any of them, either.

"So she says not to bother coming down to the sitting room, as it would just be for a short time and not worth your while."

Though far from wanting to sit with the sisters and their guests while they made more small talk and embroidered or knitted, Kate couldn't help but feel ostracized.

"I wish I could stay up here with you. The Brocklehursts are coming to visit this afternoon." Dorcas's fine features twisted into a comical scowl. "Dear Mrs. B can carry gossip like no one I have ever met—including servants who live to gossip about their employers. And her aunt, poor dear, who would prefer to be polite and speak of the weather or of events going on in town, is so soft-spoken she cannot get out three words before Mrs. B overspeaks her."

"Cannot Edith direct the conversation to more general topics?" Kate pulled her arms out of the sleeves of the bodice with Athena's help.

Dorcas rolled her eyes. "She could; however, she enjoys gossip just as much as Mrs. B—and the more salacious, the better. I will admit, I do not always try to see the good in people, but I feel strange participating in conversations relaying the worst about them, when it might not even be true."

Kate slid her arms into the dressing gown Athena held for her. She then lifted a knitted shawl—made for her by her sister Clara—and wrapped it around her shoulders. She crossed to the armchair beside the fireplace and sat, taking the warm slippers from Athena to put them on herself. But the long, extremely tight corset would not allow her to bend so far. With a knowing smirk, Athena knelt and held the fleece-lined shoes for her to step into.

"Have you ever tried inviting the aunt aside and carrying on a separate conversation with her?" Kate buttoned the dressing gown from neck to waist before tying the sash.

Athena dipped a curtsy and excused herself from the bedroom, taking the pieces of Kate's walking dress with her to be laundered.

"I . . . no." Dorcas's eyes lit up. "I believe both of us would much prefer that. Thank you, Cousin Kate!" She bounded up from the chest, gave Kate's hand a squeeze, then swished from the room.

Kate knelt as best she could and stoked the fire, hoping to make the room a little warmer before the seamstress arrived. It leapt a little, then settled back to the same sluggish blaze as before. She took her lap desk from the table and positioned the armchair so it faced the hearth before sitting and taking out the letter she'd begun to Maud and the girls yesterday.

She wrote of Lord Thynne, describing him with as much detail as she could, though without sentimentality, lest her step-mother draw erroneous conclusions.

Her pen hesitated over the ink bottle as she debated herself over the wisdom of telling them of his request to walk with her again—but a knock at the door made her quickly sand the paper dry and put it back in the cubby inside the angle-topped box.

Kate set the box on the table as Athena assisted Miss Bainbridge and her apprentices with the protective white cloth wrapped around the gown.

The silk satin glimmered in the room's soft light—with high-lights as light as a robin's egg and shadows as deep as twilight. More chills ran across her skin, but this time in anticipation of wearing so beautiful a garment.

After laying the gown flat across the bed, Miss Bainbridge joined Athena in the small dressing room where all of Kate's clothes were kept, and the two discussed petticoats. Kate ran her fingertips along the skirt of the gown, her hand tingling at its cool smoothness.

Though Kate usually detested fittings, Miss Bainbridge kept up such pleasant conversation that she found herself enjoying the process. She wished she could see how the dress looked on her, but the seamstress had placed the dressing screen between Kate and the freestanding, oval cheval mirror. She wondered if the woman had done it intentionally, to enhance her anticipation. Unfortunately, it merely served to increase her apprehension.

Rather than relegating the task solely to her two young apprentices, Miss Bainbridge joined them on the floor to pin the hem of her skirt—held to extreme fullness by what seemed to be every petticoat and crinoline Kate owned.

"While I am certain this amount of fullness is fashionable, I am uncertain I will be able to move with this many layers underneath." Kate looked down at the three women hunched like groveling penitents on the floor in front of her.

Miss Bainbridge had to remove a few pins from her mouth before answering. "Do not worry, Miss Dearing. I have a few petticoats at my shop that, with the correct starch, can hold up a skirt like this without quite so much assistance." She rose and looked Kate up and down. "Now, Athena, if you will move the screen . . ."

After making one final adjustment to where the sleeve started at the top of Kate's arm, Miss Bainbridge took Kate by her bare shoulders and turned her until she faced the mirror.

Kate gasped. Never before had her shoulders looked so creamy and sloped. And never before had she shown quite so much décolletage. Athena reached around from behind and fastened Kate's mother's sapphire-drop pendant necklace around Kate's neck. It wasn't the collar-style necklace favored by so many of her acquaintances in Philadelphia, dripping with diamonds and gemstones, but she loved it for its simplicity. The gold chain sparkled in the lamplight, and the large stone reflected the dancing flames from the fireplace as it rested just below the hollow of her throat. The petite row of white lace standing up from the neckline of the gown framed it perfectly. In fact, the gown acted as a frame for Kate herself. She turned to see her profile—a bit surprised by the extra volume of the skirt in the back, making it rise almost like a bustle from the previous century.

"Now see if Lord Thynne or any of the rest of them can keep their eyes off you at the ball," Athena said, adjusting one of the curls at the back of Kate's coiffure.

Kate's blush started in her chest and climbed to her face. "Not with Miss Buchanan or Miss Dorcas in the room."

Athena and the seamstress exchanged a glance in the mirror. "I think you'll be surprised, miss," Athena said.

Kate ignored her, turning so the seamstress could do some more pinning on the lace draping in rich folds from the short puffed sleeves. If there was a man she wanted to be unable to keep his eyes from her, it wasn't Lord Thynne. It was someone whose mud-encrusted work boots, and hands with soil under the fingernails, would never be welcome at an event like the Buchanans' ball.

Kate sighed and looked away from her reflection. If Lord Thynne was the one God had chosen to secure the Dearing family's future, she must put all thoughts of Andrew Lawton in the past.

$\mathscr{K}$ate's skin tingled as Athena arranged the final curl in the cluster that hung behind Kate's left ear and cascaded over her bare shoulder to rest in the hollow of her collarbone. In the dim candlelight, with the windows inky black from the early nightfall outside, the blue satin appeared almost indigo, with flashes of lighter blue as Kate turned first one way, then the other, to examine herself in the cheval mirror.

Now that the night of the ball had finally arrived, Kate found herself as nervous as a fly trapped in a spider's web. Not only would all of the visitors from the house party be in attendance, but additional guests would swell the numbers into the dozens, perhaps close to a hundred. All of them here to view her as if she were a wild animal in a zoological park.

When the seamstress returned with the gown earlier today, Kate feared it had been taken in too far in the waist, lowered too much on top. Yet by the time Athena, using all of her strength, had finished tightening Kate's corset, the bodice of the gown fastened easily in the back. The lace lining the wide neckline rested slightly lower than Kate was comfortable with, yet high enough to provide some modesty. The short puffed sleeves covered the points of her shoulders, making her neck look even longer than it was. And her mother's sapphire necklace sparkled against the base of her throat.

She looked like someone else.

And that, more than anything, gave her the confidence she needed to leave the bedroom. If she looked like someone else, she could pretend she was someone else—and pretend the problems that led her here did not exist.

Reaching the top of the marble stairs leading down into the grand entryway, Kate paused and took a deep breath, adjusting her gloves. Tonight, she would not be Kate Dearing, the penniless Philadelphia spinster no one wanted. Tonight, she would be Katharine the socialite, the exotic foreigner arousing every guest's curiosity, the woman who could take all the lessons on flirtation she'd learned through observation over the past ten years and use them on every eligible gentleman present.

With fingertips trailing down the carved banister, Kate descended the stairs, adjusting to the new petticoats so stiff they could almost stand on their own, careful not to let too much ankle show, even though no one stood below to see. After all, as her stepmother always said, one practiced in private to be perfect in public.

She headed toward the rear of the house. After the guests divested themselves of their wrappings and refreshed themselves from the journey to Wakesdown in the ladies' and gentlemen's receiving rooms, they would be announced as they came through the small parlor to be greeted by the family before entering the gallery, which had been cleared of furniture to serve as a ballroom.

She stopped before entering the parlor. Standing outside the door and dressed plainly with her hair in a severe chignon at the nape of her neck, Nora turned and smiled in greeting. "Good evening."

Kate paused, then smiled back at her as pleasure overcame her shock. "Miss Woodriff, I am surprised to see you."

Nora stepped back and looked Kate up and down. "You look lovely, Miss Dearing."

"Thank you." Kate thought she caught a shadow of wistfulness in the other woman's golden-brown eyes, but it was quickly masked. "It must be hard—"

"Kate." Christopher's voice broke across Kate's and she turned to greet her brother—but not before she saw a spark of warmth in Nora's eyes as she turned her gaze toward Christopher.

Dread niggled at Kate's stomach, but she bit back the almost overwhelming urge to warn Christopher again against forming an attachment. Who was she to set rules about whom he could find attractive? So long as he didn't act on it. And she trusted her brother to retain his senses and remember his responsibility toward their family.

With a nod toward Miss Woodriff, Christopher offered his arm to Kate, who bade the governess farewell before taking her brother's arm and allowing him to escort her into the parlor.

"Isn't that dress a little too . . . revealing?" Christopher whispered.

She sighed. "It's what's fashionable, I've been told. And compared to Edith and Dorcas, I'd say I'm quite modest."

"But neither of them is my sister."

Kate squeezed his arm. "I thank you for your concern. But do recall why we are here. None of the men who will be thrown my way tonight would deign to glance at me if I dressed like a prude."

Christopher glanced back over his shoulder toward where Nora Woodriff stood just outside the door. Kate's stomach dropped.

"Oh, Cousin Kate, you look beautiful." Florie Buchanan gave her a wide, toothy smile—until a glance at her oldest sister made her mask her pleasure.

"Thank you, Cousin Florie. Will you be joining us for the ball, then?"

Florie's cheeks turned pink and she ducked her chin, looking down at her plain day dress. "I wish I could, but I am not yet sixteen, and I cannot attend balls until I am."

"Florie wished to see us all in our finery." Dorcas, in pale pink satin with a much more modest neckline than Kate's, looped her arm around her sister's waist. "And now that you have, dearest, you must take your leave."

"But I haven't seen Lord Thynne yet."

"Ask and ye shall receive."

Along with everyone else, Kate turned at the sound of Lord Thynne's voice. Unbidden, her breath caught in her throat. Though a handsome man under ordinary circumstances, in his black suit, white waistcoat, and white cravat, he was extraordinary—even for a man who must be at least forty.

After paying compliments and greetings, Sir Anthony dismissed Florie and Miss Woodriff, just as they heard the first guests arriving.

Half an hour later, Kate's face ached from smiling constantly. And she'd grown quite weary of hearing Edith say, "And these are our cousins, Katharine and Christopher Dearing, visiting from America," to the dozens upon dozens of guests as they passed through the receiving line.

Beside her, Christopher kept up a stream of flirtatious conversation with Dorcas, who stood to his right, while Kate stood silent, ignored by Edith until it was time for the introduction again.

Finally, Sir Anthony indicated that the time for receiving guests had ended, and the time for dancing was now upon them.

Stephen Brightwell, who'd stood beside Sir Anthony in the place of honor and precedence in the receiving line, came to stand in front of Kate. He bowed. "I believe the honor of the first dance is mine."

Kate bent her knees in a curtsy, then took his arm. Beside her, Edith sniffed, but when Kate turned to look at her cousin, Edith was engaged in conversation with a young man with close-set blue eyes and a beak-like nose. Marquess someone or another.

Lord Thynne led Kate out into the center of the gallery. Christopher followed with a friend of Edith's on his arm. The orchestra, positioned in the far corner of the gallery, started playing what Kate thought she recognized as a newer composition by Strauss—"The Vienna Children." Her hand trembled a bit as she raised it to place in Stephen's. His other hand settled at her waist, and she rested hers on his shoulder.

The confidence with which he moved about the floor, even after it was crowded by many other couples, set Kate more at ease, and she allowed herself to be carried away by the music . . . and by Stephen's mesmerizing light blue eyes.

"Is the waltz popular in Argentina, Lord Stephen?" Kate asked.

The corner of his mouth raised, and Kate realized her mistake. But Lord Thynne spoke before she could correct herself aloud. "No. The music and dancing is somewhat different there. As you can imagine, on the ranch or the plantation, the ratio of men to women is quite large, and there aren't many occasions for dancing. When we do, it is usually with the locals providing the music. Is the waltz popular in Philadelphia?"

Kate raised her brows. "Anything that is done in Paris and London is done equally well, if not better, in Philadelphia. We Americans pride ourselves on keeping up with the latest in fashion and entertainment, even though we may be a few months behind on the newest music or books."

Lord Thynne laughed, a rusty sound that made Kate think he didn't do it often enough. She liked the way the skin around his eyes crinkled when he smiled. In a few years, Andrew Lawton's would do the same.

Her lapse of concentration almost made her stumble, but she caught herself at the last minute and moved her feet back into the correct position.

"Are you all right, Miss Dearing? You seemed as if you'd lost your balance there for a moment."

"Yes, yes. I am quite well, thank you, my lord."

"Please, you do not need to call me *my lord*."

"But what else am I to call you, other than Lord Thynne?" She smiled when his expression warmed. "It is my understanding the etiquette demands you be called by your rightful title at all times by someone like me."

"Someone like you?" This time, his steps faltered, and Kate almost tripped over his feet. He quickly righted himself and her, and continued before another couple bumped into them.

"Yes. Someone who is . . . well, not a close relation to you."

"Ah, yes." He lapsed into quiet contemplation for a few bars of the music. "But if anyone were to have an excuse to lapse into calling me by my Christian name, it would be you. After all, are not social customs more relaxed in America?"

"Not that relaxed, *my lord*. Besides, I would not want to dishonor my uncle, who has been so gracious as to extend his hospitality to my brother and me in—" She almost said *in our time of need*, but Lord Thynne did not need to know their circumstances . . . no matter how much she felt certain he would understand.

Before Lord Thynne could ask her what she'd been about to say, the music ended. She curtsied and was about to take his arm to be escorted off the dance floor when another man, this one older than Lord Thynne, approached and offered his hand to her.

Lord Thynne inclined his head and then walked away. It was several dances—and a few stomped toes—later when Kate saw him again. He led Edith to the dancing area, and Kate's cousin seemed to melt into his arms when the music started. Her black hair glistened with golden sparks of reflected candlelight as Lord Thynne moved her around the floor in another waltz.

After the song ended, the orchestra took a break for refreshments. Edith left the floor with her arm twined through Lord Thynne's, and she kept it there as they stopped to talk to another lord of something.

Kate excused herself from the third son of an earl she'd shared the last dance with and went to find her brother. Several young women, with their matrons hovering nearby, stood around Christopher, flirting outrageously.

"Ah, Kate—Katharine. Excellent." Relief filled his brown eyes as he reached his hand out to her. She took it, and he tucked her arm under his before introducing her to the bevy of beauties he'd unwillingly collected. His grip on her hand bordered on painful, though as each of the young women drifted away one by one, his clasp eased.

Only one remained when Christopher looked beyond her, his brows rising. Kate followed his gaze, and her heart gave a little leap.

"Miss Dearing, might I have the next dance?" Lord Thynne offered his arm. "I believe it is a schottische."

Kate pulled away from Christopher, ignoring the whispers of the young women and matrons standing a few feet behind them. "Yes, my lord." She grinned at him on her use of the title. "I would enjoy that." She rested her hand atop Stephen's arm and allowed him to escort her down the length of the gallery.

"To be honest, I hoped you might allow me to take you for a stroll through the orangery, since it is too cold and dark to meander about the garden." Lord Thynne slowed his pace near the door leading to the conservatory, through which they could reach the orangery.

"I . . ." She studied his face. No man had ever asked her to leave a ballroom with him. Not even Devlin Montgomery, and they'd been almost engaged.

Though she gazed into Lord Thynne's pale eyes, it wasn't his face she saw, but Andrew Lawton's. If Andrew had asked her to leave the ball to take a walk, she would not have hesitated. But Andrew was not here. Andrew could not be here. Andrew, though he made her pulse sing in her veins, would never ask her to leave a ball—for he would never be invited to one.

Stephen Brightwell, Viscount Thynne, was here. And he was asking her to grant him the honor of setting herself up for gossip and speculation by leaving the ball for a private walk. Lord

Thynne, whom she found handsome and interesting, but who did not make her pulse sing, wanted time alone with her.

"Yes, my lord. I do believe I could use the refreshment of a stroll in the orangery."

⚬⚬⚬

At the sound of footsteps coming closer, Andrew moved into the deep shadows of the conservatory, praying he wouldn't be seen. He already felt foolish enough, stealing into the house to spy on the ball like a child pressing his face to the window of a sweet shop. But when he had seen Kate take the floor with Lord Thynne, he couldn't draw himself away—and he couldn't stop the crushing disappointment that piled on him the longer he watched.

He'd grown so accustomed to seeing her in her dark cloaks, her head covered with a hood or bonnet, that he'd come to think of her as someone he could at least be friends with, someone who understood his situation, who could, one day—if he made a success of himself—even consent to live the kind of life he could offer. But seeing her now, dressed in a gown that shimmered like the sapphire at her throat, her reddish-brown hair reflecting the warm glow of the candles and lamps surrounding her, any delusion he had of a future with Kate Dearing vanished.

She looked like one of them. Like a fine lady. Like one of the privileged, entitled, wealthy aristocrats who allowed no one of mean birth to breach their sanctuary.

Soft voices joined the sound of footfalls, and Andrew moved even farther back into the corner. He should have known that once the musicians took a break from their playing, couples would take the opportunity for a private moment in the conservatory or orangery. He should have departed long ago rather than risk being caught.

Kate's skirts made a soft swishing sound against the marble tile floor. She laughed at something Lord Thynne said and responded, though Andrew could not make out her words.

Even in the dim light from the few lit sconces, Andrew could see that Kate and Lord Thynne looked quite happy together. Naturally. Kate—no, *Katharine* Dearing, like every other socialite he'd ever met, had merely been amusing herself with their meetings and walks until someone with wealth and standing came along to turn her head.

Of course, in her case, he couldn't blame her. With her family in dire straits, she must win the attention, and the heart, of the wealthiest man she could find.

The sound of their voices trailed behind them as they made their way into the orangery. With no time to waste, Andrew checked to ensure no one else came behind them and crossed the room to exit through one of the large floor-to-ceiling windows, shivering as he ducked out and then pulled the sash closed behind him.

Tomorrow he would tell Christopher that they would leave for London on Monday. Andrew had work that would keep him busy in town for at least a fortnight. That would allow Kate to secure the viscount without any distraction—and without Andrew's having to witness her doing so.

Now that Kate was alone with Lord Thynne, she struggled for something, anything, to say. "I have heard that the mountains in Argentina are much like the great Rocky Mountains in the West. So high that trees cannot grow, that snow stays on the peaks even during the height of summer."

"Though I have never seen your country's Rocky Mountains, from that description, it does sound like the mountains in Argentina. But Santiago del Estero, where the ranch and plantation are located, lies in a plain and is almost one hundred miles from the mountains. I have traveled there, though, and they are magnificent." Stephen closed his eyes and released a brief sigh.

"We have mountains in Pennsylvania, but they are not nearly so grand. The land here is flat by comparison." Kate moved closer to him to keep her skirt from catching on the spike-like fronds of a plant in a large container on the floor. At the expression on his face—soft smile, raised brows—Kate realized he misinterpreted her movement. "We really should return. I do believe I am promised to Lord Haggerston for the polka next."

Stephen returned her to the gallery and had only taken a few steps when Lord Haggerston approached, looking down his overly large nose at Stephen and taking Kate away for the dance, which had already started. From the corner of her eye, Kate watched Stephen make his way around the edge of the room, where Edith joined him. The dance's steps meant she had to turn her back to them, but when she turned that way again, Edith leaned toward Stephen, apparently telling him something of great importance—at least the frown he wore told her he took Edith's speech quite seriously. But the dance moved her the opposite direction, and the next time she turned around, she did not see either Stephen or Edith.

For the rest of the evening, Kate looked for him whenever she had a moment to catch her breath between dances. But whenever she did see him, he was turning away, speaking to someone else, or asking another woman to dance—and more than once, speaking with Edith.

Kate didn't expect him to stand around mooning over her all evening, but in a room filled with strangers, meeting a friendly gaze every once in a while would have been nice.

The dancing ended at three and everyone went into the formal dining room for a light supper. Some third or fourth son of some Lord Something-or-Another escorted Kate in. Her feet ached and she had trouble stifling her yawns. But she tried her best to keep up with the banter from the young men, and a few not-so-young men, surrounding her. Not since her first year out had Kate received such attention. If for this outcome only, the journey to England had been worthwhile.

Never would she have dreamed that when the flattery of such attention came, she would resent it—because it did not come from the one man she truly wanted.

CHAPTER FIFTEEN

$\mathcal{I}$t was almost four thirty by the time Kate returned to her room, and she would have dropped onto the bed fully clothed had Athena not been waiting for her.

Yet after such an exhausting night, Kate still woke around ten on Saturday. She dressed in a morning gown and went down to the breakfast room, where a footman was just setting out platters of food. None of the other guests or members of the family were up yet. Or, at least, none of them was taking breakfast downstairs today.

After sating her hunger on several pieces of toast with raspberry preserves and two steaming cups of tea—though she would have preferred coffee—Kate returned to her room. Athena, looking as bleary eyed as Kate felt, helped her into her walking gown and stout boots.

Outside, a bright, cold blue painted the sky. She wrapped her scarf more tightly around her neck, bringing her hood in closer to keep her ears warm, and set out into the gardens, hoping to find Andrew and see what he thought of her sketches.

After half an hour's walking, with numb feet and tingling nose and fingers, Kate finally admitted to herself that Andrew wasn't coming. And she couldn't blame him, really, not with this weather.

She walked back by way of the greenhouses and kitchen garden, to see if she could get a glimpse of him working in there today. Surely temperatures this low meant extra work trying to stave off the cold from ruining the delicate produce and flowers. But he wasn't there, either.

Disappointed, she returned to the house. Several servants stepped out of her way with bowed heads as she excused herself through the servants' wing and returned to the main part of the house. She'd just turned the corner into the entry hall when Lord Thynne stepped from the bottom of the marble staircase.

He gave her a formal bow. "Miss Dearing."

Her knees creaked like a frozen hinge when she curtsied. "Lord Thynne." She smiled up at him . . . but faltered when he didn't return the expression.

"You have been out in this cold?" His eyes rested on the mud-caked hem of her skirt.

She focused on removing her mittens to hide her embarrassment . . . and ire. "I walk every day. I told you that the first time you came upon me out in the grounds."

"What attraction could possibly draw you out on a day like today?" He crossed his arms, almost hiding his green silk waistcoat.

"Fresh air and exercise. What else?"

Lord Thynne shrugged one imperious shoulder. "So you walked alone?"

"Yes. I walked alone." Not that she had intended to. And on the heels of that thought came the suspicion that Lord Thynne might have guessed her reason for walking out in the cold. "I derive great comfort from spending time alone out-of-doors, though that time is limited to a brisk walk this time of year."

Lord Thynne relaxed his stance, dropping his arms to his sides. "Have you breakfasted yet?"

"I have, thank you. And now I must go change into something more appropriate. For if one of my cousins saw me standing here conversing with a viscount and my hem six inches in dirt, I believe they would disown me and send me packing back to America."

He smiled at her attempt at humor, but his eyes didn't twinkle as they had last night.

Kate trudged up the stairs, and worry chewed at her exhausted brain. Had she done or said something to offend Lord Thynne? Had it bothered him that she'd danced and flirted with other men after he had singled her out by taking her away from the ball for a walk?

Or had jealousy caused his haughtiness when he thought she'd gone out this morning to meet Andrew? Could Lord Thynne have come to care for her that much in just a week's time?

Athena helped her change into a blue-and-brown plaid woolen gown, layered with plenty of quilted petticoats underneath, which today not only served to add volume, but provided additional warmth. She imagined Edith would whisper complaints to Dorcas about Kate's refusal to wear bright colors, but the gown was warm, fashionable—it had been one of the last she'd had made in Philadelphia, and she'd picked the design out of *Godey's* herself—and serviceable.

She stayed in her room reading, sitting by the fire to bring life and feeling back to her limbs, for above an hour. But the book could not hold her interest. And she would not admit the reason why.

Setting the book on the small marble-topped table beside the plush armchair, she pushed herself up, straightened her skirts, draped a thick shawl over her shoulders, and went downstairs.

She bypassed the sitting room—though she could hear feminine voices emanating from there—and headed toward the recesses of the house beyond the gallery. She got a bit turned about in one of the dark corridors beyond Sir Anthony's study, ending up at the billiards room. She peeked through the open door, but the room was vacant save for a few pale rays of light through the tall windows on the opposite wall.

Now that she had her bearings, she turned down the next hallway and stopped at the third door on the right. She rapped lightly.

"Come in," Christopher's voice called.

She entered the small chamber. Leaving the door open, Kate glanced around the room. It retained much of its previous vacant state, since Christopher did not have much with which to furnish it. Only the few books he'd had room for in his trunk.

He looked over his shoulder from the desk and turned when he saw her, the Jeffersonian swivel chair squeaking as he did.

"What brings you to the dungeon, Kate?" Christopher motioned her to the only other chair in the room—wooden with narrowly spaced arms that did not invite lingering overlong.

Kate perched on the edge of the seat, knowing her layers of petticoats would be too wide to fit. "We always visit the morning after a ball. I hardly saw you last night, except for on the dance floor, and I would hear your thoughts on the event."

Christopher's chair squeaked again as he leaned back and crossed his long legs. "No, what you want to hear is if I met any eligible young ladies last night."

"I was under the impression that all of the young ladies you danced with were eligible." Kate canted her head to the side and gave him the teasing grin he usually couldn't resist.

Christopher rolled his neck and closed his eyes a moment. Slowly, but inevitably, an answering grin stole over his face. "I have a feeling that if any of those eligible young ladies express to their fathers today that they found me of interest, it would take less than five minutes for those fathers to discover just how *ine*ligible I am."

He opened his eyes and the amusement slid from his expression. "Kate, you must know it's easier for a woman of little means to find a husband than for a man to do the same." He rubbed his neck and sighed. "I'm glad Andrew and I are leaving for London on Monday."

Kate's insides felt as if she'd swallowed a bucket of snow. "Monday?"

"Yes. Andrew came to see me this morning and told me he saw no reason for further delay, so long as I could be ready to depart by then."

The snow inside her turned into a glacier, growing and expanding to fill every crevice of her being. Though Andrew had not been present at the ball last night, she could not forget the look on his face several days ago when Lord Thynne had taken her away from him at the site of the elliptical garden. He probably guessed that Stephen was paying more than a little attention to Kate.

"Shall I see you to the train station?" She hoped her voice hadn't sounded as strained as it felt leaving her throat.

"We leave on the seven o'clock train Monday morning. There is no need for you to rise so early and subject yourself to the cold. We'll only be gone about two weeks." His grin returned and he leaned forward, resting his arm on the edge of the desk. "You should be accustomed to my absences for much longer spans of time, what with my being gone for university, law school, and my apprenticeship these last six years."

She reached over and laid her hand on his wrist. "And it is those years of absence that make me want to spend as much time with you now as I can."

His expression seemed to say, *A likely story.* But he did not contradict her. He rotated his arm to turn his hand palm up and took her hand in his. "It would be better for you to stay here, snug and warm. In fact, I hope you'll think about ceasing your daily walks with the weather so drear."

Kate ran her tongue along the back of her teeth, searching her brother's eyes.

He knew.

Had Andrew told Christopher about their meetings on the grounds? Had he shared with her brother what they'd discussed? How she'd sketched ideas for him?

She pulled her hand away from Christopher's and stood. "I will keep my own counsel on if the weather is too bad for walking, thank you. Just as I will keep my own counsel on . . . whatever else affects me and me alone." The distance to the door vanished in three steps.

"Kate, I didn't mean . . ." Christopher sighed.

Glancing heavenward for calmness, Kate turned. "I know. You have only my best interests at heart with your warning. But I am not a child, Christopher. If I need your counsel, you will be the first to know."

"I love you, you know that, right?" Christopher rose and pulled Kate into a hug.

The urge to weep at the unsolicited gesture took Kate by surprise. She allowed herself a moment of weakness and melted into his strong embrace.

But no matter how much he might want to, Christopher could not solve her problems. She must stand on her own, rely on her own best judgment.

She pushed away from him before she really wanted to. "I know. And I love you too. I'll let you get back to your work."

After closing the door behind her, Kate leaned against the wall, fighting tears, fearing that Christopher would be the only man who ever said those words to her.

Sunday morning, though Andrew stood with everyone else in the small congregation when Lord Thynne and the Buchanans entered, he refused to take his gaze from the pulpit. He'd caught the entrance of the three Buchanan sisters from the corner of his eye. And he hadn't missed the fact that Edith came in by herself and not on the arm of Lord Thynne, who entered behind them.

But Thynne hadn't walked Kate in, either. No, she came in on the arm of Sir Anthony, looking quite comfortable being attended by the middle-aged baronet.

Escorted into church by a baronet; led from the ball for a private walk by a viscount. If she had her way, she'd likely be taking tea with the queen next.

Andrew clamped his back teeth together until his jaw ached. How could he have been so stupid, letting her flirting lead him to believe she might be attracted to him?

Once the Buchanans, the Dearings, and Lord Thynne were settled into their row, the vicar called the service to order. By the time it ended, Andrew's neck ached from holding his head resolutely away from Kate—difficult, since she sat in his line of vision to the front of the sanctuary—and a headache raged between his temples.

The final amen still clung to the vicar's lips when Andrew slipped out the door. Jamming his hat on his head and thrusting his arms into the sleeves of his coat, he set off down the road back to Wakesdown as fast as he could without running. He would never run away from anyone.

After a luncheon of cold meat, bread, and cheese—sent home with him by the housekeeper after supper in the servants' hall last night—Andrew tried to settle down to some much-neglected correspondence, which should have been finished long before the trip back to London. If he did not get letters out to the vendors by the day of his arrival, they might not have time to get the supplies he needed within the fortnight. And then he would have to delay his return to Wakesdown, risking Sir Anthony's irritation at the change in schedule.

But the longer he sat bent over the table, the greater the urgency he felt to get away—to move, to exert himself, to burn off the anxiety and anger building in his chest like a spring thunderhead.

Donning his hardiest work clothes, and sticking a few tapers and his matchbox in his coat pockets, Andrew left the half-finished letter on the table, not bothering to cork the ink pot, and left the cottage. He'd put off examining the folly on the far side of the fountain pond far too long. Tearing down the ivy and other vines growing over the extravagant, fanciful building would suit his need for physical exertion. Then he could start taking measurements. By the look of the clouds gathering on the horizon, he wouldn't have long before the approaching storm would send him inside the decorative building for shelter anyway.

In the gardeners' bothy, he found hedging shears and a pruning hook. Since most of the gardeners had Sunday afternoon off, he met no one, much to his satisfaction.

When he reached the folly—designed by one of Sir Anthony's ancestors at the end of the last century to look like an ancient Roman temple—Andrew gladly shrugged out of his coat, welcoming the cool breeze that penetrated his rough linen shirt. Years of neglect and overgrowth of the verdure gave the white stone structure the look of a much more ancient facade than the 1767 on the cornerstone suggested.

Though he would leave some of the decorative, flowering vines in place, Andrew began hacking away at the gooseberry and raspberry vines. The berries drew birds, and birds created mess. Limiting the appeal of the greenery around the folly would discourage flocks of them from gathering to eat the berries this summer.

As he worked, the memory of Kate's voice rang in his head, espousing the beauty inherent in the wildness of nature, trying to convince him how beauty could be found in the freedom of plants to take their own course, not in the strict structure and discipline Andrew intended for the gardens he designed.

A half-grunt, half-snort tore from him at the thought, and he grabbed a vine and chopped fiercely at it. He'd become only too well acquainted with the results of her belief in freedom and wildness, as exhibited in her behavior toward him. A disciplined woman would never have flirted with a man, toyed with his emotions, the way she had.

Andrew yanked at the pruning hook when it caught in a thick raspberry branch, but it wouldn't come loose. He knelt, wiping sweat from his face, chapped from the wind that blew dark clouds ever closer.

The first raindrop hit the back of his neck and rolled down his spine with the intensity of an ice bath. He pulled on the pruning hook until it finally gave way, gathered up his coat and the hedging shears, and dashed for the door into the folly. Unlike many, this picturesque edifice not only featured an open, columned portico around the exterior, it also had an enclosed interior—perhaps meant, one day, to be a mausoleum, but never used for it. Small statues stood in niches all around the circular walls between the windows, and a carved oak bench sat in the middle of the room.

He'd only managed to clear the vines away from one of the windows, leaving the interior quite dim. He pulled the candles and matches from his coat, took it off and draped it across the bench, and found the sconces between the statue niches.

He'd just stuck the first candle into a sconce when the door banged open with a gust and swirl of dust and detritus. He turned to close it—and then realized it hadn't blown open by itself.

Kate threw her shoulder to the door to shove it closed against the strengthening wind. Though her hood hid her face, there was no mistaking her brown cloak.

He had but a moment to school his features, to hide both his pleasure and his ire at seeing her.

Kate shook the beaded drops of water from the hood before pushing it back and stepping into the small, circular room.

Andrew crossed his arms and tried to look grave, forbidding—fighting against his instinct to move toward her. He knew the moment she saw him, for she let out a sharp gasp and pressed gloved hands to her chest.

"I do apologize—I didn't realize anyone was . . . Mr. Lawton?" She frowned and stepped sideways.

With his back to the window, the sole source of light, he must have been silhouetted. He turned away from her and struck a match against the stone wall and lit the candle. He repeated this three more times until one side of the room glowed with warm yellow light, then turned to watch her.

Kate looked around, but she had made no further ingress. "What is this place meant to be?"

"It is a folly."

"It looks like a Greek or Roman temple."

"And have you seen many Greek and Roman temples?"

Her head snapped toward him, surprise—and perhaps a bit of hurt—written in her expression at the sharpness of his tone. "I—no. Just illustrations in books."

Still frowning, she moved along the opposite wall, leaning close to examine the statues.

Andrew opened his mouth to apologize but stopped just short of speaking.

"I had hoped to find you this afternoon, since I apparently missed you on my walk yesterday morning." Kate's index finger caressed the face of one of the statues. Andrew shivered and looked away, not wanting to imagine what it would feel like to have that finger trail down his cheek, trace the contours of his ear the way she did with the image of the ancient deity.

He resisted the longing to hurdle the bench, take her in his arms, and—

"Andrew?"

He shuddered at the sound of his Christian name spoken in her soft voice. "Stop. Please, just stop."

She halted her progress around the room, dropping her hand to her side. "I apologize for using your first name. I know, it was highly American of me."

He balled his hands into fists, but that didn't help, no matter how much he liked hearing her say his name in that strange, flat accent of hers. "That is not what I'm talking about."

"Then what is it you want me to stop doing?" She moved into the center of the room, her cloak brushing dust from the bench.

"Stop . . ." *Stop making me fall in love with you.* No, he couldn't say that. "I have seen you with Lord Thynne and other men from the house party. I know you were . . . There is no reason for you to continue pretending that you enjoy my company when it is quite apparent you were just biding your time until one of the titled gentlemen responded to your flirtations."

Kate's bottom jaw dropped open and her eyes widened. "I . . . I never meant—"

"Never meant for me to think you were serious in your flirting with me? No, of course someone like you would not consider how you'd leave a wake of pain and misunderstanding behind you when you moved on to your next conquest."

To his utter astonishment, Kate burst into laughter.

She pressed a loose fist to her lips and held the other hand in the air, palm toward him. "I'm sorry. I'm not laughing at you. I'm laughing at the idea of my having conquests. Andrew—Mr. Lawton, if you are not acquainted with the real reason for my being here, then let me enlighten you."

Kate unbuttoned her cloak and draped it over the bench beside his coat. "You may have realized that I am not a yearling debutante. Not even close. I will turn twenty-eight years old in April. In the ten years since my debut, I have had a grand total of three suitors. Two of whom ended up marrying friends of mine. The third was going to marry me only for my money—that is, until my father gambled away the family fortune on a railroad land speculation and lost everything. Then he wanted nothing to do with me; in fact, he told my father that no man with use of his senses would have me." Apparently unable to contain her agitation, she marched a circuit around the room.

Andrew, standing beside the bench, turned as she walked the perimeter, fascinated with the change in her, finding it hard to remember why he'd been angry with her.

"So my father sold many of the expensive furnishings in our home, along with, I suspect, several pieces of my stepmother's jewelry, to afford to send Christopher and me here so that we could find wealthy spouses in relative obscurity."

She released another laugh, this one mirthless and painful. "I, the woman famous in Philadelphia for being the spinster with too many opinions and no talent for flirtation, was to come to a foreign country to snare a wealthy husband, with no fortune or property to entice him. Only my own charms. Ha—charms!" She stopped and threw her hands in the air. "Can you imagine me, trying to charm wealthy Englishmen who are accustomed to being around some of the most accomplished husband-seekers in the world?"

When he didn't answer, she took up her circular pacing again. "So on the voyage over, I made a decision. I could no longer be Kate, the unfortunate spinster. I had to become Katharine, the sophisticated woman who knew how to get men to pay attention to me. But as I'd never had success with it before, I needed to practice."

She stopped at the uncovered window, gazed out it a long moment, then slowly turned to face him, the frenetic expression gone. "I owe you an apology, Andrew. I did flirt with you. I needed to practice on someone, and you were the first candidate to present yourself. But . . ." She looked down and started pulling at the fingers of her gloves to remove them.

"But?" He stepped closer. Moth to flame. Bird to berry. Child to sweets. Man to woman.

Twisting her gloves in her hands, she looked up again. "But I realized that I'd made a mistake in doing so. You see . . . the more I flirted with you, the more I wanted to flirt with you—and not because I was getting better at it, but because you responded to it. You made me feel like that attractive young debutante with power over men that I never before possessed. I wanted to spend time with you because . . . because . . ."

Andrew couldn't stand it any longer. He closed the distance between them, twined his fingers in the soft wings of hair over her ears, and kissed her.

$\mathscr{K}$ate gasped when Andrew's lips pressed to hers. She held her breath until her lungs threatened to explode, then slowly let the air out through her nose. Shock subsiding, the rush of excitement pulsed through her until it infused her with enough boldness to respond, angling her head to give his lips better access to hers.

She raised her hands and rested them on his waist. Beneath the thick muslin shirt, his muscles tightened and spasmed with his uneven breathing.

"Kate." Her name in his deep voice caressed her very soul. One of his hands moved from her cheek around to her back, settling between her shoulders to draw her closer into his kiss, into his arms.

But when his chest pressed to hers, Kate panicked. Instead of embracing him, she used her hands to push against him, breaking the kiss.

Andrew stumbled back as if struck, his eyes glazed, chest heaving with his panting breaths. Kate knew she couldn't be in much better condition. They both stood, breathing hard, a few moments before either one could put voice to their thoughts.

Seeming to come to his senses, Andrew straightened, running his fingers through his hair to try to smooth it back. The unruly curls sprang right back into the riotous cloud they usually formed. "I do apologize, Miss Dearing."

"Don't." Kate smoothed her sweating, trembling hands down the front of her skirt. "You need not apologize to me. I . . . I have wanted you to do that for a while now. But . . ."

Andrew shook his head. "But it can never be. No matter how we feel for each other, we must go our own ways. You need a wealthy husband. I am in no position to support a wife, much less her family."

Tears stung Kate's eyes and regret clogged her throat. "How can God be so unfair?"

Andrew leaned against the wall, pressing his head back against the stonework. "Do you really believe God takes so minute an interest in what happens between people like you and me? It seems He has more weighty matters to attend to."

Kate turned her back to Andrew and busied herself with brushing the dust from her cloak so he wouldn't see the tears that refused to obey her internal command to stop. "I used to believe that God cared what happened to me. How many times have I heard about how God cares for the sparrows and the lilies, which means He cares for me even more? But perhaps those are just platitudes we are told to keep us from despair." She drew a ragged breath and hugged the cloak to her chest, burying her face in the damp wool.

Gentle hands took her by the shoulders and turned her around, and Andrew wrapped her in a hug.

With her arms and the cloak between them, Kate allowed herself to melt into his embrace, her forehead fitting into the curve between his shoulder and throat. As soon as she allowed herself to accept the comfort he offered, the tears ceased.

"Kate—for Kate to me you will be from now on, now I know that is who you really are—would that we could run away together, marry without thought to consequence." His chest heaved with an almost silent chuckle. "Plant our own garden and see how it grows."

She smiled at the analogy. And while she would gladly have spent the rest of the day in his arms, she couldn't. Drawing on what few reserves of strength remained to her, she pushed away and straightened her shoulders. "But we both know that garden would wither from the drought of financial ruin."

Andrew reached toward her, as if to dry the tear tracks from her cheeks, but Kate took a step back and wiped her face dry with her sleeve. She shook out her cloak and swung it around her shoulders.

"I will say good-bye now, Andrew." She wiggled the fingers of her left hand into her glove. "And farewell. When you return from London, I think it would be best if we avoided each other's company."

Andrew lifted his coat from the bench and slapped away the dust as best he could.

Kate wanted to go to him, to tell him she didn't mean it, to say she would run away with him no matter the consequences. But a picture of her three half sisters in rags, huddled together on the street corner while her father and stepmother begged for food, created a barrier she could not transverse.

"I agree. When I return, we shall see no more of each other." He shrugged into the coat, then pinned her with his piercing eyes. "Good-bye, Kate."

"Good-bye, Andrew." Rather than risk begging him for one final embrace, Kate pulled her hood up, hiding him from view, heaved the door open, and fled from the folly. The wind whipped and yanked at her cloak and skirts, and the cold rain stung her face, but she ran, down the hill and around the pond, back toward the house. She ran until her sides ached and her lungs threatened to burst.

Once she reached the grape arbor–covered path leading into the main gardens, she slowed, gulping breaths of air that had turned frigid once again. The intertwined vines overhead blocked the worst of the sleet, and her slow trudge through it allowed her time to try to compose herself before she reentered the house.

"Miss Dearing? There you are." Lord Thynne appeared at the other end of the tunnel. He strode toward her, concern deepening the lines in his forehead and around his eyes.

Why couldn't she have fallen for him instead of for Andrew?

"Miss Dorcas said you went for a walk after dinner, but when you had not returned after two hours, and the weather turned, she grew concerned. So she asked if I would come find you." He gained her side and looked her over from head to toe, as if checking for injury.

"I am quite well, my lord. But I do appreciate your concern." Despair over the loss of Andrew rose in her throat and stung the inner corners of her eyes. But she could not allow herself to give any more thought to the man she could never have. Especially not when the man who could save her family from ruin stood before her. "I am a bit tired, though, from my mad dash to shelter from the rain. Might I take your arm back to the house, my lord?"

A slow smile eased the lines in his forehead. He turned and offered his elbow toward her. "Only on one condition."

She paused, her hand halfway to his arm. "Condition?"

"That when we are alone, you agree to call me Stephen."

Stephen. She was doing a better job of remembering him by that name than by his formal title. "Are you certain it's proper?"

"No more proper than it is for us to be alone without a chaperone, Katharine." He took her hand and tucked it into the bend of his elbow. "Do I have your agreement?"

As they were of nearly the same height, Kate could look him directly in the eye without effort. She did so, trying not to contrast how his eyes seemed pale and lacking compared to Andrew's darker ones, which seemed to change color with the weather. "Yes, Stephen, you have my agreement."

❧

Too early on Monday morning, Christopher closed the door of the study behind him and slung the strap of the satchel holding the three books on railway law over his shoulder. Trying to rub away the twitch from his left eye, he hurried down the hall, hoping Andrew wouldn't have been waiting too long for him. In the middle of a cheek-stretching yawn, he drew up short at the sight of a figure hovering near the entrance to the entry hall. The slim waist, bell-shaped skirt, and absence of an apron and cap made Christopher's heart trip and miss a beat.

He moved up behind Nora Woodriff and waited for her to acknowledge his presence, but after a moment, realized she hadn't noticed his approach.

"Who are you looking for?" He leaned past her as if looking to see who might be standing in the entry.

She squeaked and jumped, the back of her head bumping his chin.

Clasping his jaw as if she'd broken it, Christopher moaned to add to the effect.

Nora's hands flew up to cover her mouth. "I am terribly sorry. But . . ."

Christopher dropped the pretense of being injured. "But what?"

She planted her small fists on her hips. "But it serves you right for sneaking up on me like that."

Christopher repositioned the strap of his bag higher on his shoulder. "Speaking of sneaking around, what are you doing hiding here, spying on the entryway?"

Nora's cheeks glowed pink. "I . . ."

"You weren't, by chance, coming to bid me farewell, were you?" He cocked his head and grinned in a way Kate had never been able to resist. Apparently, it worked on more than big sisters. Nora bit her bottom lip and ducked her head. Christopher lifted her right hand and brushed his lips over the backs of her fingers. "Will you miss me while I'm gone?"

Nora pulled her hand away. "I will miss the lessons you have been teaching Miss Florence."

Christopher gazed deeply into her eyes. "I will miss you while I am in London."

Her brown eyes blazed golden and her breathing hitched. Christopher leaned forward. Nora tilted her head back—

"Mr. Dearing, the carriage is ready." The butler stepped into the doorway and cleared his throat.

Christopher didn't miss the disapproval in the older man's expression. He hitched up the strap of the bag again. "Thank you. I will be there directly."

Both of them watched until the butler was safely on the other side of the massive marble staircase.

Rather than risk trying to kiss her again—and unsure she would accept it now that the moment had passed—Christopher ran his thumb down her cheek. "Farewell, Nora. I will think of little else but you while I am away."

She pressed her hand to her face when his fell away. "I . . . Miss Florence will miss you." Her gaze dropped to the floor.

"And you?" he prompted, unwilling to leave until she admitted she had some kind of feelings for him.

She mumbled something incomprehensible.

"What was that?"

She huffed a sigh and finally looked up at him again. "I will miss you. There. I have said it. Does that make you happy?"

He grinned at her and tweaked her chin. "Inordinately."

Before walking out the front door, Christopher turned and glanced back down the grand entryway. Nora raised her hand in a wave, then turned and disappeared down the hallway.

Christopher hurried outside to the carriage, but his haste proved to be unnecessary. Andrew trotted up from the side of the house, breathless. "I hope you did not have to wait overly long."

"I just arrived myself."

Andrew handed his valise to the footman but kept his leather-bound book with him and climbed into the carriage. Christopher's valet had brought his baggage down earlier.

The drive to the Oxford train station seemed much shorter this morning than it had the night he and Kate arrived. They took seats in the second-class car, Andrew riding backward, facing Christopher so they could both sit beside the window.

After forty-five minutes of staring at the English countryside but unable to get his mind off of Nora Woodriff, Christopher decided to do something about it. "What do you know of Miss Woodriff?"

Andrew dragged his gaze from the window as if startled anyone else was nearby. "The governess?" He shook his head. "Almost nothing. I have met her on a few occasions in the orangery—she apparently likes to sit there to read when Miss Florence has lessons with another tutor." He blinked several times as if waking from a deep sleep. "Have you . . . have you some reason for wanting to learn more of Miss Woodriff?"

Christopher shrugged, unsure now he truly wanted to discuss this with Andrew. While he considered the Englishman a friend, he was by no means a *close* friend. But with whom else could he speak? "I think quite highly of Miss Woodriff."

Andrew considered this for a moment, then made a face as if to say he could allow for that opinion. "What are the qualities she possesses which you most admire?"

The unexpected question stumped Christopher for a moment. Nora Woodriff was not a woman who would draw the eye of most men, especially around women like Kate or the older Buchanan sisters. So what was it about her that had garnered his attention the first night he walked into Wakesdown? "She has a kindness, a sweetness, about her that is . . . hard to find. Yet she is not so gentle as to allow anyone the upper hand with her. She also has a hunger for knowledge about the world—history, geography, nature, science, even religion and politics and the law—which I find invigorating. She will never be one to sit still and allow the world to change around her while she ignores it. She wants to be part of the changes, wants to know what is happening, and help it if she can."

Andrew's brows had raised slowly as Christopher talked, and a smile drew up the corners of his mouth. "You admire her because she is like you in those aspects."

"I suppose so, even if it is flattering myself to admit it." He sighed, propped his elbow on the windowsill, and rested his cheek against his palm. "Of course, it does me no good to consider the reasons I am attracted to her. I could never act on it."

"Because of her station?" The words could have been accusatory, but the understanding gleaming in Andrew's gaze kept Christopher from feeling reprimanded.

"No. Because I cannot allow the responsibility of finding a wealthy spouse fall solely on Kate. The burden weighs too heavily on her already—and if I were to marry someone of little or no wealth, I believe it would destroy my sister." Christopher rubbed his forehead. Every time he thought about this, his head started aching.

"But if you were to secure employment, if you could make your own way, would that allow you to marry where you will?" Andrew leaned forward, bracing his elbows on his knees.

"It depends."

"On what?"

"On whether the wages would be enough to support not just me and my wife but my father, stepmother, and sisters as well. Because with as much trouble as Kate had finding suitors in Philadelphia, I doubt she will be able to snare a husband here very easily."

Andrew straightened. "I find that hard to believe."

Christopher raised his head. "I'm sorry?"

Elbow against the windowsill, Andrew pressed his fist to his mouth a long moment before turning back to Christopher. "I find it hard to believe that Kate—Miss Dearing—did not have suitors lined up to court her in Philadelphia. The men there apparently cannot spot a rose among thistles when they see her."

Tempted to laugh at Andrew's gardener's analogy, Christopher paused, taking in the meaning behind the statement. "You . . . Are you in love with my sister?"

The muscles in Andrew's square jaw twitched as if he were grinding his teeth, and a flush crept up the man's face. "I . . . hold great affection for her. And I believe she feels the same for me."

Now Christopher did laugh—but only a brief chuckle. "I knew if Kate were to ever fall in love, it would not be with one of the men my father picked out for her, who could think of nothing other than business and money. So there was no way she was going to fall for one of those dandy aristocrats Sir Anthony paraded before her." He thought back to his conversations with Kate over the past few days. "Of course, I never dreamed she could be such a hypocrite—warning me away from Nora all the while she was forming an attachment to you."

"But as you just observed, she cannot choose someone like me when she has your family's financial support to consider. Sir Anthony contracted me to redesign his gardens and hothouses when I was still an apprentice to Joseph Paxton. And while I believe he is happy with my work and will provide me with an excellent reference once the job is finished, I have no guarantee of another when I leave Wakesdown. I could never do that to her." Andrew heaved a sigh and leaned his temple against his fist. "Not that it matters whether she would have me or not. We agreed to avoid each other when I return so that she can get on with the business of securing a wealthy husband. Though it is my opinion that she may be closer to that end than even she realizes."

Christopher studied his friend's expression, trying to decide if it was more wistful or angry. "What do you mean?"

"One of Sir Anthony's guests has shown a decided interest in your sister. And if she is wise, she will accept him if he makes her an offer. After all, he is a viscount and one of the wealthiest men in all of Oxfordshire."

A viscount? Sir Anthony's friend? Surely he referred to Stephen Brightwell. But he was so old. And staid. And tied to England. "Lord Thynne would do well to secure Kate's goodwill. But I cannot imagine her marrying someone she does not love."

Andrew frowned, the skin between his brows folding into a triangle. "If she wishes to save your family, she must."

Christopher pressed his forehead to the cold glass and watched the landscape fly by the window. As much as he wanted to throw caution to the wind and allow his heart to guide him, could he do that if it meant Kate's sacrificing what might be her only chance at love? There must be a way both to support his family and to allow his sister to have the happiness she so richly deserved. Even if it meant sacrificing his own.

CHAPTER SEVENTEEN

$\mathcal{T}$hough she would have preferred to stay in her room all day and mourn the loss of Andrew, Kate allowed Athena to dress her and arrange her hair, then took herself downstairs to breakfast. Although the grandfather clock in the hallway still echoed from sounding the hour of ten, a cacophony of voices drifted from the breakfast room.

Kate entered the room . . . and the voices went silent. Six women, including Edith, sat at the table. The unnatural lull in their conversation made her stop just inside the door. She glanced over her shoulder to see if someone else—perhaps one of the gentlemen—had followed her in, but she stood alone.

Dorcas opened her mouth to speak, but Edith's hand clamped down on her sister's arm, and Dorcas dropped her gaze to her plate, lips pressed shut.

Self-consciousness almost drove Kate back out into the hallway, but she rounded the perimeter of the room to the sideboard and began to serve her plate. She refused to look around at the sound of chairs moving and skirts rustling, but when she finished filling her plate and turned toward the table, it was empty.

Telling herself she was glad for the solitude so that she was not forced into trying to make polite conversation this morning—knowing that, even now, Andrew Lawton sat on a train bound for London—Kate sat down to eat. She skimmed through the newspaper someone had left on the table—most likely one of the male guests, as it was from Oxford, not one of the London papers Sir Anthony brought in every day.

Unlike Sir Anthony and most of the men here, according to what she read in the paper, most of the locals seemed excited about attending the Great Exhibition. One of the articles focused on warnings about congestion on the roads and train in the week leading up to the opening of the Exhibition on May 1, as well as precautions to ensure the safety of one's possessions and person once in London.

She made short work of her meal. After returning to her room to retrieve her coat, Kate escaped outside. Clouds made the sky a solid gray, but so far it wasn't raining, and it was not too cold. Rather than haunting all the places she'd seen with Andrew, Kate chose a path she'd never taken before. It edged several of the decorative gardens before turning away from the cultivated part of the park and into a more rustic setting. She paused when she came to a point at which the land sloped gently downward.

The vista that spread out in front of her should not be viewed alone. Andrew should be here with her, explaining to her his vision for this part of the Wakesdown estate. For she had no doubt he planned something for it—it was too overgrown and wild for him to leave it alone.

She turned around and returned to the house. She needed to finish the letter to Maud and the girls. And nothing she would see out here would take her mind off of Andrew.

In the orangery, she stopped beside one of the tables and picked up an aster blossom that had fallen. Half the petals let go and fluttered to the floor. She pulled the rest of them off and stared at the velvety yellow stamen. How could the flower still look so cheerful with all its petals gone?

Could she feign cheerfulness when she felt like a part of her was missing?

Somewhere in the recesses of her mind, something she'd heard at church came out of the cobwebs and demanded her attention.

"Therefore I say to you, Be not anxious for your life, what ye shall eat, or what ye shall drink; nor yet for your body, what ye shall put on. Is not the life more than food, and the body than raiment? . . . Consider the lilies of the field how they grow? . . . Therefore be not anxious, saying, What shall we eat? or what shall we drink? or, with what shall we be clothed? . . . For your heavenly Father knoweth that ye have need of all these things."

She was almost certain they were words spoken by Christ, and most likely from the Sermon on the Mount, one of the passages the minister at their church in Philadelphia preached from often. And she wanted to take them to heart, to trust in them fully.

But she'd seen beautifully arrayed lilies choked out by weeds, decimated by disease. The irony was that the lilies most likely to thrive and grow were those in cultivated, carefully pruned gardens—the type of disciplined landscape Andrew was so fond of and Kate railed against.

Determined to make herself stop thinking about Andrew, she dropped the stem back onto the table and brushed her gloves against the outside of her brown cloak. At the door into the conservatory, she came to an abrupt halt.

Lord Thynne—Stephen—looked up from his book, then jumped to his feet from the chaise on which he'd been lounging. "Katharine! I thought you had gone with the others."

"The others?"

"The rest of the young women walked out with the shooting party directly after breakfast. I assumed you would be joining them since you enjoy walking so much." Somehow, he managed to smile without moving his mouth at all. His eyes expressed most of his emotions.

The sense of dread she'd felt on entering the breakfast room returned. "I was not aware they were walking out with the men. Why did you not go with them?"

"Alas, I am no shooter. 'Tis a sport I have never enjoyed." He used one finger to hold his place in the book. "I am surprised no one told you of the shooting party."

Kate pressed her lips together and collected her thoughts before continuing. "The other ladies left the breakfast room as I arrived." Had that been what Dorcas wished to say to her? To invite Kate to walk out with them, before Edith stopped her? "It is just as well." She waved her hand dismissively. "I have an engagement in a few minutes anyway."

Stephen's light blue eyes clouded. "An engagement? Not an assignation, I hope." His effort at effecting a joking tone failed.

An accomplished flirt would try to stoke his jealousy further. Coquettishness just wasn't in her nature. "No, my lord—Stephen. I am to meet Miss Woodriff and Miss Florence Buchanan in the orangery for a lesson on plants and flowers."

Stephen set the book down on his abandoned seat. "May I attend also? I know everything about cotton, but nothing about decorative plants. And if I am to make Greymere a home, I need to know about these things."

She wanted to deny him. The time she spent with Nora and Florie was precious to her—some of the rare moments in this house in which she did not feel she had to put on airs or be too cautious of what she said and how she said it. But how could she say no to the highest-ranking person for miles around? "Of course you may."

Before Kate had to do more than discuss the weather with Lord Thynne, Nora arrived with Florie trailing behind. The young woman had her nose buried in a book, something Kate envied. She'd always wanted to be a reader, but the printed word held no attraction the way plants and flowers did.

When Florie looked up and saw Stephen Brightwell, Kate looked away from the knowing gleam in her cousin's blue eyes. "My lord, you remember my cousin, Miss Florence Buchanan."

From the corner of her eye, she watched Florie give her best court curtsy—she had been practicing with Dorcas in preparation for Dorcas's upcoming presentation. "My lord, it is a great privilege to make your acquaintance again."

Stephen bowed low. "Miss Florence, a pleasure."

"And this is Miss Florence's governess, Miss Woodriff."

Nora gave a much more proper curtsy and "my lord," and Stephen inclined his head to her with a pleasant greeting.

"Lord Thynne is going to attend Miss Florie's lesson with us." Again Kate avoided eye contact with Florie. "If you will follow me into the orangery, we shall begin."

Although Nora usually stood beside Florie and asked just as many questions as the young student while she sketched the various plants, today the governess stood a few paces behind her pupil and silently took notes, occasionally straining her neck to get a good view of the shape of a leaf or the number of petals on a flower. Kate was about to encourage her to come forward when she realized Nora's actions were a direct result of Stephen's presence. She did not want to embarrass the governess, so she let Nora do things her way—after all, Nora knew the rules of English society much better than Kate did.

Stephen was as attentive as Nora, but not nearly as inquisitive. He listened, repeated the Latin names a few times, then clasped his hands behind his back and listened to Kate. For her part, she tried to focus on Florie, but with Stephen's pale eyes affixed to her the entire time, she had a hard time concentrating.

She wished she could get him to go away and leave her alone. Certainly, he was a nice enough man. Thoughtful. Considerate. Well read. Concerned about the political situation in America—something no one else in England she'd met so far had shown the least interest in.

If she had never met Andrew Lawton, she might find Stephen's attentions flattering. But she had met Andrew. And more and more, she feared he might have ruined her for any other man.

After two days in Sir Anthony's London home, Christopher bypassed the empty formal dining room on the main floor and made his way down to the kitchen in the basement of the grand townhouse.

"Good morning." He grinned at the look of shock on the faces of Andrew and the kitchen staff.

The cook turned from the enormous iron stove, a wooden spoon in her hand wielded like a sword. "You oughtn't be down here, Mr. Dearing. You should be upstairs, taking your breakfast in the dining room. Sir Anthony would fire me certain if he found out I let you set foot down here."

Christopher held up his hands. "Unless you have failed to notice, I am the only person using any of the rooms above the first level of this house. Even you"—he forced a glare at Andrew, still seated at the heavy, scarred kitchen table—"have abandoned me because you feel you aren't good enough to eat with me. I've made the decision that I will take my meals down here with you so that I don't lose my mind from silence and boredom."

"No. I won't stand for it." The ample cook stamped her foot and started toward him.

Uncertain if she intended him physical harm—which she might, from the look in her eyes—Christopher backed up into the doorway.

Andrew pushed away from the table and stood, interposing himself between them. "Now, now, Mrs. Coleman. You have been trying to get me out of your kitchen since we arrived. Would it make you happier if I resolved the issue by agreeing to take my meals in the dining room with Mr. Dearing?"

The cook lowered her weapon. "Aye, Mr. Lawton, it would."

"Very well then." Andrew scooped up his journal, writing materials, and newspaper. "Mr. Dearing, would you be so kind as to bring the ink bottle?"

Christopher swept it up from the table, then turned and bowed low toward the cook. "I have been wanting to visit you to let you know how much I have enjoyed the food here, Mrs. Coleman. My compliments."

She shooed him away, but not before he caught the hint of pink in her cheeks.

By the time the food arrived in the breakfast room, Christopher might as well have spent the time by himself, with as taciturn as Andrew had become. London was making his friend terribly withdrawn. The dark circles around his eyes and the downward draw of his mouth couldn't be ignored.

Christopher shook his head. "You're just like Kate."

Andrew's head snapped up from his plate of kippers and toast. "What?"

Wiping crumbs from his chin with the back of his hand, Christopher cocked his head. "If Kate can't get outside and putter around in her garden for two days straight, she . . ." He searched for an apt description. "She wilts. Becomes reclusive and silent."

Andrew shifted his gaze to his plate. "Today shall end our confinement in this house." He set his fork down and looked at Christopher again. "This morning we shall go to Hyde Park and see the Crystal Palace. The committee is coming out to view it in its finished state—well, its almost-finished state. As they will be given a tour, Mr. Paxton thought that would be the best time for us to view it as well, as part of Mr. Paxton's group of designers and engineers."

Christopher could barely contain his excitement at the prospect of seeing the acclaimed palace.

After breakfast, he returned to his room and dressed with care—and much more formally than he had originally planned for the day when he would get to view the site of the forthcoming

Great Exhibition. From what he'd read about the engineers and architects on the Exhibition committee, he would be facing representatives from at least three major railway companies today—the Great Northern, Great Western, and Midlands. If he wanted to help his family, and determine the course of his own future, securing the approbation of these men and parlaying that into employment would be his ticket.

Clouds rolled in, and a cold drizzle started when the hack stopped at the gate to Hyde Park. The men guarding the path toward the massive glass-and-iron structure sitting atop a hill made as if to stop them from entering, but then recognized Andrew and waved them through.

Christopher gawked, open-mouthed, at the enormous structure—so long the mist hid the far end of the building. The critics in the newspaper hadn't lied. The Crystal Palace looked like a giant greenhouse.

"They finished constructing the roof of the transept in January." Andrew pointed toward the arched nave that bisected the long building.

As an example of modern architecture, the building was marvelous. As a feat of engineering, constructed in just over four months, it bordered on miraculous. Through the paned glass walls, he could see the enormous trees enclosed inside the building—Mr. Paxton's solution to the public outcry over the other proposed designs, which would have necessitated cutting down ancient elms and oaks.

After several long moments, with the drizzle increasing into rain, Christopher finally pulled his attention away from the building to his companion. Andrew stood looking up at the building—but with a distance in his gaze that made Christopher wonder what he truly saw.

"Shall we go inside?" Christopher asked.

Andrew startled and shook his head as if to clear it. "Sorry. Yes, let's do go in and get out of this rain."

Following Andrew, Christopher frowned. This morning, he'd assumed Andrew's change in manner was due to being in London, shut inside for a couple of days. But perhaps it was something else. Perhaps it was Kate. Christopher wished he were as skilled at drawing information out of people as his sister, for he'd find a way to get Andrew to talk about what was bothering him—and hopefully that would turn Andrew back into the friendly companion whose company Christopher had come to enjoy.

Inside, the Crystal Palace was even grander than from the outside. The glass-and-iron structure soared above the trees—and the sparrows that made the trees their home. And, oddly enough, a troop of soldiers stood in formation on the other side of the massive fountain in the center of the transept.

Christopher caught up with Andrew. "What are the soldiers here for?"

"A demonstration." Andrew raised his brows in a wait-and-see expression, then led Christopher up to the knot of men milling around the fountain.

"Mr. Paxton." Andrew singled out a middle-aged man with heavy side whiskers.

"Andrew, dear boy. I hope you brought the plans as you promised." He clasped Andrew's elbow when he shook his hand.

Andrew patted the satchel that hung at his side. "I did. May I introduce Christopher Dearing, the acquaintance about whom I wrote you."

"Yes, yes, the young American railway lawyer."

Christopher accepted Paxton's hand in greeting—and was surprised at the older man's vigorous and firm greeting. "Mr. Paxton, it is a pleasure to meet you. A great pleasure, sir."

Paxton clamped Christopher's upper arm and led him around, introducing him to all the other men present. Andrew had not exaggerated in the number of railway companies represented by the august gathering. Indeed, Christopher met a few Andrew had not mentioned.

The cavernous space surrounded them and soared above. Christopher spent most of the time with his head tilted back, marveling at the feat of engineering he had the privilege of witnessing.

"The building was designed in segments," Paxton explained, "each based on the structure of a *Victoria amazonia*—a water lily."

"The design is not what we are here to discuss." One of the committeemen stepped forward, arms crossed. "You still have not proven to us that the structure is sound, that the vibrations from the noise of thousands of people will not cause the glass to shatter."

"Ah, yes. Just so. Follow me, please."

Christopher trailed along behind, still fascinated with the idea of being a tadpole in a pond looking up at the underside of a lily pad.

A shouted command brought his attention back down to ground level. The soldiers came out of formation and climbed the nearest stairs, half to the north gallery and half to the south gallery. Standing in the middle of the transept, Christopher had a clear view of the balconies that looked down over the main floor on both sides of the building.

The soldiers stomped along the upper walkways, talking, shouting, laughing as they went. The noise grew and echoed. They banged the butts of their rifles against the iron railings and supports. After several minutes of this, when not a vibration was to be seen or felt in the structure, their commander shouted more commands. On each side, the soldiers fell into formation and began marching, their feet banging against the wooden floorboards as hard as possible. Even the syncopated thrumming of so many boots falling together could not get the glass and iron to tremble.

Christopher raised his hands to applaud when the commander called his soldiers to a halt, but no one else seemed willing to give Paxton such an accolade, so he dropped his hands.

Paxton turned to face the committee, triumph gleaming from his smile. Grudgingly, they admitted his demonstration to be a success, and many excused themselves to return to their other duties in town.

Prior to leaving, three of the men invited Christopher to visit their offices before he returned to Oxford. His heart, still pounding from the excitement of the demonstration, threatened to leap from his chest.

Exiting the Crystal Palace, Christopher walked backward, shielding his eyes from the misty rain. Even with water dripping down the panes of glass, no other building could be more beautiful.

Reluctant to leave, he climbed up into the hackney cab and continued to look at the marvel until the coach turned onto the road and trees blocked the view.

"Congratulations." Andrew wiped his face with a large muslin handkerchief. "I heard two of the men ask you to call on them about the possibility of a position."

"Three." He told Andrew the names. "What do you know of them?"

The rest of the drive back to Sir Anthony's house in the West End was spent with Andrew telling Christopher everything he knew about the men and the railways in which they held interest.

If Christopher could get a good position with one of them, perhaps that would be enough for him to be able to secure the attentions of a wealthy young woman—and her father's approval for them to marry. The men he met today might even have daughters in need of husbands. If he impressed their fathers with his hard work and intelligence, he might be allowed to marry one of their daughters.

Nora's golden-brown eyes and demure smile flashed through his mind, but he brushed the image aside. No matter how much he wanted to see if his future happiness lay with the Buchanans' governess, he must and would do whatever necessary to protect his sister and family. And the first step would be securing employment as soon as possible.

CHAPTER EIGHTEEN

*N*ora breathed deeply of the early spring air. The desire to spread her arms and spin around like a top, the way she'd done as a child, overwhelmed the dignity of being a twenty-six-year-old spinster. So she allowed herself two full turns—but only after looking around to make certain no one would witness it. She had two glorious hours to call her own while Florie took her riding lesson, and she intended to spend all of the time outside chasing the rays of sunshine that managed to break through the clouds every so often.

Whenever she heard voices, she diverted her path, wishing to avoid a reprimand from Miss Buchanan for being seen by their guests. Even though the rumors of Nora's desire to seduce Sir Anthony into marrying her had died down after almost five years and no shocking engagement announcement, Edith Buchanan still seemed to consider the gossip a possibility and vented her spleen on Nora every time the opportunity presented itself. So Nora had learned not to give her the opportunity.

She hoped the gardeners would not mind the flowers she picked along the way. They would brighten up the schoolroom and bring the reminder of the afternoon inside to linger a while longer once she and Florie returned to lessons.

Checking the broach watch—a gift from Mrs. Timperleigh when Nora left for Wakesdown—she sighed and returned to the house. She needed time to find a container for the flowers and to change her shoes.

Just inside the orangery door, she used the boot scraper to get as much of the mud from her boots as she could. Noises from inside made her stop, setting her foot softly on the stone floor. Recognizing Miss Buchanan's voice, Nora's skin tingled in alarm. Though no one else in the family minded if she came and went through the main entrances, Miss Buchanan would have her fired if she knew Nora had entered through the orangery rather than the kitchens.

She was about to sneak out again when a male voice gave her pause. Not Sir Anthony, but he sounded familiar. As quietly as she could, Nora edged through the orangery to one of the windows looking into the conservatory.

Lord Thynne stood near the sitting area in center of the room, arms folded across his chest. His frown drew his mouth into a tight line, and his brows hooded his pale eyes. Thankfully, Miss Buchanan had her back to the window. But Nora could hear her clearly. And what she heard made her stomach twist and chest burn with the desire to contradict the black-haired beauty.

Instead, she sneaked out of the orangery and broke into a trot around the house to reenter through the kitchens. Three maids looked at her through the windows between hallway and laundry room. The pretty blonde one came to the door.

"Miss Woodriff? What ails you?"

"Athena—oh, I am so happy to see you. Where is Miss Dearing?" Nora held on to the maid's forearm so she could concentrate on catching her breath.

Athena's eyes grew wide. "She's in her room. Why? What has happened? It isn't her brother, is it?"

"No, no nothing like that. Just something I need to tell her. Something that . . . oh, never mind. What room is she in?"

Athena told her how to get to Kate's suite. "Are you certain everything is all right? Should I take up tea or compresses?"

"No. No. But you might want to check in on Miss Dearing in half an hour to see if she needs anything." Pressing her hand to the stitch in her side, Nora gulped a few breaths, then hurried up the back stairs to the family wing of the house. She counted doors and stopped in front of the fifth. After another pause to catch her breath, she knocked.

"Come in."

Nora entered a bedroom larger than the schoolroom. She supposed it was fitting that the room chosen for Kate Dearing would be one in which the walls and furniture were covered with flowers. But Nora found it overwhelming and blinked a few times against the visual onslaught.

"Nora, what brings you to my room?" Kate stood from the small writing table, quill pen still in hand.

"I am sorry to interrupt you, but I just heard something that I thought you needed to know." Nora's lungs fought against her corset's confinement, and she concentrated on trying to regulate her breathing.

"Please, sit down." Kate indicated the second wooden chair at the table. She poured a glass of water from the pitcher beside her bed and handed it to Nora. "You look completely done in."

Nora sipped the water, then set the glass aside. "I was down in the orangery moments ago, and I overheard Miss Buchanan talking with Lord Thynne."

Kate slowly sank onto her chair.

"My mother would tan me if she knew I was carrying secrets, but you are the first person in a long time who has been friendly to me, and I want to return the favor." She took another sip of water. "Miss Buchanan told Lord Thynne that you are . . . that you and Christopher are . . ." She squirmed at the memory of how Edith phrased it. "She told him you are poor relations come to marry money, and that he should be cautious lest he be caught unawares and end up losing his fortune to . . . a money-grubber and her family." Nora rushed out the last bit, as if speed could make it less insulting.

"I see." Kate ran her fingertips along the edge of the stationery she'd been writing on. "And what did Lord Thynne say in reply?"

"He said nothing, but he looked quite upset." Nora reached across the table and covered Kate's hand with hers. "I am terribly sorry to tell you this, but I thought you should know so you might be prepared."

Kate nodded, not looking up. "Are you very disappointed in me, Nora?"

That was what had her so concerned? The idea that *Nora* might be upset by hearing about the Dearings' financial status? "Miss Dearing . . . Kate . . . I have known about your family's situation from before the time you arrived. Miss Florie told me everything."

Kate looked up, moisture glittering in her eyes. "But you do not find me ridiculous for putting on airs and trying to act like a member of an aristocratic family rather than being honest and revealing myself as someone with fewer prospects and less education than you?"

A wave of homesickness for her family took Nora by surprise. She wanted to protect Kate the way she'd always tried to protect her younger siblings. "From our conversations, I cannot believe that the female seminary you attended was not just as good or better than Mrs. Timperleigh's. As far as prospects"—she cocked her head and gave Kate a tentative smile—"I have written Mrs. Timperleigh about you and the botany lessons you have been giving Miss Florie. I believe that if you do not find a husband, Mrs. Timperleigh would consider hiring you as a teacher."

⊰⊱

Kate folded the finished letter and tucked it into the writing box along with the one to Maud and the girls she'd put aside when Nora left a little while ago.

"Miss Dearing?" Athena hovered in the doorway.

"Am I late for tea?" Kate turned to look at the painted porcelain clock on the mantel. No, only four o'clock. She turned back to Athena.

"No, ma'am. I just wanted . . . I saw Miss Woodriff downstairs earlier, and she said I should check on you."

Bless Nora for her kind heart, and Athena for worrying about her. "As you can see, I am quite well, thank you."

"Is there anything I can bring you, miss?" Athena stopped ringing her hands and smoothed them down her apron.

"No. But I have changed my mind about what I want to wear to dinner tonight."

Athena joined her in the dressing room, and the maid touched the lace hanging from the sleeve of the yellow silk gown that had been set out for the evening. When Miss Bainbridge pulled it out of the trunk, she'd laughed at the aghast expression on Kate's face, explaining that Edith had ordered it made. In addition to the jabot of red silk roses dripping down the bodice of the gown, each of the four flounces of the skirt featured rows of the silk flowers at the hem.

Bypassing the gaudy creation, Kate rummaged through the hanging dresses and pulled out the silk with the lace overlay, along with its evening bodice. "I will wear this tonight, rather than make a spectacle of myself in that."

Athena's pursed lips twisted to the side. "But . . . it's too plain. It looks almost like a mourning gown, with the purple under black lace."

"I know. But this is what I want to wear. Take that one"—she waved toward the yellow monstrosity—"and get rid of it. Keep it if you like, sell it—or sneak it into Edith's dressing room."

Laughing, Athena disappeared with the gown. She reappeared moments later to make Kate presentable for tea. She eradicated the few loose strands of hair that had escaped the sweep back to the cluster of rolled curls pinned to the back of Kate's head.

They'd go through this process again in another couple of hours, after Athena helped Kate into the dinner gown.

Kate sighed. If she married money, this would be her life— teas and dinners, house parties and seasons in London, hairdressing and changing clothes. The future stretched out in front of her in a long, boring succession of activities she found irksome.

Once assured that Kate's hair would not fall loose in the next thirty minutes, Athena curtsied her exit. Kate returned to her desk and dashed off a note to Christopher, telling him of Edith's treachery and wishing him well in his appointments with the men he'd met at the Crystal Palace.

At five, she reluctantly went downstairs to join the others for tea. But when she arrived, the female guests sat in the room, a sense of forlorn abandonment hanging about them.

Dorcas waved Kate over to join her in an otherwise unoccupied corner. She glanced furtively at her elder sister, then dropped her voice to a whisper. "I am sorry you have not been able to join us the past few mornings, Cousin Kate. We have been eating breakfast early so we can walk out with the men when they go shooting. And, I believe, so Edith can avoid inviting you. I hate to think of you spending so much time by yourself." She truly appeared saddened by the idea.

"Do not trouble yourself. I have enough to do to occupy my time." She could not bring herself to tell Dorcas of her daily walks with Stephen Brightwell through the gardens. "Did you lose the men in the park this afternoon?"

"They are just now changing, but they should join us shortly. We parted from them after luncheon, and, apparently, the shooting was so good, they stayed out late."

Kate perched on the edge of her seat, knowing better than to get too comfortable during teatime. Edith preferred everyone to move about the room rather than stay in one place. "And is there a young man of the party whose presence you particularly enjoy?"

There was nothing delicate about Dorcas's flush. Her ivory skin burned scarlet. "Edith says I mustn't settle my regard on anyone before we go to London. She told me that until I am presented, I cannot make any attachments—for I do not know whom I will meet afterward."

Kate glanced at the girl's older sister, holding court in the cluster of chairs and settees nearest the fireplace. "I see."

"Do you agree, Cousin Kate? Should I wait, not give my heart, until after I am presented?"

Kate turned back to Dorcas. "I cannot say that I absolutely agree with your sister, but in principle, yes. You are so young, have experienced so little of life. You should wait to give your heart until you are absolutely certain of the man to whom you award it." She patted her cousin's hand. "Come, let us join the others."

Kate pretended not to notice how she was ignored when she and Dorcas joined the other women, but took her seat with dignity and as much gracefulness as she possessed.

"Can you believe for three days he has chosen to stay at the house and read rather than going out with the others to shoot? And today he made up an excuse to ride to his home rather than walk out with us." Edith's blue eyes flashed, and the other women shook their heads, expressions of disgust on their faces. "It is too bad his younger brother is off in India. From what I understand, he covered himself in glory as an Army officer, and now as a member of the ambassadorial staff. He would not choose reading over sporting. And everyone knows bookish men tend to be sickly. I would imagine Stephen Brightwell will not be viscount long."

Edith's audience nodded their agreement, and she finally acknowledged Kate with a look that challenged her to contradict her assessment.

Kate raised her brows but said nothing. A stirring among the other ladies drew her attention toward the door. One by one, the male guests arrived, and the party moved to where tea had been set up at the far end of the room. Once fixed with refreshments, everyone spread out, occupying several of the groupings of chairs and sofas in the large room.

However, even with the women separated and engaged in conversation by men, the change in the room when Lord Thynne entered was palpable. He paused, swept the room with his gaze, and then walked to the tea table.

Edith bounded from her seat and intercepted him there. "Lord Thynne, I hope you had a pleasant ride to Greymere today." She poured his tea for him. It seemed an odd thing for her to say, as Kate knew through Nora that Edith had already seen Stephen since his return.

"Yes, thank you, Miss Buchanan. The work proceeds apace."

"You have the most beautiful horse, my lord. I understand you brought it from South America with you." At his direction, she added milk to the tea.

"Yes. He is a Criollo—an Argentine breed descended from the horses the first Spaniards took to the New World with them in the sixteenth—"

"And such pretty coloring. One does not often see a gray horse with black mane and tail. But he is too heavy-limbed to be a hunter, is he not?" Edith ducked her chin and looked longingly into Stephen's face.

"He is—or was—a working horse, bred for endurance during the long days on the ranch herding cattle." Stephen took a step back. "If you will excuse me, Miss Buchanan."

Edith opened her mouth to protest, but Stephen walked away . . . and straight over to take the empty chair beside Kate.

"Miss Dearing, I am sorry I could not walk with you this morning as planned. A note arrived early, necessitating a ride to Greymere to solve a problem so the work on the house could continue."

"No apology is necessary, my lord." Kate frowned at him. She didn't understand. Why would he choose to come sit beside her after what Edith revealed to him?

"I planned to ask you to join me for a walk when I returned this afternoon, but I was waylaid by some . . . unpleasant business."

Kate almost choked on her tea, assuming the unpleasant business he referred to was Edith's revelation to him of Kate's true status in this house. "And were you able to conclude the unpleasant business to your satisfaction?"

Stephen swallowed his bite of watercress sandwich. "I am attending to it. I need additional information before moving forward."

The cup and saucer rattled in Kate's trembling hand, so she set it down on the table beside her. "I see. If there is anything I can do to help . . ."

"I will be certain to accept that offer if the need arises." Stephen saluted her with his cup, then drained it. "Now, if you will excuse me, I need to speak with Sir Anthony before dinner." He inclined his head to Kate before leaving the room.

Kate wished she had not eaten the cookie with her tea, as it now roiled in her stomach and threatened not to stay there. Stephen would go to her uncle with Edith's tale. Sir Anthony would confirm all of it. And even if Stephen did not leave Wakesdown because of it, he would most definitely keep clear of Kate.

But the idea of being ostracized no longer threw her into such a whirlwind of fear as before. Not now that she had the possibility of a position at Mrs. Timperleigh's school. While it would not support her family in the manner to which they were accustomed, between herself and Christopher, they could keep them from starving.

A few minutes after Stephen left, Kate excused herself and returned to her room. Other than Dorcas, no one of the party wanted Kate there. And if she left, they could talk about her the way they'd been talking about Stephen when she arrived.

She picked up her letter to her stepmother and half sisters where she left off, trying to sound as if she enjoyed being in England much more than she really did.

At the dressing bell, Athena appeared to help her change. She suggested another gown—ivory satin with blue stripes and pink flowers—as being more appropriate to the occasion, but Kate held firm in her choice. She liked the way the dark purple accented the coppery tones in her hair, making it appear almost auburn. And the fall of black lace around the scooped neckline made her bare shoulders look creamier than usual.

"You look like you're in mourning." Athena wrinkled her nose.

Perhaps she was correct. But Kate didn't care. She loved the dress and liked how she looked in it. And with the confidence she felt, she could walk into the hornets' nest downstairs with no fear of being stung.

Amethyst jewelry and a purple ribbon woven into the intricately pinned mass of curls at the back of Kate's head finished the look. She examined herself in the cheval glass. No longer did she see a plain spinster trying to be a beautiful and captivating flirt. No longer did she see a preying, penniless woman sponging off her charitable relatives while trying to snare a rich husband. Instead, she saw a woman with hope for a future regardless of her ability to make someone like Stephen Brightwell fall in love with her.

And if she once again held the reins to her future, maybe, just maybe, she would be able to marry for love. She touched her fingertips to her mouth, remembering Andrew's lips there, and prayed that would not be the only time she kissed the man she loved.

She timed her arrival downstairs just right—following the butler into the sitting room to hear him announce dinner. As a member of the family, Kate took her place behind Florie and before the other guests in the order of precedence, escorted into the dining room by Mr. . . . oh, the one with the dark hair and bushy eyebrows who cleared his throat every few seconds.

Because of the number of houseguests and the seating arrangement being changed every evening by Edith, Kate ended up at the opposite end of the table from Stephen and her cousin, who sat across from each other at Sir Anthony's right and left. Thankfully, Florie was almost always seated near Kate.

Tonight, Kate ended up beside the Honorable Mister with the curled hair who'd flirted with her the first night of the house party. And his name . . . his name . . . something starting with an O. At least she was almost certain it started with that letter.

Mr. O—or was it his first name that started with an O?— looked around him halfway through the first course. He leaned a little closer to Kate. "I like to see a woman with a generous appetite. It seems healthier than those who take only one or two bites and are finished." He then leaned away, closer to the young woman on his other side. "Of course, women with healthy appetites do tend to become portly spinsters once they reach their middle twenties."

Heat flared in Kate's cheeks, and she took a deep breath, reassuring herself with the resulting pressure that her new corset made her look just as slender through the waist as Edith Buchanan, though Kate had more curves above and below.

"The same is true of gentlemen, of course." Kate gave Mr. O what she hoped was a sickeningly sweet smile. "Those with healthy appetites when they're young and active tend to need larger waistcoats as they age to accommodate their growing girth." She looked across the table at Florie and winked. "And gentlemen do not often make use of *contraptions* to help their waists look smaller as they gain flesh."

Mr. O—*no*, Mr. C-something—laughed, but the amusement did not reach his haughty hazel eyes. "Naturally, that is something about which you do not need to worry, Miss Dearing. A woman of your statuesque height can afford to eat as she pleases, unlike a more petite woman, like Miss Buchanan." He raised his glass in a silent toast to their hostess at the other end of the table, who glanced his direction and inclined her head imperiously, though Kate was certain her cousin could not have heard their conversation.

Once again, he leaned conspiratorially toward the woman on his other side. "Of course, men much prefer petite women when it comes to social occasions, as they are much easier to dance with and escort than those who tower over all other women. And no man wants to be with a woman taller than he. For what would his friends think?"

The petite young woman opposite him fluttered and simpered. "Oh, how droll you are, Mr. Carmichael."

Yes, Carmichael. The Honorable Mr. Oliver Carmichael. Though Kate questioned his *honorability*, given the course of his current conversational tactics.

"I must say, Miss Dearing, that I enjoy being seated at the dinner table beside a woman who speaks her mind. It makes for great entertainment." He speared a bit of meat with his fork and leaned away from Kate toward the young woman on the other side of him. "Of course, while it is pleasant for a dinner companion to speak her mind, a woman like that would not be considered suitable marriage material. For a man does not want a wife who will embarrass him by shocking others with opinions on anything other than fashion and the latest gossip from London."

"How droll of you, Mr. Carmichael." The young miss batted her lashes and tentatively touched the sleeve of his black dinner frock coat.

He kept his attention on her. "Yes, men of the world prefer conversing with women who have been out a number of years, as young misses have nothing in their heads but lace and ribbons. However, they prefer to marry debutantes." This time, he glanced around Kate and down a few chairs at Dorcas.

Kate sincerely hoped he was not setting his sights on the middle Buchanan sister. Dorcas deserved so much better.

The second course was served, and Kate, though hating herself for doing so, took less food than she wanted—conscious of the gazes of Mr. Carmichael and several other guests on her.

Mr. Carmichael looked at the woman on his other side as if seeing her for the first time. "What a lovely necklace. The emeralds catch the light exquisitely."

Miss How Droll giggled and touched her fingertips to the collar necklace. "Why, thank you, Mr. Carmichael."

He leaned toward Kate. "My grandmother favored paste jewelry as well."

Now on the receiving end, the poor miss, flushing a deep crimson that clashed with her pink dress, apparently no longer found Mr. Carmichael's cutting humor droll.

Kate had been on the losing side of this game far too often in the last ten years to be offended by Mr. Carmichael's remarks. But she still found it incomprehensible why men thought they could gain the affection of one woman by insulting another woman to her face. Even if the insults came on the heels of a supposed compliment.

Men. All men? No. Kate could not imagine Andrew Lawton toying with women's affections in such a way. This was a game of the upper crust, the set for whom courtship and flirtation were the sole occupation.

The gentleman on her left paid no attention to Kate but kept his focus entirely on Dorcas, who sat on his other side.

Kate entertained herself by imagining Andrew seated next to her instead of Oliver Carmichael. He would not insult her. Nor would he spend time cultivating a foppish air and bearing.

At the thought of Andrew sitting beside her at Sir Anthony's table—as her husband, as a valued guest and member of the family—Kate's insides tingled, and she had a hard time catching her breath. He could converse on many topics, though she knew they would talk of gardening most of the time. He had enough reserve and self-possession that his table manners would be impeccable—even though he had never dined in such company before. Or so she assumed.

The picture of him that formed in her head, dressed in formal black and white . . . Kate shuddered as prickles climbed up the back of her neck. He would be so exquisite every woman at the table would vie for his attention rather than that of Lord Thynne or the not-so-Honorable Mr. Carmichael.

Thoughts of Andrew—though she knew she had no future with him—sustained Kate through dessert, allowing her to pay no attention to Mr. Carmichael's continued attempts at flirtation. At the signal from Edith, she rose with the other women to retire to the sitting room so the men could have their brandy and cigars without them.

Kate perched on a delicate armchair beside the sofa where Dorcas sat—but just as quickly stood again when Stephen entered the room.

"Ladies." He paused and inclined his head. "I do apologize for the interruption." He stepped forward, looking at Kate. "Miss Dearing, I wonder if I might have a word with you out in the hallway. We will be in plain view of your cousins." He nodded toward Dorcas and Edith.

The rich dinner became unsettled in her stomach, but she consented and preceded him from the room. She stopped near the foot of the main staircase, where Dorcas could see them but not hear them.

"I want to apologize to you for Miss Buchanan's behavior toward you of late. I believe she is treating you thusly because of me."

Knees weak, Kate reached for the banister to steady herself. "You?"

Stephen smoothed his hands down the lapel of his dinner coat. "Yes. You see, at the ball to honor your arrival, I informed Sir Anthony of my intention to court you. His one condition was that I tell Miss Buchanan of this personally."

"That was no doubt so she could reveal to you my true status in this house. I'm a poor relation. I came here to marry money. I have nothing but my father's debts to offer a potential suitor."

The gentle smile that parted Stephen's lips made Kate feel worse rather than better. "I know. And I do not care. What good is the title and fortune handed down to me if I cannot use it to the benefit of my wife's family? And I . . . have reason to wish to marry for practicality rather than titles or estates or money."

Kate lost all feeling in her legs and sank onto the steps. Even knowing of her financial straits, a viscount still wished to marry her. By becoming his wife, her family would not only be saved, they would most likely enjoy even greater social standing than they'd had before, once Philadelphia society learned of Stephen's rank and wealth. Her younger sisters' futures and prospects would be secure—and brighter than ever. It was more than she'd hoped or prayed for.

And it was the last thing she wanted.

CHAPTER NINETEEN

 ndrew marked the last item off his list and closed the journal. He had seen everyone and acquired or ordered all of the materials and plants necessary to complete the work at Wakesdown. In six to eight weeks, he would be ready to move on, to start something new.

And moving on to a new job would help him move on with his life, as well. At least he hoped it would. Admitting his feelings for Kate to her brother had germinated the seed he'd thought he'd buried so deep it would never grow again, and thoughts of her blossomed at the least provocation. Her insistence on preferring wildness in a garden. Her love of flowers. Her sketch for the space between the arbor and the elliptical garden. The softness of her hair when he'd tucked the aster behind her ear. The bluebell shade of the gown she'd worn at the ball and how it matched her eyes. The humor with which she met life, despite the shadow of her family's misfortune looming over her shoulder.

A gust of air preceded the bang of a door slamming. Andrew pushed himself out of his chair and stepped into the hallway.

Christopher, coattails flapping, loped down the hall toward him. "Can we return to Wakesdown today?"

Andrew pulled the watch out of his waistcoat pocket. "We should have time to catch a morning train. We will need to wire ahead to let them know to send someone to meet us. Why today and not tomorrow as planned?"

"Because I need to be in Dorset to talk to Baron Wolverton tomorrow, and I need to see Sir Anthony—and my sister—before I go." Christopher ran his fingers through his sandy hair. "If I can get to Fontmell Magna in Dorset by tomorrow afternoon, and if the baron likes me, I will have a job with the London and North Western Railway company. But I need a letter of introduction from Sir Anthony. And I need to tell my sister, because if Baron Wolverton does offer me a position, I will go straight to Manchester to begin."

"Well, then, we must be away with all due haste." Andrew returned to the dingy office beside the kitchen and retrieved his journal and papers. "I have already arranged to have all materials and plants delivered to Wakesdown next week, so there is nothing more for me to do here." And he was ready to return to his cottage, which would seem spacious after staying in footman's quarters here and choosing this small hole of a room from which to work. Christopher had tried to cajole him into using Sir Anthony's library upstairs. But Andrew knew how servants talked, and he did not want word getting back to Sir Anthony that he had taken advantage of his employer's absence by gallivanting around the townhouse as if he were a family member or honored guest. Taking his meals in the dining room with Christopher was all he'd been willing to risk.

Upon arriving at the train station, Andrew sent a wire to Wakesdown to let them know of their earlier-than-planned arrival, then he and Christopher opted to save money by purchasing third-class tickets. Andrew folded his overcoat to provide some cushioning to the hard wooden bench, and settled in and listened to Christopher talk about his meeting with the railway company.

Though cold and rainy when they left London, by the time they arrived in Oxford a few hours later, the sun shone through scattering clouds. Sir Anthony's driver met them in the barouche with the top down. Andrew leaned his head back and enjoyed the warmth of the sun on his face. The first week of March was not usually so accommodating and pleasant. If the weather stayed like this, he might be able to finish in five or six weeks.

Christopher hopped down from the carriage at Wakesdown's front door and hurried inside. Andrew climbed out and took his bags from the footman, then crunched along the gravel drive toward his cottage. The grass covering the gently rolling land in the park had a pale green tint to it, which meant the ground must be almost completely thawed. He would have the under-gardeners begin digging the new planters for the elliptical and sunken gardens tomorrow.

He passed the gate to the old rose garden, stopped, and back-tracked. It hadn't been his imagination. Someone was in there.

No, not just someone. Kate.

Andrew dropped his bags to the ground and had the gate open before he realized someone else walked with her. Lord Thynne. And Kate had her hand tucked under his elbow. One of the maids—probably Athena, from the pale blonde hair peeking out from a white frilly cap—followed at a discreet distance.

A chaperone meant Kate had made plans to walk with Lord Thynne. And that meant they were courting.

Andrew clenched his hands into fists. For all that she had acted like she had feelings for him in the folly that afternoon, she certainly had reassigned those affections quickly. He closed his eyes and drew a deep breath in through his nose, then released it slowly. He had no right to jealousy, no cause for hurt feelings. Not only had Kate made her affection for him clear that after-noon in the folly, they'd both made their intentions clear—to avoid each other and allow Kate the opportunity to make an advantageous match.

Lord Thynne had not wasted the days of Andrew's absence in wooing Kate—for she appeared to be enjoying his company, laughing as the viscount spoke.

Andrew snatched his bags from the ground and went home. He would give Kate her wish and do his best to avoid her from now on. He only prayed that becoming Lady Thynne would make Kate happy.

❦

"Kate!" Christopher stopped short when he recognized the person walking with his sister.

"Christopher." Kate dropped her hand from Lord Thynne's arm and stepped forward to hug her brother. "We didn't expect you back until tomorrow."

"I know. But wait until I tell you what's transpired." In a rush, he told her everything—from the visit to the Crystal Palace to meeting Joseph Paxton to the meeting with the London and North Western Railway group this morning. "So I have to be in Dorset tomorrow. And if that goes well, I will be going to Manchester on Wednesday to start the job."

"But that's—it's so sudden." Kate chewed her bottom lip. "And Manchester is so far away."

"Less than a day by train." Christopher tried not to be angry with her. But why could she not congratulate him? Why couldn't she see this was beyond what he'd hoped for? "I know it is sudden. But that means they really want me to work for them."

"I . . ." Her eyes searched his, and she finally smiled. "Congratulations, Christopher. This sounds like just the kind of position you have been studying and training for. I know you will do well. But I will miss you."

Christopher hugged her again, all annoyance gone. "I know. But I will be traveling to London often. And you will be going to London with Uncle for Dorcas's presentation at the end of March, so I will see you whenever I am in town after that."

"Her presentation is almost a month away. There's no telling what could happen between now and then." Kate kept her eyes downcast, but only after a quick glance over her shoulder to where Lord Thynne stood a few paces away.

Frowning, Christopher looked from one to the other. Had Andrew been mistaken? Had he misread Kate's friendliness toward him as something more? Did his sister's affections lie elsewhere? And then his heart leapt. If Kate was in love with Lord Thynne, and he with her, that meant Christopher no longer needed to worry about finding a wealthy woman to marry. He wanted to hug his sister again, but she would have asked questions he did not want to answer at the moment.

And if Kate married someone with the title and position Lord Thynne enjoyed, Christopher could not only expect good things for her but for himself as well. He had not been in England long before he realized that patronage and social connections meant as much as or more than knowledge and experience when it came to success here—to a greater extent than they did in New York and Philadelphia. Being brother-in-law to a viscount could open doors for Christopher he'd never allowed himself to dream of before.

He kissed her cheek. "I'll see you at dinner, Sister." He bowed to Lord Thynne. "My lord."

Would he have to call Kate *my lady* if she married a viscount?

Sir Anthony was in his study when Christopher stopped in to see him, and he readily agreed to write the letter of introduction to Baron Wolverton. He shooed Christopher away and told him he'd have it ready for him before dinner.

That left Christopher with about an hour to kill before the dressing bell rang. He'd already talked to Matthew about packing up his belongings and had seen to his few personal items, just in case he didn't get to return to Wakesdown after tomorrow.

So when he found himself on the third floor in the oldest part of the house heading toward the schoolroom, he couldn't stop his grin. He knocked on the door, but no one answered. He opened the door. The sunlight streaming in through the tall mullioned windows had a tired, end-of-day quality to it.

"Miss Woodriff?"

The door at the other end of the room opened and a wide-eyed Nora came through. "Mr. Dearing?" Her hair hung in thick waves to her waist, ending in fat curls. She held a hairbrush like a weapon. "You aren't supposed to be back until tomorrow."

"I know." He quickly explained his early return, closing the distance between them. "And seeing you again is the main reason I wanted to come back." He lifted the thick curl that rested on her shoulder and held it to his nose. It smelled like rosewater. One of the few memories he had of his mother was that her hair always smelled like the rosewater she rinsed it in after washing it.

The orange glow of sunlight made Nora's big eyes burn with a golden intensity that bolted through Christopher like lightning. "I—" He had to clear the dryness from his throat. "I hope I might write to you if I go to Manchester."

Nora shook her head. "It would not be proper for me to receive letters from you. I am not allowed followers."

"Followers?" He lifted her hair again, this time rubbing it against his cheek.

"I may not court while employed as a governess." She reached up and pulled her hair from his hand.

"Would you be allowed to read letters I send to my sister?" Christopher picked up another lock of her hair and let the curl at the end wrap around his fingers.

"I . . . suppose so." Nora closed her eyes and swallowed hard.

Christopher released her hair and lifted her hand, lingering over kissing the back of it. "Then I will be certain to write to my sister every day."

He backed out of the room, enjoying the speechless way she watched him.

Now, only dinner tonight to get through and it was on to his future. He already missed not having to dress up to take the evening meal, which he and Andrew had decided to do in London.

The high, starched points of the collar irritated his jaw where they rubbed against it. When Matthew suggested he wear two waistcoats because he'd read about it in a publication for valets as the latest style for the well-dressed gentleman—and because several of the young men in the house party did so—Christopher balked and almost insisted on a tray in his room. But he couldn't do that to Kate, who would want to see him at dinner.

He took his place with Kate between the family and the guests in the procession leading into the dining room. Since Lord Thynne escorted Edith, Christopher knew things had not been settled between Kate and the viscount. For when she was announced officially as his fiancée, she would take precedence over their cousins. Wouldn't she? Or would that be only after they married and she became Lady Thynne? But it would be awkward if Lord Thynne could not escort his own fiancée into the dining room.

Shaking his head to clear it, he escorted Kate to her seat, then went around the table to sit between two of the Buchanans' female guests. After two weeks away, he couldn't remember their names—but he hoped it would cease to matter tomorrow.

He was called upon by Sir Anthony to provide them with the entertainment of descriptions of London and its preparations for the Great Exhibition. He told them of the structure and the soldiers, and he did his best imitation of Joseph Paxton's brusque manner. It didn't take him long to realize that Edith and her friends were doing their best to ignore him. They did not laugh along with Dorcas, Florie, Kate, and the men, and they would not look at him—nor at Kate.

Kate lingered in her seat until all the other women had gained their feet and headed for the door. She trailed behind them and then, shockingly, did not follow them down the hall toward the sitting room, but turned the opposite direction toward the back stairs.

Christopher lost track of what he was saying and had to be reminded by Lord Thynne of his story. Were Edith and the other women shunning Kate?

He glanced across the table. It probably had less to do with Kate than it did with Lord Thynne and the attention he'd been showing her, choosing her over Edith or any of the other guests who assumed themselves more worthy of becoming a viscountess than a penniless American.

When the cigar smoke grew too noxious for Christopher to take any longer, he stood. "If you will excuse me, Sir Anthony, Lord Thynne, I have much to do before I leave for Dorset tomorrow."

"Of course. I had Dibsdall give the introduction letter to Matthew, so it should be in your room." Sir Anthony stood and held out his right hand. "My sincerest best wishes in your endeavor, Christopher."

He shook his uncle's hand. "Thank you, Sir Anthony." He turned and nodded toward the remainder of the men.

"Mr. Dearing, may I speak with you a moment?" Lord Thynne followed him to the door.

"Yes, my lord." Christopher motioned the viscount to precede him into the entry hall, then followed the man all the way through the back of the house to the gallery.

Lord Thynne stopped in the center of the cavernous room, where he had led off the dancing at the ball with Kate. "Mr. Dearing, in the absence of your father, I wish to inform you of my intention to ask your sister Katharine to marry me."

Not ask his permission, but to *inform* him of his intention. Must be nice to be a viscount and not have to ask permission to do something. While the proposal would be the answer to their family's prayers, Christopher clasped his hands behind his back and began pacing. He needed to clear up a few things before he gave his consent.

"I have not known Miss Dearing above a month, but it was apparent to me from our first meeting that she and I would be compatible and go along quite well together. You saw for your-self how the other women are treating her. I believe it is incum-bent upon me to propose marriage and announce it soon so that Katharine will have the social protection of an official betrothal."

Christopher stopped, his back to the viscount. Compatible? Go along well together? Where was his declaration of undy-ing love, his inability to live without her? All of the things that Christopher wanted to say to Nora's father when he asked per-mission to marry her.

He paced back down the length of the room until he stood a few feet from Lord Thynne. "Are you aware of our family's cir-cumstances? That we would need financial support from anyone marrying in?"

"Yes. Miss Buchanan made Miss Dearing's circumstances quite clear to me shortly after you went to London. My estates are such that I am in no need of a financial infusion from a wife's dowry or inheritance. While Katharine is not of as high a social status as some would wish my future wife to be, no one can impugn her character or her social graces. She is, additionally, the granddaughter of a baronet, and if my understanding is correct, descended on your father's side from an old and respected family in Philadelphia."

Christopher wasn't sure whom he'd heard that last bit from, but he wasn't about to disabuse the viscount of that impression. "Do you love my sister, my lord?"

Lord Thynne looked distinctly uncomfortable at the question. "As I said, I knew from the first time I met her that she and I would be an excellent match."

Christopher tapped his thumbs together behind his back. "That isn't what I asked you. The question requires a simple answer. Do you love my sister?"

"I greatly admire and respect her." Lord Thynne's brows drew closer together.

"But you do not consider yourself to be in love with her."

"Not at present. However, I believe love must have time to grow and develop. And a marriage based on respect and admiration has a better chance of being happy than one based on the emotions one often mistakes for love."

Christopher crossed his arms, unwilling to accept Thynne's roundabout answer. After all, Kate's future happiness was at stake. "Why do you want to marry my sister? You barely know her, you aren't in love with her, and with your title and money, you could have any woman you wanted. Why her?"

Even though Christopher stood more than six inches taller than the viscount, the stony expression in the man's pale blue eyes and the hostile set of his face almost made Christopher back down from his insistence on an explanation.

After a long moment, Thynne sighed and his expression changed from merciless to resigned. "About a dozen years ago, when I was in my late twenties, my father decided it was time I marry. Since having completed my university studies a few years before, all I wanted to do was go to Argentina to oversee his properties there—to get away from England and all of the trappings and pretense of society and aristocracy. My father told me that as soon as I found a wife, he would let me go. So that season, I set out to find a woman to court. It did not take long. I had met Lady Henrietta two years before, during her debut season. She told me she had admired me from afar since." He paused, rubbing his temples with his fingertips.

"*Lady* Henrietta?"

"One of the many daughters of the late Earl of Norton-Mossley. The young women had been left penniless by their father's death and were dependent on their father's nephew, the current earl, for their promised dowries. Everyone knew he had not the wherewithal to provide. But my father did not need me to marry an heiress, and after many weeks I fancied myself in love with Lady Henrietta." A rough, disgusted sound escaped Thynne's throat.

Christopher dropped his arms from across his chest and tucked his hands into his coat pockets. "I take it things did not end well."

"For me, no. At the end of the season, I proposed to Lady Henrietta. She accepted. My parents invited her and her mother to Greymere for a visit so the wedding could be planned." Lord Thynne paced a few yards down the gallery, swiveled, and returned to face Christopher. "Henni came to plan a wedding. However, her plans did not include me."

Christopher frowned. "If not you, then . . . ?"

"Lady Henrietta and her mother came with their sights set on my elder brother, whose first wife died in childbirth not a year before. At first, I thought Henni was merely trying to ingratiate herself with my family." He pressed his lips together, closed his eyes, and shook his head. "I ended up in fisticuffs with my younger brother when he suggested Henni was flirting with our brother and that I should send her away before Edward took notice—and advantage. I was blinded by love for her, willing to forgive all and make excuses for her behavior."

After waiting several long moments, Christopher was afraid he wasn't going to get the rest of the story. "So what happened?"

"I discovered Henni and Edward kissing in the garden during a ball. Henrietta assured me that she did not want Edward to kiss her and it meant nothing—that she loved me and still wished to marry me. Two weeks later, a month before we were to marry, I discovered Henni and Edward . . . *in flagrante delicto* in the gardeners' tool shed."

Having studied Latin for most of his life, Christopher easily translated the phrase to *in blazing offense*. And once translated, he had no problem understanding what the viscount meant by it.

"I do not know if Henni loved Edward or seduced him because she wanted the brother with the title instead of the brother who loved her, but either way she got what she wanted. And I, in a manner of speaking, got what I wanted. By the time

Edward married her two weeks later, I was on a ship bound for Argentina."

Christopher clasped his hands behind his back and resumed pacing. "So let me make sure I understand clearly. You wish to marry Kate because you *aren't* in love with her. Is that correct?" He turned and pinned Thynne with a challenging gaze.

Thynne took a moment to think about his answer. "Yes, I believe that correctly characterizes the situation. I admire and respect your sister precisely because she has been honest with me about her family's situation. She has made no attempt to deceive me. No attempt at insincere flirtation. She has comported herself with admirable aplomb despite the treatment she has received from the other women in this house. And because of that, because she has always shown herself to be a woman of high morals and unimpeachable character, I wish to marry her."

Christopher stopped pacing. "Will you excuse me, Lord Thynne? I believe I need to speak with my sister." He took the back stairs three at a time and within moments knocked on Kate's door.

Thankfully, he'd guessed correctly that she'd returned to her room. She invited him to sit, but he did not want to keep Lord Thynne waiting long. "Kate, are you in love with Lord Thynne?"

"That is an odd question, I must say." She stood and started fussing with the arrangement of books on the shelves beside the fireplace.

"So you aren't in love with him?" He leaned over the small table. "Are you in love with someone else?"

Her hands stilled. "No."

"So if Lord Thynne were to ask you to marry him, you would?"

Kate pressed her hands to her right side as if trying to hold something in. And though she still stood with her back to him, he knew she struggled to maintain a calm demeanor. "Yes. If Lord Thynne proposes marriage, I will accept him."

"Even though you're in love with Andrew Lawton?"

She whirled so fast, her skirts flared out and knocked over the fireplace tools. "Never say that again. It doesn't matter if I've had feelings for someone else in the past. Lord Thynne can save our family. So if he offers, I will consent." Her chest heaved with her uneven breaths. "He is a nice man, as pleasant a husband as I could have hoped for. We have many things to talk about. And he wants to visit Philadelphia, so I would be able to go home and see Father and Maud and our sisters. And when the girls are older, they can come over here and I can find them rich husbands. As a viscountess, I will have access to the highest levels of society to choose from."

"Why are you willing to do this?" He straightened as Kate moved to stand in front of him, the hem of her skirts brushing the toes of his shoes.

"Because it means that you, Clara, Ada, and Ella will be able to marry for love, not for money. And that is all I have wanted for the four of you since this started." She reached up and cupped his cheek with her palm, rubbing the side of his nose with her thumb. "It means you can court and marry Nora Woodriff, Christopher. You can be happy."

"While you're unhappy? Never." He grabbed her wrist and pressed her hand to his chest, covering it with both of his. "How could I be happy knowing that you've sacrificed your happiness for me?"

She drummed her fingers against his cravat, and the smile she gave him held warmth and honesty. "I will be happier married to Stephen Brightwell than I would be as a spinster in Philadelphia knowing I could have easily saved my family—and had my own—simply by saying yes to him."

"Are you certain?" His voice came out a whisper.

"I am certain."

He kissed her cheek. "Then I will return to Lord Thynne and give him my blessing." He crossed to the door.

"Christopher . . ."

Kate's voice—in a pitch that reminded him forcibly of when they were small children—made him return to her instantly. "What is it? Have you changed your mind already?"

She shook her head, the curled wisps of hair beside her ears bouncing. "No. But . . . would you write to Father of this?"

"Why do you want me—" The expression on her face told him. "You're still angry at him. Have you not written to him the entire time we've been here?"

Her throat worked as if she were having trouble swallowing. "Christopher, before we boarded the ship in New York, when I asked him again if there were any other way to help—even offering to find a position teaching and send him all of my earn-ings—he let me know exactly what he thinks of me. He told me that his decision to send me to England to marry money was no different than his father's idea to raise and sell pigs to the army for food during the war." Her cheeks blazed red, and tears pooled in her eyes. "I said that at least now I know that he sees me as no higher than a pig to be raised for the slaughter, and that I was sorry I hadn't managed to fall on the blade and sacrifice myself long ago."

Christopher blanched at the cruelty of the words. "Kate, I'm sure he didn't mean—he loves you, of that I have no doubt. You know how he gets when he's upset. He loses the ability to speak clearly, to put his thoughts into the appropriate words. And you . . . well, you tend to take perverse pleasure in twisting his words and holding them over his head until you feel he's suffered sufficiently."

"I know I do." Kate sighed and wiped excess moisture from the corners of her eyes. "I will eventually write to him. But . . . I can't bring myself to do it yet." She looked up at Christopher, blue eyes imploring. "I'm not ready to forgive him yet, or to ask his forgiveness for what I said."

So she couldn't see how her pain affected him, Christopher pulled his sister into his arms and kissed the top of her head before pressing his cheek there. "I will write to Father and tell him of Lord Thynne's intention to propose. By the time the letter reaches him, I imagine your betrothal will be official." Christopher had also exchanged heated, accusatory words with their parent. But he would do as his sister asked—and he would explain to their father exactly what Kate was sacrificing to pay for his mistake.

$\mathcal{K}$ate had never needed to escape as badly as she did now, knowing Stephen planned to propose marriage to her at any time. She rode to the train station with Christopher Tuesday morning, but rather than returning to Wakesdown immediately, she asked the driver to take her around Oxford.

The university was beautiful beyond her imagining, as was the Thames, which ran through town. This would not be an unpleasant place to live the rest of her life, would it?

On the way back to the country road leading to Wakesdown, the driver took her down the narrow street containing Caddy Bainbridge's seamstress shop. If Kate were a viscountess, she could patronize people like Miss Bainbridge, helping their businesses grow and flourish, just like her flowers back home.

And she imagined Stephen would allow her to have any kind of garden she desired.

She would start with a well-manicured, orderly elliptical.

Pressing her thumb and forefinger to the inside corners of her eyes, Kate stopped that line of thinking. Stephen Brightwell would give her everything she wanted . . . except for the racing heart and shortness of breath that afflicted her every time she thought about Andrew Lawton.

As soon as she entered the house, the butler handed Kate a note.

Miss Dearing,

I have ridden to Greymere this morning while you were seeing your brother off at the train. I will likely not return until dinner. Until then—

S.

Kate crumpled the paper in relief and hurried upstairs to change into her walking boots. The gusty breezes were a bit chilly, and a solid canopy of gray hid the sky, but she needed to get outside and walk. For the past two weeks, she had not been able to set foot outside the house without Stephen at her side and Athena or one of the other maids trailing along behind as a chaperone, so she had not been able to fully enjoy the earliest of the buds and blooms.

She didn't think about where she would go, but simply started walking. She stopped only when she reached a very familiar place.

The dirt over the hole where the shrub had been dug up no longer looked freshly turned, but it would be weeks yet before it was warm enough for the grass to reclaim the spot.

At the sound of footsteps behind her, she groaned, then turned around with a plastered-on smile. But the person who stood behind her wasn't Stephen.

"Andrew."

He shifted the rolls of paper in his arms. "Kate."

Oh, how she wanted to rush to him, to throw her arms around his neck and kiss him until she could think of nothing else. "Was your journey to London successful?"

"It was. I have no doubt you enjoyed the guests and the dinners and . . . other activities." His voice sounded as strained as hers felt, and the skin over his square jaw twitched.

"I did. Though I was not able to get out and walk as much as I wanted." She rubbed the bridge of her nose. "Andrew, I wish—"

"I understand that you especially enjoyed Lord Thynne's company while I was gone." There was that twitch in his cheeks again.

She rested her left arm across her abdomen and propped her right hand on her waist. "As there was no one else who wished to be with me, yes, I spent time in his company."

Andrew's lower jaw moved as if his tongue wrestled with the words he wanted to say. "How could you do it? How could you move on to the next man as if nothing happened between us? Did what we shared in the folly mean nothing to you?"

Apparently honesty won over civility. "But we agreed—"

"I know we agreed." His voice deepened into a gruff growl, his words becoming more clipped and angry. "But that does not change my feelings for you."

Despite the thrilling tingle running up the back of her neck, Kate held firm to her decision. "Andrew, do you have any family?"

"My father died when I was a small child, my mother when I was twelve." His jaw tightened and cheeks pulled taut, hiding his dimples.

"Then there is no way you can understand the choice I am faced with. I must secure my family's future by marrying a man with money."

"By this time tomorrow, Christopher will have employment."

"And it will no doubt pay him a wage that would be enough for him to live on. But not a family of seven. Not in a house large enough to hold all of us."

Andrew's expression squinted into repugnance. "Please show me the respect of honesty. I think I deserve at least that much."

Stung by the accusatory tone, Kate took a step back. "What are you talking about?"

"You're afraid."

"I beg your pardon."

"You're afraid to marry someone like me, a working man, because it would mean you would have to give up all of this—a big house, servants to do your bidding, carriages and jewels and seamstresses. You would have to keep house, cook and clean, save money instead of spending it. And you would be shunned from society." The tubes of paper in his arms bent and folded at the pressure he exerted on them. "You use your family as an excuse, as a shield to hide behind so that you do not have to give up the luxuries you live for."

Heat prickled up and down Kate's body, and her breathing quickened. "And you are one of the most selfish men I have ever known. If you had any family, you would understand the meaning of love—the meaning of sacrifice. But you live only for yourself, for your own pleasure, doing what you will without having to take anyone else into consideration. In fact, you are so selfish that you are angry with me for finding someone who admires me, who is willing to take care of my family, simply because you wanted me to sit here for two weeks pining for you instead of doing what was necessary to ensure the security of those I love."

She marched past him, but whirled a few feet down the path. "You have a lot to learn about what it means to love someone, Andrew Lawton."

With every ounce of poise she could scrape together, Kate returned to her room. She locked the door before sinking onto the bed, burying her face in her pillow, and weeping until her broken heart had no more tears to release.

Andrew threw himself into his work over the next ten days, grabbing a spade and digging alongside the undergardeners and the day laborers hired on to help with construction and planting. His goal was to work so hard all day that he fell into a deep sleep as soon as he put his head on the pillow at night.

It didn't work, though. No matter how much he exhausted himself physically, as soon as he closed his eyes at night, he could see Kate's hurt expression, hear her voice, see her lithe figure.

Then he would picture her in church—not the small Wakesdown parish but the large, elegant cathedral in Oxford—standing at the altar, marrying Lord Thynne.

And then he would get out of the bed and spend the majority of the night pacing, calling himself every word he could think of for fool. A selfish, angry fool.

The Buchanans were to hold another ball, their farewell to their houseguests and to the country. For next week, they were to leave for London.

The only good thing about Kate's removal to London was that Andrew would no longer have to try to avoid her in the gardens where he, once or twice, had watched her from behind the foliage of a hedgerow or flowering tree or bush.

His pride tried to keep him from drawing the plans he'd promised Lord Thynne. If the viscount found them acceptable and hired him, how would he be able to work at Greymere when Kate was mistress there? But he could not pass up the opportunity for a job as lucrative as this might be.

A note arrived from Lord Thynne to set a time to view the plans, which spurred Andrew to finish them. On the day the viscount chose, Andrew entered the house through the kitchens, rather than taking the shorter route through the orangery and conservatory lest he risk seeing Kate. Outside Sir Anthony's study, Andrew straightened his waistcoat and neck cloth, then knocked.

"Come in," Sir Anthony called.

The baronet cleared the papers he and Lord Thynne had been looking at and invited Andrew to spread his plans out on the desk. Then he headed toward the study door.

"Will you not stay, Sir Anthony?" Lord Thynne suggested. "I value your opinion and experience."

Andrew almost sighed in relief when Sir Anthony returned to the desk. Lord Thynne's thinly veiled comments back in

Andrew's cottage had left him with no doubt the viscount knew of his attraction toward Kate. With her uncle in the room, Andrew doubted Thynne would mention it again. And the baronet's presence would help keep Andrew from accidentally admitting that most of the designs had been done with Kate's pleasure and preferences in mind, not Lord Thynne's.

Two hours later, Andrew rolled up the annotated plans so he could finalize them, and Lord Thynne promised to have a contract drawn up by his solicitor—with agreement on both sides that it would not be signed until Andrew completed his work at Wakesdown to Sir Anthony's satisfaction.

"When we next meet," Lord Thynne said, "I would like for Miss Dearing to be present."

Andrew felt as if someone had slammed him across the stomach with a shovel.

"As she is to be Lady Thynne, I want her opinion on the design before I make a final decision." Thynne's pale eyes stared unflinchingly at Andrew.

Andrew clearly understood both the command and the threat in the look—he was to stay away from Kate or risk his career being ruined. "Very good, my lord." Andrew inclined his head and left the study with as much dignity as he could muster.

The rest of the day did not go well. A letter arrived from Christopher, detailing how a landscape architect was desperately needed by the railway company and suggesting Andrew contact Baron Wolverton about it. But not even that could brighten Andrew's mood.

He'd planted his garden. Now he must tend what grew from it.

For someone very nearly engaged to a viscount, Kate Dearing did not act like a happy bride-to-be.

Nora watched her friend from the doorway into the orangery—the place they'd agreed to meet each afternoon so Kate could pass Christopher's letters to her. When she didn't think any-one was watching her, Kate allowed her true emotions to show. And those emotions hung about her in a melancholic cloak. She strolled the aisles formed by the tables and larger planters, occasionally stopping to smell a flower or to run her finger along a feathery or spiky edge of a leaf or petal. And she almost always ended up standing longest beside the purple asters.

Enough was enough. Nora cleared her throat and strode forward. Kate knew Nora's biggest secret; it was time for Nora to know Kate's.

Nora strode into the room, pretending more confidence than she possessed.

Kate's demeanor changed as soon as she heard Nora's footfalls. Her mouth curved up in a welcoming smile, and her eyes softened. She pulled a letter from her pocket. "I never knew my brother to be such an excellent correspondent. You bring out the best in him."

Nora brushed aside her own pleasure. Taking the letter, she tucked it under the cuff of her left sleeve to be read in the privacy of her room later. "Kate, I am concerned about you."

The pretense at surprise almost came across as genuine. "Why, whatever do you mean?" Kate started pulling the petals off an aster bloom.

"I've seen you when you think no one is watching. I know that you are unhappy. I would like to know why. I wish you felt you could confide in me."

Kate's chin quivered, but other than that small sign of emotion, she kept a strong hold on herself. "If I tell anyone . . ."

"You know I have no one to whom I can carry tales." Nora tried to keep her voice light, carefree, teasing. "And if you are concerned that I would tell Christopher, I promise you, I will keep whatever you tell me in the strictest confidence."

Kate tossed the stem of the denuded flower to the floor. "Lord Thynne is going to make me an offer of marriage."

Nora had inferred that from several statements Christopher made in his letters. "But you do not love Lord Thynne?"

"No." One word, one syllable. Yet filled with anguish and longing.

"You love someone else."

Kate nodded.

Nora thought for a moment. "You are in love with Andrew Lawton."

Kate's throat worked as she swallowed twice. Her blue eyes rose to Nora's, imploring. "No one can ever know."

Nora thought she understood Kate's reasoning. "You are afraid if Lord Thynne discovers you do not love him that he will not offer marriage?"

"He knows I do not love him. At least, I know he doesn't love me. But he is a good man. A man willing to take on the burden of my family. Who else would do that? For that kindness I owe him the respect of never admitting that I am in love with another man."

"And you plan to live the remainder of your life with the regret that you chose Lord Thynne over the man you truly love?" Nora's heart ached for her friend.

"I have no other choice." Kate looked down and wiped her hands together as if dusting them off. "When your family needed you to help support them, did you refuse? Did you tell them it was not what you wanted to do, that you would rather make your own choices, follow your own path?"

"You know I did not."

"Was teaching or becoming a governess the choice you would have made if your family's financial welfare had been no consideration?"

"No. I wanted nothing more than to marry and raise my own family."

"Then you can understand how I am forced into this choice by my family's circumstances." Kate's eyes met hers again, this time searching—for an answer or approbation, Nora wasn't certain.

"Has the life you've chosen been intolerable? Have you hated it? Do you regret the choices you made?"

Nora considered the last twelve years of her life. "It has not always been wonderful. There were moments, especially in the early years, when I cried myself to sleep and wished my life could go back to how it had been before my parents sent me away."

"And now?"

"Now I know why God led me on this path. It was so I could be here, in this house, when you and your brother came from America to stay. It was so I could meet Christopher." Heat flared in Nora's cheeks at admitting, for the first time, her belief that God might work in such a way.

Kate leaned back against a table, gripping the edge of it with both hands. "So whom did God send me here to meet? Andrew or Stephen? And if God truly did bring me here, why would He have put both men in front of me and forced me to choose between my own happiness or what's best for my family?"

"Perhaps . . ." Nora paused, knowing she was unworthy to speculate on God's ways and plans. But the words came unbidden. "Perhaps it is not God forcing you to choose between two men, but instead forcing you to turn to Him, to ask Him for guidance in what decision you should make. Have you ever considered that it is your happiness He wants and that He might want you to trust Him to care for your family's needs rather than trying to do it on your own?"

At Kate's prolonged silence, Nora regretted her words. "I am sorry. I did not mean to offend by speaking of things about which I have no knowledge or expertise."

"No, no. Do not apologize. I think . . . I must consider what you have said. And then I must do something at which I am no good." She gave Nora a half smile. "I must not only pray for God's guidance, I must accept it and follow, even if it isn't what I want to do."

$\mathcal{K}$ate stared into the cheval mirror. Katharine Dearing stared back at her, cinched and curled and coiffured until she looked like the viscountess she was to become.

Prayer turned out to be a pointless pursuit. She'd tried the prayers she'd learned by rote as a child. She'd tried using her own words, beginning as humbly as she could, then devolving into begging God to show her what she was supposed to do, what choice was correct. When she received no answer, she decided she would continue on as before, and take it as a sign if Stephen proposed and Andrew did not.

"'Tis good Miss Bainbridge had time to finish this dress and send it over. Otherwise, it would have been the yellow rose dress for you." Athena fluffed the fringe dangling from the short, pleated sleeves covering Kate's upper arms. In nature, Kate loved the color green. On herself, she didn't like it at all. At least on this gown, the darkest green was relegated to the swag-style floral motif woven—or perhaps embroidered, she knew nothing about such things—into the pale silver-green silk.

The color of the gown had given her a good excuse to wear greenery in her hair instead of ribbons or feathers. Athena had taken hours, it seemed, to twist, roll, and pin Kate's hair into the elaborate fall of curls that started at Kate's crown and cascaded down her neck to bounce between her shoulder blades. Ivy and white jasmine flowers peeked out through the curls and were tucked under the thin braids that created a coronet at her crown.

"You will be the most exquisite woman at the ball tonight. Miss Buchanan will be beside herself with jealousy when Lord Thynne dances with you every set."

Of Edith's jealousy, Kate had no doubt whatsoever. Stephen, however, set more stock by propriety than to dance with Kate more than three times. Or at least she assumed he did.

The only reason Kate looked forward to Stephen's proposal was to see the expression on Edith's face when their engagement was announced. Her treatment of Kate—and that of her friends still in residence—had gone from ignoring her to outright hostility . . . though veiled in biting flattery and mocking deference.

Fingerless lace mittens completed Kate's outfit, and she turned away from the mirror, but not before she caught a glimpse of Athena's concerned frown reflecting back at her.

If Kate did marry Stephen, she would ask him to let her bring Athena with her as her lady's maid. Unlike anything else in the last two hours, that thought generated a little smile.

At a knock on the door, she and Athena exchanged quizzical glances. Athena opened it and, Kate thought, hid her shock well at seeing Lord Thynne's valet standing in the hall.

"M'lord sent this for Miss Dearing." He handed Athena a box, bowed, and walked away.

Athena closed the door and carried the intricately carved wooden box to Kate. With trembling hands, Kate slid up the small brass latch and opened the lid. Inside, nestled on a bed of black silk velvet, lay a beautiful diamond-and-emerald collar necklace with matching drop earrings.

Her breath caught in her throat. She could not accept such a gift. But Athena had already removed the simple gold chain and earrings Kate had chosen and set the new necklace around the base of Kate's throat. "Won't be long now, miss, until you're a viscountess."

Kate hooked the earrings into her lobes and, holding her breath, turned back toward the mirror.

Surely Queen Victoria herself did not have jewels so exquisite. And Queen Victoria would never wonder how much they were worth and think about how that money would be put to better use in helping her family.

Athena fluffed Kate's sleeve fringe again. "You're all ready to go, my lady." She grinned and bent her knees in a shallow curtsy.

"Oh, don't call me that!" Kate shuddered. She hated the formality required by her current position. How would she cope with the additional deferential treatment of being one of the aristocracy?

Arriving downstairs, she almost laughed at the irony of worrying about deferential treatment in the future. As soon as Edith caught sight of the jewels sparkling at Kate's throat and ears, her mouth drew into a pucker, her eyes narrowed, and she turned her back, ushering her friends into the parlor without a word to Kate. Perhaps deferential treatment would be better after all.

"You are so beautiful." Florie's breathless voice made Kate turn. The young woman still wore her day dress, and the longing in her blue eyes made Kate's soul yearn to be in her position again—fourteen and her biggest concern being not attending a ball because she wasn't out yet. No responsibility. No anguish over the possibility of marrying one man when she had feelings for another.

Kate did her best attempt at a court-presentation curtsy, having seen Dorcas and Florie practice it so often. "Why, thank you, Miss Florence."

Florie giggled, then reached out a hand to help steady Kate when she came back upright a bit wobbly. "Lord Thynne will not be able to keep his eyes off you tonight. Nor will any other man in the room."

Kate reached up to touch the necklace that pressed the base of her throat.

Because this ball was not in her honor, Kate attended as a guest, which meant she did not have to stand in the parlor in the receiving line. She moved into the gallery and accepted the salutations of those she'd met since her arrival in England. Unlike Edith and her friends, all the other guests acted as if she were already viscountess—a few acknowledging her with bows and curtsies. She held her head a little higher and pretended to enjoy such attention. It was the least she could do for Stephen's sake.

Kate had almost reached the end of the long room when a discernible change in the demeanor of the guests and a buzz of whispers caught her attention. She excused herself from Lord and Lady Someone and turned to look back toward the entrance.

Stephen, his white waistcoat and cravat glowing in the light of hundreds of candles, received the deferential greetings of those nearest the door with his usual grace, moving purposely into the room, yet not in such haste that anyone could construe it as rudeness.

Kate's pulse pounded, and the necklace and earrings weighed heavily.

Those standing around her split their attention between watching Kate and watching Stephen. It did not take him long to traverse the room.

He bowed to Kate.

She curtsied.

He lifted her right hand to his lips.

She trembled.

He tucked her hand under his elbow.

She walked sedately beside him and greeted each person introduced to her with the decorum and serenity she imagined a viscountess—or a potential future viscountess, in her case—needed.

Because Kate wasn't the guest of honor—nor officially the fiancée of a viscount—Edith Buchanan had the honor of leading off the dancing.

Without asking, Stephen led Kate out for the waltz. Behind them, before the music drowned them out, whispers swelled, confirming the rumor that Lord Thynne intended to marry Sir Anthony's American niece.

"I am pleased you did not change your mind and choose a different gown to wear tonight." Even though the corners of his lips hardly rose, his eyes crinkled in a smile. "I went to great lengths to ascertain what color you would be in so I could choose jewels to match."

"Thank you for these, Stephen, though I should never have accepted them." Kate's skirts flared as they whirled around to make their way up the room in the thronging circle of dancing couples. "I do not deserve such generosity."

"Do not presume, Miss Dearing, to tell me of what you deserve. You are deserving of all the world has to offer. And once I put my question to you, I will endeavor to try to lay that world at your feet."

Once, as a girl, Kate fell into a patch of stinging nettles. The tingling in her skin now reminded her of that feeling. "And what if my answer is not what you expect?" She managed to force enough of a teasing tone into her voice that he did not look at all concerned.

"Then I shall put the question to you now and see how you respond."

Kate's body went numb. Had it not been for the support of Stephen's arms and his expertise as a dancer, she would have been on the floor in an ignominious heap.

"Katharine Dearing," he said without pausing or faltering in his steps, "will you do me the honor of becoming my wife?"

Was this the sign Kate prayed for? Could God have remained silent, deaf to her pleas, because there really was no choice but this?

Every fiber of her being urged her to break away from his arms, to run from the manor and down the gravel drive to the cottages, and to tell Andrew Lawton she wasn't afraid of hard work, that she was indeed using her family as an excuse and a shield.

"Stephen," she said as though the words were no effort at all, "it would be my honor to become your wife." Her throat burned with the desire to deny what she'd just said, to take it back. Tears pricked the inside corners of her eyes. But she'd committed herself. She could not take it back.

"Shall we have your uncle make an announcement tonight?"

And let word get back to Andrew while she still had the chance of running into him and telling him herself? Not a chance. "Do you mind if we wait until . . ." When? She did not want to overshadow Dorcas's presentation, yet the sooner they married, the sooner she could end her father's anxiety—not that he deserved it after what he'd said to her. "Do you mind if we wait until the dinner my uncle is giving the week after we arrive in London? There will not be as many people present, but it will suffice for a public announcement, will it not?"

"And we can have it put in the *Times* for the following day. My mother will not arrive in town until after Easter. But I am certain she will want to hold a celebration in your honor."

The music ended, and they bowed and curtsied to each other.

"Shall we tell your uncle the question is settled?" He extended his arm to her.

"Yes. But please ask him to tell no one until the dinner."

"Not even your cousins?" Stephen gave Edith, now dancing with Oliver Carmichael, a pointed look.

"Well, yes, perhaps they should be told. After all, they are family, so they have a right to be in on the secret."

"That was my thinking as well." Stephen reached over and squeezed her hand where it rested in the crook of his elbow. "I hope you will not think me overly presumptuous, but after I spoke with your brother about my intention to propose marriage to you, I wrote to your father. He should be receiving the letter soon."

Kate inclined her head to the Dowager Something of Somewhere and swallowed her resentment. "Should we wait until he replies to make a formal announcement?"

"Do you fear he will not give his consent?" Stephen leaned his head closer to Kate's. "You are of age to make your own decision, after all."

"And have been for lo these many years. No, I . . . I just thought that if he asked something of you that you are not agreeable to . . ."

"You are concerned he will request too much money as a marriage settlement."

Kate couldn't raise her gaze from the parquet floor, not wanting him to see that she hoped her father would relent and tell her she did not have to marry for money. "Yes."

Stephen squeezed her hand again. "Do not let that bother you. Your father and I will negotiate those details. You need not concern yourself with your family's financial situation ever again."

Kate stopped, frowning at Stephen. "What if I want to take an interest in my—in *our* family's financial situation?"

"I meant no insult, Katharine. I meant only that you no longer need to worry." Stephen gently tugged her arm until she started strolling beside him again. "Your father and I will discuss the settlement. Your only focus should be choosing new fabrics and furniture for all of the rooms at Greymere—it is in desperate need of refitting."

She smiled at him as if she wished to do nothing more in the world. Her future was set. She would never need lift a finger to do anything. No more digging and planting her own patch of ground, tending her own flowers. Servants to attend to every whim. A life of boredom in which—except for bearing the next Viscount Thynne, and hopefully a spare or two—her education, thoughts, and ideas would become obsolete and worthless.

Sir Anthony beamed at Kate when she and Stephen drew to a stop beside him.

"As you may have surmised, sir, I have asked Miss Dearing to become my wife, and she has accepted." He stopped her uncle from calling for the music to cease by stepping into his path. Kate dropped her hand from Stephen's arm. "Miss Dearing has asked that no public announcement be made until the dinner you are having in London after your daughter's presentation."

Sir Anthony looked ready to weep from the disappointment of not being able to announce his niece's engagement to a viscount immediately.

Kate stepped up beside Stephen. "I do not want to usurp Dorcas's time of celebration, Uncle. She should be the focus of attention when we arrive in London. There will be plenty of time for your friends and acquaintances to wish us joy after that."

Stephen took her hand and tucked it through his arm again. "I would not say plenty of time, my dear. I do not plan to make this an extended engagement."

Kate's heart pounded. "When did you want the wedding date to be?"

"I must return to Argentina soon to meet with my steward and settle some business affairs now that I will no longer be living there. I will be gone for two months at the least, and I do not want to wait until after I return to marry you. I thought, if you agree, you might go with me. It can be our honeymoon. After I settle affairs in Argentina, we can sail to Philadelphia for a brief visit to your family before returning to England."

A flash of gratitude lit her heart . . . then her mind settled on the word *brief*. Only a brief visit with her family?

She hated herself for taking offense over everything Stephen said tonight. It was not a good way to start her life as his wife.

Yet the longer the evening wore on, the more annoyed she grew. His voice—had it always been so nasal? And why could the man not smile? His eyes were so pale that from across the room they appeared almost colorless—something that unnerved her. And no matter where she went or with whom she was dancing, she could feel his gaze upon her.

He chose his three dances carefully—ensuring he was her escort into supper at midnight. They sat with the dotty Dowager

Countess . . . Wimpole? Wimbledon? Wimple? Kate berated herself for her problem with recalling names and promised to work on improving her skill. Although, given that the dowager called her Miss Darling when they parted, she did not feel quite so bad about her lack.

At the end of the ball, Stephen held Kate back until everyone departed and the few remaining houseguests retired to their rooms. He escorted her to the foot of the staircase.

"Now that we are betrothed, may I kiss you, Katharine?"

Kate nodded, unwilling to speak lest she deny him the privilege of a fiancé.

Stephen leaned forward, closed his eyes, and pressed his lips to Kate's. She didn't have time to close her eyes before it ended.

"Good night, sweet Katharine." He ran his thumb along her jaw, bowed, and disappeared into the back corridor toward the stairs to the wing where the male guests were accommodated.

Kate trudged up the stairs, fingertips pressed to her lips, remembering a kiss. But it was not Stephen's kiss she thought of.

Athena, who'd been asleep in the shepherdess chair beside the fireplace, helped Kate out of her gown. Afterward, she dismissed the maid, assuring her she could unpin her hair and put on her own nightgown without assistance. Yawning, Athena thanked her and left.

Too tired to reach up to remove the pins, but knowing she wouldn't be able to sleep, Kate tied the belt of her wrapper and curled up on the window seat to watch the sunrise.

From this window, on a clear day, she could see almost all the way to the folly.

Suddenly, she didn't care what anyone would think if they discovered her impetuous action. Dressing herself in a heavy wool morning gown, boots, and her cloak, she sneaked out of the house and hurried through the silent gardens and park, around the fountain pond, and to the folly.

Her nose, ears, and cheeks tingled from the cold, but the brisk walk kept her warm. Legs tired and ready to give out on her when she topped the steps to the folly's portico, she yanked the door handle. It did not give. She rattled it, pushed against it with her shoulder. But it wasn't stuck. It was locked.

She sank onto the top step and buried her face in her hands, a sprig of ivy and a few jasmine blooms falling from her hair to the stonework beside her. Stephen had proposed. Andrew had locked up the place in which she had expressed her feelings for him.

She supposed she could not ask for a clearer answer than that from God.

CHAPTER TWENTY-TWO

March 30, 1851

My dearest Nora,

You will be in London tomorrow, so this note might not reach you before you leave Wakesdown, but I could not let the day pass without writing to you. I received a letter from my father today. He had not heard of Kate's engagement to Lord T when he wrote it, or he might have written to her instead.

I met with the landlord this morning and signed a lease on the flat. I have written the address below. If you are able, please write to me once you arrive in London and when you are to leave for Manchester.

I long to see you.

All my love,
Christopher

Nora closed her eyes and recited the note in her head again. She could not keep her eyes closed long, though, or the swaying of the train would make her ill.

Florie still prattled on about everything she would *not* get to do in London. "It is *so* unfair. I will be fifteen in four months. I have read of ladies who are *married* by the time they were fifteen, sixteen at the latest."

"Do you want to be married when you are fifteen?" Kate asked her cousin. They shared the forward-facing seat in the private compartment.

The little upturned nose wrinkled. "No! But I would like to go to balls and the theater and be presented at court."

"I know I will sound like old Dowager Countess Wimbly—"

"Wigston," Florie corrected automatically.

"Are you certain?"

"I was spying from the top of the stairs when she arrived." Florie turned a glare on Nora. "Before *she* made me go to my room."

"For the second time," Nora reminded her.

"For the second time."

"Oh. Well, I know I will sound like an old dowager when I say this, but enjoy the years you have before your debut. Learn all you can. Play your instruments. Make friends. True friends, not just those girls others around you deem proper company for you. Fly kites and run barefoot in the mud. Because in three very short years, you will be forced to be proper and put away those things in favor of hunting for a husband. If you are fortunate, you will fall in love with a suitable man who will love you back and who will allow you to continue your pursuits."

"Like Lord Thynne." Florie wrapped her arm through Kate's and leaned against her, gazing up at her cousin in adoration.

Kate's expression hardened—but she smiled again so quickly Nora wouldn't have seen it if she hadn't been watching for it.

Nora hadn't seen Kate since their talk in the orangery. When Florie burst into the schoolroom the day after the ball with the news that Kate and Lord Thynne were engaged, Nora hoped Kate had made the right decision.

Apparently, she might not have.

But Nora had spoken her mind, had given Kate advice. Whether or not she followed it was between Kate and God.

The train slowed as they entered London. Florie kept Kate occupied by pointing out sights of interest. Nora had made this journey too many times to find the buildings and parks of interest anymore. And the train did not pass close enough to Hyde Park for them to see what did interest Nora—the Crystal Palace.

The idea of the Great Exhibition had fascinated Nora since its announcement. But now that she'd read Christopher's first-hand account of touring the Crystal Palace and of his several trips to the site since then to view the arrival of goods and machinery from all over the world—though all he was able to see from the park were crates and boxes—Nora was almost as anxious as he for the opening of the Exhibition.

Two coaches met them at the train station.

Sir Anthony took Kate by the elbow and led her to the first one, in which Miss Buchanan and Miss Dorcas would be riding. "Come, Katharine, you must ride in the first coach. Take my seat. I will ride in the second."

Kate pulled away gently but decisively. "No, Uncle. You ride with Cousin Edith and Cousin Dorcas. I am perfectly content to ride with Florie and Miss Woodriff again."

"But you should be in the first carriage. It would not do for the fiancée of a viscount—"

Coloring, Kate held up her hand. "I do not mind, I promise." She lowered her voice. "And as the engagement is not public knowledge, it would be better if I kept to the place of precedence befitting my public position."

Nora glanced around, making certain no one was close enough to overhear Kate's conversation with her uncle.

Sir Anthony rubbed his forehead. "If you are certain . . ."

"I am." Before he could change his mind, Kate climbed into the second carriage.

Nora tried to talk her out of taking the backward seat, but Kate almost pushed her into the front-facing seat. "I would rather not have you get sick all over me, Nora. I may not want the honor of riding in the front coach, but I would like to arrive with some dignity."

Face burning with embarrassment over her physical aversion to traveling, Nora gratefully took the better seat. Florie chose to sit next to her cousin—so she could point out all the sights of London, she said. Nora had a feeling Florie also did not want to be in close proximity to Nora should her stomach rebel again, as it had half an hour into the train ride.

Florie's prattle continued on the drive through town, and Kate dutifully looked out the window at each of the young woman's exclamations of "Look, there."

For all of Kate's patience with her cousins—with Florie's incessant chatter and with the ill treatment from Edith's hands— she would have made a good governess if she had not agreed to become the wife of an aristocrat. Though, now Nora thought about it, both positions took that kind of tolerance.

"What will you do on your holiday, Miss Woodriff?"

Florie's question startled Nora back into the present. "I will spend it away from prying busybodies who want to know every-one else's business." She smiled to soften the rebuke. "I will go to Manchester to visit my parents."

"And Christopher. He will still be there, will he not?" Florie looked from Nora to Kate and back.

"I am not certain. I know he plans to come to London in time for the dinner your father is giving after your sister's presen-tation. We may pass each other in different trains coming and going." Nora could not meet Kate's steady gaze. If Kate knew, or even guessed, what she and Christopher planned . . .

"Perhaps you should wait to make your visit to Manchester until after the dinner. Then you and Christopher could take the same train back."

Kate's suggestion made Nora feel all the more guilty.

"Yes, Miss Woodriff. That is a wonderful idea. Then you can be here for Dorcas's presentation *and* for the dinner when Father announces Kate's engagement." Florie's eyes sparkled across the dim interior of the coach.

Nora almost laughed at Florie's implication that Nora would be present at those events, when Florie herself would only be allowed marginal attendance. "Or I could go as soon as I get you settled in, Miss Florie, and then perhaps Mr. Dearing and I could ride down from Manchester together in time for him to attend Sir Anthony's dinner." The shocking part of this conversation was that neither Kate nor Florie had voiced the obvious—how highly improper it would be for Nora to travel anywhere with Christopher Dearing without a chaperone, even on a train in a public car on a one-day journey.

Did Kate suspect . . . ?

The carriage heaved to a stop. Nora waited until Florie and Kate were out before lifting her skirts and climbing down. She immediately made her way to her quarters on the fourth floor of Sir Anthony's massive Mayfair town house, set her valise on her bed, then went down one floor to Florie's room.

The chambermaid looked up from unpacking Florie's trunk. "Miss Florence went down to the sitting room."

"Thank you." As suspected, Florie did not need Nora here. Nora went down to the ground floor and stood outside Sir Anthony's study a moment before knocking.

"Come in."

Nora slipped in, leaving the door ajar behind her.

Sir Anthony stood from the large chair behind his desk. "Ah, Miss Woodriff. Do have a seat." He motioned her toward the armchair that faced the desk. "I take it you have come about your holiday?"

She sat on the edge of it. "Yes. I wondered if I might take my leave beginning tomorrow. I would return Friday next."

"I believe that is the day my nephew plans to come down from Manchester." Sir Anthony tapped the forefinger of his left hand against his chin. "Yes. Yes, do go home tomorrow. Then you can return Friday, and perhaps you will see Christopher on the train. Though you cannot travel with him, it would be a relief to me to know he is on the same train should anything happen and you need assistance."

Nora's breath came in short gasps. "Thank you, sir."

"While you are gone, I will discover what the best agency in London is, and when you return, we will start looking for another position for you." His face crumpled into a comically sad expression for a moment. "You have become like part of the family, Miss Woodriff. I know it will be difficult for Florence to part with you."

"I hope she will not forget me and even consent to write to me from time to time."

"I am certain she will." Sir Anthony stood, and Nora rose also. He extended his right hand to her, and Nora shook it. "We will see you in a week."

"Thank you, Sir Anthony. And if I may, I would like to go down to the telegraph office to wire my parents and let them know to expect me tomorrow night."

"Yes, yes, of course. Do you want the carriage to take you?"

"Oh, no, sir. It is a pleasant day, and I feel the need to walk."

He nodded. "I understand. Enjoy your holiday, Miss Woodriff."

"Thank you, sir."

Upstairs, Nora tied on her bonnet and made sure she had enough money in her reticule to cover the cost of two telegrams.

Half an hour later, she walked into the telegraph office. While waiting on the three previous customers to complete their business, she studied the train schedule. Fourteen hours on a train made for an arduous day. If Sir Anthony had not insisted Nora accompany Florie on the journey to London, she could have left from Oxford and eliminated nearly three hours from that time. But what did that matter now? She was here, and she had permission to go home for a week. Five days, once she accounted for traveling all day tomorrow and next Friday.

She sent the message to her parents first, telling them to expect her on the late train. Then she pulled out the scrap of paper on which she'd scribbled her carefully worded message for Christopher. After writing down the address of his leased flat on the form, she wrote out the message in clear block letters and handed it to the operator.

Now, to make it through the night without letting anticipation get the better of her.

Andrew pounded the soil around the tussock of ornamental grass. Its feathery fronds waved in the gentle spring breeze, and the long grass blades swayed. He sat on the ground and wiped the sweat from his face with his sleeve. Kate had suggested using *Cortaderia selloana* as a border for the elliptical garden and he had to admit, she was right.

Around him, undergardeners and day laborers worked on the final touches to the area. Once this was finished, Andrew's work at Wakesdown would be also. And though he wanted Sir Anthony's approval, he also wanted to wait a few weeks to make sure none of the plants or trees they'd planted over the past weeks would die.

By late afternoon, he'd paid the laborers and sent them home. He and Wakesdown's gardeners would inspect everything tomorrow and make any last-minute repairs or changes before Andrew left Wakesdown.

In a way, he hated that the job was complete. Now what would he have to occupy his hands and try to keep his mind off of Kate and her engagement to Lord Thynne?

Kate. Engaged to Lord Thynne.

Andrew slammed the front door of his cottage and threw his work gloves across the sitting room. He'd gone to the folly the morning after the ball, something in his gut telling him he should go. But instead of Kate, all he'd found were two wilted jasmine blooms and a piece of ivy on the top step.

She must have been there. Where else would the flowers have come from? But if she'd accepted Lord Thynne's proposal at the ball, as all the servants said she had, why would she have gone to the folly hours later?

He wanted to believe it was because she regretted her decision, that she wanted to change her mind. But if he allowed himself to believe that, he would have to take responsibility for fighting the urge to go until two hours after he'd first woken up with the idea. If he'd gone when he first awakened, would she have been there, waiting for him? Could he have stopped her from marrying Lord Thynne?

Time rendered speculation pointless. He hadn't responded to the urge to go until too late. Now she was gone, out of his reach.

Early the next morning, the head gardener pulled up to Andrew's cottage in the work wagon. Sir Anthony had told Andrew to have the butler order one of the carriages to take him to the railway station, but Andrew did not care for the butler and did not believe the butler had taken too kindly to someone who wasn't firmly under his command.

He tossed his small trunk and valise into the back of the wagon and climbed up onto the seat beside Tom. Neither spoke as Tom drove through the grounds. What a change eight months had wrought. What was once dry, brown grass was now green and lush. Vignettes and settings created by landscaping made a feast for the eyes and invited one to spend time in each.

"Stop here a moment please, Tom."

Andrew jumped down from the wagon. He opened a gate in the low stone wall, went through the gate, past a tall wall, and into the main gardens. He jogged down the path that led through the arbor and stopped when he came to his favorite spot in the entire grounds.

A small boxwood shrub surrounded by purple aster flowers stood in a large stone pot beside the path.

Andrew picked one of the flowers and threaded it into the buttonhole in his lapel. He could not stay long, but he paused a moment longer, eyes closed, remembering.

He ran back to the wagon, cupping his hand over the flower to keep from losing it. He slowed when he saw a man on a horse beside the wagon, talking to Tom.

"Andrew, this man has a wire for you. He went down to the cottages, and you weren't there. So he was going to the big house—but saw me sitting here and thought he'd ask after you."

Andrew raised his eyebrows, and he tried not to let his excitement show. She'd changed her mind. She wanted him, not Thynne. He took the missive with trembling hands, and the messenger rode away.

The excitement did not last long. Before reading the message, he scanned down it and found, to his disappointment, that it was from Sir Anthony, not Kate.

"I hope it isn't bad news."

Andrew folded the telegram and slid it into his pocket, then mounted the wagon again. "No. Sir Anthony wants me to pay him a visit when I arrive in London."

"He say what for?" Tom jiggled the reins and the heavy-limbed workhorses trudged down the road.

"No. Maybe he wants to introduce me to someone who needs my services."

Though grateful for the baronet's patronage, Andrew could not abide the thought of entering the house where Kate was staying. However, meeting someone else who might want to hire him could be his escape from working for Lord *and Lady* Thynne.

The train to London was more crowded than usual, and most of the passengers talked of the Exhibition and their plan to find accommodations by arriving almost a month early. Andrew did not want to inform them that any place they thought they might get a room had been booked a long time ago. He was grateful for Mr. Paxton's invitation to stay with him while in town for the opening. Even though Andrew had not been Paxton's apprentice since before Paxton drew his plans for the Crystal Palace, his mentor wanted him to be there, by his side, on opening day.

Some might think Andrew would be able to enjoy a few weeks of rest until then. But if he knew Joseph Paxton at all, he would be working on drawing plans for all of the visionary projects Paxton could imagine.

Andrew's first evening in London consisted of a riotous dinner with twelve of Paxton's closest acquaintances and a few former apprentices, like Andrew. He paid careful attention to who was whom and what connections they had. And when he returned to his room, he wrote down in his journal the names of those who might be helpful to him in the future.

At one o'clock the next day, Andrew knocked on the front door of the Buchanans' Mayfair town home. He hated cities, with their unadorned blocks of stone and brick facades with little to no vegetation to break up the monotony.

A butler who looked annoyed by Andrew's existence opened the door. Andrew handed him his calling card. "Andrew Lawton to see Sir Anthony Buchanan."

The butler let him into the hall. "Wait here."

The house seemed different than when he and Christopher stayed here. The presence of more household staff and the sound of voices coming from the front parlor probably contributed to that feeling.

Andrew tapped his hat against his leg, knowing each moment he waited could result in an unwanted run-in with Kate. Moments later, though, he entered Sir Anthony's study without encountering any other member of the family.

"Andrew, do come in. I would ask you to sit, but what I need to talk to you about is best if you see it for yourself." Sir Anthony led Andrew through the back of the house and out into a courtyard that opened up into a small garden.

"As you can see"—Sir Anthony swept the yard with narrowed eyes—"our garden here is in as much need of your services as those at Wakesdown were. I know I did not contract you for this, but would you be willing to redesign this garden before you move on to your next patron?"

And increase his chances of seeing Kate if he were to come here daily? He hesitated, though Sir Anthony did not seem to notice.

"There is a back gate here. I will get you a key so you can come and go as you please, and so you can let the workers in and lock up behind them when they leave in the evenings."

He would not have to enter the house. And if he did, it would be through the back hallway that led directly past Sir Anthony's study before it got to any of the public spaces. He would never have to see Kate.

"I will be happy to redesign your garden, Sir Anthony."

They shook hands, and the baronet led Andrew back into the house, where he wrote up an agreement they both signed.

The butler looked down his nose at Andrew in the front hall, but Andrew did not care. He would have employment, and it would be for someone who liked his work and found very few faults with anything he did. And he would not have to enter through the house.

The front door swung open.

Dorcas Buchanan stepped in, pulling off her gloves. "Why, Mr. Lawton. I did not think we would be seeing any more of you now that we're in London."

Andrew was about to lift his hat to her, but remembered just in time that he still had his hat in his hand. He inclined his head instead. "Miss Dorcas. Your father asked me to redesign the back garden here."

The young woman's smile showed she could be coy without trying. "That will be lovely, I am certain. Have you seen Kate? She and I are supposed to be going to Hyde Park this afternoon, but my gown fitting ran late."

Andrew jammed his hat on his head. "No, I have not seen Miss Dearing. Good day, Miss Dorcas." He skirted around her and exited the house. If God would listen to his prayers this time, he would not see Miss Katharine Dearing again. Ever.

CHAPTER TWENTY-THREE

*N*ora, I do not believe I have ever seen you so agitated."

Nora dropped her spoon and it clattered against the ceramic saucer under her teacup. She looked up, having almost forgotten her mother sat at table with her. "I know. I . . . I am simply overjoyed to be home for the first time in so long." She reached across the corner of the kitchen table and squeezed her mother's hand.

After allowing Nora to sleep late this morning, Mama had asked nothing of Nora other than to sit with her and keep her company while she worked on mending some clothing for a few of the bachelors who worked with Father. Now they sat at the kitchen table, indulging in a first cup of tea before Father returned home from the mill expecting the afternoon repast to tide him over until dinner in another couple of hours.

"We've had a letter from John. He has sold his mercantile and is coming home."

The news of her brother broke through Nora's distraction. "Coming home? But in all of his letters, he went on about how much he loves California. Did he say why?"

"Apparently, someone offered him more money to buy it from him than he could turn down. Combined with the profits he has already made, your brother is coming home a very wealthy man."

A couple of months ago, Nora would have heard such news with blinding envy. Now, however . . . "I am happy for him. He deserves his success, after all of his hard work."

A frown pinched Mama's thin eyebrows together. "And what of your father's hard work? Or your sister's or your other brother's? Why should John be the only one rewarded for toiling away?"

Nora rubbed her hand across the back of her mother's, then lifted it and kissed each rough, cracked knuckle. For years, Mama had taken in washing to make extra money to augment Father's reduced wages at the mill after his hand was injured and he became a bookkeeper—quite a step down from his former position as mill foreman. "I am not saying that none of the rest of us deserves success. But at least someone in our family managed to find it." She clasped Mama's hand in both of hers, leaning halfway across the table to do so. "And since it *is* John, you know that he will love nothing better than to come home and do whatever he can to make you and Father comfortable, perhaps even allow Father to stop working such long hours just to put food on the table and oil in the lamps."

Mama's frown eased, and she reached up to caress Nora's cheek. "You have grown up, girl. Last time you were home, when John was packing to leave, you railed against the injustice of John's going and leaving you behind."

Heat climbed into Nora's cheeks. She straightened, pulling her hands back and settling them in her lap. "That is because . . . Mama, there is something—"

Nora jumped at a knock on the front door. "I'll get it." She leapt up from the table and hurried from the kitchen and down the central hall, smoothing her hair, loose from the band of ribbon at her crown, back over her shoulders.

The door swung open at Nora's yank. Two large hands cupped her face, and Christopher Dearing leaned down and kissed her. Nora lost all sensation in her body except for the exquisite pressure of Christopher's lips on hers, and the heat flaring in her chest. She clung to the doorknob with one hand and to Christopher's lapel with the other to keep from crumpling to the floor.

Christopher ended the kiss and gathered Nora up in his arms, lifting her so her toes barely touched the wood planks. She wrapped her arms around his neck, one hand buried in his sandy-brown hair.

"Oh, I have missed you." His breath against her ear made her whole neck tingle.

"And I have missed you. But Christopher, the neighbors . . ."

He stepped into the hall, keeping her in his arms, and closed the door behind them. She let the embrace continue a moment longer—until she heard a chair scrape against the floor in the kitchen.

"Put me down. Put me down," she whispered. She barely had time to straighten her lace collar before her mother appeared in the hallway.

"Nora, who was at the door?" Mama stopped short when she saw Christopher standing beside Nora.

"Mama, this is Mr. Christopher Dearing, nephew of Sir Anthony. Mr. Dearing is a lawyer for the London and North Western Railway and works from their offices here in Manchester. I"—Nora glanced up at him—"wired him yesterday before leaving London and invited him to come for tea this afternoon."

"Mrs. Woodriff." Christopher extended his right hand toward Mama. "It is a great honor to meet you. Nor—your daughter has spoken of you quite often."

Mama looked at his hand a moment before shaking it. "I wish I could say the same, lad, but this is the first I've heard of you."

"Won't you please come into the sitting room, Mr. Dearing?" Nora's voice came out high pitched, her words faster than normal. "I am certain Father will be along shortly."

"I heard the whistle from the mill as I rounded the corner." Christopher ducked to keep from hitting his head on the low lintel of the door into the small front room.

"You sound American, Mr. Dearing." Mama motioned him to take Father's favorite chair, nearest the fireplace.

"Yes, ma'am. From Philadelphia, Pennsylvania."

Nora took Christopher's hat and coat. "I shall go and finish preparing the tea tray, Mama, while you and Mr. Dearing become better acquainted." She escaped to the kitchen, where she draped Christopher's coat across the back of a chair and set his hat in the seat. She held on to the chair and focused on calming her breathing.

He was here. In her house. About to . . . about to ask . . .

The clatter of the front door brought her to her senses, and she took the kettle off the fire, added fresh tea leaves to the teapot, and poured the water in. She set it on the large tray with four matching ceramic cups, of the set she and her sister had scrimped and saved for two years to buy for their mother for Christmas several years ago, and carried it into the sitting room.

Father and Christopher were shaking hands when she entered. "Father, you have met Mr. Dearing?"

A burly man with bushy gray sidewhiskers to make up for the lack of hair on top of his head, her father turned to greet her, his brown eyes twinkling. "Aye, Daughter. I met your beau. But I'll not be taking kindly to his having my chair." He winked at Nora and stepped forward to take the tray from her. "No food?"

Nora laughed and kissed her father's cheek. "It's on another tray. I shall go get it." Joy swelled through her and made her want to sing and skip and spin as she returned to the kitchen for the tray of sandwiches and biscuits.

Back in the sitting room, her father had indeed ousted the usurper from his chair, and Christopher sat alone on the small settee, with Mama in the adjacent armchair. Leaving only the spot on the settee beside Christopher vacant.

The nerves under her skin waltzing to the rhythm of her heart, Nora poured tea—adding sugar and no milk to Christopher's, just the way he liked it—and handed everyone a plate with a cucumber-and-watercress sandwich and two biscuits.

Christopher looked up at her when she moved beside him to sit, and Nora almost swooned from the surge of affection— dare she call it love?—that overwhelmed her. She sat beside him, sipped her tea, and picked at her food while Christopher answered her parents' questions about his background and family and new job.

Her father finally set his empty teacup and plate back onto the table and braced his fists against his knees, leaning forward. "What are your intentions toward my daughter, Mr. Dearing?"

Nora could have screamed with vexation. Her father enjoyed making people uncomfortable, and she'd hoped he would refrain from trying it with Christopher.

Rather than appearing intimidated, though, Christopher grinned and also set his plate and cup and saucer on the table. "Sir, I assure you my intentions are quite honorable. You see, I came here to ask your blessing and for your daughter's hand in marriage."

Nora bit her bottom lip, trying to keep her heart from leaping up into her throat. She exchanged a glance with her mother— and both broke into wide smiles.

Father rubbed the gray stubble on his chin, making a rasping sound that grated on Nora's already frayed patience. "And this job of yours—it pays enough for you to support a wife?"

Nora closed her eyes and shook her head at her father's persistent interrogation.

"Yes, sir—and because I am brilliant and can ingratiate myself to anyone, I am certain that I will rise quickly in the firm and not only be able to support Nora and our family, but to do so in a handsome manner." The lilt in Christopher's deep voice made it sound as if he would break out in laughter at any moment.

Father stopped rubbing his chin. The corners of his lips twitched, but he squinted at Christopher. "So you intend to stay in England and not abscond with my daughter back to America?"

Nora took a breath and opened her mouth to insist her father stop with his falderal, but Christopher took hold of her hand and squeezed.

"Mr. Woodriff, I am committed to staying with the London and North Western for the next four years. After that time, if I do end up returning to America, I will make sure that Nora returns home to visit at least as often as she has been able to for the past twelve years." Christopher's brown eyes held a challenge for her father. Nora knew Christopher resented the fact that she'd been sent away from home at age fourteen to find work to help support her family, but she'd hoped he would not make an issue of it. After all, it was something that was not only unchangeable now, but a blessing in disguise, as it had put her in the Buchanans' home so she could meet him.

Father looked stunned for a moment at Christopher's brash words—then threw his head back and laughed. "I like him, Nora. Of course you have my permission to marry her."

Christopher squeezed her hand again. "Excellent. Thank you, sir. But there is one more thing I need to ask you."

Nora squeezed his hand back and started praying harder than she ever had in her life.

Kate marveled at the structure of the Crystal Palace—and the number of people gathered along the roads bordering Hyde Park this afternoon to look at it and to watch as scores of workmen unloaded wagons of some of the largest crates Kate had ever seen. Other wagons drove directly into the building to be unloaded.

Florie looked at the paper in her hand. "Cousin Christopher said that the gardens are there"—she pointed to her left and the long side of the building facing southeast—"along with the terraces, the Grand Center Walk, and the cascades and fountains."

All of which was hidden by trees. Kate sighed. She'd have to wait the few weeks until the Exhibition officially opened to be able to see them.

"Then . . . the model of the cottage for the working classes is not far from the gardens." Florie waved her hand again and kept walking.

Kate paused at a yank on her elbow. Dorcas—who had held on to Kate's arm ever since they climbed out of the carriage and entered the crowd to try to get a closer look—had stopped, but her attention was not on the building. "Is that—why it is!" She dropped her hand from Kate's elbow and dropped into an abbreviated curtsy. "Good day, Lord Thynne."

He inclined his head. "Good day, Miss Dorcas, Miss Florence." He finally looked at Kate. "Miss Dearing."

Kate's stomach lurched, but not in the exciting way it did when she saw Andrew. She'd grown to dread seeing Stephen—not because of anything he had done, other than propose marriage to her, but because the more she thought about actually marrying him, the worse she felt about her decision to say yes.

"Have you come to see the Crystal Palace?" Florie asked. "Can you get us into the park to see it?"

Stephen smiled at her with his eyes. "No, Miss Florence. Even my influence as a peer of the realm cannot convince them to let us pass through the gate."

"Mr. Lawton could probably get us in." Dorcas sighed after her softly spoken statement.

A wave of chills rushed down Kate's arms at the mention of Andrew's name. For all she knew, he could be inside that enormous greenhouse at this very moment. So near, yet impossibly distant.

"If you ladies have not yet had tea—and if you are not expected home soon—might I ask you to join me at Thornbury

Lodge Inn? It is a bit of a drive from here, but because of that it should not be too crowded."

Kate wanted to deny his request, to escape his presence, but how could she without raising questions in his and her cousins' minds? "I am willing if my cousins are."

Both Dorcas and Florie nodded their heads.

"Very good." Stephen offered his arm to Kate. "I shall walk you back to your carriage and give the driver the directions."

Whispering and giggling, Florie and Dorcas hooked arms together and fell in step behind Kate and Stephen. Kate tried resting her hand as lightly as possible in the crook of Stephen's elbow, tried to stay far enough away that her skirt barely brushed his leg, but the press of the crowd did not allow her to keep that much distance between them.

After handing Kate and her cousins up into the open barouche, Stephen told the driver how to find the inn.

"Will you not ride with us?" Florie asked him.

"My curricle is not far from here. I shall meet you there. I fear leaving it for too long. Although the newspapers report that there has been less crime in the city in the past weeks since the influx of visitors began, I still do not want to take the chance of leaving my horse and carriage longer than necessary." Stephen touched the brim of his tall top hat, his eyes crinkled in his smileless smile.

Florie, who sat in the backward-facing seat with Kate, wrapped her arm through Kate's and sighed. "He may not be young, and other men might be more handsome, but he is such a *nice* man. You are so fortunate, Cousin Kate, to be marrying such a man."

Kate laughed in spite of herself. "Would you say so if he were not a wealthy viscount?"

Her cousin gave the question serious thought before answering, chewing her bottom lip. "Yes. I think I would say so—because I like him. But it is better that he is a wealthy viscount."

Kate pulled her arm free and put it around Florie's shoulders, giving the young woman a hug. In less than five years, her half sister Clara would be this age. Perhaps Father and Maud would consent to sending her to England for finishing school. Or, if not, sending her a few years after that so that she could debut in a London season when she turned eighteen.

A sense of emptiness had settled in her chest the moment she'd accepted Stephen's proposal, and it grew larger and threatened to consume her every time she thought about her future as Lady Thynne. If she dreaded being near Stephen now, how would she feel in six months—a year, ten years?

"Kate, are you unwell?" Dorcas leaned forward and touched Kate's knee. "You look faint."

If that was Dorcas's delicate way of saying Kate looked as if she might be sick to her stomach, Dorcas was quite right. Kate took a few deep breaths and cleared her mind from all thoughts of the future. She shuddered as the nausea passed.

"I am fine. Do not worry yourself, Dorcas." Kate pressed her hand to her right side, where her corset boning dug into her ribs.

Dorcas leaned back, nodding as if she understood why all color had drained from Kate's face. If Dorcas wanted to believe it was shortness of breath from her corset being laced too tightly, Kate would let her. She had confided in Nora her true feelings about the viscount—her future husband—but no one else could ever know.

The carriage rolled to a stop a few minutes later in front of a quaint building that looked as if it had been built during the Tudor era, with its whitewash and rows of dark-wood planks across the facade.

Neither Dorcas nor Florie had ever taken tea in a public hotel before, so Kate led the way in with more confidence than she felt. The matron who greeted them set her at ease and led them to a table near the fireplace at the rear of the dining room.

"Brisk wind today, aye?" The matron wiped a few crumbs from the table with a cloth she tucked back into a voluminous apron pocket. "Tea for three, is it?"

"Four," Kate corrected. "We have another joining us."

By the time the matron returned with a silver tea service, delicate china cups, saucers, and plates, and trays of all kinds of sweets and sandwiches, Stephen still had not arrived.

Kate did not touch the tea or food. She had no money with her, and she imagined Dorcas and Florie did not have enough with them to cover such a spread should Stephen not appear.

Her fear lasted a few more minutes, until Stephen arrived, windswept and looking rather dashing, if Kate did admit it rather grudgingly.

"I do apologize for my late appearance." He allowed the matron to take his hat and coat before sitting. "It is good that you left the park when you did. I had just gained my carriage when a fight broke out amongst several rapscallions, causing a great melee in the crowd. It was nigh on a quarter hour before the police could settle it and clear the street."

Thankful they'd missed the scene, Kate smiled over Florie's disappointed expression. But the young woman quickly recovered. As she did so often with Christopher, Florie launched into questioning Stephen—about Argentina, about his cattle ranch, and about the *vaqueros*, or cowboys, on it.

"In Argentina, they are not called *vaqueros*, but *gauchos*. They are the best cattlemen in the world—and they breed excellent horseflesh." Stephen went on to talk about his cowboys for the next several minutes. Kate finished two lemon cookies and a second cup of tea before he finished.

She wished she could find his passion for Argentina and cattle ranching as fascinating as Florie did. But after a few minutes of listening to him, her mind began to wander—wondering what the landscape was like, what kinds of flowers grew wild on the Argentinian plains.

Of course, if Stephen had his way, she would not have to wonder much longer, since they would be in Argentina by June. They had settled on the third week of May for the wedding, giving his mother almost two months to plan the wedding breakfast and make certain everyone knew of it—though she would keep the invitation list exclusive, Stephen assured Kate. Two days later, they were to sail for Argentina.

Kate's stomach clamped down on the food and drink she'd just put in it. She still had time to end it. To come clean with Stephen about Andrew. To tell him she could not marry him when she loved someone else.

Anger bubbled up along with the acrid burning in the back of Kate's throat. Anger directed at her father for putting her in this situation. And at Andrew Lawton for not being the wealthy viscount instead of Stephen.

Oh, yes, and she was angry at God. For abandoning her, for not answering her pleas for help, for leaving her in a field full of weeds, even though she could see a beautiful garden on the other side of the wall.

While she could make the decision to go into the garden—to be with Andrew instead of Stephen—she would then be doing the same thing to her family that God had done to her: leaving them lost among the weeds. And she couldn't do that.

She hoped the resentment that had become her constant companion ever since leaving Philadelphia would eventually go away. But looking across the table at Stephen, she had a feeling that wouldn't happen for a very, very long time.

$\mathcal{C}$hristopher tucked Nora's valise onto the shelf over their seats. Nora waved at her parents, who stood on the platform and waved back. The train jerked, so Christopher sat before he lost his footing.

"I'm glad I had a chance to get to know your parents this week." He leaned forward to rearrange the back of his suit coat so that it didn't restrict his movement.

Nora blushed—something she'd done quite a bit of in the past six days. "I am happy they like you so well. Of course, I never doubted they would."

Christopher raised a brow before chuckling. "I think you had your moments of doubt, my dear. Especially about your mother." Leaning forward, he took her gloved hand in his. "But once she was convinced of how much I loved you, I believe she came around to liking me well enough."

"They had reason for concern, given what you asked of them within the first hour of meeting them." Nora looked around, then pulled her hand away and folded it with the other out of his reach.

Christopher leaned back and stretched out his legs, careful not to brush his shoes against Nora's skirt. It was so good to see her out of the somber browns, grays, and blues she wore in her role of governess. The pink gown with tiny yellow flowers all over it flattered her rosy cheeks. With her hair curling over her ears and a pert hat pinned atop another pile of curls at her crown, she looked years younger—and she drew admiring glances from other men at the station and even now on the train. "But they said yes. Don't tell me you regret your decision to accept my proposal."

"Of course not." Nora pulled yarn and long knitting needles out of her bag and started to work. "What will you do once we reach London?"

He watched, fascinated with the way her hands manipulated the yarn and needles to create a woven fabric. "Naturally, we will go to my uncle's house. Tomorrow, I need to take the satchel of correspondence to the office in London. Tomorrow night is Uncle's dinner, at which Kate's engagement will be announced. Then back to Manchester until the end of the month, when we'll go to London for the opening of the Great Exhibition. And you? Does Florie have lessons when you are in town together?"

Nora stopped, unraveled a few stitches, pulled up a dropped stitch from the row below, and started forward again. "No formal lessons, but we do try to practice her French and Latin daily. And I ensure she has appropriate reading material."

This led into a discussion of Christopher's favorite book, and they spent the next few hours talking about Daniel Boone, Davy Crockett, and other folk legends from America. When Nora started nodding off, Christopher moved to sit beside her, took the knitting needles and yarn out of her hands, and let her rest her head on his shoulder. Whenever the train stopped, they got out and walked up and down the platform, their bodies becoming stiffer and slower as the day progressed.

"Sir Anthony was the only person who thought it would be inappropriate for the two of us to travel back to London together. At least, he was the only one who voiced his concern." Nora accepted the hand Christopher offered her and gingerly came down off the high train-car step. He tucked her hand under his elbow, and they fell into the promenade of other passengers stretching out after a couple of hours of sitting on uncomfortably firm seats.

"He's probably right. You do have your reputation to think of. What proper family will ever hire you now, if they learn that you traveled unaccompanied to Manchester and then a week later traveled back in the company of a young man to whom you were not related?"

"Who would recognize us to know they could ruin me by spreading such rumors? After all, London is a big city." They both inclined their heads to the older couple who'd been sitting across and two rows in front of them in the car. "Anyone who would know Sir Anthony would not be riding in the second-class car."

"Except for people like us. We both know Sir Anthony."

"That's not what I mean, and you know it." But Nora laughed anyway.

The conductor called for passengers to board the train. Christopher helped Nora up the steep steps and walked behind her back to their seats.

Five hours later, the train creaked to a stop in a dark London station.

"Wait by the baggage. I'll go get us a cab." He found one willing to take what Christopher could pay, especially since they had only two valises with them.

As soon as they arrived at the Buchanan house, Sir Anthony called for a cold supper to be served and invited Nora to join them at the table. Edith was the only person who declined to join them. Christopher did not miss her company at all.

After escaping his sister's hug of greeting, he sat down and started stuffing cucumber sandwiches into his mouth. The food available along the train ride had been good, but expensive, so Christopher and Nora had not eaten much more than the basket lunch her mother sent with them.

As soon as his stomach stopped rumbling, Christopher asked for everyone's attention, but he looked at his sister when he started talking. "Kate, you've always told me that I should follow my heart in every circumstance, that I'll never go wrong that way. Well . . ." He reached beside him and clasped Nora's hand and lifted it to rest on the table. "Nora became my wife four days ago."

Kate still thought she might be sick. She bypassed the dining room, even though she knew Christopher left for work early this morning. Nora was not likely to impose her presence on the family until they'd reconciled to the idea that Christopher and the governess had married secretly. And no one else in the family would be down for at least another hour.

She wasn't certain which bothered her more—the idea that Christopher did not feel he could tell her of his plans, or the fact that she now had no choice but to marry Stephen Brightwell.

Sir Anthony's initial burst of anger had been formidable. Kate hoped Nora would not judge their whole family on their uncle's outburst and his insistence that Christopher and Nora leave the townhouse immediately. Thankfully, he'd relented before they could make it out the door. He apologized, congratulating the couple and insisting they stay with the family for the two nights until they went back to Manchester, and again when they returned to London at the end of the month to attend the opening of the Great Exhibition.

Kate wished she could accept their news so easily.

She unlocked and pushed open the back door. The fresh air did little to quell her discomfort. She glanced around, but, as she'd hoped, the garden was empty. Everyone in the household still kept country hours, not rising for breakfast until ten o'clock or later.

She had no business begrudging Christopher his decision. After all, she'd told him he could marry Nora—that she was marrying Stephen so he could be happy. Why did she now feel as if she hated him? Why did her heart cry out against the injustice of his ability to marry whomever he pleased when she could not?

Kate needed the open spaces she'd become accustomed to at Wakesdown. Though the garden was larger than the entire yard behind their home in Philadelphia, its walls threatened to close in around her and smother her with regret over her recent decision.

At seven years old, she'd spent seven glorious months on her grandfather's farm near Harrisburg, Pennsylvania, when her mother decided she wanted her third child born there instead of in the city. Kate had fallen in love with the outdoors. She'd sought comfort in the pasture behind the stables after her mother passed away. The orchard beyond the garden was where she'd hidden to try to keep her father from taking her back to Philadelphia. Cities reminded her of everything she'd lost.

She turned the corner around the small gazebo that blocked the southeastern corner of the yard from view of the house. Her room overlooked the street, and because each day had been full of visits, shopping, and receiving callers, she had seen only a bit of the back courtyard and flower beds from the windows in the back parlor when the family took tea there on their at-home days.

She drew up short at the sight of a gardener with a wide-bladed shovel, his back to her, digging up a tree stump. Kate tried to slip away, but her shoes rustled the dry leaves and twigs scattered through the new-growth grasses. The man straightened, turned, and, seeing Kate, swept his hat from his head.

"Good morning, miss. Sorry if I disturbed you. I thought I would get an early start on this." He jerked his thumb over his shoulder at the stump. "I can lay off if you want, come back later."

"No, it is I who am disturbing you. Please, do not let me keep you from your work." Kate lifted her skirts and continued around the path encircling the gazebo, relieved yet anxious all the same.

She pulled a few weeds from a flower bed. But most of the beds lining the walls and surrounding the gazebo looked as if they were in the middle of being dug up and replanted, so she did not disturb anything else, lest the gardener get annoyed with her.

The heat rose with the sun as it ascended higher. Kate's stomach growled, and even though she had not yet found the relaxation she sought, she decided to go inside for breakfast.

She reached the back entrance and set her hand to the knob, but it twisted and the door pulled away from her before she could turn it. She glanced up, ready to thank the footman or maid who'd seen her coming and opened it for her—but the words died in the back of her throat.

Andrew blanched at the sight of her.

She nearly swooned as she gazed at that square jaw, darkened from the whiskers that lay just under the skin. The curly hair, always in need of a trim. The eyes reflecting the greens, golds, and browns of nature. The dimple in his chin. The perfectly shaped mouth.

Her lips tingled in memory of the way his felt against them. So different from the terse, dry pecks Stephen gave her. She closed her eyes and shook her head. She would not let thoughts of Stephen ruin what might be her last chance to say good-bye to Andrew.

"I am sorry," he muttered.

"You were right," she said at the same time. Kate opened her eyes. Had Andrew just apologized to her?

"Right about what?" He stepped through the door and out into the courtyard.

She followed him away from the house, where they risked being overheard, and out into the yard. "I was afraid. I did use my family as an excuse."

"I was wrong for saying that. You are one of the bravest women I've ever known, willing to sacrifice your happiness for your family. But . . ."

"But is it a sacrifice I truly need to make?" Kate sighed. "Believe me, I have been mulling that question over since the moment I learned Lord Thynne intended to propose marriage to me."

Andrew's shoulders drooped. "And you have come to the conclusion that you do need to make the sacrifice. I prayed for a different outcome, but"—he reached out and stroked her cheek—"because I love you, I must honor your choice."

The tears she'd managed to hold at bay since her private outpouring after their argument in the garden at Wakesdown released and flowed down her cheeks. "If I could think of some way to change things . . . to make the circumstances such that . . . But I cannot."

Andrew withdrew a handkerchief from his coat pocket and wiped her cheeks, then pressed it into her hand. "I know."

Before she could consider her actions and the consequences thereof, Kate stepped forward, hooked her hand behind Andrew's neck, and kissed him. She tried to communicate all of her longing, regret, and grief through the gesture.

Andrew's hands settled on her waist and he drew her close, embracing her tightly. He slanted his head and deepened the kiss, branding her mouth—and her entire being—as his.

She broke away, trembling. With a shudder, Andrew pressed his forehead to hers. "I will never forget you," he whispered.

"And I will never forget you." Though it was the most difficult thing she'd ever done, Kate pulled away from his arms and ran into the house.

She stayed in her room the rest of the day, lying atop the bed, staring at the walls and ceiling, trying to find a way out of marrying Stephen Brightwell. But by the time Athena arrived to help her dress for dinner, no new solution presented itself. Apparently God was still not in the mood to talk to her.

The muted pinkish-purple of the silk gown provided the perfect setting for the heavy gold embroidery along the neck, waist, and hem. It was a dress fitting for Katharine Brightwell, Viscountess Thynne—too elaborate, too expensive for a plain Miss Kate Dearing. Which was why she had never worn it before.

Athena seemed to sense Kate's mood and kept silent throughout the process of dressing her and arranging her hair. Neither of them were too surprised at a knock on the door moments before Kate was ready to go downstairs.

Stephen's valet handed Athena a small box. "From m'lord for Miss Dearing."

Athena closed the door and handed the box to Kate. Inside lay a ring—a large emerald surrounded by small diamonds. An engagement ring.

Athena frowned. "Shouldn't he have given you that himself, not sent his valet with it?"

Kate shrugged and tried to slide the ring onto her finger over the tight silk glove. It wouldn't fit. She handed the ring back to Athena and pulled off the gloves. "I'll wear the lace mittens again."

Athena retrieved the fingerless mitts from the wardrobe and put the silk gloves away as Kate slipped the lace over her hands. Kate took the ring back. It was still too tight to fit on the third finger of her left hand.

"Apparently my hands are too large. It must mean I am not fit to be a viscountess." Kate laughed, trying to sound as if she jested, but her heart cried out in agreement with her words. She was not meant to be a viscountess. Was not meant to marry Stephen Brightwell.

She smiled and thanked Athena for her ministrations, then tucked the ring into the palm of her hand and carried it downstairs with her.

Stephen met her at the bottom of the stairs. "Do you like it?" He reached for her left hand.

She opened her fist to reveal the ring lying there. "My finger is too big for it."

Plucking the ring from her palm, Stephen turned her hand over and tried to make it fit. Kate winced and pulled her hand away.

Stephen sighed. "I shall have to take you to the jeweler so we can have it refit." He tucked it into the watch pocket of his waistcoat, then offered Kate his arm. "Shall we?"

Allowing him to escort her into the sitting room, where all the guests gathered before dinner, was part of the theater of the evening. They would enter together. Stephen would escort her into the dining room at the head of the line. They would be seated across from each other at her uncle's right and left hands. And after the first course, Uncle would stand, raise his glass, congratulate Stephen, and wish Kate all happiness.

At least that's how Sir Anthony and Stephen explained to her the evening would transpire. The schedule did not allow for Kate to become sick all over her uncle's expensive carpets or on the silver and crystal at table.

"Cousin Katharine. Lord Thynne. Do come meet the baron and baroness." Edith beamed at them. Taken aback at Edith's friendly—no, *sisterly*—demeanor, Kate lagged behind Stephen until he practically pulled her by the arm. She recovered herself and regained his side.

Once all of the guests arrived, Edith graciously positioned Kate and Stephen at the door to lead everyone in to dinner.

"It isn't like Edith to be so pleasant," Kate whispered. She dropped her arm from Stephen's arm so he could pull out her chair.

"Perhaps she has reconciled herself to our marriage." He waited until Kate's nod before going around to take his seat across from her.

Or perhaps it was because Edith had placed herself beside Stephen when making the seating arrangement. She smiled across the table at Kate as if there had never been any enmity between them.

Kate took one spoonful of soup, and her stomach nearly rebelled. She spent the first course stirring it and pretending to listen to the elderly baron—she'd already forgotten his name— tell her of his adventures fighting Napoleon as a young naval offi- cer. He'd just launched into a story about going to Jamaica to fight pirates in 1814 when the footmen cleared the soup course and the butler refilled everyone's wine glasses. Everyone's but Kate's, since she had not touched hers.

Sir Anthony stood and raised his glass. "Friends, thank you for coming. Three days ago we celebrated my daughter Dorcas's pre- sentation at court, and many of you joined us here for the recep- tion afterward. Ladies and gentlemen, Miss Dorcas Buchanan."

Wishes for health and happiness followed the raising of glasses. Dorcas blushed prettily. Between her beauty and her bid- dable nature, if her cousin were not engaged by the end of the season, Kate would be shocked.

Several people put down their glasses but picked them up when Sir Anthony raised his again. "Tonight, we have more good news to celebrate. Please join me in congratulating Lord Thynne, whose proposal of marriage to my niece, Miss Katharine Dearing, has been accepted."

The guests tittered and wished Kate happiness and congratu- lated Stephen, just as planned. The roiling in her stomach began to calm.

Sir Anthony had just regained his seat when Edith stood. "Father, may I say something?"

The little Kate managed to eat today rose to the back of her throat. Though Edith smiled, her eyes remained cool and cal- culating—almost menacing—when she gazed across the table at Kate.

"Yes, Edith, of course. I am certain your cousin and Lord Thynne would be happy to hear your best wishes." From his tone and expression, he obviously had no insight into his daughter's jealous tendencies.

Edith raised her glass. "To my cousin Katharine. You came as a poor relation to snare a rich husband, and you performed beyond everyone's expectations."

Gasps and whispers followed this statement. Sir Anthony stood. "Edith, that is quite—"

"And to Lord Thynne. May you find happiness in your choice of wife. And may you be ever ignorant of her true nature—or at least possess the ability to turn a blind eye when you find her sneaking out of the house to carry on an affair with the landscape architect you have hired to redesign your gardens."

"Edith!" Sir Anthony bellowed.

"I've witnessed it with my own eyes, Papa. As has my maid." Edith shot Kate a sickeningly sweet simper. "Cousin Katharine and Mr. Lawton kissing, on more than one occasion. Including this morning, in the back garden of the house in which we sit."

Her uncle sank into his chair, visibly shaken. "Katharine—is this true?"

Kate couldn't breathe, and she feared she would lose what little she'd managed to eat if she opened her mouth. She closed her eyes and nodded.

From his place across the table, Stephen—Lord Thynne rose. "If you will please excuse me." He tossed his napkin down and left the room.

The flat tone of his voice, the deadly calm in his pale eyes, pierced Kate's soul. She didn't love him, didn't truly want to marry him. But she hadn't wanted to hurt him, either.

He would never forgive her. And she couldn't blame him. She would have a hard time forgiving herself.

CHAPTER TWENTY-FIVE

$\mathscr{K}$ate cringed as the door closed behind the final guest. The smell of the uneaten dinner lingered in the dining room, bringing Kate ever closer to being sick all over her gown and the table linen.

Tears burned the corners of her eyes. The need to find Stephen and drop to her knees and beg his forgiveness made her legs twitch. But she seemed rooted to the chair.

Nora, wearing the yellow gown Kate had asked Athena to dispose of—elegant now that Nora had removed most of the silk roses—slipped into the chair beside Kate and took Kate's hand in both of hers. Christopher added his support, standing behind Kate with his hand on her shoulder.

Edith still sat across the table from Kate, preening in her success. Dorcas had fled the room in tears shortly after her sister's speech. Florie, who had not been allowed to attend the formal dinner, would be sorry she missed all of this.

The urge to laugh came out as a strangled cough. Why should the thought of Florie's reaction be so amusing? As quickly as the urge hit, Kate's fear and remorse drowned it. She turned to her sister-in-law to apologize for ruining Nora's first social event as part of the family, but her mouth would not form words.

Stephen returned, walking the length of the dining room in silence. He stopped to stare into the fireplace behind the chair in which Sir Anthony sat slumped, hand over his eyes. "I must speak with Katharine alone."

Kate flinched at Stephen's soft voice. Christopher squeezed her shoulder, then held his hand to Nora to assist her up and escort her from the room.

When Sir Anthony lowered his hand, Kate's heart wrenched. Her uncle looked like he'd aged twenty years in the past twenty minutes. He pushed himself unsteadily to his feet and started around the table—but stopped and took Edith by the hand, almost dragging her up from her chair and out of the room.

The silence that followed their departure pressed painfully against Kate's ears. Her body grew heavier and heavier with dread until she was certain the chair legs would crack and she would fall to the floor at any moment.

After what seemed like hours, but could have only been minutes, Stephen turned around and rested his hands on the back of Sir Anthony's vacant chair. "Have you nothing to say for yourself, Katharine?"

When she was a child and was being reprimanded, her mother or father always called her Katharine, not Kate. Hearing it fall from Stephen's lips felt different only in that she knew she deserved whatever punishment he meted out. And like a child, she could not raise her eyes to his. "I am sorry, my lord. I never meant to hurt you."

He sighed. "I have told you many times that I wish you to call me Stephen."

Kate's gaze snapped up to meet his. "But . . ." Words jumbled and created a dam in her throat.

Stephen pulled out the head chair and sat, his back stiff and straight. "Katharine, I am under no delusion that you have feelings for me beyond friendly affection. At least I hope you feel that way toward me."

She nodded, unable to translate a coherent thought into words.

"And it does not come as a surprise to me that you have expressed . . . romantic sentiment toward Mr. Lawton." He swiped his hand across his eyes as if trying to wipe something from his memory. "I saw you with him and heard you speak of him, too often not to realize you had formed an attachment."

"I never wanted to deceive you, Stephen." Her voice crackled as she forced the words out. "And I never meant to develop feelings for Andrew—Mr. Lawton. My duty in coming to England has always been clear. And that duty means that it does not matter if I have developed an affection for him. There is no future for me with Mr. Lawton. I told him so when I saw him. I am not certain what Edith thinks she saw—or what someone told her was seen—but the kiss I shared with Mr. Lawton this morning was one of farewell. I could ask for your forgiveness for the pain and humiliation I have caused you by that action, but I do not deserve it."

Kate dropped her gaze back to her hands, clasped in her lap. She picked at a loose thread in the lace mittens, and it started unraveling. Just like her life.

Without another word, Stephen stood and left the room again. Kate leaned her elbows on the table and buried her face in her hands. He would never forgive her. The engagement was over, and Kate would have to return to Philadelphia in shame and try to explain to her father why they would lose everything. All because she could not control herself around Andrew Lawton.

She looked up at a noise at the door—then sat up straight, dropping her hands to her lap when Stephen entered with Sir Anthony.

Her uncle sank into his chair again, only now curiosity had replaced resignation and anxiety in his expression.

Stephen stood behind the chair directly across the table from Kate. "Katharine, when I spoke to your brother of my intention to propose marriage to you, I told him that I wanted to marry you because I am *not* in love with you. Nor did I believe then that you were in love with me—which has been proven. You have just told me that your . . . indiscretion with Mr. Lawton this morning was by way of saying farewell. I take that to mean that you do not intend to see him ever again. Is that correct?"

All of the air left Kate's lungs. Hearing Stephen say it—that she would never see Andrew again—made her nausea return. But she nodded. "Yes."

"Do you still wish to marry me?" Stephen held the newels at the top of his chair in fists so tight, Kate expected to see them reduced to sawdust at any moment.

Tears flooded her eyes. Regret, relief, remorse, recrimination all vied for dominance. "If you will still have me, my lord, yes. But . . . why? Why would you still want to marry me after what I've done?"

Stephen sighed and began pacing again. "I am forty years old. I am Viscount Thynne, member of Parliament, peer of the realm. My elder brother died childless after two unhappy marriages. My younger brother has made many choices—not the least of which is his marriage to a commoner, the daughter of a soldier—which make him ill-suited to be the next viscount should anything happen to me. So I must take a wife."

He stopped behind his chair again, his expression resigned. "I have not the stamina nor the patience to try to make a woman fall in love with me. You have been honest—mostly honest—with me from the beginning. You did not hide your family's financial situation from me, and I respect that. Yes, many will mock me for marrying a fortune seeker, but I do so with my eyes wide open, rather than being manipulated and led to believe it is a love match only to learn of the deception after the wedding, as many men do. There is not anything else you need to reveal to me, is there?" He raised his left brow, his thin lips pressed together.

"No, nothing else, my lord."

He looked put out with her use of his title again, but with Sir Anthony as witness, she would not be so presumptuous as to call him by his Christian name.

"Obviously, we will now have to wait to marry until the gossip dies down. The announcement of our engagement will be printed in the *Times* tomorrow as planned—'tis too late to stop it now. But rather than marrying in May, I shall go to Argentina sometime in the next week to conduct my business there. If you agree to my terms and keep them, then upon my return, we shall marry."

Kate's heart thudded. "Terms?"

"Yes." Stephen looked at her uncle. "Sir Anthony, this is why I asked you to come back in, so that you can serve as witness."

Sir Anthony nodded. "Shall I fetch pen and parchment to write it down?"

"No. I trust that a spoken agreement will suffice."

Kate nodded. The last thing she wanted to do was sign a contract, official or not. But she would, if it meant Stephen would still help her family.

"Good. Then let us begin."

The mournful tune Andrew whistled died on his lips at the sight of a footman standing at the back gate into the Buchanans' garden.

"Sir Anthony wishes to see you." With no further ceremony, the footman marched through the garden and into the house. He did not stop at the door of the study but went all the way to the door into the front parlor.

Andrew walked past him into the room, frowning. He had just spoken with Sir Anthony yesterday about the progress on the garden. What could be so urgent as to require such a sudden beckoning?

Sir Anthony stood beside the fireplace. Miss Buchanan sat in a throne-like chair flanking him. Andrew's scalp tingled.

"Andrew, though it pains me to do so, I have hard questions to put to you before I come to a decision." For the first time since Andrew met him, Sir Anthony looked old and tired.

What questions? What decision? He said nothing—especially given the hint of a smile playing about Edith's pursed lips.

"Edith, tell him what you told us last night."

Hands folded in her lap, Edith gave her father a sweet smile. "Before Mr. Lawton and Cousin Christopher came to London in February, my maid, enjoying a walk in the park on her Sunday afternoon off, saw Mr. Lawton and Miss Dearing enter the folly near the fountain pond. The door was closed, so my maid peeked through the window to make sure Miss Dearing was not in any danger. She witnessed this man and Cousin Katharine in a passionate embrace. As Lord Thynne had not yet started courting Katharine in earnest, I thought I would keep my cousin's secret. However, I myself saw Katharine and Mr. Lawton in a similar passionate embrace in the garden here just yesterday. Yesterday—the day Katharine knew her betrothal to Lord Thynne was being announced. On that very day, she engaged in compromising behavior—"

"That is quite enough, Edith. You may leave us now." Sir Anthony waited until his eldest daughter's footfalls disappeared up the stairs out in the entry hall before he broke his pose and showed his agitation. "I cannot believe this is happening. First Christopher goes off and elopes with the governess, and without asking my leave. But for his station in life—as a working man—a woman like Nora Woodriff suits."

Yes, Christopher had come to Andrew yesterday to tell him of the elopement before going to the station to purchase their train tickets to return to Manchester today. But what did that have to do with Edith's spying on Kate and seeing her kissing Andrew?

"Do you deny what Edith says?"

To protect Kate's reputation, to allow her to have the marriage she needed to support her family, Andrew almost lied. But no doubt Kate would have told them the truth. Wait . . . why wasn't she here, facing the accusation with him? "Where's Kate?"

Sir Anthony's brows shot up. "You presume to call her by her familiar name?"

"Where is she? What have you done with her?" Andrew took a step forward, then stopped. Threatening physical repercussions would not help him at all in this situation.

"I have done nothing with her. After Edith revealed at dinner—in front of all of my guests!—how my niece had been compromised by the landscape designer I hired, Katharine admitted to the truth. She is . . . she left this house an hour ago."

"Where did she go?" He needed to find her. Kate had told them the truth—that she had feelings for Andrew and couldn't marry Stephen Brightwell. She was no longer engaged to be married to another man. His heart raced with anticipation. He could not offer her the riches of Thynne, but a poor husband was better than no husband, which is what she'd have if her situation became widely known.

"Do you deny you compromised my niece?"

"Answer my question and I'll answer yours." Andrew crossed his arms.

Sir Anthony looked as if he would continue to argue, then deflated and sank into the chair Edith had vacated. "Andrew, please. Do I not deserve the truth from you?"

Andrew's breathing hitched. His respect for the baronet made the words tumble from his mouth. "I did not compromise your niece. We kissed, twice. Once in the garden folly—we were trapped due to the storm outside, and I was trying to convince her that I loved her. The second was yesterday, when I came upon her in the garden to wish her joy in her marriage to Lord Thynne. It was a farewell kiss, nothing more." It had been a farewell kiss . . . oh, but so much more.

Sir Anthony rubbed his forehead. "I cannot tell you where Miss Dearing is. Lord Thynne is making arrangements to leave for Argentina next week to conclude some business there. When he comes back in two months, if in that time Katharine has stayed where we sent her—away from you and your seeming intent to ruin her reputation—he will marry her as planned. If she leaves that place and is seen in your company, Lord Thynne will withdraw his offer of marriage . . . and the generous financial settlement he planned to give her father. A future viscountess can have no hint of scandal about her."

"And Kate agreed to that?" Andrew took a deep breath and moderated his tone. Yelling, like physical violence, would get him nowhere. "She will still marry him after all of this?"

"Perhaps you do not understand the severity of her family's need."

"I don't understand? My mother died in the poorhouse when I was twelve years old. If anyone understands a dire financial situa-tion, I do." And Kate had once again shown she would choose her family over her own happiness—now even over her own honor and dignity. Andrew pounded his fist against his palm.

Could he be the loving, forbearing man of yesterday, under-standing and supporting her choice to help her family? Or would he be the unreasonable, jealous Andrew of the garden, losing his temper and accusing Kate of treachery?

Kate had made her choice. Andrew must make his. "I will stay away from her. I will not interfere again. I will have no contact with her."

"Not even secretly, through her brother? I know you and he have grown close."

"Not even through Christopher."

Sir Anthony bobbed his head. "Good. You will finish the job on the back garden within the week. At the end, you will have your promised payment. However, I will hold on to the letter of reference I wrote for you until after Katharine's wedding. It seems only fitting I have some measure to ensure you stay away and do not interfere, do you not agree?"

Andrew swallowed his anger. "Yes, sir, I agree."

"And I do not think you will be surprised to learn that Lord Thynne has hired another architect to design his gardens."

No surprise there. Andrew had not wanted to work for him anyway. "Until I receive the letter of reference, what am I supposed to do?"

Sir Anthony looked truly sorrowful. "That is up to you. But so long as you stay away from Katharine, I will do what I can to help you, short of giving you a reference. As you and my niece are both coming to learn, your future can be either built or ruined on your reputation."

Reputation. For someone like Andrew, his livelihood depended on cultivating a good one. He couldn't believe God would allow him to fall in love with Kate if it meant destroying any chance at building his career.

"Be thankful you live in this modern age, Mr. Lawton. In my grandfather's time, a man of Stephen Brightwell's status could— and most likely would—have you transported to Australia for something like this."

From everything Andrew had read in his life, Australia had very interesting and unique flora. Perhaps transportation would not be a bad option—if Kate were sent with him. If only things were done that way still.

He bowed to the baronet. "I will follow Lord Thynne's rules. And the day after his wedding, I will be here to collect my letter of reference. Good day."

CHAPTER TWENTY-SIX

*K*ate hated rain. She hated fog. She hated London. She hated Mrs. Headington. And she most especially hated Headington House for Wayward Women.

"I never would have suspected. Mousy little thing you were when I saw you on that ship." Mrs. Headington clasped her fingers over her ample abdomen and rocked back in the desk chair. Its mechanics groaned in protest. "And everything I heard about you when I was visiting my sister in Philadelphia, how the men would not go near you because of your dour expressions and penchant for serious conversation. You, a wayward woman!" The woman clucked her teeth and shook her head.

Kate drummed her fingertips on the arm of her straight-backed wooden chair. After fourteen of these daily tête-à-têtes, she was starting to get used to the unnaturally upright posture the chair forced her into. Every day, Mrs. Headington began with the same monologue.

It had seemed providential to meet Mrs. Headington on the ship from America. Edith Buchanan's former governess told them much of the family's background, filling in holes in Kate and Christopher's knowledge of the family history, since their mother had not told Kate much in the eight years they had together, and Father claimed to know even less about the Buchanans than his children. So Christopher befriended Mrs. Headington and encouraged her to tell them stories of the years she had served them as governess.

"And how shocking that your brother eloped with the Buchanans' governess. I left service a year before I married Mr. Headington, God rest his soul. After he died, I started Headington House for Wayward Women, to help all of you wicked young women who did not have the benefit of a strong moral hand to guide you in your childhoods."

If Edith Buchanan served as testimony to Mrs. Headington's strong moral guidance, Kate wanted none of it.

"Two weeks and still nothing to say? Well, we shall continue our little visits until you understand the natural wickedness in your soul that led you to throw yourself on the altar of sin and degradation. Only when I believe you've made a full recovery from your wicked ways will I give you the letter of recommendation you need from me so you can marry Lord Thynne."

Kate had the wicked thought that the next time she heard the word *wicked*, she would scream. She and the three other wicked wayward women in residence at Mrs. Headington's House for said wayward wicked women had taken to using the word to describe everything, from a stocking that needed darning to Mrs. Headington's cat—however, in that instance, the epithet fit.

Though not confined to the house of ill reform, Kate had not ventured farther than the small patch of garden in the back since Sir Anthony escorted her here fifteen days ago.

She thought of leaving, of using what little money she had left to purchase a train ticket to Manchester and go stay with Christopher and Nora. Or even return to Oxford and see if Mrs. Timperleigh would hire her to teach at the seminary on recommendation from Nora.

Then she remembered her father. And her stepmother and little sisters. Christopher sent home what money he could, but it amounted to a pittance since he now had a wife to support.

So if Stephen would still take her, she would do whatever was necessary to meet her part of the agreement. "I admit it. I had wicked thoughts in my heart, which led me to wicked actions. But I am sincerely sorry for them."

The joy that gleamed in Mrs. Headington's eyes indicated she had not noticed the touch of sarcasm in Kate's voice. "Have you prayed, repented of them, asked God to show you a better way?"

That was the rub, wasn't it? Kate had tried praying but received no answers. "I will pray harder."

"My mother always said that if your knees weren't bruised, you weren't praying hard enough." Mrs. Headington reached into a desk drawer and pulled out a ledger. She wrote something on the page with Kate's name written across the top, then put the book back in her desk and locked it. "You may go now, Miss Dearing. We shall meet at the same time tomorrow. My prescription for you is at least one hour of prayers tonight before bed, and two hours tomorrow morning before breakfast."

Kate gave her a tight-lipped smile and escaped the study. She trudged upstairs to change from her plain brown morning dress into a similarly plain blue tea dress. At least here no one minded Kate's old gowns and muted colors. She'd left her new, expensive gowns behind at the Buchanans' home, with the exception of the purple gown with the black-lace overlay, for which she'd brought both the day and evening bodices. Just in case she needed to be seen publicly.

"How was it?" Jane, one of the other wicked wayward women, asked.

Kate told her about the prayer prescription.

"Do you pray?" Jane asked.

"I've tried. Over and over I've tried. I've asked God to show my father how to get his money back. I've prayed that God would make me fall out of love with one man and in love with another. I've begged to be delivered from my circumstances time and again, with no results." Kate turned so Jane could unbutton the back of her bodice.

"Perhaps you just don't know how to listen for an answer." Jane went to her dresser and pulled a pamphlet from the top drawer, which she handed to Kate. "In here, you will find many verses that talk about prayer. It isn't the words we say or the length of our prayers that God listens to. It is the heart. Sometimes praying is being silent, listening. Waiting for God to reveal His will. One of the verses in there says that if we pray, God will give us the desires of our hearts. If we truly learn to pray, God reveals the desires He has placed in our hearts. Not what we want, but His good and perfect plan for us."

Reluctantly, Kate took the booklet. "If prayer is so efficacious, then why are you still at Mrs. Headington's house?"

Jane's rosebud mouth quirked up in a half smile. With her beauty, Kate could easily understand how the younger woman could have found herself in circumstances that would have led her family to send her here.

"I came because my family insisted, before I good and truly compromised myself—and with a married man, no less. But that was months ago. Now, because of this"—she touched the Bible on her nightstand—"I am here of my own accord. She doesn't seem it, but Mrs. Headington has been a great help to me in rearranging my thoughts and ideas about how to behave around men. And I enjoy the companionship of you and the other *wicked women.*"

Kate laughed. She stepped out of her morning dress and Jane helped her into the tea dress. When Kate first arrived at Mrs. Headington's, she'd been annoyed to learn she was expected to share a room with a stranger. But as they had no lady's maids, it was a great help to have another woman to help with bodice buttons and corset laces.

After Jane buttoned Kate's bodice, Kate helped her new friend change into an ivory-and-rose striped silk gown of which even Edith would have been jealous.

"Are you coming?" Jane paused at the door.

"You go on ahead. I'll be down in a minute." Kate waited until the door closed between them before picking up the pamphlet again.

She skimmed the first page. According to the booklet, if she prayed and truly believed God would answer, He would. But like a good father, God did not give His children what they wanted whenever they asked. Instead, He gave them what they needed.

Kate had already prayed for guidance and God did not provide it. So what was it that she really needed?

Over the next few days, Mrs. Headington daily asked Kate how many hours she'd spent in prayer the previous twenty-four hours and recorded it in her ledger. Thankfully, she did not ask to see Kate's knees as proof.

Kate practiced praying in her own way. Every morning, in the hour she'd used to take her walks at Wakesdown, she sat on her bed, eyes closed. She pictured images of flowers and plants in her head, thanking God for each one. This, of course, led to thoughts of Andrew. Instead of asking for guidance, for a push one way or the other, she prayed for him. Prayed for his happiness. Prayed for the future success of his business. Prayed he might one day forgive her for involving him in her mess of a life.

She prayed for Stephen as well. For safe travels. Equitable and fair business dealings on all sides. For his future, whether it was with her or not. For him to feel about his future wife the way she felt about Andrew.

Yet even after spending an hour praying for the two men instead of for her own confusion, Kate still had no answer.

Was being trapped in a situation the same as receiving God's guidance?

Andrew stood in the middle of the transept with Joseph Paxton and marveled as tens of thousands of people milled about, seeing and being seen. Queen Victoria and Prince Albert and their children toured the displays in the Crystal Palace like every other family in attendance.

More than the building or anything showcased in it, the most marvelous part of today's opening of the Great Exhibition was that Andrew was in the same room as the queen of England. He had been only a few dozen yards away from her as she gave her speech declaring the Exhibition open and honoring Prince Albert for his vision.

He, Andrew Lawton, who'd spent half his childhood in the poorhouse and the remainder of his life trying his hardest to avoid going back, had sat in the gallery with many of the engineers and committee members and other invited guests.

"Go on, lad. Enjoy yourself." Mr. Paxton nudged Andrew's elbow. "Go find your friends."

Oh, yes. In the excitement he'd almost forgotten Christopher and Nora. Getting his bearings, Andrew started down the wide corridor toward the east entrance. Flags and banners hung from the galleries above to show what was being displayed and where it was from. Andrew walked . . . and walked. Past enormous marble statuary and displays of art, textiles, and machinery—and the elm trees no one had wanted to chop down.

A giant lion towered over the Zollverein displays, followed by textiles from Denmark and Sweden on his right and china and porcelain from Russia on the other side. But the entire section at this end of the building had been reserved for the United States.

The American delegation still worked feverishly at unpacking crates and setting up displays. But enough was out to promise guests spectacular sights—the next time they came.

He found Christopher and Nora looking at glasswares in the southeast corner of the American section. Nora exclaimed over the beauty of the pieces she liked, and Christopher pointed out anything labeled as having come from Pennsylvania.

"How was your journey from Manchester?" Andrew shook hands with Christopher and bowed to Nora.

"Oh, Andrew, please. Do not be so formal." Nora laughed and held her hand out to him. He shook it as well.

"The journey was long. I was rather surprised at the warmth of the greeting that we received at my uncle's house, but he seemed to genuinely miss us while we were gone." Christopher and Nora exchanged a glance Andrew was fairly certain he understood. They had been informed of Kate's agreement with Lord Thynne and had agreed not to mention her in front of Andrew.

He and Christopher took Nora around, telling her what they remembered of the place from months ago, when it had been empty.

"There she is!" Nora stepped back, pulling Christopher with her.

Andrew stopped, then quickly joined the people crowding the side of the walkway, all conversation now hushed. He bowed low, but peeked to watch the family walk by. From his seat in the box looking down on the podium earlier, he had not realized just how tiny Queen Victoria was.

Nora and many of the other women around twittered and cooed over the queen's pink silk gown, her coronet and the white feathers hanging from it at the sides, how handsome and well behaved her children were, and how dapper Prince Albert appeared in his red-coated uniform.

After spending nearly an hour wandering through the exhibit of agricultural and horticultural machines and implements— although Andrew would have been happy to cut the time shorter—Christopher finally gave in to Nora's soft sighs and asked her where she would like to go next.

Nora consulted the diagram of the exhibition spaces in the commemorative booklet. Her eyes sparkled with mischief when she looked up. "Why don't we go upstairs?"

Directly over the machinery were displays of jewelry, embroideries, lace, silks, and shawls.

Christopher groaned. "Aw, Nora."

"I looked at machinery with you. You can look at these with me." Both laughed, and Andrew admired the easy friendship between them. He and Kate had—

No. He could not think about Kate.

"Do you believe cotton will someday overtake linen and silk for clothing, Andrew?" Nora asked, fingering an artfully arranged bolt of colorfully patterned silk. "Since it cannot be grown in England, and we are dependent on importing it, can it ever gain in popularity?"

Aside from wanting to understand the principles of growing, harvesting, and processing cotton, Andrew had taken some time to familiarize himself with experts' writings on the future of the humble plant product. "If the Americans can continue growing it in the quantities they do now—or increase production, as they have over the past decades—I cannot see why cotton would not become just as popular as silk and linen."

Beyond Nora, in the lace and embroidery area, his gaze fell on a woman in a dress too tight and juvenile for her ample form. Something about her struck Andrew as familiar. He moved around Christopher and Nora to get a better look.

Four other women followed behind her, heads covered in bonnets, dresses obscured by shawls long enough to touch the floor in the back. Her daughters, most likely.

"What are you looking at?" Christopher moved to stand beside Andrew.

"That woman over there, in the green plaid dress. I feel I should know her."

Christopher followed Andrew's gaze.

At his friend's sharp intake of breath, Andrew looked at him. "Do you recognize her?"

"Who?" Nora joined them.

"The woman . . . there, in green."

"Oh, why, that's Mrs. Headington. She was the Buchanans' governess when Edith was a child." Nora's nose wrinkled. "And I cannot say much for her methods, given the results."

"Yes. Ka—" Christopher gave Andrew a furtive glance. "I met Mrs. Headington on the steamer from New York. And I think I would prefer to avoid her if we can."

Christopher communicated something to Nora with an intense expression, and she nodded. "I do believe I am ready for something to drink." Nora hooked her hand through Christopher's arm. "Shall we return to the refreshment court downstairs?"

Getting to the stairs necessitated walking past the section where Mrs. Headington and her companions now examined silver platters and plates.

Whispered conversation stopped Andrew at the top of the stairs.

". . . betrothed to Viscount Thynne."

". . . heard she had a liaison with the gardener."

". . . he might marry her regardless."

Andrew turned. A cluster of women huddled together like hens on a winter morning. He followed their line of sight—right to where Mrs. Headington and the women he'd supposed were her daughters stood. He watched for a long moment.

The tallest of the four younger women stood at an angle that allowed him to see her face. His stomach twisted and skin tingled.

Kate.

He was halfway to her before he remembered the agreement that sealed their fates. He could not speak to her. Could not be near her.

Turning, he almost plowed into Christopher and Nora. Both wore horrified expressions.

"I did not talk to her. You do not need to worry that I will compromise her further. I am leaving, immediately." He lurched past Christopher, but his friend stopped him with a viselike grip on his arm.

"Wait. There's something I need to tell you."

CHAPTER TWENTY-SEVEN

$\mathcal{K}$ate wondered when Mrs. Headington would realize she'd slipped away and send one of the constables to find her. She had not wanted to come to see the Great Exhibition, but her jailer—hostess—insisted. The press of thousands of people made Kate's insides tremble and her skin crawl. The noise of brass bands and choirs, squalls of exhausted and bored children, and adults' voices raised to be heard over all the rest, thrummed through her head in a sharp ache.

Mrs. Headington, enraptured by the cases of priceless jewels, had waved her hand with a grunt when Kate mentioned she needed to visit the ladies' room—on the first level. The other three wicked wayward women seemed to understand Kate's need for escape. They nodded as if to say they would keep Mrs. Headington occupied so she would not notice Kate's disappearance.

Kate promised herself she would not stay away long—it wouldn't be fair to the other wickeds if she did not help provide the same opportunity for each of them.

She hurried past the long queue of women waiting to enter the ladies' room, past the giant locomotives and fancy carriages, across to the other side of the building and out through one of the doors on the south side.

The cool drizzle soothed her upturned face. Before her stretched the terraces leading to the Grand Center Walk through the gardens. She nodded to other walkers—most headed back inside and out of the misty drizzle—as she descended the steps to the lower terrace.

A sign explained that the Crystal Palace Gardens had been designed by Joseph Paxton in the Italianate and English styles. As Kate looked around her, she realized how wrong she'd been in calling Andrew's style Italianate. The precise terraces, square flower beds, ornate fountains, statues and urns, and low, carved stone walls raised her tension rather than relieving it.

She sped her pace, hoping not all of the areas of the garden had been designed in this style. A few dozen yards farther down the path, past the large circular ponds with fountain features in them, she slowed again. The Italianate style softened. Flower beds took on rounder, softer shapes. Colors mingled, hue blending into hue. Trees were no longer cut into unnatural geometric shapes but had been trimmed to reveal their full beauty.

It reminded her forcibly of Andrew's drawings for the gardens at Wakesdown, and she wondered if his name should be alongside Joseph Paxton's on the plaque.

The rain began to soak through her shawl and into her dress. If she planned to relieve the other wickeds, she must hurry. But she needed to see the rest of the garden—at least what she could from the main promenade.

A man offered Kate his umbrella, but she declined with a smile. For all that it chilled her to the bone, the rain had a cleansing effect on her mind, clearing it as certainly as a river carried away the leaves that cluttered its surface in autumn.

But as she walked farther, her thoughts started jumbling again. She stopped and examined her surroundings. Here, the garden looked unkempt, overgrown, untended. She snorted, startling a young couple sharing an umbrella as they hurried back toward the building.

She should feel right at home in this part of the garden. Nature as it was meant to be surrounded her. Wild. Untouched. Free to grow its own direction at its own pace.

Seeking shelter under one of Hyde Park's original ancient elm trees, Kate contemplated what she'd seen.

Too much attention, too much discipline, and a garden was unnatural, harsh.

Too much freedom, and it was chaotic.

With the correct blend of discipline and freedom came true beauty. In a garden and in a person. She closed her eyes and started to pray, filled with an understanding and peace she'd never known.

"Kate?"

She gripped the tree trunk behind her to keep from falling over. The voice seemed to answer her prayer. Slowly she opened her eyes.

Andrew stood several yards away on the path, the pole of an open black umbrella resting on his shoulder.

"I prayed you would come."

He took two steps toward her. "I almost did not find you. I saw you upstairs, and I tried to leave, tried to honor your decision. But when I changed my mind and returned, you were gone."

"Did you speak with Mrs. Headington?"

"No. I found one of the young women whom I'd seen with you, and she said you needed a breath of air." He blinked, and a slow smile pulled the corners of his lips up in an expression that made Kate's knees weak. "I knew then that I would find you in the gardens."

"I understand now."

He took a few more steps toward her, cutting the distance in half. "Understand what?"

"About gardens and discipline." She shared her conclusions. "I think you and I started out as the two opposite styles, but through knowing each other, we have balanced out our natures. And God has used us to prune each other into the people He intended us to be."

He took three more steps, then stopped. "Kate, if you still want to marry Lord Thynne, tell me now, and I will leave so that no one sees us together."

Kate reached up under her chin and untied the ribbons of the straw bonnet. Its wide brim would prevent her from doing what she wanted most in the world to do. She pushed away from the tree, pulled off the bonnet, and met Andrew under the umbrella.

His free arm encircled her waist and pulled her close, and his lips claimed hers in a scorching kiss that threatened to consume Kate's physical being until only her soul remained and melded with his.

Ending the kiss, Kate wrapped her arms around his waist and rested her cheek against his shoulder. "I *am* a wicked, wicked wayward woman. And I cannot marry Stephen Brightwell, no matter how magnanimous he was to agree to marry me even after I'd proved I could never love him."

"You, Kate, wicked? Never."

She laughed. She would tell him all about Mrs. Headington later. For now, all that mattered was the two of them. She raised her head and locked her eyes with his. "I have learned over the past few weeks that it was not strength that led me to sacrifice my happiness and agree to marry Stephen. It was a lack of faith. I did not believe that God could give me joy *and* provide for my family. I thought that responsibility fell on me. But in learning how to pray—no, it's more how to *listen* to God—I have come to see that God did not want me to come here to bear a burden never meant for me. He brought me here to give me more happiness than I could ever hope to deserve. He gave me you."

"I love you, Katharine Dearing."

"Kate. Please. *Katharine* Dearing was a woman who could not understand the difference between pride and obstinacy and who was blind to God's gifts. Katharine Dearing was betrothed to a viscount. *Kate* Dearing loves you, Andrew Lawton." She leaned in for another kiss, this one gentle and filled with healing for the months of longing and heartache and years of solitude and loneliness.

He pressed his forehead to hers. "*Kate* Dearing, I am not a wealthy man. And because I have broken my promise to your uncle, I might have difficulty finding work. But if you are willing to face an uncertain future with me, will you be my wife?"

She tilted her head and kissed him again. "I will be your wife, because I have faith that God will provide for our needs."

They stood in an embrace a few moments longer, then Andrew pulled away, his arm still around her. "You are soaked through. We need to get you home and changed into warm, dry clothing. But first we need to find your brother."

"Yes, I hoped to see Christopher and Nora today." Especially now that she could share the most wonderful news with them.

Andrew led her back into the Crystal Palace, then closed the umbrella and returned it to the constable standing at the entrance. "Thank you for that, Jack."

"My pleasure, Mr. Lawton. I see you found what you'd lost." The constable inclined his head to Kate.

"A little damp, but yes. I found her. And I will never lose her again."

Kate beamed at her fiancé—that word no longer filled her with dread—and took his arm. The noise and press of the crowds no longer bothered her. In fact, she rather appreciated the excuse to walk closer to Andrew's side than propriety would normally have allowed for an unmarried couple.

He led her to the refreshment court, and they found Christopher and Nora sitting at a table with several strangers, all discussing what they'd seen so far and using their booklets to plan what to see next.

Nora closed her book and jumped up to hug Kate. "You are all wet. Come, we must get you back to Mrs. Headington's house before you catch a chill."

"I take it from the smiles on your faces that all went well?" Christopher stood and took his sister's hands in his. "Will I soon be introducing Andrew to others as my brother-in-law?"

"As soon as possible would be my preference." Kate slew her gaze at Andrew, and he grinned at her.

He flourished a bow. "Your wish is my command."

Christopher let out a cowboy whoop that drew admonishing stares and amused laughter from bystanders. He hugged Kate, lifting her from the floor and swinging her around. "I am so happy for you, Sister. When I thought that by my marrying Nora, I had forced you into a decision that would make you miserable for the rest of your life, I was beside myself. Just as you say you've only ever wanted happiness for your younger siblings, I have only ever wanted happiness for my sisters. Especially you."

Christopher released her and settled his hands on her shoulders. "And now, there is something you must know." His brown eyes bore into hers, his demeanor shifting from jovial to serious. "I received a letter from Father the day before we left Manchester to come to the Exhibition."

Kate trembled. She was about to learn the consequences of her decision to trust God and not marry Stephen.

"The land commission confirmed their original ruling and will not open up all the land in question for development. The railroad company is out of business."

Kate's heart sank. She'd brought her family to ruin—

"But before he even knew the verdict of the company's appeal, Father had already made a decision. He has sold the house in Philadelphia. He, Maud, and the girls are moving to the farm in Harrisburg to start over. It will be difficult—building up the herds and breaking ground to plant. But you know Father. He prides himself on coming from a long line of self-made men. He . . ." Christopher pulled the letter out of his pocket and handed it to Kate. "Well, you read it."

Kate had trouble breathing. She opened the letter and scanned the first two pages, reading the details of what Christopher had just told her. It wasn't until she got to the final page that she found what he wanted her to read.

> *Tell your sister I was wrong in saying what I did, and that I beg her forgiveness. That I love her more than life itself and pray for her daily. I only hope this doesn't come too late for her to find true happiness instead of forcing herself into a loveless marriage because of my greed and recklessness. I can only pray that I have not lost her love forever.*

She couldn't read the rest of the letter for the moisture welling in her eyes, and she handed it back to Christopher. "I will write to him tonight."

Christopher squeezed her shoulders and broke into a wide smile. "The Dearing family will be all right, Kate. You'll see."

Tears streaming down her cheeks, Kate allowed Andrew to pull her into his arms. After a moment she pushed away. "Christopher, why didn't you tell me this last night at dinner?"

His bottom lip pulled down to one side in a sheepish grimace. "Well . . . I had planned to meet Andrew here today. And I knew you would be here. And I hoped to be able to bring the two of you together—but I didn't want this to influence your choice. If you knew about Father's decision, Andrew would never have known that you chose him because you truly loved him enough to be willing to give up Lord Thynne's fortune and the possibility of securing that money for the family."

Kate glared at Andrew. "You knew?"

"Christopher told me when I tried to leave after seeing you with Mrs. Headington. Telling me that I would not bring about the financial destruction of your family by completing your ruination was the only way he could get me to come after you." He made a face reminiscent of the little boy he had once been. "Can you forgive me for keeping it from you?"

Kate wanted to torment him, to make him wonder if she were truly angry with him, but his comical, childlike expression wouldn't allow her to keep her laughter inside. "Of course I forgive you."

"There's more, Kate." Christopher exchanged an unreadable glance with Nora. "I told Andrew of this weeks ago. The railway company wants to hire a landscape architect to design gardens at several of their train stations for passengers to walk in when the trains stop for water and fuel. I have recommended Andrew, and he is to go to Dorset tomorrow to meet with Baron Wolverton. If the baron likes him, Andrew will be employed by the London and North Western Railway and share an office with me in Manchester. What do you think of that?"

Laughter bubbled up in Kate until she could not contain it. Though it generated a stir, she kissed Andrew right there in the refreshment court in the middle of the Crystal Palace at the Great Exhibition.

"There is something we need to do before anything else. We must go see my uncle." Kate ran her fingertips down Andrew's cheek, feeling the twitch of the muscles as he ground his back teeth together.

"Must we do that today?" Andrew captured her hand, kissed her palm, then lowered it to tuck under his elbow.

"Would you rather he hear it from someone else while you are off in Dorset?" Kate rested her free hand on Andrew's arm, ready to pull him with her if need be. She owed her uncle—and Stephen—the absolute truth.

"No. You are right. I merely hoped we could take a walk in the gardens before we go."

"Well . . . we can probably get a hackney cab on that side of the park more easily than here near the building."

"We shall find you later—if not at Sir Anthony's house today, at the train station tomorrow," Nora called, pulling Christopher away, toward the Egyptian exhibit.

The continued drizzle meant that Kate and Andrew had the secondary paths through the gardens almost entirely to themselves. Neither minded their damp clothes—in fact, Kate appreciated how it cooled her skin after one particular pause beside a patch of purple pansies.

"We should go, before I am thoroughly compromised," Kate murmured against Andrew's lips, her arms encircling his neck, fingers twined in the curls that lay over his high collar.

In the cab on the way to her uncle's townhouse in the West End, Kate told Andrew of Mrs. Headington—meeting her on the boat, then having Sir Anthony suggest her home for Wayward Women as the place for Kate to stay until Stephen returned from Argentina.

"I am sorry you had to go through that because of me."

Kate wrapped her arm through his and rested her cheek against the damp wool of his overcoat. "Don't be sorry. If I had not gone, I wouldn't have learned how to listen to God instead of just telling Him what I want and what I think I need."

"You will have to tell me of this lesson you learned." The carriage jolted to a stop outside the Buchanan house. "Some other time."

Kate's heart raced, and her knees wobbled when Andrew helped her down from the coach.

The butler's usually impassive face broke into shock when he saw Kate at the door—and horror when he recognized Andrew behind her. He said nothing, only led them into the empty front parlor and disappeared.

Moments later Sir Anthony entered, his expression stormy. "What is the meaning of this?"

Kate stepped forward. "Uncle Anthony, what happened when my mother announced to the family that she planned to marry my father?" She'd read her mother's diary often enough to have her version of events memorized.

"She . . . your mother refused a proposal from the second son of Baron Poppelwell. When our father tried to cajole Louisa into accepting, she announced that she was in love with Graham Dearing, the American who had taken the London season by storm, that he had proposed, and that she planned to marry him.

My father refused. Louisa left the house, eloped with Dearing, and they sailed for America the next week." His fiery eyes softened. "My father never heard from her again. It broke his heart."

"My mother taught me that I should always follow my heart, especially when it came to choosing the man with whom to spend the rest of my life." She reached out and touched his sleeve. "So I must follow in my mother's footsteps and marry for love, not for duty. Will you—can you understand that, Uncle?"

Sir Anthony covered Kate's hand with his. "Yes, child. I do understand. And, to be honest, when your brother shared the contents of your father's letter with me yesterday, and told me of the employment opportunity for Mr. Lawton, I suspected I would be receiving this visit from the two of you today. And"—he sighed—"as I did for your mother, so I will do for you. I will support you in whatever decision you make. Granted, it would have been quite the social boon for you to marry a viscount rather than the landscape gardener." His kind smile at Andrew softened the rebuke. "But you are my family. My sister's daughter."

He pulled a letter out of his pocket and handed it to Andrew. "Christopher asked me to write this—a letter of introduction for you to take to Baron Wolverton tomorrow. If he does not approve your hiring, come back, and I will give you your letter of reference and help you find another position."

Andrew turned the sealed letter over and over in his hands, staring at it a long moment before he looked up. "Why would you do this?"

"Family is more important than social connection, more important than wealth. And though I have not known Katharine long, she is my family. And the longer I thought about her unhappiness in marrying for duty rather than love, the more I regretted what happened that night I helped force her into an untenable situation." He squeezed Kate's hand. "Can you forgive me for not seeing my way clear to help you break your engagement to Lord Thynne that night?"

"Only if you can forgive me for bringing humiliation on you and your household."

Uncle Anthony pulled her into a tight embrace. "I am glad you will be staying in England. You are so like Louisa, it is as if I have my sister back." He stepped away from Kate and extended his hand to Andrew. "May I be the first to welcome you to the family and wish you joy?"

Andrew still wore a confused, stunned frown, but he shook the baronet's hand. "Thank you, Sir Anthony. I shall endeavor to deserve your forgiveness and your well wishes."

"Katharine, I shall send to Mrs. Headington's for your things. You will stay here until you marry and move to Manchester." Sir Anthony headed toward the door, apparently ready to set everything in motion immediately.

"Actually, Uncle, may I ask a favor?" Kate shifted her weight to lean into Andrew's side when he put his arm around her.

Her uncle turned, brows raised in question.

"I would prefer to go back to Wakesdown to wait. After all, I am more a wayward woman now than I was before, and I would not want to bring any hint of scandal to Dorcas . . . or Edith . . . by my presence here during their season." Besides, she wanted to get away from this city, get back to the place where it all began. The place where she fell in love.

"Of course. I shall wire the housekeeper to expect you on the noon train tomorrow. That way, you and Andrew can take your leave at the train station near the same time. Does that suffice?"

Kate pulled away from Andrew and flew to her uncle to kiss his cheek. "Thank you for being so understanding and accommodating. I do not deserve it."

"You are my niece. Of course you deserve it." With a nod, he disappeared up the hall.

Kate returned to Andrew and stepped into his embrace. For months she'd begged, pleaded, railed at God, and accused Him of not listening. But now she could see His hand at work in everything from the moment she overheard Father's conversation with Devlin Montgomery. She'd only had to stop talking at Him long enough to be able to listen to Him.

Andrew bent to kiss her, and Kate returned the sweet, soft gesture. She still needed to write to her father and to Stephen, but for the moment that could wait.

She thanked God for bringing Andrew into her life. And she thanked Him for showing her how to truly follow her heart.

Dear Reader,

Throughout the process of developing this story and writing it, I've often been asked, "Why the Great Exhibition? What drew you to that particular historical event?" Well, it all started with a couple of movies. A couple of TV mini-series, to be precise.

In 2001, I watched *Victoria & Albert* on A&E and fell in love with the love story of these two monarchs of England. But that wasn't the only thing I took away from it. I was also fascinated by the scenes which portrayed the planning and opening of Prince Albert's Great Exhibition in 1851. Then, a few years later, I watched another mini-series: *North & South*. No, not the one about the American Civil War, the one based on the classic, but little-known novel by Elizabeth Gaskell. It also has a scene that takes place at the Great Exhibition. Once I saw that, I was hooked—on the era and on the event.

The historical significance of the Great Exhibition cannot be overlooked, but is rarely remembered. In the late 1840s, the world was on the cusp of a great leap forward. Being a man of science and industry, Prince Albert wanted to see this potential fulfilled, and so planned what was the first true world's fair. It's a time period that readers of historical fiction will find at once familiar and unique. There are all of the trappings we come to expect in nineteenth-century romances, yet there is also the excitement of the era's move into the Industrial Age, including train travel, steam engines, and new inventions like the telegraph and the daguerreotype arriving on the scene.

In *Follow the Heart*, I take a closer look into one aspect of what this new growth and technology meant to individuals and families. For while many were making their fortunes, others were gambling theirs away on speculations and failed inventions. For Kate Dearing, the result of her father's desire to be part of the growth and spread of the railroad industry becomes an unreasonable and nearly unbearable burden of obligation. For Christopher Dearing, it may be just the push he needs to make his own way in life instead of following in his father's footsteps.

As I wrote it, it became a lesson on using prayer as a time to *listen* to God instead of just telling Him what I want. It also made me stop and evaluate my own life—to see if I am simply fulfilling obligations or if I am following my heart in the choices I make.

I hope as you read this, you will also spend time listening to God and determining if you are following your heart.

DISCUSSION QUESTIONS

1. What expectations did you have when you began reading the book? Were your expectations met? Were you disappointed with anything in the story?

2. What did you learn about the time period that you didn't know before reading this book? What did you learn about how people lived/what life might have been like? Was there anything you didn't understand (terms, social customs)? Was there anything you expected to see but didn't?

3. In this story, there is a lot of talk about duty and obligation versus following the heart. In what ways did you see this happening and with which characters?

4. Kate and Christopher must hide the truth of their family's financial situation in order to try to make good marriages. Is reputation—what is known or assumed about someone's background—as important today as it was then?

5. When Lord Thynne proposes to Kate, she makes the decision to marry him because it will save her family, even though it's not what she wants. Would you be willing to do that?

6. In this era, it was unseemly for a woman to discuss politics or religion or anything other than fashion, the weather, or the latest gossip in the presence of men. Why do you think this was the case? Has this changed in 150+ years?

7. Much of what Kate and Andrew argue about in the beginning is the philosophy of how a garden should be tended—with Kate for letting it grow wild and Andrew for pruning and trimming everything neatly into order. Which kind of garden/landscape do you prefer? Do you agree with Andrew's statement that people are much like gardens, wild and chaotic if not properly tended?

8. Was Christopher right in not telling Kate the contents of their father's letter before she reconciled with Andrew?

9. What did you think about the way in which Jane explained prayer to Kate—saying it was more about listening and less about talking? Has there ever been a time in your life when, like Kate, you felt like God was ignoring you or had abandoned you? What happened to show you that He still loves you and answers your prayers?

10. Read Matthew 6:25–34. How is this passage exemplified in this story?